The Constant Progression Of Clouds

By: S.P. Hodde

Your Coach for College, L.L.C.
1424 Meadow Drive
Walled Lake, Michigan 48390

www.yourcoachforcollege.com
sphodde.com

Table of Contents

SPECIAL OFFER!
Get Your Free Short Story!

I would love to be able to let you know about upcoming book launches, promotions, and giveaways, so I invite you to join my author mailing list.

As a thank-you for joining my list, I would love to send you my short story entitled "Pretzel Crumbs & Wet Sand." This is the first in a series of short stories that will eventually be published as a collection centered around the theme of family.

Please see the "Free Short Story" section at the end of this book to sign up and download your free story, which I sincerely hope you'll enjoy!

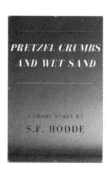

Synopsis:

When a typical holiday weekend turns into a nightmare, Dana and her friend Kate experience terror they could never have imagined. As Dana tries to hustle the children to safety ahead of a monster storm, they are carried away on the wings of the wind and she has the fight of her life to save them. Can they all survive it? Will it tear the family apart or bring them together?

Dedication

For my sons, James and Michael.
Thank you with all my heart for being my constant sources of joy
and inspiration.

I will love you, always and forever.

CHAPTER ONE

Precipice

"Either define the moment, or the moment will define you."
—*Walt Whitman*

"It's either get strong or die." That phrase kept taking jab punches at my mind, fighting with the lump in my throat and the ache in my heart. I glided morosely back and forth, nestled in my daughter's saddle-swing in the backyard, rocking on the heels of my bare feet, digging into the earth beneath me. "Is there no third choice?" I wondered again and again. Neither of the two I saw before me seemed at all viable. Get strong or die? I had no idea how to do either. That, plus I'd have to do the former in order to carry out the latter anyway. I was terrified to do the latter, but at that point, it did have its appeal.

But I couldn't die. The baby *was* dead, but my daughter was alive, and I couldn't leave her. Who would protect her, teach her, love her... if I escaped by taking the easy way out? It would be too selfish. If it weren't for Reagan, ending it would be the certain option.

I wrapped my arms gently around my midsection, planting my feet to stop the swing. I had to try to come to terms with it yet again. The baby I'd carried for almost three months with such hope, joy, and love was dead. I had to forcefully remind myself: my baby was still inside me, but he – I was certain sure he was, had been, a boy — was undoubtedly, undeniably, irrevocably dead.

When the doctor confirmed my suspicion earlier that morning, my heart cracked and broke into thousands of little crystal tears that rolled around inside me, clinking and clanging against all my other broken bits of self.

When I dropped down into the saddle-swing after arriving home from that horrible appointment, alone, as usual, I could see nothing other than that single choice before me: either follow my baby to the grave or follow my living child into the world. I, myself, felt neither alive nor dead, but like I was wandering, lost and alone, in some horrible lost limbo in between. I felt like an elephant balancing, teetering, with one foot on the point of a pin. A fall was inevitable one way or another, and soon.

My womb was a tomb. I couldn't get that refrain out of my head.

Reagan, at sixteen, was *very* much alive. I couldn't figure out how it had all gone so terribly wrong with her, but as I began once again to attempt to soothe myself with the gentle movement of the swing, I knew that no matter how painful everything was at the moment, no matter how defeated and alone I felt, I could never desert my daughter, my lovely little girl. At least she *had* been lovely in the days when she *was* a little girl and it had been her tiny little feet sanding off the grass under that very same swing.

For the previous year and a half, though, she had been far from lovely. Still, there was no one else who would love Reagan and care for her like her mother could, even a mother who had fallen as low as I had, and I was certainly not going to leave any of that to my husband. Richard (Dick as I'd called him for quite some time) had indulged and spoiled Reagan to the point that the girl was practically impossible. "I can't do anything with either of them," I thought. "They may not hate me, but they surely do not love me. In fact, I doubt very much if either of them thinks much about me at all. Maybe they *would* be better off without me." The easy answer tempted me once more.

But the other option -- getting strong -- how the hell would I manage that? I could just as easily fly to the moon on the back of a bird. I had never been anything even remotely resembling strong; everybody knew that. Now I was stuck in the mire up to my tear-filled eyes and the more I struggled, the deeper I seemed to sink.

I tied my thin tawny hair into a knot behind my neck in an attempt to cool myself down, but it immediately unraveled and hung limply across my shoulders once again as I continued to try to sort things out.

There was no one to whom I could turn for help. I had no siblings, my father had died years before, my mother had remarried, moved to Phoenix, and was making a new life for herself there. We had been close when I was young, but we'd grown apart as her life took off and mine stagnated and started to crumble. Besides, I had a strong feeling that my mother didn't think about me all that much any more, either, but that was okay —she was happy now. I had always kept my personal life to myself at work so…no… there was no one there either. I was on my own.

I wiped a loose tear away with the sleeve of my sweatshirt and vaguely wondered what time it was. I really had no earthly idea. I pulled myself out of the hug of the swing and plodded back toward the house. I couldn't indulge myself all day. I needed to make this decision, then get back to taking care of everybody.

So I chose: Live. But how? I truly had no idea. I suddenly realized that, rather than heading back to the house as I had intended, I had begun pacing back and forth along the backyard fence, absent-mindedly, for what seemed like hours, but could just as easily have been minutes or days. My sense of time had utterly vanished. I became aware of the hollow pit in my stomach and realized that I was famished, but that was no surprise or sign of anything. I was always hungry.

It was late may and the afternoon was warm. The scent of the lilac bush just outside my back door brought me some measure of pleasure as I passed it. I instinctively thanked God or Allah or the Universe or whoever the hell was in charge of the lilacs for giving me that moment of pleasant distraction. I always felt so thankful for everything, but was so unsure of whom or what to thank. So, I made my traditional generic prayer of gratitude. At least I still had that.

Even though I had twisted a lilac from the bush, intending to bring it inside and put it in water to brighten the house (and hopefully my mood), I found myself rambling past the back door and roaming toward the front of the house instead of going inside and doing so. Few cars ever passed down my street so it was peaceful and quiet most of the time.

There was a streetlight at the end of Palmer Street, which dead-ended into my street in front of the house next door. I'd always liked that streetlight. It stood at the intersection of the T formed by the two roads, and I always felt like it was welcoming me home, like some convivial sentinel who was always on duty to greet and protect me, especially after dark. When Reagan was little, she thought it looked like a friendly alien and she named it Louie, Louie the Lamppost. I tried to explain that it was a streetlight, but she didn't really care about the distinction. It always made me smile when she said, "Hello, Louie!" as we passed or, when she was a little older, referred to knowing that she had to be home before Louie lit up in the evenings, or when she pointed out that the bugs were dancing with Louie in the halo of his light. I so missed that creative, adorable little girl. Even though Louie technically stood on my neighbor's lawn, we had adopted him as our own.

In spite of, or maybe because of, the peace and calm of the neighborhood and the tulips and daffodils stubbornly hanging on to their blooms in my neighbors' front yards, heartbreaking thoughts began to chase each other around in my mind again, so I forced myself to focus on the azure sky, dotted and streaked here and there with fluffy pulled-apart cotton candy clouds, the singing of the birds, and the beauty of my neighbors' artful entryways and gardens. "That's it," I thought. "Focus on outside things, just for a minute. Just for a break."

I was just starting to feel better and ready once again to try to puzzle out how to proceed, how to get strong, when Dick pulled up in the driveway, early for a change. He hated when I called him Dick, so I never did so to his face or within his hearing. I know it's cliche, but he

11

really was a dick to me most of the time so it seemed fitting. He leapt from his immaculate F150 (his pride and joy) like a bullet from a gun, strode purposefully up to me and softly said my name while trying to take me into his outstretched arms. "He must have heard," I thought, otherwise he would not have been home before dark and he certainly would not have been trying to embrace me. I hadn't called him. He didn't care about my poor baby at all. I knew it. In fact, I hadn't spoken a word to him for almost a month. Why would he expect an embrace from me now? I pulled away and held him at arm's length. "My mom called and told me," he said by way of explanation. "Are you okay?"

"What an ass," I thought, but I delivered the expected answer. "Sure, I'm fine. They'll do a D&C on Friday. You don't need to take off work. I can go with your mom. I think she'll take me. I'll need to get someone to watch Reagan, though."

"I'll take you, and Reagan is sixteen. She doesn't need a babysitter," he answered, but then, seeing the expression on my face, he added, "Mom can watch her, or she can stay with a friend." I could tell, based on his perturbed expression, that he was thinking, "Why won't she give it up? One little comment three weeks ago and she closed up like a tight fist ready to strike." Even as the words entered my mind, I knew it was a foolish notion. First, I knew that Dick would never have said anything remotely like that because using a smilie would have been out of character for him. He didn't have a creative bone in his body. Also, he knew, we both knew, that I would never strike. I didn't have it in me. I hadn't been avoiding him to be mean. I had been avoiding him because being anywhere near him just hurt too damn much. It was self-preservation. Before today, I'd had my baby to divert my attention from his cruelty and neglect. No more, and I couldn't stand to look at him just then.

I turned and went inside, still carrying my lilac, now in a tightly clenched fist, between aching fingers. "Fine," I mumbled as I walked away from him. I didn't care who took me. I didn't want to go. I didn't want my son scraped out of me. I wanted him in my belly, kicking me, sitting on my bladder, keeping me up at night with his vivacious summersaults. I wanted him in my arms. I wanted to nuzzle his little face against mine. I wanted… I just needed to stop carrying my dead baby around inside me. It was too much. I couldn't really breathe, so I had no energy to pretend to be fine for Dick, even though that's what he'd become accustomed to and expected.

I had no feelings for Dick any more, when once, not that long before really, I had loved him to distraction. At least I thought I had. Now, though, he had hurt me so deeply, so many times, in so many ways that I had become numb. I suspected that I still loved him, deep down somewhere, but I could not feel it because that feeling was hidden under the thousands of insults, hurtful comments, broken promises, decimated dreams, lost chances… all crowding in on that love and weighing it down until it was flat and lifeless. It was no longer recognizable as the love I used to feel. It was still there, still hanging on to life somehow, this pulverized love, but it had been beaten beyond recognition.

CHAPTER TWO

Realization

"Things do not change; we change."
—*Henry David Thoreau*

My baby had been dead for two days; more than that really — I had only *known* for two days — and I still had an entire endless day yet to wait for the D&C. Carrying my dead child. Trying to pretend everything was fine. I don't know which was worse, which was harder to do. Dick seemed to have pretty much forgotten about it all and had gone back to forgetting I existed. He'd made it clear that he hadn't wanted another child anyway. I really doubted that he'd ever wanted kids at all. He'd just humored me to shut me up, hoping that once I was occupied with a child, I'd expect less time or attention from him. That's how it felt to me anyway.

At least we were talking again. We'd been shadows sharing a house for the past three weeks since he'd hurt me, again. He never hit me. It wasn't that. He was just very neglectful, of both me and of Reagan, although to a lesser extent, but when he came home from work that night three weeks ago, he crossed a line, even for me.

I had been working outside in the warmth of that early afternoon, enjoying the uncharacteristically hot Michigan May weather, cutting down the burning bush that the previous owners had planted right in front of the picture window. They had let it get so overgrown that it severely obstructed the light and the view of the yard from the living room. I always craved light and color and so intended to plant a perennial flower garden in its place. I had asked Dick to help me get rid of that bush and its companions a hundred times over the last ten years or so, but was not surprised that I'd had to do it myself. It really should've been pulled out by the roots with a truck and a chain, but I was going to dig it out the best I could. I was sick of waiting for help that I knew would never come, and I wanted my baby to enjoy sunshine and flowers instead of the darkness caused by the obstruction.

Dick always acquiesced to any request I made, said whatever he thought I wanted to hear, then proceeded to do exactly nothing, leaving it to me to handle whatever needed to be handled. I didn't mind too much because I enjoyed the outdoors and the hard work, but being so disregarded by Dick was hurtful. That, plus my doctor had not been able to completely convince me that the intense labor involved in that undertaking hadn't been the reason I lost my baby. I still had guilt about that day, praying that it hadn't been my fault that my baby was gone. I'll admit that, deep in my psyche, I was also trying to suppress an inexplicable urge to blame Dick. It was easier than blaming myself, but I knew blame wouldn't change anything. Nothing could change anything.

That afternoon had been especially hot and humid and I had put in several hours in the garden in spite of the morning sickness that had slowed my start. After I'd attacked that bush, I cleaned up and showered, then sat down with a bowl of frozen yogurt to cool off and rest while Reagan was in her room on the phone again. When Dick came in and when he saw me, his only greeting to me was, "You know, if you get fat again, I'll find somewhere else to be."

He couldn't have chosen a sharper arrow with which to pierce my heart. He knew that I was sensitive about my weight. All through my childhood and adolescence my father had made jokes about how fat I was… and now my husband habitually made comments in the same vein. He also knew that I felt neglected and unloved because of the long hours he already put in at work, the time he spent at bars drinking with his buddies, or the hours he spent putzing out in the garage on the rare occasions that he *was* home. It seemed that he'd do almost anything to avoid being with me, and here he was insulting and threatening me in the same short breath.

My throat started to constrict, but I knew that crying would be the worst thing I could do. Dick rarely took me seriously, and never gave me the time of day when I showed any emotion at all, so I stopped the tears before they dropped. I had learned how to do that early in my childhood. My father was the same way: tears equalled weakness, so I had learned years before to put a stopper in tears that really needed to flow, but couldn't.

The frozen yogurt that I'd been so enjoying immediately rioted in my stomach and I felt ill. I got up and put the untouched bowl in the sink. I hadn't spoken to Dick since, and he loved it. It was no skin off his nose whatsoever, which only made me sadder.

Now, though, plans had to be made to deal with my poor baby. My poor little baby. I reiterated my decision: I couldn't die, so I had to find some way to get strong. I still had no idea what that even meant, really.

Still, I vaguely sensed that, while I waited those three days for the D&C, carrying the tiny corpse within me, waiting for him to be taken from me, scraped out of me…the seed of something else was set down in his place and was beginning to germinate… split… cell divide… take shape… grow. Whatever it was, it was taking on a life of its own to replace the tiny one just lost. I didn't know whether to be thankful or afraid.

Dying was definitely not an option for me now, though. I'd made my choice. I'd *have* to find a way to get strong because things could not, would not, stay as they were. If they did, it would surely kill me, if not physically, then mentally and emotionally, and what good could I be to Reagan then? Spiritually, I already felt dead. That would also have to be revived somehow, I thought, because I was going to live. Dick's blasé response to what was such a tragedy for me solidified that. I was going to live, and live whole, even though I had no idea how.

"Where can I turn for help?" I asked myself for the hundredth time. I had no role models of strong women. My mother had been weak for as long as I could remember. It wasn't her fault. It was how she was brought up. Having grown up in the sixties and seventies myself didn't help much, either. True, you saw the occasional strong woman on television back then, but she was the odd duck, or else she was exceptionally beautiful, and I certainly didn't have that going for me, especially if my father and husband were to be believed.

CHAPTER THREE
Aftermath

"The only thing grief has taught me is to know how shallow it is."
—*Ralph Waldon Emerson*

I placed my hand on my belly instinctively as I awoke, but there was no kick, no life, just a hollow-pit emptiness that reached all the way around my heart and deep down into my soul. I choked back the sob that was creeping toward my throat because I could sense that my daughter was trying to wake me, unsure whether or not she had succeeded. She saw the tear roll down my cheek before I could stop it. Reagan put her warm, soft finger against my face and caught the tear in a rare moment of compassion, or, more likely, curiosity. I saw her hold it up to the light that was coming in through the living room window and it glistened as if with a light of its own. I thought, as I watched through the lashes of my half-closed eyes with my heart in my throat, that maybe some of my baby's light lingered in that tear, just long enough to make contact with his sister, before fading away. It was with Herculean effort that I stifled sob after that thought, but I didn't want to upset Reagan. She was my priority now.

I had come home from the procedure groggy and desperately in need of a nap. Even though it was most likely that Reagan was waking me because she wanted something from me, the innocence with which she had rescued my tear threatened to move me to tears again. How could I ever have thought about leaving this beautiful, wonderful girl? Reagan gave me a small dimpled smile when I opened my eyes, and it warmed me where I had been chilled to the bone only a moment before, filled me with a love strong enough to restore me, at least temporarily. I did love this girl, more than anything, in spite of everything.

Reagan had just been dropped off after spending the after school hours with her friend Melanie. I suddenly realized that I had no idea what time it was and that I could've been sleeping on that couch for hours. It was still light out, though, so it couldn't be too late. I hoped Melanie's mother hadn't noticed me through the window (now unobstructed) looking comatose on the couch in the middle of the day. What would she have thought of me? Selfishly lying on the couch in the middle of the afternoon? What the hell?

Dick had stayed with me during the procedure that morning, but as soon as he deposited me at home, he left to go to work. He was a police officer, which was another reason I called him Dick. He didn't have a glamorous job, like the "private's dicks" in the old movies, though. He had wanted to study criminology, but couldn't handle four years of college. He ended up getting his Associates Degree at community college then he went into the Academy once he realized that he'd had all the education in which he was interested. I sometimes wondered if part of the reason he neglected and berated me so much was that he was jealous of the two degrees I'd earned myself. Who knows? Maybe he really was just a dick.

Anyway, he hadn't lasted long on the beat either. He'd gotten into some kind of trouble (he would never tell me exactly what). He'd tried to lead me to believe it had been a voluntary move, but I highly doubted that. He was the kind of guy who thought he knew absolutely everything about absolutely everything. He had a habit of pointing at people and telling them what they should do and was more likely to make demands than requests. I'd always suspected that he somehow pissed off one of his superiors, but I never found out the truth. Now he was a dispatcher for the Novi Police Department. I was actually glad he made that move. I didn't want Reagan to have to live without a father if anything ever happened to him with such a dangerous job.

So, he didn't actually *have* to go into work. He just preferred hanging out at the station (or in his garage man-cave working on some project or watching sports) to being with me. It had been like that since right after we got married, so I was used to it. I didn't even wonder anymore if he might be having an affair. Our own intimate relations had ceased years ago (with one obvious exception) and, frankly, I didn't think he had it in him. He also might have gone out for beer with the guys. Even though it was kind of early for that, it wouldn't have surprised me. Who knew? Who cared? So, with him gone and with me trying to escape myself on the couch, the house really did look deserted.

"What kind of a mother *am* I?" I silently chastised myself again. What kind of a mother wouldn't be awake, ready to welcome her daughter home with hugs and treats and questions about her day? I pushed my guilt aside and tried to wake entirely. "Where's your daddy?" I asked Reagan, who by this time had wiped my tear on her jeans and was staring at me with a look of disdain.

"*I* don't know," she snapped with the familiar confrontational attitude in her voice which had, sadly, become more and more frequent of late. "I didn't see him, so how should I know?" Well, it had been fun imaging her as my wonderful girl for a little while anyway, before reality came back from wherever it had been hiding.

"Did you see his car in the driveway?"

"Yeah. What's he doing home?" Garage. For sure. Why couldn't she just have told me that without my having to drag it out of her? I'd have to tell Reagan about the baby. Dick couldn't do it. He wouldn't know how. Would she be sad? She was so excited at first about a baby sister (or brother, if she had to, she'd said), but she had become so self-centered and selfish lately that I really wondered if she might even be happy about our loss. My loss. Was I the only one who'd mourn this baby?

CHAPTER FOUR

Logan

"A friend may well be reckoned the masterpiece of nature."
—*Ralph Waldo Emerson*

The next Sunday, two days after the D&C, I was still struggling and very much alone. Questions assailed my thoughts constantly. How would I get over the loss of my son? How would I get strong? I had no idea and trying to figure it out was wearing me down. Sometimes I was sad, then the anger would come exploding through me like a tornado. Those two emotions consumed me. Sometimes they danced, sometimes they dueled. All the time they hurt. As I walked out into the mild May afternoon to escape the oppression of the house, I found that even the birds grated on my nerves. What usually brought me such joy, even that, seemed to have turned against me. I fumed further at the thought. I didn't deserve this. I didn't care how horrible a person I was, no one had the right to sink me so low that I lost the birds.

As I sat, bare heels digging into the dirt under the swing once more, propelling myself morosely back and forth in the rubber saddle (how long had it been since Reagan used this swing, I wondered), I heard a new sound. A soothing tune and a lovely voice singing in a language I had never heard. I was so moved and intrigued that I stopped the swing and rose to follow the sound. It was so faint, now that I was trying to locate its source, that I wondered if I'd really heard it at all. Then, when it drew my attention again, I wondered if *it* hadn't sought *me* out, called me to it. How could I have heard such a soft sound amidst the trill of the birds (who were suddenly sounding musical again) and the dull drone of my own dark thoughts?

I realized that it was coming from the house next door, which had been recently vacated by some neighbors who kept to themselves and who we never really got to know. It had been occupied two weeks earlier by someone I'd been "too busy" to seek out for an introduction. This was awkward. I so wanted to know what he or she was listening to, it was such a welcome and pleasant distraction, but I had been such a poor neighbor that I hesitated to intrude.

In those days, I often put off doing things that I might enjoy, like meeting new people, under the guise of being too busy. I made time for all my obligations and for all the people who needed things from me, but I very rarely made time for myself. I was too busy to do that. Too many lessons to plan, quizzes to write, essays to grade... Funny how I didn't feel too busy just then, when I felt a desperate need, and it was actually about *me* and not about being kind to new neighbors.

I pushed the guilt that surfaced about that down into the recesses of my mind, or wherever it was that I shoved guilt and doubt and hurt and all the unpleasant things when I didn't want to deal with them, and walked over to the fence to listen.

As I leaned slightly forward against the fence and toward the house next door to better hear the music, I was startled when a woman stood up from behind the fence-high hedge on her side and almost bumped into the parts of me that were leaning over to encroach upon her space.

"Oh!" I exclaimed as I pulled back in utter terror that I had been discovered and might be considered rude. Terror might sound like an extreme word to use, but that's how I was back then. Terrified of not being liked, of not fitting in. It took less than an instant for me to realize, however, that this was not the case here. The woman was in her early sixties and had a face that was as peaceful and serene as the music that was still lilting through the air and over her hedge into my dark world. Her smile was warm and welcoming. It felt like the sun does on your skin when you walk back out into it after strolling through several blocks of shade.

"Good Morning," she said pleasantly.

"Good Morning," I replied. "I didn't mean to startle you. I saw you working there and thought I'd finally stop by to introduce myself and welcome you to the neighborhood." I have no idea why such a lie came out of my mouth! I absolutely abhor dishonesty, so why would I say such a thing, especially since it was so obviously untrue and I was so sure that she knew it?

"Thank you so much," she replied and, even though neither her voice nor her manner betrayed none of it, I was certain sure that she had my lie well in hand and was quite aware that it had been I, and not she, who had been startled. For some reason, I wanted to start off right with this woman, maybe because I felt that, since nothing else in my life felt right at that moment, maybe this one thing could.

"Truthfully," I said, trying to cover my deceitful tracks, "I heard that enchanting music coming from your house and felt irresistibly drawn to it, which is kind of odd since I'm not really a music aficionado."

"It has that affect," she answered. "It's Sanskrit, and they're mantras set to music."

"Really?... and her voice is enchanting, so well suited to it... ha, listen to me! I sound like a critic!"

"You are," she said pleasantly. "Everyone is, whether they know it or not!" She meant this kindly, as though everyone had the talent, the right, and the opportunity to evaluate such things. She was beginning to interest me more than the music. "Her name is Deva Premal," she continued. "I'd be happy to loan you her CDs. I've got all her stuff digitally now, so the CDs just sit there. You're more than welcome to them. I'll be right back." She turned before I could answer, and I watched as her slender body moved gracefully away from me and she went in through the sliding glass door just across the lush green lawn that carpeted her yard. She was wearing a bright yellow T-shirt under short denim overalls and had a blue bandana tied around her neck. She removed her linen sun hat as she went through the door. I saw her wipe the perspiration from her forehead with her forearm before the door closed behind her.

As I waited, I looked over her yard with interest. Her gardens were full of blooming spring flowers, very colorful, eclectic. Some were perennials, some annuals, some still in flats waiting to be set into the ground to bloom later in the summer. A large bag of potting soil stood guard nearby, overseeing an assortment of ceramic and terra-cotta pots and the various garden tools that were strewn about. A two-seated glider was positioned in one corner of the yard so that one could relax there under the shade of her Maple tree and take it all in. All it needed was a waterfall and it could have been Eden itself. I realized that for the short while that I'd been there, the sights, sounds, and fragrances of this place had soothed me and had driven my troubles from my mind. I could feel my shoulders ease down, my neck elongate, my breathing slow down and deepen a little bit, just by taking it all in.

As I contemplated the unexpected change in my physical and emotional state, my new friend reappeared with the CDs and a warm bran muffin. Add a fourth sense to the three already pleasantly stimulated here! I could tell from the look of it that the muffin would be delicious. I should've been welcoming *her* to the neighborhood with food and flowers, but she was welcoming me back to sanity with that and so much more, and I didn't even know her name.

"I baked these this morning," she said, "and, since I live alone, there are plenty to share. They aren't quite as good out of the freezer so I like to get rid of them while they're fresh! Enjoy it… and the CDs." She smiled so sincerely as she handed them over the hedge to me that I wanted to hug her! It occurred to me that if I had, that would've been the fifth of five senses that had come alive for me there by the fence, when all had seemed so dry and decidedly dead just moments before. It felt almost like a resurrection.

"I'm Sunny," I said, as I set the CDs down on the ground beside me and pulled a piece from the muffin, unable to resist the warm, tantalizing, homey aroma any longer. "Well, actually Allison."

"Logan," she said, extending her hand over both bush and fence to me. It was small and warm, but her grip was firm and confident, like a miniature hug. That fifth sense had come into play after all, and I wasn't disappointed. I felt done, like the muffin; perfectly baked, warm, and delicious. She had that affect on me then and forever after.

I was so taken aback by the sudden change in my state of mind that I was at a loss for what to talk about next, so I thanked her again for the loan of the CDs and for the muffin. I told her how much I had enjoyed meeting her, and turned to depart. She stopped me only long enough to return the pleasantry, and added, "Why don't you stop back by the hedge tomorrow afternoon? I'll still be planting. The weather is supposed to be fabulous again and I'll probably overdo it if someone doesn't make me take a break. Maybe we could chat again. I'd enjoy that."

I told her that I would and I realized as I walked away that it was true. It wasn't one of those automatic parting statements where someone says, "Oh, we'll have to get together" and then nothing ever comes of it. I was already looking forward to it. I knew that I'd even rearrange my schedule to make it happen if that became necessary. I didn't know then what it was, but she worked on me like a drug and lifted me up somehow, and I felt better for hours afterward, until my family came home.

CHAPTER FIVE
Reagan

"Children are all foreigners."
—*Ralph Waldo Emerson*

I had been quite revived by my short time with Logan and, as I began again to ponder what the hell I was going to do with myself, I found that I was able to think it through a little less darkly and a little more logically.

There was no way I'd get pregnant again so it would just be me, Reagan, and Dick. I thought maybe it was my pulsating sense of loss that had made me feel so alone, so apart from them, but I knew it really wasn't that. They just had no use for me beyond what I could do for them: clean the house, make dinner, do laundry, bring in half the income. That was my life. Head in to school, teach my five English classes, come home, grade papers, plan lessons, and take care of the house and those two. I'd forgotten how to have fun. I hadn't even realized that until just then. I'd forgotten how to take care of myself.

Once inside, I put the CDs down, finished the last of the muffin, and poured myself a glass of Chardonay. I drank a silent toast to my angel child and to my devil child. Dick got nothing. It was slowly dawning on me that I hated my life. Maybe it came to me as a result of the anxiety and agitation of my life compared to the peace and serenity I'd sensed next door. I don't know, but it was a frightening realization, wherever it had come from.

I'd been so depressed those last several days. I tried to distract myself from the debilitating thoughts that were threatening to intrude on me again with the wine, a half a bag of potato chips, and a magazine, but it wasn't working. I got up and went into the kitchen to grab some chocolate chip cookies. "I deserve this," I thought, and then, unbidden, came the truth: I'd better watch it. The last time I'd finished off the cookies, there'd been hell to pay. "Fuck it," I thought, and I went back to "I deserve this." I swear, for a good portion of my life, there were two different people in my head fighting over stuff like this. It was infuriating, maddening, and exhausting.

Armed with my drink and my second snack, I sat back down in the armchair and just sat. And sat. I couldn't keep my thoughts at bay, so I thought I might as well just let them spar with each other until some of them got knocked out. "Who knows?" I thought. "Maybe one of these thoughts will eventually win the fight and I'll know what to do."

How it broke my heart as I realized that my family was what had been pushing me down, down, down into cold, dark water and holding me there, pinning my arms so I couldn't breathe, couldn't swim to the surface, only letting me gasp at the occasional short breath of life. I had never seen it clearly until that day, that moment when each of them walked into the house and punctuated the sentence that had been forming in my mind: *I hate this*!" I was three glasses of wine and six cookies in by the time they came home.

With the help of my alcohol and sugar, I had become comparatively light-hearted (and light-headed) by that time. I kept remembering my little slice of afternoon with Logan, which had truly been a breath of fresh air.

I eventually gave up trying to succumb to my rioting thoughts since I was obviously getting nowhere with that and I cleaned the house, even Reagan's room. I tackled the laundry and then allowed myself some time to read. I never did that. It felt wrong, at first, to take this time for myself, but I justified it by saying that the house was clean and that ordering pizza was Reagan's favorite thing for dinner anyway — and who knew if Dick would even show up, or in what condition — so I tried to read that magazine again for a while before I decided to really treat myself and search for a novel. A novel! It had been so long!

I realized as I sat down with the book that I was actually caring for myself for once, and looking forward to something again, albeit something as small as sitting in a chair and reading for half an hour. I had been trying to drink less and not binge as often, but today I was *doing* something for myself, instead of *not* doing something. It felt different. I felt at peace, a little. I was starting to feel a little bit happy again, until…

Reagan walked through the door first, apparently also in a good mood. She said hello to me and gave me a weak hug, something she didn't condescend to do very often any more, even when she wanted something. Maybe she had a little residual sympathy for my recent ordeal. Not likely. She was on her cell phone chatting with a girlfriend the whole time, so I knew I wasn't her focus, but hey, I'd take what I could get. After she extricated herself from my embrace, she sauntered past me without looking at me, went to her room, and closed the door.

Two minutes later, the screaming began.

"What were you doing in my room?" she hollered as she flung her door back open.

"Nothing but cleaning up a little for you, Reagan." I could feel the pin pushing into my happy bubble, the puncture and deflation just moments away.

"You have no business in my room! This is MY private stuff! You stay out of here!" SLAM! I'm surprised the door jam survived the assault. I was torn apart by a sudden barrage of emotions that were pulling at my limbs, trying to draw and quarter me. Shock, anger, disillusionment, fear...

How to handle this? React as a human adult who'd been insulted -- with anger? Whose kindness had been abused — with hurt? As a parent trying to teach someone how to behave like a civilized adult -- with authority? Like a teenager trying to reach her on her own level -- give in and apologize? Add to the drama? I stood there, just stood there, and as the volume of her music increased, and the size of my heart decreased, compressed into a pulsating pea-sized pain.

I winced at the harsh, blaring music (if you could even call that music) coming from Reagan's room, shattering my peaceful afternoon — a peace that had been so hard-won for me. The memory of the serene, cheerful music that had glided over the hedge from Logan's house that morning gently prodded me to realize that what was in front of me did not *have* to be my experience. There were alternatives. I had options That explosion of sound vibrating Reagan's bedroom door must have been deafening for her, so I could only assume that it was intended to annoy me. Logan's music had been designed to elicit peace and tranquility and it had brought me joy. I knew the cacophony assaulting me from down the hall was designed to piss me off, but miraculously, I noticed that now it blew right past me and the serenity from my encounter with Logan reasserted itself somehow, sort of wrapped me in strong arms, and I remained calm. I found myself almost gliding toward her room.

I opened her door. I walked slowly and deliberately up to her and took the phone out of her hand as she looked at me in disbelief. She was tall, like her father, and was already at eve-level with my five-foot self. Another year and she'd probably tower over me. I snapped the phone shut and put it in the back pocket of my jeans. It was so uncharacteristic of me to enter without knocking, let alone confiscate anything, that she'd had no sense to prepare herself to stop me or even to protest. I couldn't believe she could actually hear anyone on the phone over that horrendous, ear-splitting noise anyway but, apparently I'd interrupted an important conversation because, after the momentary shock wore off, she proceeded to scream at me hysterically once more.

As she rebuked me with shrill teenage angst, I silently walked over to her speaker and unplugged it. She stopped yelling, probably in shock once more, and I turned to face her. I stood there, looking her into her eyes, saying nothing, breathing deeply, just waiting for it to play out. She recovered enough to begin her assault once again, but I was unfazed, to the utter amazement of us both. I knew, though, that she'd have to run out of steam eventually, and I felt unnaturally relaxed and energized at that moment. "What had Logan put in that muffin?" I wondered, amused. It was really weird, the whole thing. Reagan eventually realized that she was having no affect on me whatsoever, so she stopped hollering and said, "What?"

"This is my house," I said casually. "I'll clean it if and when I want to. I really don't care how you feel about it, but you will treat me with respect in my house, or you will probably not like the consequences." I turned, intending to walk out the door. I have no idea how I knew to do that. None of it was planned, or even briefly contemplated. It just came out of nowhere.

"Hey! Gimme me back my phone!" she shouted after me as I walked past her toward her door, indicating pretty clearly that the encounter was over.

"It's *my* phone," I reminded her over my shoulder. Then, just as I reached the hallway, I stopped and turned to face her again as another thought occurred to me. "I'll be happy to show you the name on the bills. If you'd like me to allow you to use my phone, you can sincerely apologize for disrespecting me, thank me for cleaning up your pit of a room, doing your laundry, buying your clothes and food, and feeding and raising you for the last sixteen years." I knew it sounded cliche, but I didn't care. Then I had another thought and said, "In fact, you can start cleaning this room yourself, on a regular basis, and doing your own laundry while you're at it. So when all that happens, and when you apologize for and get over being a spoiled, disrespectful, ungrateful brat, I might let you use my phone again." The look on her face was... awesome! I don't know where any of this had come from, but I didn't care because I felt wonderful!

"You BITCH!" she screamed at me. Oddly, rather than being offended or hurt by her attack as I typically would have been, I felt a small smile tug at the corners of my mouth. It didn't bother me at all and, unbelievably, I wasn't bothered by guilt for talking to her the way I had either. I had, after all, spoken calmly and rationally -– okay, maybe I did call her a few nasty names, but hey, they were all true. And I didn't feel that her label for me was accurate, so why get upset by it? I finally felt like I was a grown-up, a level headed adult, not any kind of bitch. "Oh my God," I thought. "I just had someone insult me, my own daughter no less, and I don't care!" I didn't care what someone else thought of me! *That* was new. At that moment, I only cared what *I* thought of me and I thought I was pretty damn cool just then! It was only one very small victory, not over Reagan, but over myself -– over my own anger, my hurt, my fear of losing her. It felt wonderful, like I was an entirely different person. I didn't realize it then, but it was the first tiny baby step to becoming one.

As I crossed the threshold into the hallway, I stopped, caressed the door jam, and said, without looking back at her, "Maybe I should take my door off this room, too, and really start teaching you what you have to be grateful for." I could feel her anger in the air. It felt like a hurricane and I was in the eye. I turned to her once again and said, "Feel free to get your own phone if you don't like my conditions. I'll show you how to do laundry tomorrow after school. If you don't show up or don't pay attention, you can shrink all your stuff or turn it all pink, then you can get a job so you can replace it. It's your life now, baby girl." I walked out and headed back to my wine and my novel. I felt so absolutely free!

Reagan literally wailed in exasperation, unintelligible, jumbled syllables of frustration, and it was so gratifying to me! It was like the sound I had heard in my head all the time when trying to cope with *my* life, but the frustration, for once, wasn't mine.

Then, as I made my way down the hall toward the kitchen, taking her phone from my pocket and tossing it up and down with great satisfaction, she hit me with it: "I'm SO telling dad!" she bellowed, and I knew that the battle had been won, but the war was just beginning.

CHAPTER SIX

Dick

*"People have a hard time letting go of their suffering.
Out of a fear of the unknown,
they prefer suffering that is familiar."*

—Thich Nhat Hanh

Dick would take her side, of course. He always did. She was his baby
no matter how little time or attention he gave her of his own accord.
And he was her hero, in spite of the same. And I was there to serve and
please them both, not to make waves or worry about my own sorry
self. That's how it had been in my home for years. Exactly how long,
why, or how this had come to pass I had no idea, but that was it and I
was done.

I headed through the kitchen toward the backyard, pausing when I
noticed my reflection in the microwave mounted over the stove as I
passed it. My hair was pulled back in the pony tail I'd secured before
Reagan got home, and my glasses were smudged, both of which were
what I normally saw when I looked in a mirror. This time, though, I
swear, I saw two of me reflected in that black glass. The meek, timid,
oh-please-love-me me, and the woman standing up straight, shoulders
back, cell phone rising into the air and falling back into her palm to the

rhythm of her heart. These images weren't side by side, but were superimposed. I held the phone up, opened it, and then closed it with a snap, and the former version vanished into darkness at that satisfying sound. I looked at the remaining image and smiled. I pulled the elastic tie from my hair, let it fall over my shoulders, and tried to fluff it up a little bit. I took off may glasses and cleaned then with the bottom of my shirt. Tomorrow, I'd see if I had any make-up left in the house, and maybe I'd try to squeeze into those old jeans again.

I smiled, in spite of the memory of the extra twenty pounds I was carrying that I so, so hated. I couldn't myself see below my neck in the microwave, so the memory of my overweight (and the accompanying shame) came from within me rather than from my reflection. I shoved the shame away and focused on that square-shouldered woman in the black door of the microwave. I liked her better.

I walked out into the backyard, shut Reagan's phone off, and pitched it into the hedges between Logan's house and mine, about twenty feet past the spot where I'd first met her. Then I went back inside to pour myself another glass of wine (I'd earned it!) and order the pizza. "Veggies – not a modicum of meat, tonight," I thought. Then I laughed. It was a little thing. Such a little thing, but it would make a very big impact on my carnivorous family, I had no doubt. I felt like I was fighting back, for once, even if in the smallest possible way. For a fleeting moment, I worried that I was becoming vindictive, but that evaporated like mist in the breeze and I realized that I really and truly did not care anymore.

I went back inside and found my own phone. All of a sudden, just as

I was about to dial Hungry Howie's to order the pizza, I knew somehow, I just knew, that I *could* take care of myself. After just that one episode with Reagan, that one encounter with Logan, I felt stronger and a little more ready for the storm that I knew for certain sure was approaching. I felt ready — I somehow knew that this time I'd be the palm bending in the gale, not the tree that snaps and falls to the ground as I had always been in the past, and as I used to think I always would be. I almost welcomed the coming drama as an opportunity to prove it to myself.

What had *happened* to me that day? I didn't know, but I felt different, like I could finally breathe all the way into the bottom of my lungs, like I didn't care about anything or anyone but myself and, while that kind of selfishness would formerly have triggered tremendous guilt, today it triggered nothing but pride and a sense of strength. My darling boy had left a hole in my heart, but it felt like a kind of light was filling that in now and I was slowly learning to be whole again. Even if this were fleeting, even if it were merely momentary, I felt it, loved it, and wanted to nurture it as I had wanted to nurture my poor sweet boy.

Could all this have come from some Sanskrit mantras and a bran muffin? I didn't know. I didn't care. I smiled. I felt like I couldn't ever be hurt again. Ever. It was wrong, of course, but it was pretty heady stuff!

Reagan's excessively loud music actually pleased me, even though it was chosen and played at a volume designed to aggravate me even out in the yard, because I knew I had struck a chord. She would run to daddy, as usual, and he would be her hero and lash out at me, but I'd smile and say I didn't know where the damn phone was (which was sort of true). I found myself chuckling at this, at my vain attempt to maintain the honesty I valued so much. The feeling pushed out beyond the smile and I found myself actually laughing out loud! This was getting freaking funny! I *could* control a thing or two! Dick would buy her a new phone, of course, but I decided that I'd just take it again. She'd either learn to be nice or it would become a game. I couldn't really lose either way, I figured. I was actually having fun.

I returned to the house, even though I seriously would rather have gone to find Logan and hug her. I don't know how much she had to do with any of this, but before I met her I was worthless even to myself and now I felt free, alive, empowered, even after having so recently been so devastated. Even it if didn't last another minute, it had been so wonderful that I felt indebted to her forever. I wondered what she was doing. I already felt like she was a friend. I put my legs up on the coffee table, took another sip of my wine, opened my novel, and smiled again.

Then, even over Reagan's damn music, I heard Dick's diesel engine rounding the corner past Louie the Lamppost. Then I heard the car door slam, and knew it was the bell to start round two. I put up my fists and took a couple of jab punches at the air like a boxer and laughed out loud again at how silly that would have looked had anyone seen me do it.

It was about eight o'clock by this time and I was just draining my third (or fourth?) glass of Chardonay when he sauntered in through the front door. He never parked in the garage, and neither could I, since he had turned it into his man cave. As usual, he stopped to putz in there for a while before coming inside to see his family so it was a good forty-five minutes before I actually saw him. Reagan must not have heard the car door over her obnoxious music when he pulled in, otherwise she surely would have met him in the driveway with her complaints about me.

I must've looked like I was three sheets to the wind because when he came into the room he stopped in his tracks and looked at me hard. I realized later that what had puzzled him so much was that I was just sitting there with my feet up, smiling — not grading papers or planning lessons or cooking dinner or folding laundry— just sitting rather than reacting to the audio-tantrum coming from Reagan's room. I had actually gotten used to it over the last hour or so, so it didn't bother me at all by the time he got there, although it must have been deafening to him.

"What the hell is going on?" he shouted over the noise.

"Welcome home dear," I thought to myself. I just pointed toward Reagan's door with my empty glass and left it at that.

He went to her and the decibels decreased a little, but not enough for me to be able to hear their exchange over the music. I didn't need to listen to their conversation to know what was transpiring. They'd be whispering, conspiring, but I knew how it would play out.

I would be the horrible, clueless imbecile who understood nothing. He would reassure her that he'd get me to see reason, blah, blah, blah. It was all so comical to me now. "He really will think I'm wasted," I thought to myself, stifling another round of light laughter and walking

41

to the fridge to refill my glass. It was so ironic that sanity finally achieved should appear like intoxication. Well, to be honest, it really was quite intoxicating (and the wine hadn't hurt either)! Another low laugh-out-loud escaped me.

While Dick was listening to Reagan's complaints about me, I went into the kitchen to pour my fourth (or fifth?) and final glass of wine. Dick was over six feet tall, balding, and had been growing a beer belly for years that threatened to overhang his belt sooner rather than later. He came out of Reagan's room, frowning, with the beer he'd brought in from the garage still in his hand, and walked toward me. He had a fridge out in his man-cave so he could drink all the beer he wanted without having to come into the house. I'm surprised he didn't put in a bathroom and a cot out there. Then he would never have to see us at all.

He paused at the juncture of the hallway and the living room, which was part of the long open area of our house that extended through the kitchen, so he could watch me. "Oh," I thought to myself, "don't bother to come over to me. Just stand there twenty-feet away and carry on with your judgment."

"Really?" he said in the sardonic, condescending, sarcastic tone he always used as he watched me re-cork the empty bottle and toss it into the trash. He was still in his uniform, and I couldn't help but notice the marked contrast between the crisp clothing and the slovenly body that was stretching the fabric taunt.

I decided not to even answer him. What was the point, really? I was feeling too damn good at the moment and I didn't want to ruin it. I turned my back on him and walked out into the backyard once more to remove myself form the negative atmosphere and, surprisingly, he followed.

CHAPTER SEVEN
Revelation

"Disobedience is the true foundation of liberty. The obedient must be slaves."
—*Henry David Thoreau*

I barely had a chance to park myself in the swing before Dick accosted me. I was facing away from the house so he had to walk around the swing set in order to confront me. He was over a foot taller than me and, since I was sitting and he was standing over me, I felt even smaller. I momentarily entertained the hilarious thought of swinging powerfully back on the swing, then forward, and kicking him clear into the yard behind us. I was rocking slowly on my heals again so would no way have had the necessary momentum to create even a scaled down version of that scenario (and I'd never do anything remotely like that anyway), but it made me laugh out loud to envision it. He must have thought I was insane!

"What the *hell* is wrong with you?" he demanded, looking down at me as if I were a timid child to be reprimanded. "Why do you have to go causing trouble? Why can't you just deal with her?"

"I *did* deal with her," I said, looking up and continuing to rock back and forth on my heels. I couldn't quite look all the way up to his eyes, though. In spite of my violent fantasy, I was becoming that timid child again under his angry gaze. I could feel it. I felt all my resolve evaporating. I started second guessing how I'd handled the situation, but that didn't last for long.

"Ally-cat," he said, "were you drunk when you took her phone? Where is it?"

"No, and I don't know where it is."

"You're lying." He didn't know me at all. If I'd said that I had no idea where it was, I'd have been lying, but the truth was that I didn't know where it really was. Splitting hairs, I know, but it made me feel better.

Before I could answer, he took my glass out of my hand, dumped the remaining wine out on the grass, and said, "Alley-fat," (that was not accidental, I knew, because he'd called that many times before), "I can't do everything around here. You need to straighten up and get your shit together."

That did it. It was the frozen yogurt incident all over again, except this time it wouldn't be the silent treatment he got. It was as if all the hurt from the past nineteen years was coiled up like a snake and his cruel words were the stick that poked it.

"Fuck you!" I said in a low voice, but obviously spitting venom. The look on Dick's face was priceless. I had never spoken to him that way, ever. I planted my feet and stopped the swing. Oddly, as I stood to face him, it occurred to me that my whole life had been like that swing — vacillating back and forth, back and forth, between misguided attempts to make my marriage work, between decisions, between

myself and who I was trying to be for him, for them. All I needed was
to plant my feed and the swinging stopped. All I needed to do was
stop swinging and stand up. I had reached another decision. I was
done putting up with his shit.

"Now I know you're drunk, Alley-fat," he laughed, relishing the
insults that he knew would hurt me most.

"I'm not drunk, you dick," I said, and his face turned dark at being
addressed that way. Before he could protest, I reminded him, "You just
insulted me, *again*, so don't you say a word to me about it." I walked
the few paces that separated us and, this time, looked him right in the
eye… well, at least as much as possible from twelve inches below him.
"You are fucking toxic, you know that?" I said. I stopped the tirade
gurgling up inside me before it started. I decided to reign it in and not
go on and on about how he'd neglected and abused me for years, how
he spoiled Reagan rotten, how he was a terrible husband and father… I
knew he would neither listen nor care and there was nothing to be
gained by escalating things.

All I needed was for him to understand that he no longer had power
over me, could no longer control me. "Stay the fuck away from me and
don't ask me for anything ever again," was all that spat from my
serpent's tongue. He was so stunned that he didn't even realize that I
had grabbed my glass out of his hand. I turned my back on him and
walked into the house. I had intended to pass the refrigerator and
head… where? I realized that I didn't have any place to go. No place in
that house was mine. Nowhere to run. Nowhere to hide. Nowhere to
lick my wounds.

This revelation stopped me in my tracks, right in front of the fridge. I opened the door, grabbed another bottle of wine, went out the front door, and headed to Logan's. It was an impulse, but she seemed genuinely happy to see me, even though I'd turned up unannounced. I don't know how she knew, but she apparently understood that I was upset and that I'd had more than enough wine already so she took the bottle gently out of my hand when I walked in but, rather than opening it or putting it in her refrigerator, she unscrewed the top and dumped the contents down the sink. Had she been anyone else, I would have protested (probably vehemently), but I just let her do it. "Come on," she said. "Let's take a walk around the neighborhood and you can tell me all about it."

It was a beautiful, balmy summer night and I noticed myself cooling down (both literally and figuratively) before we even passed Louie The Lamppost. We set off at a reasonable clip. I don't know if Logan wanted me to burn off calories or frustration but, as it turned out, both objectives were accomplished. She was out of her gardening overalls and was wearing a long, full, multi-colored skirt, flat strappy sandals, a white gauzy, flowing top, and a beautiful fringed scarf with a floral pattern of burgundy and white. Not what you'd really want to work up a sweat in, but we maintained a decent pace nonetheless.

As we walked, Logan listened as I related the events of the day, not interrupting at all until I'd run out of steam. We had circled the block twice by then and, when we came back around to Logan's house, she stopped under the streetlight. Louie would be coming on any minute, I thought.

The walking and venting had done me a world of good, but I still didn't want to go home. Logan said that she'd invite me to spend the night at her house, but not until I'd settled this issue. "Running away from a problem only makes it chase you," she said. I knew she was right, but the last thing I wanted to do was go back to that house.

"Look," she reminded me, "you told me that Dick always just acts like nothing's happened when something like this happens, right?"

"Nothing like *this* has *ever* happened!" I pointed out. "I've always been compliant, obedient, submissive, subservient. I thought it might make him care about me, love me, but it hasn't, for certain sure it hasn't."

Logan gently took my hand, looked into my eyes, and said, "You've finally figured out what doesn't work. I haven't met Dick, but based on what you're told me, I'd be surprised if anything ever would."

"So what can I do? Tonight? Tomorrow?"

"Well," I could tell she was thinking out loud, "why don't you go home and act as if nothing happened, too, like he always does?"

"I hate when he does that so why on God's green earth would *I* want to behave that way?"

"Well, I'm just thinking that since that's what *he'll* do, you *not* doing that will just cause more conflict, tension, aggravation and hurt — for *you*. I'm thinking that, now that you've made your decision not to put up with his abuse any more, you'll need some time to figure things out and that's better done in peace than in chaos, with positive energy rather than negative energy."

That made sense. I didn't want to see him and I *certainly* didn't want to share his bed, but Logan's thoughts made sense. It wasn't given as advice. I could tell that she would support me no matter what I decided to do — I knew she'd even let me sleep at her house if I asked her to — but it was getting late and, now that the false wine-energy had dissipated and I had exerted a little effort during our walk, I really was feeling better, thinking more clearly, and getting kind of tired.

It was 9:30 before I got home. I walked around back just to... I don't even know why. Maybe I was afraid to run into either of them, which was more likely if I came in through the front door. That was foolish, though, because I knew that Dick would be back out in the garage and Reagan would be in her room. The living room and kitchen area would most likely be vacant. Still, I stayed out back for a while and, as I strolled around the yard, I noticed the moon shining overhead. It was beautiful, not quite full, but almost. Just like I was not quite strong, but almost. It made me happy to think that I had something in common with the moon. She changed all the time, and so could I.

I stopped to watch it for a few minutes. Gray clouds, thin and long, almost transparent, were moving slowly across her face, but they couldn't block her shine. I thought about the revelation I'd had earlier about the swing. It was comforting and felt nurturing somehow, but the swing was always in one place, even as it moved back and forth. It would always keep me relatively stationary. The clouds, though, they were moving, almost meandering, across the face of the moon toward the East. They might be dark, and they might be trying to block part of what I wanted to see, but they were moving. They wouldn't always be there, stuck in one place, and I decided that neither would I. They wouldn't always be gray and neither would my mood. I stood watching the clouds cross the face of the moon, thinking about this, and I decided that the time for swinging back and forth was done. It was time to move forward in one direction like the clouds and never go back. Things might get dark, or stagnate, or get scary, but as long as I was moving forward, I would be able to handle them.

"I can handle it!" I said the words out loud and permitted myself a mirthful little shake. I went into the house (empty for all intents and purposes, just as I'd known it would be) and I kept repeating this mantra to myself over and over again. I still had no idea what I was going to do or how I was going to do it, or where I was going to go or how I was going to get there, but I made a commitment to myself then and there and I would keep repeating that mantra to myself until it was truly true.

CHAPTER EIGHT
Rebirth

"Circumstance does not make the man. Circumstance reveals man to himself."
— *Ralph Waldo Emerson*

The next day, I awoke in one of the best moods I'd been in for a very long time, in spite of the events of the previous day and the hangover that was pinpricking behind my eyes and making my mouth dry, and in spite of the snoring Dick beside me.

I got up without waking him (no surprise there), poured myself a cup of coffee, and resolved to *do* something. What? I still had no idea. So much had happened just the day before that changed everything! My encounters with Logan, Reagan, and Dick all served to pull the black cloth of oppression off my eyes, and I started to contemplate where my life would go from there. Nothing was as it had been even twenty-four hours before.

I decided to call in sick. What the hell, right? I had taken Friday off for the D&C so I really should have gone in, but I didn't care. I threw together some lesson plans for the sub and that was that. After the Terrible Twosome left for the day (neither of whom even bothered to ask why I was still at home when I should have been long gone), I poured myself a third cup of coffee, toasted a bagel, and went to sit outside for a while before the approaching dark clouds could move in and drop their rain on me. I pulled the sides of my sweater together across my body to fend off a morning chill and set my sights on figuring out my life. I had been trying unsuccessfully to do this for days, but I felt like I was somehow in a better place from which to figure it out now. Besides, I'd resolved not to give up until I figured something out.

As I snuggled into the swing saddle seat (the only thing in the yard on which to sit) and wished the clouds away, I thought, "The only things I know for sure that I have are intelligence and determination." How I knew I had these things when most of my life I'd been told otherwise, acted otherwise, I had no idea, but I knew.

Looking back, I bet it was my job that gave me what little confidence I had. I was really good at my job and I knew it. I loved my students. I loved my colleagues. I loved my subject matter. I really liked and respected teenagers and they picked up on that, I think. It felt really good to remember that I was good at something and appreciated at least a little bit.

I knew this because I'd kept all the emails, cards, notes, and letters from students, parents, and colleagues that I'd received over the years. How could they all be wrong? I decided that the next time I was feeling down, I'd organize and compile them into a binder. I'd have to remember to put "buy binder" on my to-do list so I'd be prepared when the time came. I'd call it my "feel good" file. There, that was one thing I could do for myself to remind myself that I was, in fact, a worthy person, no matter what the Terrible Twosome thought of me.

In spite of all this, work had become almost unbearable over the last few years due to constraints put upon teachers and the focus having shifted from teaching and learning to data collection. Four years into "No Child Left Behind" (which we dubbed "No Teacher Left Standing"), we were all struggling to do the superfluous crap (testing, testing, testing) required of us by the powers-that-be *and* give kids the real knowledge and skills we knew they needed in a way that would help them actually learn. There just weren't enough hours in the day or days in the week. That, coupled with class sizes upwards of thirty, was knocking us all down. We were working harder and were being forced to be less and less effective than we knew we could be, and it was frustrating and demoralizing beyond belief.

I still loved it, though, in spite of having my hands tied again and again by people who had apparently never met a teenager. Remembering how much I loved my job in spite of all this helped more than I thought it would. I knew it would have to be enough. I was too young to retire and there was no sense trying to start over somewhere else and take the inevitable pay cut and seniority step-down. I'd have to make it work somehow.

I left the swing and walked the long length of my backyard, watching the gathering clouds, contemplating still. My whole childhood had made me weak. My greatest fear — being alone — had become my reality. I'd have to endure that and figure it out for myself. But that was okay. What the hell else did I have to do besides raise my daughter now, and keep up at school? I knew that whatever relations

I'd had with Dick in some drunken stupor (the only times he ever showed any interest in me) would never happen again so could never result in another pregnancy. I'd get back on the pill anyway, just in case. He'd be happy about that. "There," I thought. "Another decision made."

The raindrops finally began to eek their way out of the clouds and to fall gently down around me. I continued to walk and ponder, even as the rain diluted the coffee in my cup. I eventually headed back into the house, dumping the dregs of my cold, watered-down coffee in the sink and putting my plate in the dishwasher as I passed. I walked into the living room, in a strangely contemplative mood. I normally didn't have much time for introspection, even though I'm an introspective person by nature, so I was enjoying this.

I realized yet again that I needed to move my life in another direction, but which? And how? The dream I'd cradled and nurtured of a happy family was long gone. I knew that now for certain sure. I'd made a really lovely home, I thought, and I tried as hard as I could, but I could't make that dream happen alone… but there was plenty I *could* do alone, and my pain and grief fueled my determination to find out just what that was.

I realized that my happiness was in my *own* hands, not Dick's, and no one else's, and I reasoned that if I felt confident enough to raise Reagan (and didn't my utter and complete love and devotion to my child guarantee that?) and to take care of my students, then I could somehow summon the same love and devotion for myself and raise myself as well. That was it: I may have been thirty-nine years old, but I definitely needed to re-raise myself, re-define myself, re-invent myself. It was like a project. Looking at it that way made it seem way less scary and much more possible, which surprised me. It really didn't seem like such a daunting task after all.

I went to the front picture window to watch the rain pummeling the sidewalks and the street. I could see Louie standing tall and strong on the road verge between the street and the sidewalk in front of Logan's house. He didn't seem to mind the rain at all, I noticed with a chuckle, so why should I? "Into each life little rain must fall." Hadn't I heard that again and again over the years?

I watched the fat drops splash in the puddles already dotting the sidewalk in front of my house where the cement had buckled slightly over the years to leave little basins for the water to fill. It was actually so cool. I hadn't taken time to consider things like that in a very long time. Odd, that as I tried to contemplate my future, I remembered things from my past, like my introspective spirit, my love of nature, of reading… all the things I'd let slip through my fingers and out of my life.

As I stood there, thinking about how much Logan's flowers would love this gentle shower, I continued to puzzle it out. Why should I be afraid of being alone? Hadn't I been alone for the last eight years since my mother remarried and moved to Phoenix? Hadn't I been alone among Dick's friends and their wives doing shots of tequila and playing video games in the early years of our marriage? I had tried for a while to join in and keep up, but succeeded only in realizing that alcohol would be the death of me if I did, and that I didn't want to live that kind of life. Still, I managed to consume more than my fair share of wine for certain sure, but somehow that felt different. Hadn't I been alone since most of my friends had vacated our lives, not enjoying Dick's brand of boozy socializing?

I stepped away from the window and paced back and forth between the kitchen and the living room, the knuckle of my thumb absentmindedly between my teeth. I was enjoying my introspection and I really felt like things were looking up, so I didn't want to really *do* anything at the moment. I hadn't planned on calling in sick, so there was nothing on my to-do list that needed to be done until later. I decided, strange as it seemed to me, that I'd put on my boots and raincoat, grab the umbrella, and head out for a walk in the rain.

By the time I got outside, the weather was warming up in spite of the drizzle. I walked past Logan's house and, on a whim, when I reached Louie the Lamppost, I did a Gene Kelly move and held on to it with one arm as I waltzed around it, *Singing in the Rain* style. I hoped that Logan hadn't seen me do that from her window, but then I realized that she most likely wouldn't have thought that weird at all, and would probably come out to dance with me.

I suddenly realized that I really *wasn't* alone anymore! I'd met *her*, and I somehow knew that there was a budding friendship there, and I *so* needed a friend. It revived me like a tonic to realize that I wasn't alone. My weak self tried to tell me that I'd only known her a day so… but I told that self to shut the hell up and I continued down the street, stifling the urge to jump in all the puddles as I walked away from my house feeling a little bit cleansed and still sure in my heart that Logan and I would become friends. I hadn't trusted my intuition in a very long time and it was time to revive that as well.

In my own home, I felt like an outsider. I think I had always felt like an outsider, except with Reagan, my darling girl, when she was younger and still darling. That's where I'd placed all my hopes and dreams and where I had derived my greatest sense of purpose, satisfaction, and joy. But as Reagan got older and learned to manipulate Dick to get her way, she was moving away from me. I had thought the new baby would fill the widening hole in my heart, maybe even bring my fractured family back together again, but now that hole just had jagged edges.

So, I would continue to raise Reagan the best I could, I'd hold down my job, I'd nurture a friendship with Logan (and I *would* do my part to do that, I promised myself!), and I'd try to save my marriage, unlikely as that seemed. I was too stubborn to let it go without a fight and I vowed to leave no stone unturned before giving it up for lost. I could just imagine how Reagan would react to the news if I failed and it deteriorated to the probable conclusion.

I returned home after just one turn around the block. I came in, shook off the rain, and decided to distract myself. All this contemplation and reflection had turned out to be quite tiring. As I settled into the recliner that faced the window, I put my hand on my empty belly again (I had to stop this from becoming a habit if I intended to move past this heartache) as I picked up the novel I'd left on the coffee table and settled in to read. I really should have been grading those hundred and sixty essays that had just come in, but I didn't have it in me. I just didn't.

I opened the book, then closed it again. I tried not to think of all the books I wouldn't be reading to my lost child. Maybe my son. I'd always wondered if maybe a son wouldn't have made Dick more interested in his family. Now I'd never know. I felt so full of emotion, but yet so empty and devoid of everything else at the very same time. Misty eyes again. My son.

"It's probably for the best," I thought as I put the book down for the third time and started pacing the hallway, walking past Reagan's room, past the room I shared with Dick, past the half prepared nursery. I paused in that doorway and looked at the tiny clothes I'd laid out across the railing of the crib, the elephant and giraffe mobile that no one of mine would ever reach for now, the box of newborn diapers in the corner... "I wouldn't have been a very strong role model for you, would I?" I whispered, gently caressing my empty belly.

I was so, so sad, yet it began to dawn on me as I walked into that room that the old saying must really be true. This must have been meant to be for some reason as yet unknown to me. I ran my hand along the railing of the crib and straightened up the teddy bear that had slumped in the corner where the railings met. The crib had been Reagan's so long ago and was set up and ready with little elephant/giraffe sheets, even though my boy would have been in a bassinet for a while at first.

Dick had insisted on keeping all of Regan's baby furniture so that if we ever did have another child, we wouldn't have to spend a lot of money on new stuff. I pulled the string on the mobile and it began to rotate to the tune of *Twinkle, Twinkle, Little Star.* "My little star has gone back to the heavens," I thought, as a tear wiggled itself free from the corner of my eye despite my best efforts to contain it.

As I left the nursery, I found myself thinking that it was better for the child to have died than to have lived with me as his mother. "No!" I actually spoke the word aloud as I closed the nursery door behind me. I couldn't let myself think like that. I wouldn't let myself believe that. I was weak, yes, but I was a good, loving, honest, caring person, wasn't I? I had strived to be all those things all my life, so how could I not be, at least a little? That had to count for something, right?

I found myself wandering aimlessly around the empty house again. "Maybe I should get a dog or a cat," I thought. Something to love me… There must have been a reason for the Universe to have taken my baby. Maybe it was so yesterday would happen, so this day could happen.

The rain had stopped, the clouds were disappearing into the East, and the morning sun was trying really hard to peak though the stragglers. I decided to head back outside to encourage it and to wave goodbye to the clouds. I walked back to the swing, which had become a real place of comfort for me for some reason, even though I'd recognized that it did, indeed, keep me in one place, vacillating, not moving forward. Even though I'd committed to moving myself forward, I thought about how that swing soothed me and provided me with some momentum, not to kick Dick across the yard as I'd envisioned the night before, but to propel me into my uncertain future.

I wiped the rain off the seat with a paper towel I'd brought out for that purpose and, after rocking back and forth for a few moments, I lifted my eyes from my folded, wringing hands and saw that the sunshine really was looking around the side of the last few clouds now for the first time that day and it dawned me. It *was* so this day could happen! My baby died so that I could live. Not just exist as I had been, but to *live*. This day was my rebirth. I *could* change and be the strong role model Reagan needed. I hugged myself tightly around the middle and dropped tears of a different flavor.

"Oh thank you, little one," I whispered to myself, even as I felt silly and ridiculously melodramatic for doing so. "I'm so sorry you didn't make it into the world. You never even drew a breath, but you've already saved a life. And I promise it won't be for nothing. I *will* get strong and *will* raise your sister to be strong, too, all alone if I have to. And I will somehow make this world a better place before I leave it." I knew I sounded like an idiot, but I didn't care. There was no one to hear me. Somehow, this all needed to be said out loud, I think to cement it in my mind, heart, and soul. "I'll make you proud," I continued, "and you won't regret giving your little life up for me, I promise. We'll have a cup of tea together in Heaven someday." I had a quick, unbidden thought that, had this child been born, he might just as easily have ended up drinking tequila with his father in Hell, and the vision of saving him from that soothed me as well. Melodramatic or not, that ridiculous little monologue and the accompanying thoughts really soothed me.

Six days before, when I'd found out that my baby was dead, I hated Dick, really hated him, but with these thoughts that hatred left me like a long-necked crane floating from rock to air — fluid and graceful. It left nothing in its place — just a huge void. No hate, no love, nothing. I had a void in my heart where Dick used to be and a void in my womb where my son used to be and a void in my soul where I used to be. "Nature abhors a vacuum." Where had I heard that? Probably from my mother, who was great with the philosophical sayings, touting them often but living by them rarely. Well, the void in my womb would never be filled, but I determined then and there that I would find a way to fill my heart and soul with something, something wonderful. I headed down to my basement office, sat down at my desk, and started grading those essays.

Dying was not an option.

CHAPTER NINE
Decision

"Once you make a decision, the universe conspires to make it happen."
—*Ralph Waldon Emerson*

I was surprised by how many essays I got through before Reagan came home from school. I wasn't nearly finished, but I'd managed to put twenty of them in the "done" pile. She still wasn't talking to me, but that was fine. I knew she'd have a new phone (thank you, Dick) by the end of the day and that soon she'd need something from me and would forget the whole episode. I was fine with that, but I stuck to my guns. When she came in after school, I told her that she had a half an hour to get her dirty clothes together for her first laundry lesson. If looks could kill, I wouldn't have stood a chance.

Surprisingly, she did show up downstairs in the laundry room at the time I'd specified and grudgingly learned to do her laundry. Check off one success! All the contemplating I'd done that morning had really settled me down and cheered me up, and I made a commitment to myself to regularly take time to figure things out in the future, rather than just doing what I'd always done or what others wanted me to do. It was freeing, and now my laundry chore had been reduced in the bargain. Maybe I'd stop doing Dick's laundry, too. That was something to think about!

Once I had come to all my rain-walk realizations, things seemed a little easier. My heart had been tied into so many knots by Dick's behavior in the past that it couldn't *be* tied any tighter, so what was the worst that could happen? We fight? Well, I needed the practice. He leaves me? Well, I was worried about that anyway so if it happened, it'd be one less worry, wouldn't it? Have a confrontation with Reagan? Hadn't that actually proved effective not so long ago?

Apparently, my typical behavior hadn't gotten my life to a place where I was happy, so maybe it *was* time to rock the boat. In any event, I somehow knew that I had to in order to begin to make myself whole again, to give my life some kind of meaning. Then to take the next step, then the next, then the next until I found myself on the right road. I knew that there'd be roadblocks and detours along the way, but I was becoming anxious to get on with it anyway.

After mulling things over and over continuously for several days I came to another life-changing realization and subsequent decision: I had some needs that I had to met. Me. I left Reagan in the basement to sort her laundry, grabbed a pencil and small legal pad and began to think and write a list, hoping that it would lead me to the road for which I was searching. I laughed when I visualized myself skipping along yellow brick to the tune of singing munchkins. I didn't have any munchkins in my life anymore, singing or otherwise, but I would follow the road once I found it, wicked witches be damned.

First, I needed more than just Logan in my life. Second, I needed to feel like I was doing something important and valuable, beyond what was left in my teaching career. Third, I realized on a visceral level that even as I was trying to fill the void left by the death of my son, I was suffering from another void where my relationship with Reagan had once been. She was her daddy's girl through-and-through now and didn't give me the time of day anymore unless I'd failed to do something she expected of me or did something of which she didn't approve (like clean her damn room for her).

Looking over this short list, an idea was born that I thought would cover all three points and put that road in view, but I knew for certain sure that there'd be hell to pay for it on all fronts at home.

CHAPTER TEN

Reaction

"He only is a well-made man who has a good determination."
—*Ralph Waldo Emerson*

When Dick came in the door the next evening, it was apparent that he'd already been drinking. No surprise there. No better time than the present, though, to tell him about my decision. Trying to time what I did or said to correspond with the appropriate level of his intoxication hadn't proved effective in the past anyway. "Hi," I said, jumping right in. "I have to tell you something." I was so proud of myself for having said "tell" rather than "ask," as I would have done just a few days ago.

"Can't it wait? I have to make a couple of phone calls."

"It could, but then I might not get around to it again and you'd wonder where I am." That got his attention.

"What are you talking about?" I smiled at the silly notion that flew through my head that he might be worried that I'd leave him. He was still under the impression that he had me solidly under his thumb. Too bad he never paid attention to anything but himself and his work; he might have been more aware that his life was about to change.

"I'm signing up to be a Big Sister. I'm going to mentor a teenage girl who doesn't have a mother."

He actually laughed out loud. "You're kidding! You can't even control the teenage girl you've got. What do you want another one for? Are you a sucker for punishment?"

"I don't really have a teenage girl anymore," I replied steadily "You've taken her over and have spoiled her to the point where I have no affect on her at all any more and she hates me for trying, so I give up."

"You give up?" I hated when he repeated me or asked stupid questions, which was pretty much all the time. "Great. What kind of mother *are* you?"

"A better mother than you are a father. At least I have an eye toward her learning something with everything I do. You fly by the seat of your pants and give her whatever she wants no matter what she learns from it, as long is it's a minimum bother to you." I was surprised that he had no reaction to that, so I continued. "The only father I've ever seen or heard of who's worse than you is my own." My father had been an alcoholic, too, who constantly put me down whenever he wasn't neglecting me. It always amazed me how I had inadvertently married my father, in spite of the fact that I had so wanted to escape him. A shrink would have had a blast with that!

My father had passed away years before. My mother had always tolerated all his bullshit. There was so much that she had to put up with! She never had the nerve to leave him. After she met Phil, I realized that I'd never really seen her happy at any time in my life until a couple of years after my father passed, after she got over the guilt of being happy that he was gone and after she had found someone who treated her well. I *so* didn't want my marriage to be like hers.

"Thanks a lot," he said sarcastically. "Sorry you don't appreciate me. Do whatever the hell you want. Just don't ask me for money."

"I won't," I retorted. "I'll just take what I need." He raised his eyebrows at that one. "I contribute more than my fair share to this household and, even though your spousal and parenting skills are similar to his, you are NOT my father. I don't have to ask your permission for anything. I'm only informing you as a courtesy. Reagan's old enough to stay alone, even if she isn't mature enough, thanks to you. And thanks for the support, by the way. As usual I got from you exactly what I expected — not a damn thing."

He turned his back on me as if I weren't worth another moment of his time, and walked out to the garage, grabbing a beer from the fridge on the way, and closing both the refrigerator and door to the garage with exaggerated slowness to illustrate his utter lack of concern about any of it — including me, I thought.

I'd had my fill of Dick, yet I still felt so very empty. I had made a decision to move forward, to do something to help myself, but I still loved him. I still wanted him. Still wanted to make it work. I'd do anything to make it work, but that didn't matter. I could't make it work without his help and he seemed hell bent on denying me that. I'd have to live in a marriage in which there was no love, no joy, no connection, or I'd have to admit failure, give it up, and be alone.

I went back out to the swing to deliberately give myself an attitude adjustment. This was becoming a habit for me and it amazed me how much it really helped. Plus, being outside had the added bonus of the possibility of hearing or smelling something amazing coming from Logan's. I rocked back and forth on the swing, heels in the dirt, like I was rocking myself in a big hug, slowly deepening the crater beneath me, like a river creating a canyon. For some reason, this place, that action, still helped me calm down and think more clearly. I decided not to think of the swing as a symbol of stagnation any longer. Now, it was a symbol of solace and contemplation, a place for me to rest until I was strong enough to stand up or jump off once again. That crater was deep enough. Stand and jump I would, but I'd take comfort when I needed it.

The more I thought about it, the more I wondered yet again what it was that scared and worried me so much about being alone. I remembered my realization from a couple of days before that I was already alone for all intents and purposes. I did everything by myself, even going to Dick's family functions without him. (At least I wasn't the only person he neglected.) I ate alone. I spent my evenings alone. I spent my weekends alone, especially now that Reagan was a teenager and always out with her friends. Why the hell was I the least bit concerned about being alone? I realized that it made absolutely no logical sense. Then I realized that I didn't *have* to be alone, especially now that I had Logan and would soon have a Little Sister to spend time with. I knew it would be fatal to keep to myself with all that was going on in my head and in my life, so I was determined to nurture those relationships.

Considering these things made my concerns seem so foolish all of a sudden. I could do this… but if I eventually left Dick, I'd lose half my income. Money was never that important to me, and I made a decent living, so what the hell? I seriously began to consider the real possibility of it. Still, I hated the idea of failing at the marriage and breaking up Reagan's home. I decided that I'd give it one more year and really try to make him care about me. After that, if I failed — if *he* failed — I'd move on, knowing I'd done everything I could do to make it work.

There. Another decision. Not bad for a doormat. I was making progress. I needed to get busy filling myself back up.

CHAPTER ELEVEN
Proceeding

"Do the thing you fear and the death of fear is certain."
—*Ralph Waldo Emerson*

As I walked into the Big Sister agency the following Monday afternoon, I had no idea what to expect. I opened the heavy glass door, greeted the receptionist, took seat, and recalled the questionnaire I had been asked to complete. It made the kind of inquiry you'd expect. No, I had no felony convictions; no, I wasn't a drug user; no, I'd never been accused of child abuse. I wondered if it ever occurred to anyone how easy it would be for someone to lie on that form. I hoped for the sake of the kids that they did great background checks. Would they reject me when they found out that I was weak, timid, and unsure of myself? Dear God, what was I doing? Whatever made me think I'd be qualified for something like this?

I didn't run, though. How different my life would have been if I had. I alternated between sitting in the reasonably comfortable chair and pacing the outer office, looking over the spines of the books on the tall oak shelves as I passed.

After about half an hour, I was called into a small office, lined with several high, five-drawer, mismatched filing cabinets. Some of the drawers were pulled partially out and there were papers and file folders sticking up here and there. The apparent disorganization unsettled me even more. Still, there were gingham curtains hanging on either side of a bright window behind the desk, which I thought was more homey than blinds would have been, so I tried to push my aversion to chaotic spaces out of my mind. The sounds of the Detroit traffic outside were audible (with the occasional honking horns and sirens), and the office had a musty lots-of-old-paper aroma, which was not at all unpleasant.

The agent who greeted me with a slight, lilting southern drawl as I entered was an elderly woman, probably in her late-seventies, whose salt-and-pepper hair was pinned back in a tight bun. Her name was Eunice something (I don't remember now) and she introduced herself to me with a warm handshake and a genuine smile. It was obvious from her smile and her bearing that this wasn't just a job for her. I could tell that she had a passion for this like I used to have a passion for teaching, but she didn't seem marred or burned out like I was. I envied her.

She was so welcoming and pleasant that I felt immediately at ease. She insisted that we start out on a first-name basis and I soon forgot about my apprehension, the disarray of the office, and the ridiculous nature of the stock questionnaire. I felt for the first time that maybe this could work out after all.

Eunice interviewed me casually, as though we were old friends, and seemed to see through all my insecurities and to find someone worthy

71

beneath it all. I secretly hoped that it wasn't just because they had more little sisters than big sisters or had some God-awful quota to fill, and so had to suck up to any idiot who might apply. Why must I always think the worst of myself? I wondered that even then, when I really was stepping out of my comfort zone and trying, trying *so* hard, to get strong.

Once we'd both ascertained that this was something that I really wanted to do and was apparently qualified for, Eunice told me a little about the family with which I was to become involved. Since we'd spoken previously on the phone to set up the appointment and to get some basic information and logistics, Eunice had already pulled the file of a potential Little Sister for me. As she searched around her cluttered desk to locate it, I had a clear moment of sadness because I realized that it was because I was devolving within my own family that this was even happening, and I suddenly felt like a failure again. How could I help this girl when I couldn't even handle my own daughter? I shook it off and listened as Eunice spoke to me about Micah and her family.

"Well, the younger daughter is more conducive to having a Big Sister. She's quiet. She's pliable. But the older girl is the one who really needs it. She's seventeen and has been driving her father crazy with worry. She's running around with people she shouldn't be running around with and there's a boyfriend that's trouble. Her father's not sure if she's taking drugs or not. He doesn't think so, but he's concerned that it may happen eventually and he's trying to prevent it."

"What about her mother?" I asked, then immediately realized that it was a stupid question. Obviously the mother was out of the picture or we wouldn't be having this conversation. The specifics were none of my business.

"We like to leave that up to either the father or the sister to divulge. We don't want people going in prejudging…"

"Oh, I totally understand!" I interrupted. "It really doesn't matter anyway. I'm just looking for some way to make a connection with her."

"The very last thing you want to do is try to replace her mother, no matter what the story is. You'll always be resented if you do."

"Of course." I decided that it would be better to just shut up and listen. Keep my foot out of my mouth. "I have training and experience with teenagers, so I should be okay," I blurted out in spite of myself. "I teach high school English." Eunice already knew this. Why was I telling her again? I wondered who I was trying to convince, her or myself .

"There is no training or experience for this," she said. 'You may be an educator and you may be a parent, but this young lady is neither your student nor your child, and she's likely to resent you from the get-go. It happens a lot with the older ones."

"I only meant that I feel comfortable with teenagers. I *like* them, so I don't mind taking the older girl instead of the younger. I don't pretend to have a clue what I'm doing here," I admitted.

"Good. Then you have a good chance of doing well. You know they say that the worst thing in the world to be is an expert — then you're set in your ways and aren't open to anything new. Your openness and your willingness to stay that way will be your greatest asset." Hmmm.

I'd never thought of it that way before. "Let that give you confidence. Even if you have a teenager at home where things aren't working out so well, it doesn't mean that you won't make a difference to someone else, even if it's not this girl. God doesn't always match family members up right. We try to do it a little better here."

I was surprised to hear such a blasphemous remark, especially from a woman wearing a large gold cross around her neck. Eunice noticed my discomfort and saw me glance at the crucifix on the wall behind her desk, and she smiled. "Oh, God doesn't mind when I say that!" she laughed. "He knows that we know he's working with a larger clientele and has human free will to contend with as well. Even though we have a better filing system, we still can't beat his track record, but it'd be a blind God indeed, or a dishonest one, who couldn't admit that not all the families he makes are functional ones!"

"How did you know that I'm having problems with my daughter?" I asked. Was I that transparent?

"Oh, you're not the first person who's come in here looking for a replacement," she remarked.

That got my dander up and I started to protest, "I didn't come here for a replacement."

"Not a replacement for your daughter," she clarified, "a replacement for the relationship you have, or used to have, with her. She'll always be your little girl, I know that, but my guess is that she's becoming a young woman and you miss the old relationship you had with her when she was a child. You'd be surprised how often that happens." She'd hit that nail right on the head. "That's why most women would

74

want the younger sister — a second chance. You're not only taking the harder road with the older sister, you're running a big risk that you won't be able to find that good ol' relationship that you miss so much — you might just be running your ship aground on the same old shore. But you're smart, and you're strong" — was she kidding? –- "so you'll take the older sister." Well, that settled it. Even if I had wanted to change my mind, I didn't feel like I could now that Eunice had, for all intents and purposes, told me what I was doing and that I was capable of doing it. I wondered what had made her think I was strong?"

"If nothing else," Eunice continued as she walked me to her office door and took my hand in a friendly double-handed embrace at the end of our interview, "it'll make you value your own daughter more, no matter what she's doing or not doing that's making you crazy. It might also make her value *you* more. With the right attitude, only good can come of whatever comes of this." I eventually added this to my growing list of mantras that I had starting using at Logan's suggestion to help me get through tough days. "Only good can come of whatever comes of this." Logan would like that.

Eunice left me at the door with the family's contact information, a smile that made me feel more comfortable and confident than I really was, and a promise to check in with me at the end of the June. That would give me one month to either get settled into this or to run screaming. She reminded me that I could call her at any time with questions or concerns.

I left thinking that Eunice just might be right. No matter what happened, I'd have to find the good in it because I had to get away from my family. My family — it broke my heart to realize yet again — was toxic and I needed to do something good, for myself and for someone else, as the antidote to a reality that had been slowly poisoning me. I hadn't seen even a shade of this truth until I lost my little son, but now it was clear as day, and it kept washing over me like a tidal wave trying to knock me down.

I had come here because I had assessed what I knew, what I loved, and what I was good at, and all that had lead me to this path upon which I was about to take my first tiny, tentative steps… away from my toxic family to… who knew where or what? No matter what happened though, good or bad, I had taken a step… a step to getting strong, a step to taking care of myself, and that was really something.

With the interview over and things about to get underway, I found myself feeling a little proud of myself as I headed back to my car, even if I was still incredibly apprehensive and, I had to admit, scared to death.

"But I might do just fine," I told myself as I snapped the seatbelt. I planned to call the girl's father and set up a meeting with him so he could "interview" me, too, and decide if I would be a good fit with his daughter, as Eunice had instructed me to do. We'd decide on the specifics then. I made a vow to myself not to let any of them down, realizing that I'd already let my own family down. Dear God - what was I thinking?

CHAPTER TWELVE

Leap

"Whatever you do, you need courage.
Whatever course you decide upon, there is always someone to tell you
that you are wrong."

—*Ralph Waldo Emerson*

I made the call as soon as I arrived home that afternoon, but got no answer, so I had to leave a message. I had come right in, put my purse on the hook by the door, took a deep breath, sat down at the kitchen table to steady myself, then hesitantly punched in the number on my phone. I knew I needed to take the plunge before I could talk myself out of it.

The voice on the answering machine must have been the younger daughter. She was very proper and businesslike and I followed her instructions to leave a message. When I hung up, I felt like I'd sounded incredibly lame, but I decided that it was what it was. I was who I was. It would either work out or it wouldn't. I got up from the table to grab a root beer and a cheese stick and managed to convince myself that if it didn't work out, I'd figure out something else.

Three days later, just when I was beginning to think this family didn't want me, the phone rang. Once he ascertained that he'd reached the proper person, he said, "My name is Desmond… Desi. I'm Micah's father." His voice was smooth and clear, intriguing. It was deep and gruff, like a farmer's who had worked outside his whole life, but simultaneously soft and warm, like a poet's. I couldn't summon up a matching image to save my life. "For heaven's sake, stop being such a sappy romantic," I though to myself, but those were the words that came immediately to mind to describe his voice: farmer and poet. Weird, right?

He had what I at first characterized as a slight African American accent that was tinged with a sophistication that I hadn't expected for some reason. I realized immediately that I'd made my first mistake. In spite of the fact that I prided myself on my acceptance of others and my abhorrence of bigotry in any form, there I was thinking stereotypically. "Oh dear God, what's wrong with me?" I moaned to myself again. I realized that I was embroiled in these thoughts instead of listening to him and chastised myself for that as well.

"I'm sorry," I said. "Could you repeat that, please? I was just distracted by something." I couldn't tell him by what. I couldn't make up a specific excuse for my inattention because I couldn't convincingly lie to save my life… and I had been distracted after all.

"Yes, of course," he said. "I was asking when it might be convenient for you to meet with me about my daughter."

"Certainly. I'd love to. I'm so glad you called. I'm so looking forward to meeting you and, hopefully, your daughter."

"Eunice *did* tell you that it's Micah I'm interested in having you meet, not my younger daughter, right? Just to clarify. It seems like not a lot of people are willing to take on the challenge of an older girl, a teenager. She's seventeen, a junior at Pontiac High School."

"Yes. It's Micah that I'm looking forward to meeting."

"I'm so glad. I've been praying and praying that someone would come to care about her besides me and her sister, and that damned boyfriend I'm so worried about. I love her so much, but I'm not what she needs at this point in her life and I can't seem to reach her. I need help. I need help." That repetition, the desperation in his voice, simultaneously caused me concern and broke my heart, and I found myself wanting sincerely to provide the help which he seemed to so urgently need. I only hoped I wouldn't be a disappointment, or worse.

"I'll do whatever I can to help, I promise. Where do we go from here?"

"Well, Eunice suggested that we meet for coffee. I'm working two jobs (which is why it took me so long to return your call — sorry about that), and it's a little hard to schedule things sometimes, but we'll make it work. What's good for you? I've got a couple of hours free in the middle of Sunday afternoon. Will that work?"

"I'll make it work. When and where?"

"You decide. Make it convenient for you." I was tempted to throw the specifics back to him, which is what I usually did, but I remembered how often Dick had faulted me for what he perceived as my inability to make a decision, when I was really just trying to make him happy.

"Is Starbuck's on Fourteen and Decker too far for you?" I asked.

"Not at all. What time?"

"2:00."

"Perfect. See you then. Give me a shout if anything changes, okay?"

"You too. See you Sunday," I said.

I had just finished saving his contact information on my phone when I realized that I had already promised to drive Reagan to a rollerskating party on Sunday afternoon. I had a moment of panic about how to be in two places at once, then suddenly realized that I didn't have to be and that I didn't care. I was going to meet this man at 2:00 and Reagan could just work around it.

Just as I was beginning to feel a little guilt about having such thoughts about my daughter, Reagan slammed a door and screamed at me about doing her laundry, so the guilt dissipated like the dew under a hot morning sun. She knew I wasn't doing her laundry anymore and her attitude blew that guilt out like a candle in a gust. Reagan could just ask her father to take her to her Jordan's party on Sunday. In fact, she could ask her father to do her laundry, too, if she didn't want to do it herself. I patted my muffin top and said, "Son, are you watching me? I *am* getting strong!" and I swear at that moment a warm breeze wafted in through the open kitchen window, bringing me the aroma of the lilacs outside. It felt like it was gently caressing me. It felt like a hug.

CHAPTER THIRTEEN
Pushback

"Our strength grows out of our weaknesses."
—*Ralph Waldo Emerson*

It didn't go over very well when I told Dick that he was going to have to deal with getting Reagan to her rollerskating party on Sunday because I had plans.

"What do you mean you have plans?" God, I hated when he did that! How many things could that possibly mean? I wondered if he realized how stupid that question made him sound.

"I told you that I am going to be a Big Sister. I'm meeting the girl's father for coffee so we can discuss how this'll all work and make some arrangements. It's at 2:00 on Sunday and that's when Reagan needs to be at Bonaventure for her party. I don't think my meeting will take very long so I can probably pick her up after, but you need to get her there. Either drive her, give her your car, or make other arrangements."

"Great, so you're going to meet some guy for coffee and I have to screw up my Sunday babysitting."

Sometimes he just made me boil, so I slowly enumerated all things he'd gotten wrong. "First, Reagan isn't a baby; and second, you can't babysit your own child; and third, it's a 20 minute drive so you'll be spending a shade over a quarter of an hour, max. Deal with it. And fourth, this isn't 'some guy.' Pay attention." I was starting to feel like I was talking to one of my less than stellar students. "I'm meeting the father of a girl who needs some help. He's taking a lot more time for his daughter than you seem to be willing to take for yours."

"Just go. I'll figure something out." The look on his face was precious, like he didn't even know me. Well, he didn't, so there!

"Good," I said, leaving the room. I no longer had any desire to breathe the same air as that man.

* * * * *

Reagan was livid about the situation, to put it mildly, when I told her about it later that day. "Whadya mean dad has to take me?" She had acquired Dick's habit of asking ridiculous questions. "Why can't I just have your car?"

"I just told you that I'm using my car. Pay attention," I said, getting really exasperated. I realized that I'd had to say "pay attention" to both of them and that, really, they never *did* pay attention to me. Well, they'd have to now, and I was proud of myself for telling them so.

"Great," she spat. "I told Jordan and Ashley that we'd pick them up, so you'll have to tell dad."

"You volunteered my time without checking with me? Was that nice? Would you appreciate it if I did that to you? *You* tell your dad. I'm not involved in this."

"I hate it when I have to borrow *his* car. All he does is bitch and tell me not to go 'joy riding'." She said that last with a smirk, a small shake of her head at each word, and a tone of complete contempt. I wrestled with anger and a horrible feeling of futility, but only momentarily.

"Don't talk to me like that Reagan," I commanded. "If you don't like it, then get a job and get your own car. And don't forget about gas and insurance. You might want to thank you father for whatever he ends up doing for you or you might find yourself with no rides at all. Try to be a little more grateful and just deal with it." I just couldn't stop myself. I was on a roll, so I went on. "You've never had to deal with anything in your life because you father's always bailed you out. I wouldn't alienate him if I were you because you're on my last nerve and I'm not about to bend over backwards for you any more." God that felt good! I didn't know where it had come from, but it felt really good. I didn't feel like a bad mother, either. In fact, for the first time in a long time, I felt like a good mother. "Go talk to him because I have plans for Sunday afternoon and am not available. I am not at your service. Period."

"You have *plans*? What do you mean you have plans?" Ugghh!!! "Whadya gonna do, meet your other daughter?" She dragged out the last word as if it were the most vile form of profanity.

I refused to take the bait. "I do not have another daughter. I told you where I'm going and what I'm doing and I don't particularly care one way or the other what you think about it. We're going to discuss how I might be of assistance to this family."

"Great. Assist everybody but me."

"What assistance do you need besides me waiting on you hand and foot? When was the last time you said even one nice thing to me,

Reagan? When was the last time you weren't downright mean and insulting to me? Why on earth would I want to even be around you, let alone 'assist' you? I won't play your games any more. You're on your own. Until you can treat me like a human being, you're on your own," I repeated. Then, in a perfect imitation of the way Reagan and Dick always acted toward me when they'd had enough, I turned on my heel, keeping eye contact until the last second, and then turned my head to face forward and I walked out of the room. I could feel myself growing taller as I squared my shoulders, took nice long, confident strides, and smiled from ear to ear. I laughed at myself because it was ridiculous that standing up to a sixteen-year old girl should actually make me feel so good about myself, but it so did.

It occurred to me that, up until the incident with the phone a week ago, I'd never done that before. I had let her control me all those years when it was *me* who was the parent. I had a momentary flash of sorrow and guilt, and regret that I may have truly been a terrible mother, but I decided to put those thoughts inside an imaginary pink balloon — Logan told me that pink is the color of good health —and I released it into imaginary air and watched it float up into imaginary clouds, snuggle in there, and drift away with them as they moved slowly across an imaginary sky, away from me.

It seemed silly at first, this imaginary farewell to unwanted feelings, but it worked incredibly well and I allowed myself to feel good about myself. What a freakin' novel concept! I almost laughed out loud again! If I kept doing that, they'd think I was crazy for certain sure, but I didn't care about that either. Neither of them would even notice, most likely. "Laugh away," I told myself. I wondered if all my recent laughing was functioning like bicep curls, but for the inner strength I was sure I was acquiring, bit by bit, one decision at a time, one confrontation at a time, one laugh at time.

It was an emotional roller-coaster afternoon, and not long after my confrontation with Reagan, I found my pendulum swinging the other way again as self-doubt tried to creep back in, so I headed out to the backyard to swing it all away.

CHAPTER FOURTEEN
Work

"A life of labor does not make men, but drudges."
—*Ralph Waldo Emerson*

After having revived myself in the swing for a while, I went back inside and went downstairs to my office to try to get some work done. The next week was final exams and I had to have *everything* done by a week from Friday: the hundred forty remaining essays, a hundred sixty-two final exams, and a not insignificant trickling of late work that desperate kids would turn in at the last minute trying for partial credit. Then, of course, there would be the barrage of phone calls and emails from parents who wanted to know what their kids could to do raise their Es to passing grades in two days. One of my friends always answered that question with, "Invent a time machine," but I didn't have the balls to actually say that to anyone. As usual, I was too nice and would spend a ton of time responding, trying to talk them down, and dealing with the fallout.

The *Romeo and Juliet* rewrites that I was working through had come in two weeks prior and, since I hadn't finished grading them yet, the kids were bitching. I was usually pretty good about getting essays turned around within a week, but I'd had shit to deal with recently, so they'd just have to wait. They'd had ten days to write *one*, but expected me to grade a hundred and sixty in a day. At least this batch was all rewrites, so it wouldn't take me quite as long as first-submissions. First-time essays usually sucked because, in spite of having had over a week to work out a good piece of writing, a lot of kids still waited until the night before and then turned in complete garbage. I had *so* much to do! hadn't finished planning Monday's review sessions for third or sixth periods, either, so I headed downstairs toward those tasks and got busy.

As I separated the remaining essays into piles of ten (which made tackling them seem like less of a chore somehow), I decided that I wasn't going to stress about this. There was no time for another round of rewrites before the end of the school year, so I could skimp on the comments (which about two-thirds of the kids obviously didn't read anyway) and just check to see if they had made the required improvements. I would just check off the appropriate boxes on the rubric and make a note that they should see me if they had questions. If it was per usual, probably only five or six of them ever them would.

Very few kids these days understood that *learning* was more important than grades, in spite of my constant repetition of that fact. I kept telling them that if the learning happened, the grades would follow, but since a good number of parents cared more about grades than about learning, that was that. Grades were so inflated by that time anyway that I worried about how the kids would fare in college since so many of them would be shocked by real grades and many of them hadn't acquired the necessary skills, despite my best efforts. I loved my kids, all my kids, and I did worry about them.

I missed the old days when class sizes were maxed out at twenty-five and when *real* teaching and learning happened. Now that there were up to thirty, thirty-five kids, in every class, it was more like whack-a-mole. "Jason, stop talking. Brenda, put your phone away. Ella, wake up. Robert, sit down." There was no time to conference individually any more and it broke my heart to see so many kids falling through the huge cracks that the District and the State had opened up… "Stop it!" I scolded myself. What was the sense in ruminating about this? There was nothing I could do but the best I could do. "Another mantra to add to my list," I thought. The best I could do *was* the best I could do, after all. And during *this* of all weeks, the best I could do maybe wasn't as good as I would usually have done or would have liked to do, but it *was* the *best* I could do. I popped the top of a diet root beer, grabbed my green pen (red always felt like yelling to me), opened the bag of pretzel sticks that would sustain me through the chore, and picked up the first pile of ten.

It was so hard to concentrate. In spite of my best intentions, I kept brooding on the fact that work just wasn't fun anymore. I felt more like a tester than a teacher, more like an evaluator than an educator. Teaching to the test (especially one that I didn't write!) really pissed me off, but that was the order of the day. I found myself thumbing through memories of the "good ol' days" when it had been so much fun, and the kids had learned so much, the days when I so often saw lightbulbs going on above their heads as they learned to think and discuss and formulate opinions and to support them… back when the essays used to be good. These memories distracted me from the task at hand so I sent them off in another pink balloon and finally got down to work.

I made good progress and got the lessons planned for Monday and Tuesday, and I only had about thirty-five essays left by the time I gave it up at around midnight. You can only grade so many before your brain turns to mush. I took my mushy brain back upstairs, poured myself a glass of wine, and grabbed a couple of peanut butter cookies out of the jar. My reward. I'd worked through dinner rather than eating with the Terrible Twosome and it only took the one glass of wine to fuzz up my head. I got to bed about 1:00, which meant I'd be teaching on four hours' sleep the next day…again. We were all sleep derived this time of year.

I banged through a dozen or so essays (leaving the rest for the weekend) during sixth period on Friday while the kids, in this class at least, loved me now in spite of still not having their essays back because I'd decided to just push play that day. They quietly watched the Decaprio version of *Romeo and Juliet* while I worked, but my heart just wasn't in it. A hundred and a half essays all on the same lame topic was *so* boring. Were it up to me, I would have given them a choice of topics so they could have more control over and interest in the task and so that I'd have a more enjoyable variety of papers to read. Oh well, it wasn't up to me anymore, was it?

When the last bell rang I couldn't get out fast enough. The secretary in the office looked perplexed and concerned as I rushed by at two-thirty, having rarely seen me leave the building that early. I usually didn't get out of there before four or five, sometimes even six. I had decided that I would just finish the film during sixth period on Monday and have the kids in the other hours do group review for finals (or silent reading if they were too rowdy for that) so I could finish everything up. I never would have resorted to this in the past. Now it was a coping technique necessary to survive in the new reality, and all that grading had to be done by Tuesday so I would have the last three afternoons free to score final exams.

On the way home, I swung through McDonald's for an order of fries and, while I was waiting in line, I marveled yet again at how incredibly clueless the general public was about a teacher's life and the disservice that some parents and the powers-that-be were doing to their children. I was almost sorry (almost) that I had fought Dick about putting Reagan in private school. I had wanted her to learn in a more diverse environment. I only won the argument when I reminded Dick about how much a private education would cost. After that, he backed down and I chalked it up as one of the very few times I actually got my way.

I had wanted to get my Master's Degree and maybe eventually move to teaching at one of the nearby community colleges, but Dick bristled at the cost of that as well, so I was treading water and saw no real prospect of improving my work situation any time soon. At least summer vacation was only a week away. It felt like I was dragging myself up the last huge sand dune before the oasis.

CHAPTER FIFTEEN
Desi

"Be curious, not judgmental."
—*Walt Whitman*

How they worked out the rides that Sunday, I never knew because, in spite of the cold shoulder and dirty looks I got from both of them for the remainder of the week, I left the house at 1:30 on Sunday to drive to Starbuck's, leaving them to their own devices.

I had been so looking forward to Sunday that the three days since I'd spoken with Desi had just dragged by, especially since my only diversion was finishing up those boring essays.

When I pulled into the parking lot at Starbuck's, I looked around, wondering what kind of car Desi was likely to drive. Traffic had been light and I was twenty minutes early, so I planned on sitting in the parking lot to wait and watch for him. Would he be driving a junker? A beat-up POS car (as my father used to call the pieces of shit some of his subordinates drove)? Would the car signal to me that some poverty-stricken Pontiac-ite was pulling in? Was I acting like a stalker? What the hell was wrong with me?

I chastised myself for thinking like that. I consistently tried to be non-judgmental, but it wasn't always easy. For all I knew, this guy could be worth a million dollars. That wouldn't mean that he could't live in Pontiac and have a troubled daughter without a female role model. Look at *my* family for Christ's sake! We were solidly middle class and we were falling apart at warp speed. I hadn't been able to be a good female role model for *my* daughter, even though I had read everything I could get my hands on and made every decision concerning her with an eye toward how it would turn her into strong, confident, caring, independent young woman. Boy had I blown that one! I had a fleeting thought about looking into a Big Sister for Reagan. How ironic would that be? I thought about Dick. He was a lost cause.

I decided that I'd take whatever came for what it was. Logan had told me, more than once in the several conversations we'd had over the hedge in the week since we'd met, that staying in the present moment and accepting whatever came along, and being grateful for it whatever that might be, was the real path to peace and happiness. In fact, she was the one who told me about the pink balloon, and that shit really worked! The first time she'd mentioned that was the afternoon I'd informed the Terrible Twosome that I wasn't going to be a chauffeur on Sunday. Even though I had tried to stay strong, the events of that afternoon had shaken me, and I found myself once again in the swing trying to sort it out.

Logan saw me there and called me over. We sat together on the glider in her yard drinking camomile tea and noshing on some roasted nuts she'd just taken out of her oven. She must have been able to tell that I was upset because she was staying unusually quiet as we rocked back and forth. As it always did, that motion calmed me down, and I started to feel quite at home there. After several minutes, I felt compelled to break the silence and I spilled the whole story as Logan sat and listened in silence. No need to tell *her* to pay attention.

She didn't say anything. Didn't give me any advice or encouragement. She just listened and, when I had finished my tale of woe, she reached over and took my hand. That was it. We just sat like that and rocked. Ten minutes later I had to head home and, as she walked me down her side of the fence and I rounded it to head down my side of the fence to my own back door, she told me about the pink balloon. That had come in handy many times already.

I decided not to wait in the car for Desi after all. That suddenly seemed weak and I wasn't having any more of that if I could help it. I walked in and ordered a small hazelnut coffee and was able to grab the two upholstered chairs near the window. I thought it was a good bit of luck that they weren't already occupied because sitting there would make it seem more like two friends conversing than like an interview with two people across from each other at a table. Even though I knew this *was*, for all intents and purposes, an interview, I didn't want it to feel like one for some reason.

When he walked in, I was immediately taken aback. Looking cautiously around the room, obviously a little nervous, was the most stunning man I had ever seen, black, white, or any color in between. It wasn't that he was particularly handsome. It was more a presence that he exuded, something emanated from him that had a power I couldn't really discern or explain to myself. It was a strange mixture of strength and vulnerability.

He was even taller than Dick and had kind, concerned eyes, but what made my heart stop was the smile he cast my way when he somehow recognized me as the woman he intended to meet. Our eyes locked and we gave each other a small nod of confirmation, at which he beamed a full-face smile that seemed to flow right out of his eyes. It actually made me catch my breath. His expression as he walked over to join me was a mixture of happiness, worry, relief, and about thousand other emotions –- on his *face*! I'd never experienced that before. Dick could've been carved in stone for all the emotion he ever exhibited (and most days I truly believed he was!). The chemistry of that smile hit me before we'd exchanged a word. I was immediately enthralled by this man.

He was wearing a nice light sweater, blue and gray, and some good-fitting jeans that made it impossible not to look at his body, which was lean and solid. He was clean-shaven, clean-cut, with short black hair. As he approached me, his face took on a look of serene concern and hopeful expectation. I found myself afraid to hear him speak, afraid that adding that farmer-poet voice to the person I saw before me might just be too much for me.

"God, stop it!" I said to myself. "This isn't a date; it's a business meeting." I suddenly regretted my choice of seats, but he seemed glad of it as he sank down into the cushions of the chair beside me as though he really needed to rest. Then he leaned forward in his seat to shake my hand, a gesture so formal yet simultaneously so intimate that it confounded me. He was so full of contradictions, it seemed. He smiled at me again, that disarming smile, and said he was so pleased to meet me. He didn't say more in the way of greeting, but the look in his eyes made me think he was hoping that I'd be the answer to his hopes and prayers.

I suddenly felt like I was under a great deal of pressure and became nervous, but he put me at ease right away. It was that smile. It was a warm, melting smile that dissolved my fears and inhibitions and made me remember that, in some way, I was hoping that his daughter might help answer some of my prayers as well. (How freakin' selfish could I be?)

He made no move to get up to order, so I jumped right in and asked about Micah.

"Well," he said, "I'll let her give you the details because I don't want to cloud anything up with my perspective, but the bottom line is that her mother ran out on us several years ago and Micah immediately took it upon herself, at *way* too young an age, to become the woman of the house, take care of it, take care of her younger sister, who's a special girl" — he didn't elaborate on this — "take care of me... For a while, she was taking care of herself as well, but as she got older and the demands on her -- not from Bria or me but from herself -- intensified, she started getting a little lax in that department." I sat silently, taking intermittent sips of my coffee, as he continued. I was so proud of myself for not interrupting him, which was usually a huge fault of mine. I wondered if I was learning to listen better the from the way Logan always listened to me.

"I know her love and concern for me is what's kept her at her studies and out of trouble so far, but she's getting tired of worrying about me I think (finally!) and her friends are becoming more important in her life. The problem is that the friends aren't good people and will certainly lead her down some dangerous paths. She's started telling me that I don't understand her, and I don't. I was hoping that maybe a woman's perspective, a woman's ear, a woman's... I don't know what... might bring back my little girl." He paused for a moment and continued. "No. I really do know that that's done. She'll never be my little girl again, I know, but maybe you can help me save my young woman. It's better said that way, I guess. I don't know. I just don't know."

He must have seen the look of concern on my face and mistaken it for fear of failure, but this was one time when my own failure was not on my mind. I was filled with compassion for this obviously loving man who, in his helplessness, could so easily admit his lack of power and knowledge. I'd never met a man so open before.

"Please don't get me wrong," he continued, possibly misreading my expression. "I don't expect miracles. I won't have any hard feelings if this doesn't work out or even If it makes things worse, God forbid. I just have to do *something* and I don't know what. This was all I could think of."

"Well, I don't know what to do either," I said, smiling at him in an attempt to resurrect his smile and smooth out the crease in his brow, "so we're both in the same boat. But I think we'll be able to figure something out. Let's just take it one step at a time." Oh my God... I was pretending that I knew what the hell I was talking about. "I'm going to hell for sure!" I thought.

"She was only twelve," he continued. "She wasn't young enough when her mother left for it not to hurt, and it did hurt -- badly," he said. I couldn't tell if he meant that it hurt Micah or him. Probably both. "My younger daughter has dealt with it by becoming very introverted and speaking very rarely. She's a loving, intuitive child, my Bria, my baby, and I worry about her too, but she's an old soul, if you know what I mean, and she's strong in her own way. She's processing. You can see that she's processing.

"She was seven when her mom walked out so she had five fewer years of memories than Micah did. It was really hard for her, but Micah.. she's been hurting these past five years and she's angry… and getting angrier it seems." Again, his worry and concern were written plainly on his face. "She tries to bury it by working so hard, at home, at school, but it never erased the hurt for that girl. She's spiteful. She's vengeful. She's pissed. I really think the only thing that's kept her from making any really bad mistakes up until now is that she knows Bria loves her, looks up to her, and would be hurt or disappointed if Micah didn't live up to… what? Her expectations? *We* have no expectations, really. Micah drives herself, but I'm afraid she's headed for a cliff." This poor man. I could relate to so much of what he was going through, but certainly not to all of it, so I continued to give him my undivided attention and decided that I would for as long as he needed it.

"She loves me and knows how hurt I was, am, by all that's happened," he continued, "but she's getting older and her priorities, naturally, are changing. I don't blame her, but I have to help her — somehow."

I kept sipping my coffee every now and then, letting him talk, restraining my natural tendency to interrupt with stories of my own. That became easier to do as I listened to him because such strong emotion poured out with every word, concern caressed every clause, sentiment surrounded every sentence that he uttered. I was exposed to more pure emotion in that one hour coffee date (date? Was it?) with Desi than in the entire nineteen years of my marriage to Dick. But this wasn't a date.

"I don't like her friends," he went on, "but I've been trying to work two jobs to keep body and soul together –- not that I'm complaining — and that makes it harder to monitor what she's doing or who she's with. I work as a painter (residential, commercial) and I freelance as a handyman when I can get work. It's a lot, and I know how lucky I am to have a job at all, but it means that I'm not around as much as I would like to be to keep an eye on her, to guide her…to protect her, if she'd even let me. And I can't give her the female perspective on anything, obviously. One time, I tried the old line about how guys are only after one thing and you'd think I'd said the stupidest thing in the world. And I can't make her see that the guy she's dating is bad news, really bad news, when all her girlfriends think he's the livin' end, that he's so hot, and that she's so lucky to have him. Damn it."

His frustration rode the expletive like a jockey on a racehorse breaking free of the gate. He immediately apologized and I put his mind at ease by informing him that English teachers typically swear like truck drivers so he should have no concerns about profanity around me. "And that boyfriend," he continued, "he terrifies me. Why can't she see through that kid? She even asked me one time if I realized how lucky *she* was to be able to get with *him*. To *get with* him! My God, she doesn't have a clue about her own worth. She doesn't take me seriously. I just don't know what to do."

I could tell he was lapsing into despair again so I tried to reassure him, even though I was apprehensive myself about my ability to do anything to help. This sounded like a very troubled young lady, but I knew telling him that this was just typical teenage angst wouldn't help and might even seem like I was dismissing or diminishing his concerns, his very real fear. I had been thinking about using that old cliche about boys myself! What new perspective could I bring? And I didn't have a clue about my *own* worth, so how could I help his daughter see hers? I had no idea what or how to do anything!

It seemed like he needed a break, which I totally understood since I knew from personal experience how draining a barrage of emotions could be. He got up to get a coffee, then settled back into his chair to continue, looking somewhat revived I thought.

"She's smarter than any woman I know," he said after taking a sip of his coffee and setting the cup on the small table between us. She doesn't fit in with this crowd she's hanging with and she's trying to change herself, downplay herself, so that she can. She hides her intelligence so she'll fit in and it's such a waste! I know you're going to say that I'm just saying that because I'm her father, but when you meet her, you'll see what I mean."

"So I passed the interview? I get to meet her?" I interrupted, unable to stop myself. "I've said so little I was afraid you'd think I wasn't able to be helpful."

He laughed lightly and said, "It's probably because you're such a good listener that I feel certain that you'll be a wonderful help, but really, there's no pressure. Just whatever you can say or do for however long you can say or do it. Anything. Anything at all."

"I'll do whatever I can. I've known girls like her. I've taught high school students for a couple of decades and it's always unsettling to see young women who devalue themselves. Girls who think the only way they can define themselves is by the boys they date or the clique they can get into. It breaks my heart. It's taken women so long to come as far as we have and I see so many young girls taking us back fifty years with that kind of thinking…. Not that I mean Micah!"

"No, I understand," he interjected to put my mind at ease. "Do you teach in an integrated school?"

"It's becoming more diverse. When I started, it was as white bread as they come, but it's getting better… and I think some things are the same in all races, especially when it comes to adolescents. Black or white, teenagers all have the same harsh issues to deal with. I wouldn't go back for a million dollars!"

"Me either, and I agree. I think you're right, but you throw some black on that mix, and there's a whole host of other problems of which you can't possibly be aware. It definitely adds complications, as does a home that was broken the way ours was." I was so relieved, even impressed… I don't know…that he didn't seem predisposed to the idea that I was predisposed to any idea of him or of Micah. I had thought discussing race would get awkward, but so far, it didn't feel that way.

I held back and didn't ask for specifics about how their home had been broken. I knew I'd get the story later if I needed to know it. I said, "I'll be open to that, and I hope you won't hesitate to share with me anything you think might help me, even if you're afraid you might offend me. I have pretty thick skin," I lied in spite of myself, adding the truth, "and I do have an open mind. I'm not going to pretend to know or even understand the issues Micah has to deal with, but I'll remember that they're there, and I'll stay open and on the lookout."

"Thank you. Thank you so much," he said. These were the six most heartfelt words I'd ever heard in my life.

"What is it that you think I should do with her, to start?"

"Her, specifically, I have no idea. I know she's my daughter, but she's been moving away from me lately and I don't feel certain of anything. The lady at Big Sisters said that a Big Sister could take her out to lunch or to the mall – not to buy her anything – I have that covered — but to maybe just talk, point out what clothes are appropriate and which ones aren't…that kind of thing. Go to the movies, or have 'em visit with their families…I have no freaking idea."

I shook my head. "My family couldn't help her. My husband and my daughter would only make her worse." I have no idea why I was being so candid, but I continued. "To be totally honest with you, part of the reason that I want to do this is that I need to escape my family and I want to escape into something good. I want to escape into helping somebody if I can. I want to escape into some new friends. I want to escape from the pain of my own house." I stopped myself short, realizing that I was saying too much, too soon, but I felt so comfortable around him already. I leaned slightly toward him, involuntarily, and said, "I hope you don't think that the fact that I have weak relationships with them means that I'm not going to be any good for Micah because it doesn't. I'm not going to say that it's all them and not me but… but it's all them and not me!" I ended with some levity that got us both smiling again.

"You don't need to tell me about weak family relationships," he offered, leaning forward in his chair with his elbows on his knees. "At least none of yours have snapped in half." I wondered what that could possibly mean. It seemed so violent, painful, and permanent.

"No," he continued, "the fact that you're this honest and open about it makes me think that you'd be the perfect person for my girl. She needs some honesty. She needs some openness. She needs some reality. You know, maybe seeing that adults have problems, that white people have problems, too, might make her take better stock of her own. Maybe it'll help her see them, deal with them, rather than running away from them with those… I don't know what to call them… those…"

"White trash kids who happen to be black?" I supplied with a smile, then second guessed myself about using that label.

"That sounds about right!" he laughed, glancing over the fact that I had just inadvertently used a stereotype when I'd pretty much just pledged not to resort to stereotypes.

I continued, trying not to sound too judgmental or superior. "It's hard to label people because doing so is always shallow and superficial at best, but I know sometimes for the sake of clarity, generalizations have to happen. I do understand what you mean, though."

"I think you do," he said as he returned my smile, sat back in his chair, and continued. "I don't expect her to ever understand her mother. I don't understand her mother. She doesn't have to understand anything. I just want her to have some joy out of life and there's no joy there now at all. Just anger, and something that seems like desperation. I don't know. I just don't want her to make any bad decisions and waste the wonderful gifts God gave her.

"Well, I can't promise anything for sure, but to do my best. That I do promise."

"Well, there's one little hitch."

"I'll betcha ten bucks I can guess what it is: she doesn't want to do this."

"Ah, you *do* get teenagers. No ma'am, she does not. She thinks I'm getting her a babysitter and she feels insulted by that. She's trying so hard to grow up before her time that this looks to her like I don't appreciate or trust her. She just needs some guidance, but she doesn't see any reason why she'd needs this. She thinks...."

I finished his sentence, even though I'd promised myself that I'd refrain from doing that "...she thinks that everything is just fine and that adults don't understand jack."

"Absolutely," said Desi.

"Well, then, she's pretty much like my other hundred and sixty kids so there's no surprises there!" We chuckled again. We were slowly becoming very easy with each other, I could feel it. "How about we find a time when I can come pick her up. She knows we've met, right?. I mean I know she knows I'm from Big Sisters but, I mean… we could say we're friends."

"Absolutely. We're friends." He turned that beautiful smile on me again.

"…and we'll go out to… what do you think would be better, lunch or coffee?"

"Well," he answered, "the girl likes to eat!"

"Lunch it is then. We'll go out and we'll see if we can hit it off."

"I think that's a good place to start. Let me tell you that, already, even if it doesn't work out, I appreciate you giving me this afternoon, and I appreciate you being willing to, wanting to, do this. You're like an angel. I love my daughter. I love my daughter so much. If I could have kept her mother from running away, I would have." Oddly, it made me kind of sad to hear that. "But some things are out of my control. So many things are out of my control."

"Oh, believe me," I chuckled, "I understand what *that's* like! I'll do whatever I can, I promise."

Well, we'd see, because we decided that I'd pick Micah up the following Saturday and we'd go to lunch, just the two of us.

CHAPTER SIXTEEN
Binge

"The road to wisdom is paved with excess."
——*Walt Whitman*

The week I had to wait before I could meet Micah absolutely sucked. The last week of school was always so filled with emotion. I was freaked out because I couldn't see how in the hell I'd get all my work done by the Friday afternoon deadline. I was so excited that summer was finally almost here. I was sad because I'd miss the kids I'd grown so fond of over the last nine months. So many emotions square dancing around my heart and through my psyche.

I spent Monday and Tuesday reviewing for finals with the kids and then grading papers late into the night. The essays were almost done, but there had been more late work than I'd expected. I was happy, though, that I'd have no more lesson plans to do. That used to be one of my favorite things. I could get creative and come up with stuff that the kids would love and that moved them forward. I used to love seeing their eyes light up when they figured things out on their own or when insights dawned on them. I loved the long class discussions when you could just see them learning how to *think* and how to communicate. Now, most of that was gone and we had to teach what we were told to teach, how they told us to teach it. It was so very sad. Summer vacation could not arrive soon enough.

I finished the rest of the essays over the course of Wednesday and Thursday nights, but it rendered me exhausted and sleep deprived. I got the late work and some of the parent emails done Wednesday and Thursday afternoons after morning final exams were over. When Friday came, I felt like I was hanging by a very thin, fraying thread. I spent Friday afternoon finalizing and entering grades, and finishing up the last of the parent emails. It never failed to amaze me how some parents, many of whom had never bothered to answer *my* emails to *them* during the semester, just came out of the woodwork with demands to break the rules and give full credit for late work, or worse, just up the grade for no good reason. When I left work on Friday, I was both exhausted and elated. I was relieved to have the school year behind me and very excited to see Micah on Saturday.

I wasn't sure, but I was beginning to think the Terrible Twosome were finally coming to understand that things were really beginning to change. They were accustomed to me being insane during the last week of school, but they weren't used to being as ignored by me as I always was by them.

When I walked into the house after school that Friday, I could hear Reagan's music blaring from her room and I knew Dick would head to the garage as soon as he got home (whenever that might be). We really were more like three roommates than a real family by this point and it so hurt my heart. I had, by then, however, realized that I couldn't fix things on that front all alone, so my priority *had* to be myself.

I went into the kitchen, poured myself a glass of Chardonay and popped a bagel in the toaster oven. I smothered that with butter, then I took it all into the living room and enjoyed them while treating myself to a relatively short binge of a few re-runs of *Law & Order, SVU*. I always did something frivolous, something that was brain-candy, after school on that last day. It seemed like a necessary decompression. Some of the other teachers were going out for cocktails after school, but I decided I didn't want to be fuzzy for my sister-date with Micah the next day, so I passed on that, much to the surprise of many of my colleagues. We weren't really close, but I usually never missed the opportunity to have a cocktail. I wonder how many of them guessed that I'd be sitting down with wine when I got home anyway.

The carbs and alcohol did seem to take the edge off the harrowing week but, as usual, it wasn't enough, and I couldn't stop imbibing and noshing once I'd started. I made four more trips to the kitchen, lamenting my apparent inability to comfort myself. So much for not being fuzzy. If I hadn't been buzzed and on the edge of a food coma by the end of night, I might have realized that drinking and binging were not the answer to either my need to celebrate or to alleviating the things that pained me. Logan had been subtly trying to teach me this and, as I finally climbed into bed and faded into sleep around 9:00 after the sixth episode, I resolved to really, really try to meditate or walk or do some yoga or one of the dozens of other things Logan had introduced me to already during our now almost-daily encounters that would prove to be far more helpful and less fat and fuzz producing.

As I tossed in my bed feeling horrible and waiting for sleep to release me, I remembered the night I binged for the first time. Dark, mid-summer. Crickets singing in the back yard. Television talking at me from the front room. Who knew it would be my last night as a child and my first as a confused, disturbed adolescent?

My dad. That night. The memory sort of enveloped me as I fruitlessly waited for sleep to show up. I almost felt like I was there again, it was that vivid. I think I was about thirteen, maybe fourteen, just a little younger than Regan. He had come home sober, oddly enough. That should've been a big signal right there. The old trusted patterns weren't in place. My mom, however, and also oddly, was thoroughly inebriated and was upset at the lateness of the hour that marked his return, something about which she would never have cared at all had she been sober. Normally, she was more pleased by his absence than by his rare timely arrival. This night, though, alcohol had prompted her to combativeness. Unfortunately, my father had no such aggressive general on his side of their battlefield this night and only looked tired, sounded tired.

Already defeated by his day, he seemed ready to surrender, which was so not like him. I don't remember him ever backing away from a conflict.

It was about 10:00 p.m. and he had just finished an afternoon shift, standing in front of an 1800 degree furnace for ten hours at the heat treating shop where he worked, and he was done in, seemingly more than usual in light of the events that followed.

He reheated some leftovers while my mother pelted him with

harshly slurred angry words about what a horrible husband, father, and person he was. He remained silent, trying to stomach, if not enjoy, the dinner in front of him, while she droned on and on. She could see nothing through the fog of her stupor, so she continued to press forward, harrying his silence, until he cracked. Had she been herself, she would have remembered that his cracking was a foregone conclusion and was never pleasant and was sometimes even down-right dangerous.

Remembering this made we wonder for the millionth time how it was that I had ever taken a drink at all but, in spite of what I should have learned from my father, I fell in love with my Chardonay anyway. Having lived with these parents, you'd think I'd avoid alcohol like the plague. Nope.

Finally, he rose slowly, frighteningly slowly, from his chair to face her, infuriated but still struggling desperately to control that which he could never before control: himself. He might have succeeded this time, he was trying so hard, but my mother perceived his hesitation as weakness so she foolishly chose to thrust a blade into that newly plated armor he appeared to have donned to protect himself from her onslaught and to prevent him from exploding.

She made a quick grab at his ashtray, which was right next to his plate and was full to the brim as always, and she upside-downed it over his dinner. That was it –- the charge has been sounded. His rage was palpable. I could actually feel its energy in the atmosphere around us.

I had been a silent witness to all this, which was the only way to survive in that house, but waves of apprehension and fear washed over me as I sat nearby, out of sight. I was sitting about half way up the stairs that led to my bungalow attic room, behind the wall that hid the stairs from the kitchen. Right through the wall I felt it. I didn't see her dump the ashtray, but I could feel that a line had somehow been crossed because it became excruciatingly silent. No words were spoken at all. My mother even stopped. She felt it too, even through her boozy brain. I scooted down to the bottom step where I could see her better. There was a look of defiance, confusion, and terror on her face, as she slowly realized what she'd done.

After a stand-still moment, he bolted, still silent, past her and into the room they shared. He reappeared almost instantly, a rifle that I didn't even know was in the house expertly aimed between her glassy, half crossed eyes. Still no words. Still no sound other than the beating of hearts. The air settled into a thick stillness. Even our breathing was silent and in slow motion. He didn't shake. He stared down the barrel of the rifle that wasn't but twelve inches from her face. I didn't move. She didn't move. The very, very real danger of the moment penetrated even her stubborn stupor and she froze. It was an eternal moment.

After however long (who can remember?), I slowly got up from that bottom stair and very cautiously went to him. I figured, what did it matter if he shot me? What kind of whack-ass world was this that I should want to live in it anyway? This is not how parents were supposed to act. I watched television. I had friends. I knew what families were supposed to look like. So what if this crazy excuse for a family fell apart? Was it ever even together? Could it ever be? I knew the answer to that.

I don't remember being afraid for me at all. I remember being afraid for *her*. She was so clueless at the moment, and she usually wasn't like this. She, too, must just have been at her breaking point is all, I thought.

So I approached him, slowly, thinking that nothing really mattered but that, if I could get the gun, it might not be such a messy night. I said silent prayer as the gun began to shake almost imperceptibly in his hands as he just held it there, pointed at her. He paid no attention to my approach. God only knows what was going through his mind. If he had been drinking, it would have all been over, doubtless, but since he was sober, he was desperately trying to reign in his rage.

I laid my hand gently on his shoulder from the side, afraid I'd startle him if I came up from behind. Without moving any other muscle, he slowly turned his head and locked eyes with me. I just held his gaze and kept repeating silently to myself, talking to myself rather than to him, "I love you. It's not worth it. I love you. It's not worth it." I don't know if he read my mind, but after several more silent, still as death moments, he slowly lowered the gun.

My mother had turned into a statue during all this. She was way too familiar with his hair trigger temper and the events of the night had sobered her up enough to realize that she had put herself (and possibly me) in very real danger. But he looked at me. He saw only me. Still no words — out of any of us. It seemed as if someone had spoken, the spell would be broken, the gun would discharge, and we'd all be gone.

The tension in the air still seemed to be pulsating, but it dissipated by degrees as he slowly pointed the barrel toward the floor then slowly handed the gun to me. "I'm going out," he said in a quiet, otherworldly voice.

"That's good," I replied, my hand still on his shoulder. I gave him a minuscule squeeze and smiled. "Be careful. See you soon."

He turned heavily and walked out the front door, fishing his car keys out of his pants pocket as he went. My mother still stood there. She didn't seem to be able to speak yet or move. I think she was trying to figure out what the hell had just happened. As soon as the front door closed behind him and I saw through the picture window that the headlights were receding and then moving down the street, time sped up. Until that moment, it had stood still as death, but when I knew it was safe, I snapped to life and moved with more speed than I thought I'd be able to muster after such an emotional choking.

I leaned the gun against a chair and grabbed my mother's wrist. I hope I wasn't too rough with her because I did pity her, but I had to get her out of there. I tugged her into her room, grabbed her robe from the hook behind the door, managed to wrestle her into it and cinch the belt. Then I dragged her back out, grabbed the rifle in one hand, still holding her by the arm with the other, and half pulled, half dragged her, stumbling and stammering, down the front porch steps, down the walk, down one curb, across the street, tripping and recovering up over the next curb, up the walk and several porch steps to the home of Sally and Sam, our hippy neighbors across the street.

All this time, my mother wasn't real to me. She had started talking again, but I heard nothing she said and wouldn't have understood it even if it had been intelligible. I perceived only muffled sounds as my heart beat in my ears. She complained in my wake me as I dragged her along on our short journey. It seemed like a hundred miles to me, especially since I was running on instinct and had no idea what I intended to do after invading the privacy of these good people with the insanity of my situation. But mom was cold, she was angry, she was tired, she didn't deserve to be treated like this... this was the ilk of her grievances I was sure, but I heard it only as a low hum and not as actual words.

Sally was a friend even though she was over a decade my senior. She and her family were kind of free spirited and lived with a small commune of others in their modest home, members of a band, others who came and went. My girlfriends and I sometimes babysat for their three year old daughter and we'd become somewhat close. I wasn't sure how, but I knew she'd help me.

When Sally opened the door, she saw me there with my half dressed, drunken mother and a rifle, but she didn't say a word. She just opened the door and motioned us inside. She agreed to keep mom overnight and to do something — anything -- with the rifle. I never found out what she did. I never saw that gun again. I appreciated that so much, especially since she had a child in the house. To be honest, I can't say that I would have been as helpful were the situation reversed. She waved away my protests and told me not to worry, but to get back home and wait for my dad. I figured that was probably the best advice and, since mom was snoring away on the couch within minutes, I left.

Sally was a true friend. She'd listen to my mother in the morning, give her some cereal and coffee, and send her back to whatever peace I'd be able to make at home, which turned out to be easier than I thought it would be.

When I got back to the house, I ate twelve pieces of bologna right out of the package. After that, I started in on the nearly full jar of peanut butter which I ate with a spoon, and opened a new bag of chips.

* * * * *

Two and a half hours later, he came back. By that time, I had also finished the rest of the Oreos in the cookie jar. About half a package, I'd guess, had vanished.

He smelled of beer and cigarettes, but he was still mostly sober… and destroyed. He asked where she was. I told him. He asked about his gun. I told him. I told him it was gone forever. "Good," he said. I suggested that he go to bed and get some rest. I was worried in case Sally couldn't keep my mom as easily as she kept the gun. If mom woke up before she sobered up, Sally might have to bring her back.

To my utter shock and infinite relief, he agreed. I followed him into the room he shared with my mother. He sank down onto the edge of the bed, put his face into his shaking hands, and sobbed. I never thought I'd ever see such a thing. This tough, big, burly, ex-marine was falling apart before my eyes. I had never seen him cry. I was surprised to learn that he was even capable of it. I was no longer a child with a father to protect her. I was a teenager with a man-child who needed to be protected from himself.

I went to him and knelt down in front of him, drawing his forty-five year old head onto my fourteen year old shoulder. His sobs were silent, but they wracked his body and I wondered if he had ever done this before in his life -– in the war when his buddies were killed or when his parents or younger sister died or when he was scared. I didn't know he could get scared, but he was now. He was frightened to death. I wondered who in his past had cradled his head, hugged him, and told him not to worry, that everything would be all right, as I was doing now. It was so surreal. So very surreal.

After about ten minutes, he had no more energy left and he grew silent and still. I knew he was slowing getting reading to speak to me, and that it would be hard for him to disengage himself and regain his hard-ass persona after what had just transpired. I knew I'd have to help him do that. I'd have to reassure him that he was still a scary-as-hell bad ass in spite of this episode between us. It would be as if it never happened. I knew that's how it'd have to be. This wouldn't bring us any closer. It was a only dream.

I also knew that he would have killed her had I not been there to stop it. He knew it, too. I knew that, if he had done it, it would have killed him. Having *almost* done it had driven him to distraction. It had turned him into a person I didn't recognize. He knew all this as well as I did.

"It'll never happen again," he whispered when he finally got himself under control, lifted his head from my shoulder and looked at me with red-rimmed eyes. "I will never see that gun again -– make sure of that," he said in a tone that clearly laid out my responsibility in the matter. I felt great relief at this because I had been sure that he would have made me get it back. "I'll just leave, first, before… You'll understand if I just leave?"

"I'll be proud of you for it," I replied. "I was proud of you tonight." He knew what I meant so I didn't need to elaborate. How odd that he and I, who had never understood each other before, were practically reading each other's thoughts now that our roles had been reversed. I knew he meant that he'd remove himself from the situation, not that he'd leave for good. He knew I was proud of his self-control, not of what he'd done.

I rose slowly after giving him a reassuring hug . I don't remember ever having hugged him before that and I never did afterward. He was not an affectionate man. I helped him to his feet and walked him around to his side of the bed. I turned the covers down for him, patted his shoulder after I'd pulled the covers up to his chin, then I left the room, gently closing the door behind me.

I saw the line of light beneath the door disappear a minute later as he turned off the bedside lamp, and I heard the springs creak as he settled in. I listened at the door until his soft, regular breathing assured me that he had fallen asleep.

I looked out the front window at Sally's house and observed that it was dark and the porch light had been extinguished, a sign that all was well and that mom wouldn't be home until morning.

Everyone was asleep but me. I finished the bologna, the jar of peanut butter, the bag of chips, the Oreos, and a sleeve of Ritz crackers before I was able to slump into a food coma on the couch and wait for Act II in the morning. I've never been the same.

CHAPTER SEVENTEEN
Micah

"What we fear doing most is usually what we most need to do."
—*Ralph Waldo Emerson*

The week just dragged by, and I circled around and back between confidence and trepidation, between excitement and apprehension, about my upcoming meeting with Micah. It almost made me dizzy. Neither of the Terrible Twosome spoke to me the previous Sunday afternoon when I returned from meeting Desi, which was just fine with me. I had grabbed the half bottle of wine from the fridge and headed over to Logan's. We'd grown close enough that I was never worried about popping in. I could trust that if it wasn't a good time, she'd let me know, and she could trust that I wouldn't take offense at that.

I knew she didn't drink and I usually didn't imbibe when I was at her place, but that day, I felt the need to both soothe and celebrate. I told her all about the afternoon (downplaying my inescapable attraction to Desi). She seemed genuinely interested and suggested that maybe she could join Micah and I on one of our adventures. That's what she called them — adventures. I hoped she was right.

Saturday finally arrived and it was another glorious, sunny summer afternoon. As I drove up Woodard Avenue, I realized yet again how fortunate I was, even in the face of so much loss. Even though Dick still lived with me, for all intents and purposes he was gone from my life. Even though Reagan still lived with me, she was gone too. It was ironic: even though my baby boy was gone, I felt as if he still lived in me, while the two living people who should love me were, for all intents and purposes, nonexistent. I tried to think all this through on my way to meet Micah, but to be honest, the only thing that was really occupying my mind was Desi. I pushed thoughts of him out of my head again and again, but they kept creeping back in like mice in the night.

When I arrived at their home, I was stuck by the look of the place. It was on a typical suburban Pontiac street, most of which were populated with homes that were run down and unkempt, as I'd expected, having driven through Pontiac many times before on my way to visit my mother in Auburn Hills before she moved to Phoenix.

The street was straight and the branches of the large trees that lined both sides reached out toward each other high overhead, forming a canopy to shake the road. The tar-covered cracks all over the street looked like interconnecting veins. I saw ouses with peeling paint, garbage cans littering curbs, children's toys strewn about in driveways and on sidewalks here and there — not the professionally landscaped, groomed, manicured subdivisions of my world.

But their house, even though it was basically cut from the same cloth as all the others (drab, dusty gray, as if it had been painted a century before with ash) somehow stood out. It looked more kept and swept. It was like the whole neighborhood was lined with cookie-cutter Boo Radley houses, but this one stood apart like Miss Maudie's somehow.

The house couldn't have been more than ten or eleven hundred square feet, but it had a huge, somewhat elevated, front porch that spanned the whole front of the house. The front door was located at the right side and there were a few steps leading up to it. The long front flower bed in front of the porch was overgrown with weeds, but there were a couple of pots of neglected marigolds, just starting to brown and dry, up on the half-wall that surrounded the porch. They reminded me of Mayella Ewell's geraniums, her sad attempt to incorporate some beauty into her dismal dump existence. Just a little attention would have those marigolds looking beautiful in no time, and I bet Logan could transform that flower bed in a heartbeat.

I wondered if it'd be like that with Micah — all that was needed was just a little care and attention. And I wondered if her father ever found himself considering his daughter that way — as just needing a bigger pot, some fresh soil, and more tender loving care than he had the time or capacity to render, no matter how much love he felt for her. He was working two jobs after all. His daughters were certainly things of beauty that he had brought into the world, and yet did he not have the wherewithal to tend those flowers the way they needed to be tended in order to flourish in a harsh environment... so that they could reach their full beautiful bloom. Maybe that's why he contacted Big Sisters. Is that what I was to be? His gardener? His Miracle Grow? Was I up to this?

I parked on the street in front of the house, avoiding the two strips of payment that ran up the right side of the house and served as the driveway. I walked up the steps to the porch, which was devoid of any decent outdoor furniture upon which someone with leisure time could comfortably sit and enjoy the sights and sounds of the neighborhood after a hard day's work, as they did on the street on which I lived. There were two old metal folding chairs, the kind with plastic strips woven into a back and a seat, but that was it.

The whole atmosphere was so foreign to me. I suddenly felt intimidated, but I refused to give up now. Besides, my desire to see Micah's father again was undeniable, so I knocked on the front door in a way that I hoped sounded both confident and friendly.

Desi answered with the same beautiful smile that I remembered from our first meeting and it completely disarmed me once again. I felt like a teenager. What the hell was happening to me?

"I'm *so* glad to see you," he said, shaking my hand. "Please come in." He greeted and welcomed me in such a way that I felt he was proprietor of a manner house rather than the owner (renter? I didn't know) of a small, run-down residence on a dilapidated street in Pontiac. I could tell that this man took great pride in what little he had, and the fact that it was meager, by the standards of my ilk at least, apparently meant nothing to him. We didn't know it yet, but the Great Recession was creeping toward us in the dark and it seems to have knocked on the doors in this neighborhood sooner than the rest. Desi was doing the best he good to say afloat.

I was impressed by the dignified way that he stood aside and motioned me into the front room. He asked if he could take my jacket, and I found this utterly charming, and charming was disarming because it was so foreign to me.

Once inside, I noticed immediately that everything was clean and arranged in a very pleasing way to take maximum advantage of the space and of what natural light there was, and I immediately felt welcome. There wasn't much light because the roof that sloped down over the front porch blocked a good deal of it, but the frayed curtains were pulled all the way back to let in as much as possible. Desi left the front door open as well, which let in still a little more, and the warm summer breeze followed me into the room.

The room was spotless. Throw pillows on the couch had been fluffed up and placed at attractive angles against the worn arms, each of which was covered by a pretty dish towel, apparently to hide the wear and tear. The faded wall-to-wall carpet had obviously been recently vacuumed and there wasn't a spot of dust anywhere. I noticed the sweet aroma of apple spice coming from the jar candle that was glowing at the center of the dark wood coffee table. I wondered if all this was his doing or if his daughters had taken the initiative or had been assigned the tasks necessary to achieve the pleasant atmosphere.

I handed Desi my jean jacket as I walked past him into the living room and noticed a slight young girl about twelve years old seated on a well-worn wing-back chair, apparently so absorbed in the book she was reading that she hadn't noticed me at first. After a moment, she somehow sensed my presence, glanced up, and saw me smiling at her. She gave me a shy smile in return, reminiscent of her father's, but more hesitant, not suspicious really, just less exuberant.

She put her book down on an end table, left her chair, and approached me timidly with her hand outstretched in a practiced, focused manner. I took her hand and introduced myself. The girl was not necessarily fearful, but she was wary, uncertain, yet determined to do what she had apparently been taught was the right thing to do. She gently shook my hand and said in a very small voice that was almost whisper, "Welcome. My name is Bria."

"Bria? What a beautiful name! I don't think I've ever heard it before, and it's like a song."

This caused her smile to widen and brighten a little bit, which made me notice her eyes. They were the most soulful, penetrating eyes I'd ever seen on anyone, let alone on someone so young. I almost wished I had come to be *her* big sister. Those bright brown/gray eyes, the color of tree bark, drew me irresistibly in somehow. I knew at once that this was a special girl.

Her father gave Bria a beaming smile of approval, patted her gently on her head, crouched down to match her height, and kissed her on the cheek, saying, "You're wonderful, kiddo. You can go now." She obviously basked in the praise, but not because it was rarely given. Father and daughter seemed to have a very special, loving bond. She hugged him tightly around the neck and then skipped out of the room. Desi stood back up as she left, looking after her with a smile. I couldn't imagine a scene even remotely like that ever occurring between anyone at my house.

I looked around nervously, looking for Micah. She was nowhere to be seen.

"She's sulking in her room," Desi said, rightly reading my concern.

"Oh, oh. Starting off with sulking, huh?"

"Well, that's better than yelling and screaming," he said. I felt immediately more at ease once I realized that he was going to be completely honest with me and not try to hide any of Micah's reservations in an attempt to keep me interested. A completely honest and forthcoming man… something with which I was not at all familiar. I found that I was liking him more and more by the minute and hoped against hope that Micah didn't prove to be more than I could handle — and hoped against hope that the attraction I was feeling for Desi would be short-lived and nothing I'd actually ever have to deal with later. I chalked it up to the thrill of being needed and taken seriously for once, and hoped I'd just become accustomed to it and that this weird yearning I was feeling would fade out over time.

"I'm surprised, though," he continued, "because she's too smart to act like this. She knows it won't get her anywhere." In two sentences he'd managed to compliment his daughter and raise himself in my estimation yet again as a father who had some measure of control and common sense about raising children. Micah apparently didn't have *him* wrapped around her little finger the way Reagan had Dick twisted around hers like a coiled pipe cleaner. I felt like I was breathing fresh air here. I could already tell that I so wanted to be a part of this family — a good, really good part. I already wanted to help this girl for her father's sake, even though I had not yet met her and there were already obvious issues on the horizon.

"At least at this point, she's still dependent on me so she has to toe the line, but that won't last forever. That's my concern. That's why I'm so worried. She's getting older. She's hooking up with people who might meet some immediate needs she feels she has but who are leading her away from me, from us, as I mentioned to you before. And you know how it is… if I try to forbid her to see them, especially that boyfriend, she'll just rebel harder and faster and I'll lose her. I can't lose her. I just can't. It'd be a such a waste and the world would be so much more worse off for not having her — the *real* her, not the her she's pretending to be —in it. I just can't lose her."

I was touched once again by his passion, his love, his sense of helplessness. I had those same feelings, but I had to admit to myself that I also had a lot of negative feelings for my own daughter, which he apparently did not have for his. Reagan had hurt me so badly so many times, and she could be so mean and vicious when she wanted to be, which was almost all time these days. I had a fleeting memory of her catching my tear on that horrible day… I immediately felt like he was a better father than I was a mother, so I wondered again who I thought I was to be inserting myself into their lives when my own life was in such dire straights.

He motioned to the comfortable looking wing-back chair that Bria had vacated and I sat down, sinking a little too deeply into the soft cushions. Was that because the chair was old or because I was fat? "Stop it!" I silently admonished myself.

He took a seat on the sofa to my left, moving one of the pillows out of his way absent-mindedly. "I'm desperately afraid that they'll succeed in leading her down the wrong road and then I'll have no influence whatsoever," he continued, leaning back and running his hands over his buzz cut hair. He had started a bit of a beard since we'd last met and it was close shaved as well. At that moment, I thought he looked a little bit like Derek Morgan from *Criminal Minds*, but with a wider smile, bigger eyes, and a few more crow's feet around his eyes and worry lines along his high forehead. Dick looked more like a tall Dwight Eisenhower with a beer belly. Could two men *be* more different, in every possible way?

"Not that I'm a control freak," he continued. "I'm really not. Okay, maybe just a little when it comes to my girls, who are the only things I have ever even had the illusion of having any control over! It's just that I *do* know what's better for Micah way more than she does, or than her friends do, or that boyfriend." I noticed that he never used a name for this apparent bad seed.

"Oh yeah, I totally understand that," I said. "Don't even think that you have to explain yourself to me. I told you about my daughter…" I stopped myself. This wasn't a date. He wasn't interested in my problems. He was worried about Micah. I had to stop talking about myself all the time and learn to listen better.

"You know, maybe the two of us should go have coffee again sometime and maybe compare notes on these girls of ours. We might be able to learn something from each other," he smiled.

I thought, "Oh my God! Did he just ask me out?" Would that make me happy, afraid? I felt a shiver run up and down my spine, then across and out my shoulders, and it took me completely by surprise.

This was an amazingly attractive man and I was a married woman! Nothing could *ever* come of it, I reminded myself (several times that afternoon, I must admit). I was far too honest and loyal for that, even in spite of my horrendous marital circumstances. But I knew that I wanted him all the same. There was no denying it.

I hadn't had even a basic interest, let alone love or passion, from a man in so long that I was experiencing feelings I could scarcely remember. I couldn't help noticing a little leap of the heart at the idea that someone might be interested in me, might find me attractive, might want to spend some time with me, might want to… To be honest, my heart was not the only part of me that was feeling stirred up at that moment. I had no idea how I felt, except that I had butterflies – or bats – fluttering through my body, and I felt that I must be visibly shaking. I thanked the Universe once again that I'd had the sense to have taken four years of acting in high school because I apparently pulled my response off without alerting him to all this nonsense running through my mind and body.

"That'd be great. So when do I get to meet Micah?" Best to get back down to business, I thought.

"I'll go get her," he said with another disarming smile. "It might take me a couple of minutes."

"No problem. Take your time."

I took the wait as an opportunity to look around the room a little more closely. I noticed a line of photographs in frames of various sizes, colors, and shapes carefully positioned along the mantel of a brick fireplace against the wall opposite the couch. In many of them, a strikingly beautiful woman was smiling, either up at the photographer or down at one of the two young girls who were with her. She was African American, but with lighter skin than Desi, who reminded me of milk chocolate — leave it to me to compare his complexion to food. What the hell?

The frames varied in size from five-by-seven to tiny silver-plated thumbnails. There were pictures of the family when the girls were small and I could see that when Micah was Bria's age she looked quite a bit like her, but she didn't have those same piercing, mysterious eyes.

In one of the larger frames, their mother held Micah, who was probably six or seven, high in the air. Micah's outstretched arms looked like she was trying to hug the whole world and I could almost hear the giggles that she must have tossed into the sky from her wriggling body — it really looked as though her whole body was laughing — as she was held aloft by this woman who, judging form the look on her face, loved this child to distraction. I walked along the mantel, absentmindedly running my hand along the edge as I strolled, contemplating the photos.

As I moved from left to right, it was as if I were reading the life story of this family. The girls in the pictures got older and the story the photographs told began to change as I moved along the fireplace considering them all. There were probably twenty of them crowding the mantle, small ones in front, larger ones behind, all positioned so that they could all be easily viewed by anyone who cared to look.

The woman's beauty faded at what must have been a remarkable rate based on how much the girls had grown, and the happiness in her eyes and in the eyes of the girls diminished and faded as the years passed. I wondered why Desi kept this chronology so prominently displayed when it obviously told such a sad story, and why he wasn't in a single photograph. He was probably the photographer, but even I (*my* family's photographer) managed to sneak into a picture or two here and there. To someone who didn't know what I knew, it would have appeared that Desi wasn't part of that happy family at all. I was glad that I knew he had been.

I didn't have time to contemplate it further because Desi emerged from the back of the house followed by a young woman who was quite obviously displeased and was acquiescing under duress.

"Hi," I said, holding out my hand. It was immediately apparent that Micah wasn't going to be as compliant as her younger sister. She kept her arms folded across her chest and adopted a wide-leg stance that could only have been intended to convey both protection and defiance. She was wearing jeans with holes in the knees, well-worn black and white sneakers, and a hunter green T-shirt with one pocket. She had her dark brown hair up in a ponytail at the back of her head. I guessed it to be about shoulder length, but it was hard to tell. It was thick and looked soft and, even though I could tell that she hadn't seen the inside of a salon in quite some time, it looked nice. She glared at me and said, "Okay, let's get this over with."

"Great," I said with as much pleasant enthusiasm as I could muster in response to such obvious resistance, trying not to sound like an idiot who couldn't read body language, but any fool could have seen through that pretense. I could tell at once that this girl was no fool. I was certain that I was the one who sounded like an idiot, too stupid to properly respond to her obvious attempt to put me in my place. I knew she was hoping she could get me to high-tail it out of there. I thought maybe I should do just that, but I am so glad I didn't. I didn't realize it at the time, but my very life depended on staying this course.

I don't remember the awkward moments before I left with Micah, but something must have happened to get her to accompany me. I'm guessing it was a look I saw Desi give her. Man, I wish I could get through to Reagan with just a look! She ignored my looks just as thoroughly as she ignored my words. Still, Micah grabbed her jacket from the coat stand by the door as Desi returned mine to me, and she marched out the door ahead of me.

I shook hands with Desi (a warm, strong hand) and followed her out. We walked single file down the porch steps and the walkway and over the road verge to my car. Micah stood stoically on the grass next to her door, her arms still folded, still glaring, as I started to go around to the driver's side. I hesitated when I saw that Micah had no intention of moving.

"You want me to open the door for you?" I asked in what I hoped was a pleasant, friendly tone, rather than the sarcastic one that I really felt like using. I could tell this was going to be a long afternoon. Here I was, trying to grow out of my subservient habits and I end up having to play chauffeur to a snotty kid.

"You want me to go, you gotta do the work. I'm not into this. I have more important things to do."

"Okay," I said, not taking the bait. I walked back around to Micah's side of the car and opened the door for her. I was so tempted to put my hand on her head as she ducked to get in, the way cops do when they load unwilling suspects into the backs of their patrol cars, but I was sure Micah would have smacked my arm away — or worse, that Desi was looking out the window and would see me degrading his daughter. I chastised myself for even considering doing such a thing. I felt like I was making unfair judgments about her –- prejudgments -– and I admonished myself for that as well. Who did I think I was? Micah had every right to be pissed. In her mind she *did* have better things to do than hang out with some old lady who apparently had nothing better to occupy her time than to poke her nose into another family's business.

But Desi had asked me to do this, and so I would give it my best shot. If Micah would only meet me a quarter of the way… I decided that I'd really, really try to be nice, at least until Micah pushed me over the edge. I wasn't going to subject myself to constant hurt and annoyance the way I did with Dick and Reagan. An unbidden thought surfaced as I clicked my seatbelt: why *did* I put up with their shit anyway? There was no time to dwell on that then, however, but I suddenly felt exceedingly proud of myself because I realized that I did, indeed — *finally!* — actually have an edge to be pushed over! I laughed out loud at this notion as I put the car in drive and began to pull out. Micah passed a suspicious glance my way, not understanding this random outburst of mirth. I got myself under control and we proceeded down her street in silence. I knew I'd have to be the one to break the tension.

"Where do you want to go?" I asked.

"I don't care. Are you not getting this? I don't want to be here. I have nothing to say to you. You're not my mother. You're not my 'Big Sister.'" She spat those words out like they were poison. "I'm only doing this to keep the old man off my back. Let's go. Let's eat. Let's go back. I have crap to do."

"Great," I said, with feigned politeness that I hoped didn't sound feigned, even though I knew it did. "You know, you don't have to be mean to me," I said.

"What the hell do you know about mean? Look, I don't know you. I don't want to know you. I don't like you. I don't care about you. Get the idea yet?"

"How can you not like me? You don't *know* me. You just said that yourself."

"Look, people prejudge people all the time. Trust me, I know. I'm in a different world than you." Had Micah somehow sensed my earlier doubts about this? Oh no!

"I know that. So, you're prejudging me because you think I'm prejudging you?"

"No. I'm prejudging you because I don't care if you're prejudging me and because it seems like the fastest way to get rid of you so I can get back to what *is* important to me. But since you admit to prejudging me and we're both doing it, why don't we just call it a draw and you can just shut the fuck up and drive." There was no emotion in her voice, no passion, no violent edge. Just a finality with which it was difficult to argue.

At least Reagan wouldn't have used that kind of language with me I thought, at least not yet. How long would it be, though, until she didn't care and employed expletives as a matter of course, like this young woman seemed to do? When would *she* just tell me to fuck off?

"How old are you?" I asked, trying to change the subject and get some kind of communication going.

"I'm seventeen, goin' on forty." I sensed an odd mixture of resentment and pride in her voice.

"Looking forward to eighteen?"

"Are you the queen of stupid questions? Oh, sorry. I forgot you can't handle mean. Yeah, I'm looking forward to it. It can't be soon enough. Happy?"

"Why is that?" Another dumb question, I knew.

"Because as soon as I'm fuckin' eighteen, I am outta here!"

"Why are you waiting until you're eighteen?"

"You *are* the queen. What am I supposed to do when I'm not legal?"

"I don't know. Get a job. I teach high school. I've known kids who've been emancipated."

"I can't afford to get emancipated. I don't even have time to look into that. Do you realize that I'm the woman of that house? I have to raise that little sister of mine, I gotta try to keep up my grades in school, I gotta try to make sure the old man doesn't have a fuckin' breakdown. Why do you think I said seventeen goin' on forty?" Then she said, under her breath, "I just wanna be a fuckin' kid once in a while."

"What's wrong with your dad? He seems pretty nice, pretty stable,"

I said, letting that last remark slide.

"He's a good guy," she seemed to soften a bit when talking about him. "He's a really good guy, but he just gotta get over the fact that my bitch of a old lady left him and it wasn't his fault and he's doin' the best he can. He beats himself up too much… Why am I telling you all this shit? Like you care."

"Maybe I do."

"Why? You don't know me."

"Maybe I'd like to get to know you. Maybe I really would." I didn't intend it, but even I had to admit that last part sounded as if I were speaking to myself rather than to her.

"You sound like that desire surprises you," she said, giving me a little side-eye from the passenger seat and surprising me with her apparent ability to read me.

"Well, it does a little. You kinda scared me there for a while."

"But not no more?"

"Yeah, still a little." Honesty had always worked best for me in the past, so I thought I'd stick with it now. Micah seemed to respect that because she turned slightly toward me in the seat and relaxed her hold on herself just a little bit. That she'd given up that much told me that this girl probably really could use someone to talk to. Her guard was down only for a split second, though, before the tough girl resurfaced. She immediately resumed her former posture and said, "Just drive. I'm not telling my biznez to a total stranger."

"Well, maybe by the end of lunch we won't be *total* strangers. Where do you want to go?"

"Are you deaf? I said I don't care about twelve times. I DO NOT care. Go wherever you fuckin' wanna go."

"Okay." I decided to ignore the language. "There's an Olive Garden not too far from here and I like their salads and breadsticks. Don't let me order the Alfredo."

"Jesus Christ! You worried about yo' fat ass? I wish I had your white lady problems... and quit talkin' to me like I was yer girlfriend. Jesus Christ."

At that point I realized that Micah was just going to stay confrontational so I backed off and let her stew for a little bit as we turned onto I-75 North and headed to Auburn Hills. I couldn't really think of anything to say to her or to ask her anyway that wouldn't draw the same kind of response I'd been getting so far. Silence was golden, after all.

After about ten minutes, we pulled into Olive Garden and I walked around the car and opened the door for Micah since it was apparent that if I didn't do so, she'd just stay in the car. I opened the restaurant door for her as well. Once we were inside, I asked for a booth by the window pretending not to care how Micah felt about that.

"Why you care where yo' seat's at?" she asked.

"It's a beautiful day and I want to suck up as much sunshine as I can before the gray days come back in the fall and winter. Too many of them in a row, even in spring and summer, and it gets to me. I know... another white lady problem, but you asked."

"Nope, that's one problem we share," she said, "but shit, it's only the middle of June, for Christ's sake. A little early to be gettin' anal 'bout that, don't ya think?" It was the first time Mica had asked me a question that wasn't rhetorical (or was it?). I felt a slight stirring of hope either way. I found that I really did want this girl to know me and maybe like me, at least a little.

"Look, I don't mean to get in your business." I thought it might be time to dive right back in. "I just know when I have shit goin' on, sometimes it helps to talk about it, and I don't really have anyone to talk to a lot of time. I just thought that if you needed someone... and your dad obviously thinks you might need someone cuz he called Big Sisters."

She seemed to soften a little again at the thought of her father. "Yeah, he worries about me. I wish he'd knock that off."

"Not gonna happen," I said. "It's so very obvious that he loves you more than you'll ever know, more than absolutely anything. I've only talked to him twice before today, but there's no doubt about that. When you love someone that much, you never back off. It's impossible." I paused, but she didn't jump back in. "Look, we're gonna sit together for an hour or so and we're gonna have some food and, like I said, sometimes it helps to talk about your problems, or about anything."

"Look, I ain't no therapist for yo' problems and you ain't no therapist for my problems, so why don't ya just order your damn salad and be quiet." Back to square one.

I decided at this point that Micah might be right about this being a futile endeavor, but I'd gotten at least something out of her and I wasn't going to push it, so we sat in silence while we looked over the menu. I ordered the Alfredo. I knew I should leave the wine for another day after entertaining a fleeting thought that it might help me in this situation, then immediately realized that it so would not.

I couldn't stand the pressure of the silence while we waited for our server to materialize so I decided to do what I considered the lamest thing possible and talk about the weather. It was safe at least. "God it's gorgeous out today." Micah rolled her eyes as if I really had said the most ridiculous, stupid thing she'd ever heard.

"The weather, really? That's the best you can do?" She was pretty quick on the uptake.

"Yeah. Don't you even like the weather?" I asked.

"What do you care what I like or don't like?" This felt like round two. I realized then that most of Micah's questions concerned the validity and extent of my caring.

"I don't know," I said. "I'm just sensing this serious attitude from you that I didn't do anything to cause. All I did was show up and offer to buy you a goddam meal. Why can't you just be civil for the duration. Jeeze." I had wanted to say something to show her that I did care, but I was getting a little exasperated.

She lowered her menu, behind which she had sort of been hiding, and asked, "Why you here?" She looked me in the eyes with the question shining brightly in hers. They almost looked like Bria's eyes then, but not quite. Micah's eyes were the same soft gray/brown with the same long, dark lashes, but hers were much older and way too much wiser than her little sister's. Far more intense and searching. She really wanted to know. She wasn't just lobbing another phrase at me designed to make me say something she could insult, which seemed to have been the game she'd been playing up to this point. Who knows what prompted her to ask a serious question. Who cares?

"You really wanna know?" I asked

"You're the one who pointed out that we have an hour to kill." Well, she had me there.

"Why do you care?" I replied. "You said you weren't a therapist for my problems." Why was I resisting now that she'd finally gotten serious?

"You're here cuz *you've* got problems?" she muttered, apparently exasperated. "That's just great. That's just what I need." How intuitive was this kid?

"Listen, all I ..." At that moment the waitress came up to the table. Micah said, "I'll have a glass of your house Merlo and a water."

"She'll have a water and a Diet Coke," I corrected her in an authoritative tone, "and I'll have the Chardonay and a water with lemon." Even though I had previously eschewed the idea of having alcohol, and I wasn't even sure it was permitted on a "sister date" (although I was pretty sure it wasn't), I felt the need of a little liquid support. Jumping in and amending her order, then ordering almost the exact same thing, had the affect I intended, though: Micah was sufficiently reminded which of us actually had the power in this relationship. No matter how Micah might assert herself, by virtue of my age and affiliation with her father, Micah was lower on this totem pole.

"I'll have a just a water," she said, apparently feeling the need to correct me and maintain control at least to the extent that she could. She rolled her eyes at my obvious pulling of rank. I smiled to myself again when I realized that I actually *had* asserted authority! I wondered if I could have done it differently, less obtrusively… Damn it! Here I was, second guessing myself again. Well, there was no way I could have let Micah order wine. For an instant, I reconsidered my own Chardonay, then thought, "What the hell. Maybe it'll loosen me up a little." Did I think about having to drive Micah home after having had a drink? To my utter and everlasting shame, no, I did not. I resolved with everything I had that I would only have the one.

I said to her, "Okay look. Let's do this. I'm sorry that I just did that. I'm still having the wine though." I thought I saw the slightest twinge of a smile on Micah's face. "I just did it because I wanted you to know that I have privileges and abilities that you don't have."

"No shit," she spat, enunciating each word pointedly and slowly, like a growl, as she glared at me. "You think you gotta treat me like a child to make *that* point? Like I need to be reminded of that. I'm reminded of that every God damn day in every aspect of my little life a hundred times over, except with my man. He loves me. *He* understands me. *He* appreciates me."

"Alright. I'm gonna want you to tell me about him eventually. Because I'm *interested*. It can't be out of the question for you to think that something might interest me, especially about someone who makes such an obvious difference in your life, a life you don't seem too happy with otherwise, by the way. But for now, let's go back to where we were. You wanted to know why I'm here. I felt bad just now about how I treated you and I promise not to treat you like a kid again (but I can't let you drink!)." I saw that minuscule, momentary smile sneak in and out once again. "If I accidentally do treat you with less respect than you deserve, you can let me know without being mean, okay?"

She didn't respond to that but said, "Yeah. I wanna know why you're doing this. I wanna know what you expect from me, and I wanna know what you expect for yourself. What you getting' outta this? White lady, with a good job, and according to my old man a solid marriage and a girl of your own -- a girl of your own! – little white girl of your own! What the hell do you want with me?"

Before I could answer, Micah had a thought that apparently upset her because she charged ahead. "Are you trying to 'save' me? Do you think I need to be 'saved'? You know so much that you can solve all my black-ass teenage girl problems? You know nothing -- nothing -- about the world I live in, what my life is like, what the hell... I can't believe my old man is forcing this on me, after all I do for him. Doesn't he have any respect for me at all?" She took a deep breath and then came back to herself, and turned the topic back around to me to keep herself from getting upset further. "No one is selfless. You're in it for something. Don't lie to me. What is it?"

She was so forthright, and so absolutely right about it, that I fell back on total honesty once again and told her. "A friend. I want a friend. That's the honest truth and I couldn't have told you that ten minutes ago. I used to think... maybe it *was* to save you, or someone, I don't know... I used to think it was something good I could do in the world. Some way to give back, some way to show the Universe that

I'm grateful for everything I have been blessed with, but now... I just want a friend."

"A friend? You got no friends? What's the matter with you?"

"I have friends," I explained, not taking offense because I sensed that she hadn't intended any. "But they know only what they see, and they don't see me. Neither does my husband or my daughter. I want a friend who can know what I know and what I feel and help me figure out who I am."

"And you expect a seventeen year old black chick from Pontiac to be able to do that?"

"No. I was hoping a young woman with a different view on life might be able to give me some perspective, some different things to think about, or some different ways to look at the things I've been thinking about but can't figure out. I'm not doing this to save you. I'm doing this to save me and if you get something out of it like a free meal once in a while, I don't see why you have to be such a bitch about it." I could fee myself getting worked up so I took a breath and resumed, trying to be a little nicer. "It'll make your dad happy. It'll get you out of some homework or housework once in a while and there's no pressure — if nothing comes of it, then nothing comes of it. Maybe we each will have heard some interesting stories, I don't know. Why are you so against it? It is because you feel like you don't have a choice? You do. I won't be offended if you bail. I promise."

"You don't get it." She paused while the waitress opened the stand and set her tray down next to our table. As she served our food, Micah was apparently mulling over what I said. Her body language changed

140

slightly and she appeared a little more relaxed. Some of her belligerence kind of evaporated with her tension and she became smaller. For some reason, this made me kind of sad.

Neither of us spoke as we began the meal and I was determined once again to overcome my aversion to long awkward silences and my propensity to fill them with chatter, and wait for Micah to be ready to tell me what it was that I didn't get.

After a few bites of the salad she had allowed me to put on her plate for her from the large bowl on the table, she spoke. "I love my father. You have no idea what a wonderful, amazing man he is." I thought that if Micah hadn't been so hell bent on maintaining her tough street-kid persona, I might have seen a tear slide down her cheek, such was the passion in her voice. "When my old lady left, she damn near killed him -- and I mean literally. I'm not goin' into details. Suffice it to say that I do *not* have a choice. If it'll make him happy that I do this, then I do this. It's as simple as that."

"Wow. I wish my daughter cared a tenth as much about my feelings as you do about his."

"Look. If I agree to do lunch with you again, will you agree to treat me as much like an equal as your limited resources allow?"

"Agreed, as long as you agree to try to curb the mean and work on the nice." We were in negotiations.

"Fine. You agree not to pry."

"Deal. You *can* pry. I might need it. And we both agree not to judge, pre- or post — you have no idea whether my resources are limited or not." Her expression told me that she was a little sorry she'd said that.

"It's a bargain." She extended her hand, then withdrew it slowly. "One more thing," she said as she hesitated. "One hundred percent confidential. One hundred percent trust. We don't know each other and have no reason to trust each other, but we have no reason not to either. I will tell you truly that I'm an honest person, and I never lie, and I never hold back, so you'll just have to deal with that. The minute I can't be myself, or the minute I feel like confidence or trust has been betrayed, we're done." Sounded reasonable to me.

"Give me your hand," I said with more confidence than I'd felt in a long time. "If what you've just told me about yourself is true -- and I believe it is because you added to the accord that we trust each other — then we have more in common than you know and I'm honored to shake on this deal. And, I promise, still no pressure, although I'll admit that I'm feeling a helluva lot better now than I did an hour ago."

Micah extended her hand again, shook mine with a firm grip, and smiled for the first time, and again her father's smile invaded my mind. "Not scared of me anymore?" she asked.

"Not at all. Now I'm scared of myself!" I let loose the tiniest little laugh.

"Can we just eat for a while?" Micah asked as she fished a breadstick out of the basket. "I'm starving and this looks great." She didn't offer any to me, but she didn't make another comment about my fat ass either so I was satisfied.

I thoroughly enjoyed my Alfredo and my Chardonay. I managed to keep my mouth shut and let Micah eat, think, and proceed with this new accord at her own pace.

When Micah had almost finished, she put her fork down gently across her plate and said, "Okay. Spill it. Tell me what the hell your deal is."

"Well," I began, but then realized that I didn't really know and was just figuring it out as I went. "My deal is that don't know who I am, or what I want, or what I'm supposed to do, or how to survive." This girl somehow had the ability to make me cut through all the clutter and chatter in my brain and release the raw, undistilled truth. Maybe that's why I chose to confide in her. I didn't know that it would, but doing so seemed to clarify so much. Maybe it was because she really knew nothing about me and had no history through which to filter my words, no common friends or acquaintances with whom she could compare notes about me. I was laid bare, but that didn't concern me for some reason.

I started telling her about Dick's alcoholism (and I couldn't help but notice her glance at my wine glass when this topic came up), about his taking Reagan's side all the time, about him turning her into a spoiled brat so I couldn't reach her any more as a mother, as a friend, as a disciplinarian, as anything… that I had lost her and my heart was breaking. I told her about my crazy upbringing, about the father I couldn't please and the mother who thought I could do no wrong. I told her about my whacked out sense of self, about how work used to give me such joy and a sense of purpose, but was more an exercise in frustration than the calling it had once been. I went on and on, even though it was the short version, until I fell silent. It had exhausted me. Micah sat silently attentive the entire time.

"You are fucked up," she said matter of factly, almost as if she were just an incredibly blunt therapist.

"Yep. Good thing you aren't a shrink. I probably couldn't afford you." For some reason that struck her as funny and she laughed out loud. She couldn't help herself. It all did really sound so ridiculous, and it was ludicrous that Micah, a seventeen year old high school student, was the listener rather than me, which is how I'd envisioned our encounter playing out. Our roles had reversed right away and that, I thought, made Micah happy, or at least comfortable enough for her to let her guard down a little and try to enjoy herself. Her laugh sent me into a fit of laughter as well. Micah tried to return to her stoicism, but watching this grown woman across the table laughing uncontrollably after spilling her guts to a kid she didn't even know apparently got to her, and she had to laugh again as well. We laughed and laughed for a full minute or two before it played itself out. The tension had broken and, even though the bond hadn't yet formed, the foundation was laid. We'd crashed through the first barrier and I don't mind admitting that I was terribly happy about it.

I paid the bill and drove Micah home. It was later than I'd planned to be out, but I didn't care. I had just spent one of the most interesting and enjoyable afternoons and almost-evenings that I'd had in a long, long time. We agreed that we'd meet again the next Saturday for lunch. It was the first time I felt a smile in my heart in what seemed like forever.

CHAPTER EIGHTEEN
Tea

"The only way to have a friend is to be one."
—*Ralph Waldo Emerson*

I enjoyed my day with Micah so much that I wanted to share it all with Logan. Also, I enjoyed myself so often at Logan's house that I wanted to reciprocate, so I decided to invite her over for tea. Still, the very idea of entertaining was unsettling to me and trying to compete with Logan, trying to give her an experience at my house that in any way even came close to what I experienced at hers, seemed like an impossibility. I was not good that that type of thing. Not only couldn't I cook, but having Logan over would most likely necessitate her having to meet the Terrible Twosome and that frightened me a little, too. Okay, it frightened me a lot.

I decided to tackle these fears in my journal after dinner that night. Logan had suggested that journaling would be a real help in my efforts to get strong. I made myself some tea and snuggled under a blanket in my bentwood rocker in the living room. I turned off the overhead lights and wrote under the softer light of the table lamp. I picked up my pen, turned to the next blank page, and began moving thoughts from my mind, out through my arm and hand, and down onto the page. Soon enough, I found that I had managed to talk myself down from the encroaching panic I'd experienced when contemplating entertaining.

It was Logan, after all. She was the least judgmental person I'd ever met and even if the Terrible Twosome embarrassed me, I'd get over it. Logan was my neighbor and was fast becoming my dearest friend. I reasoned that, if I tried to hide anything from her, whether it be my crumbling family or my domestic inadequacies, I wouldn't be holding up my end of the friendship bargain. That would be blatantly unfair and I couldn't take that chance.

I put down my pen and called her to ask if she was free the next afternoon to come by for tea and snacks. I think I was secretly hoping that she wasn't available, I which case I could put off the stress of entertaining her, but she said that she couldn't think of anything she'd rather do, so that was that.

Of course, Logan offered to bring something. She liked to cook and knew that I didn't. When I told her not to worry and that I'd figure something out, she suggested that I not bother making anything and that I should just pick something up at the market and keep it simple. I felt like I needed to make an effort for her, though, albeit a small one. I was grateful that she didn't argue the point. I have a feeling that she knew I wanted to do something for *her* for a change.

After we agreed on 3:00 the next afternoon, I put my phone back on the table and resumed writing. This time, however, I started making a list of things I needed to do in order to pull off this feat; that's what it felt like to me. I'd need to clean the house, make the tea (well, maybe I'd buy that, too), get something to snack on, and hope for the best.

* * * * *

The next morning, I thoroughly cleaned the house, with the exception of Reagan's room, which I had no intention of ever entering again if I could help it. I decided to buy some iced tea and make a new pineapple cheesecake dip that I found in one of my dozens of cookbooks. I never cooked, but I loved to look through the books! Weird, right? Anyway, I served that with graham crackers, mini-pretzels, and apple slices and, to my surprise and delight, it was wonderful!

It was Sunday afternoon, but we had the place to ourselves since Dick was in the garage and Reagan was at the mall with some of her friends. The house was spotless. I made sure of that, and I made sure Reagan's door was closed so that disaster area was impossible to view.

Over ice tea and munchies that day, we became even closer. I found out that Logan was sixty-two years old and had worked most of her life as a massage therapist, yoga instructor, and meditation teacher. No wonder she was so good at this stuff, and so able to help me learn it.

"Wow, can I pay you for some massages?" I asked excitedly. I'd only had a couple of massages years ago before I got married. I loved a good massage, but Dick always said we could't afford it. Even though I explained that my insurance covered it, he bitched about the deducible and the co-pay. I had been too weak to argue.

"Sorry," she answered, looking really, truly sorry. "I had to give that up. After doing it for a couple of decades, my body just couldn't handle it anymore. It's more physical than people realize. About twelve years ago, my carpal tunnel got so bad that there was no way I could properly serve my clients so I had to let it go. I most certainly will do yoga with you though, and we can meditate together."

I was little bummed about no massages, but the rest thrilled me. It seemed to me like yoga and meditation could be stepping stones for me, could maybe help me find myself, help me get stronger, enable me to better move forward. Logan agreed. It was worth a try for certain sure and any time I could spend with Logan... well, she was becoming like a sister to me already and those times were the best times, other than the time I'd spent with Micah. "It was truly a rewarding part of my life though, and I was sorry to see it end," she continued, "but things end." Like careers, marriages, and daughters being sweet little girls, I thought.

As the afternoon progressed, Logan told me about how exciting the '60s had been and how she was so involved in the Civil Rights Movement and the Vietnam War protests. She had never been to college, but she had lived in Ann Arbor for quite a while and so was very comfortable on the campus of the University of Michigan, and had made lots of friends there. It felt really good to finally be giving her my attention and listening to her for a change. It seemed like all I ever did was whine and complain to her, but when I mentioned this, she told me it didn't seem that way to her at all. I don't know if she was just trying to make me feel better, but at any rate, she did!

I was just at the point of asking her for more stories from those by gone days, when Reagan and Dick both walked in at the same time.

Apparently, when Reagan was dropped off, she'd wandered into the garage to say hello to her dad and, when Dick told her that "that hippie neighbor" (as he called her) was over, they decided that they wanted to come in and check her out. It's to my everlasting shame that Dick didn't have the common courtesy to come in earlier and greet our guest, but it didn't really surprise me.

When they reached the kitchen where we were comfortably seated at the table, I introduced them both to Logan. She stood up and shook both their hands and said how wonderful it was to meet them. Then there was an awkward silence. I was mortified. You'd think they would've said something like, "Nice to meet you, too," but no. It reminded me of how lovely Bria had been when I'd first met her. So polite, so grown up. I cringed with embarrassment at how my family reacted, or rather didn't react, to my new best friend.

Reagan at least said small hello, but Dick was silent. They both walked past us over to the refrigerator to get something to drink, and I was at a loss as to how to proceed in my conversation with Logan with them standing there, listening. Luckily, and unsurprisingly, Logan knew how to handle the situation and she just continued her tale as if nothing had happened. The Terrible Twosome left, one with a Diet Coke and the other with a beer, which surprised me because Dick had a small refrigerator out in the garage which was always stocked with his drug of choice (well, one of them - I'm pretty sure I'd smelled weed out there a couple of times, not that I really had an issue with that, other than the fact that it was illegal). I think coming inside for his beer was just his sad attempt at a ruse, an excuse to come in, as if meeting a new neighbor wasn't excuse enough.

Once they left the kitchen and were out of earshot, Logan paused her story. She looked at me and said, "Allison, I know you've been really open with me and you've told me a lot about both Reagan and Dick, and I never doubted you for a second, but even having met them for that short amount of time just now helped me understand your situation a little bit better. When they were in this room, the negative energy was palpable. The only way to get negative energy to dissipate is by infusing the space with positive energy. Lucky for you, I'm an expert at that!"

"Well," I laughed, "I will welcome all the help I can get! I'm so sorry that they were rude to you, Logan, but you've got to trust me when I say that it's not you. They're fine around their own friends, but not so much around mine, although I don't really have a lot of friends anymore, and the ones I do have I wouldn't invite over just because I wouldn't want them to have to experience what you just did. You so did not deserve that, and I'm so sorry."

"Why is it that you don't have any friends?" she asked, dismissing my apology. "That absolutely amazes me because you're such a warm, intelligent, interesting person," Logan wondered.

"Well, I don't know about any of that, but most of my friends fell by the wayside once they spent a little bit of time with Dick, and I can't get close with his friends because their whole purpose in life seems to be getting shit-faced. I know that I drink too much wine, and I'm working on cutting that back, but that's a few glasses a few times a week to get me through the stress of my job and the stress of my house and the stress of my family and the stress of my life," I rambled. "It's not the same as what they all seem to be into."

"I can almost guarantee you, Aliison, that once you start meditating, doing some yoga with me, finding some other interests, you won't need that wine and you will attract friends like bees to a flower!" I didn't really believe that, of course, but I really, really hoped that hanging out with Logan and learning whatever it was that she could teach me might help me in my quest to get strong and pull my life together. "Why don't we start walking together in the mornings," she suggested, "now that school is out for the summer?"

I couldn't think of anything I would enjoy more, so we made a pact to walk at least around the block but hopefully farther (depending on the time we both had and on the unpredictable Michigan weather) every morning at eight. We decided to cement the pact by going for a walk right then and there.

I didn't bother telling the Terrible Twosome where I was going because I knew that they could not have cared less. We went out my front door, down the front walk, and turned right to walk past Logan's house. We stopped for a minute there to look at her late-season lilac bushes, which were just about done and losing their blooms, and at her budding rosebushes. Tiny red, pink, and yellow buds were just peeking out at the ends of their stems. When I remarked on these, Logan said, "Well, if you would like some flowers for your yard, I should have some for you within the next few days to a week. I love them, but I don't like how that cyclone fence runs all the way around the perimeter of my house, enclosing even the front yard, and I'm thinking about taking it down. That means the rosebushes and lilacs will have to come out. I'll move some of them to spots in the back, but I'd love the rest to find a good home and I can't think of a better place than your yard!"

"Oh," I said, concerned, "I can almost guarantee you that if you pull that fence down Dick will sue you, not because he gives a shit about the fence, but because he's just a troublemaker!"

"Okay, "said Logan, "I'll leave the fence between your driveway and my front yard, but I can certainly take down the part that runs across the front of my house without antagonizing him because that is not on his — your — property. That'll still leave several bushes along the front fence that'll need to come down and doing that will still open up my space and give me rosebushes and lilacs to give to you."

"I would so love that!" I loved the lilac bush I already had at the back of my house. The idea of having more of the kind of beauty and fragrance in my yard that Logan had in hers brought me instant joy. "It really doesn't look very groomed, does it, the way it is?" I observed. "The people who used to live here really kept to themselves, and I think they put these lilac bushes in the front and let them get so overgrown to sort of hide their house from the street. Based on how your backyard looks, I have no doubt that you can turn this front yard into an Eden as well. I'm serious though, Logan, when I tell you that if you don't let me help you, I'm going to be very disappointed. School is out for summer, I have all kinds of time, and if I could learn to garden like you, I would be in seventh heaven!"

"Good deal," Logan responded, smiling at me. She put her arm through mine and we continued strolling down the street, critiquing the gardens of the neighbors, and talking about ideas for her front yard, and where I might put the lilacs and rosebushes that she was going to give me.

When we had come full circle and were back standing between our two houses saying goodbye, I told Logan the story of Louie The Lamppost and she got a real kick out of it. We decided that we would dig a small bed around him and decorate Louie with flowers as well.

When I got back home, I was feeling good again, in spite of the rudeness of my family that had so mortified me. Logan hadn't been phased by it, so why should I be?

I got dinner on the table and was surprised when Dick came in to eat with us. He usually stayed in the garage and just reheated whatever was there before he went to bed. This night, though, he sat at the table with us and, as we began the meal, he said, "Well, *she's* interesting."

"What's that supposed to mean?" I asked.

"Well, she's like a damn hippie, right? I wouldn't be surprised if she were a communist or a socialist."

"Jesus, Dick," was all I could say.

"I don't think she's good for you," he said after a pause. That was a surprise. Since when did he care what was good for *me*? Then I realized that he meant she was not good for *him* because I wasn't the old me anymore.

"What the hell is your problem, Dick?" I could sense Reagan tightening up. Confrontation between us was almost nonexistent in those doormat days.

"She's changing you," he said. "You were having tea today instead of wine? You're certainly not yourself around here anymore, and you're not doing your job very well either."

I couldn't help it. I just laughed out load and I seriously think I scared them both. "Fine," I said, "I quit." Still smiling, and feeling SO proud of myself, I picked up my plate and my water glass and headed out to the backyard.

"Hey, get back here. We need to talk about this," he shouted after me.

"Fuck you," I sang as the storm door shut softly behind me. I felt so empowered. I wasn't even scared. I didn't even feel the need to run over to Logan's to have her talk me down. I was up! I *was* getting strong and that knowledge made me even stronger. I remember thinking that I *could* be a good friend to Logan, and I *could* be a good mentor for Micah. I could even be a good mother to Reagan, and I could ignore Dick enough to keep him from ever hurting me again.

CHAPTER NINETEEN
Saturday

"The language of friendship is not words but meanings."
—*Henry David Thoreau*

"What is the bug up your butt?" Micah asked me as we sat in a window booth at Dave & Amy's the next Saturday for our second sister-date. I hadn't realized that I'd been lost in thought, essentially ignoring her. The week had gone relatively well. Even though I'd managed to stay away from Dick, I'd had a run-in or two with Reagan and had been ruminating about that, mulling it over, wondering if I'd handled things the best way... I immediately felt contrite and apologized, saying that I hadn't meant to be rude.

"Screw rude," she said. "What the hell's up with you? I'm forced to have these fuckin' visits with you, and I do it so the old man'll stay offa my ass -- the least you could do is tell me what the hell is eating you instead of sittin' there like a dummy."

"Hey! That wasn't nice!" I said.

"I mean like a mannequin — you know: no life!"

"Oh, sorry," I said. Then I figured, what the hell? She was right. It *was* my doing that she had to give up her Saturday afternoon. I should at least make it entertaining for her, show her how someone who is supposed to have it all together was actually falling apart and was being terrorized by her own family. I *was* getting stronger, but I wasn't there yet for certain sure.

So I told her. I expanded on what I'd told her at our first meeting, including all that had happened the previous week. I told her about Reagan's tantrums and her constant whining to her father. Told her about Dick always taking her side. Told her about how Dick followed me out into the backyard that night, so soon after I lost my beautiful baby (although I kept that part to myself), to scold and harangue me for fifteen minutes, trying to intimidate me, and basically succeeding. Told her how Dick reacted to meeting Logan. Told her how I told him to go fuck himself. Told her about how I felt about it all, my changing attitude, my determination to get strong, my fear of failure, all of it.

She sat in silence, listening intently, judging I was sure, but she said nothing until I had exhausted myself. She was a lot like Logan that way. She nodded almost imperceptibly and said, "You go girl."

That surprised me. Support! Form a teenager? I was really taken aback.

"You don't side with Reagan and think I'm a horrible mother/person/whatever?"

"Hell no. No offense, but she sounds like a spoiled bitch."

At first I felt the maternal defense mechanism engage, but instead I was surprised when a small laugh escaped me instead. "She is," I said, "and I don't know what to do about it. Her dad feeds her with it ever day. All he wants is peace and quiet, to be left alone, so he gives her whatever she wants to shut her up. He doesn't care what she learns or doesn't learn from it or how it affects anyone besides him. She doesn't care about anything because she doesn't have to. Daddy takes care of it all. I have no idea what to do."

"You do so know what to do about it. You've don't it already, a couple of times. It'll get easier. Frankly, there is nothing else *to* do about it. It is what it is. She's too old to be re-raised. You just gotta worry about you now. Screw her and him. It be all 'bout you now, awright?"

"Why do you talk like that?" It came out before I realized how condescending it was and how superior it made me sound, so I jumped back to clarify before she could pounce.

"I mean, you're obviously so intelligent, articulate, insightful, well-read… and you know the right way… sorry, the socially acceptable way…. Sorry… what the hell… to speak. I hear and see it in you, sense it in you. Why do you use such… substandard language. I'm sorry. I can't find a way to say what I mean without being insulting… insensitive… offensive… shit."

"Don't worry about it," she said. "The fact that you didn't start that sentence with 'I'm not racist, but…' means something. I know what you mean, Allison." Her using my name that way didn't sound disrespectful to me at all. It felt like a warm hug. "Anyway, I talk like that, sometimes, for the same reason you put up with shit you don't deserve. It's how we survive. Don't… doesn't make it right, but we do what we do. Being who we really are has consequences we're not ready to deal with… has consequences with which we're not ready to deal."

That simple corrections she made spoke volumes to me. This girl was consciously spanning two worlds, trying to navigate them both at the same time, and trying to figure out where she fit, where she wanted to fit, where she should fit... How hard must that be for her? "But you," I said, "you could open so many doors for yourself if you allowed your potential to be expressed."

"Doors to your world, maybe, but what about mine? I have to live here. *You're* even afraid of doors in your world. What would happen if you dumped that lush fuck who doesn't treat you in any way right? Quit the dissin' daughter and stood up for yourself? You'd lose what you know, and what you know is safe. Same with me. That's that."

"Safe maybe isn't always best."

"There's hurtin' either way, and safe is easier."

"How did you get to be so wise? You're nothing like Reagan and you guys are almost the same age."

"She's spoiled. I'm not. 'Nuff said."

She had a point there. No doubt. "Would you tell me your story? It might help me deal with mine. We might live in different cultures, be different ages, different colors, but I think you just pointed out one serious-ass similarity –– maybe we can help each other to move beyond safe, to whole, or to… something."

"That might be possible. You're a lot more interesting when you spillin' your guts. My story's not that interesting –– well, maybe to you it will be, but for me, a lot of it is typical –– stereotypical –– bullshit. The most important aspect of it is my dad. If it weren't for him, God only knows where I'd end up. My bitch of a mother nearly killed him and now he lives for us, Bria and me, and the fact that I love and appreciate him is what keeps me out of trouble for the most part."

It seemed as if Micah was finally going to open up to me. I suggested sharing dessert and she agreed. We ordered pretzels and queso, which is supposed to be an appetizer, but we both agreed that it would hit the spot better than something sweet. Micah was quiet while we waited for our server to bring it. I thought she was gathering her thoughts, so I gave her the courtesy of silence, as she had given me for so long while listening to me without interrupting. The ability to do that is quite a rare trait in a teenager. Hell, I couldn't do it myself half the time and, once again, she impressed me.

As it turned out, she wasn't quite ready to tell me her story that day. We had only been together for a couple of hours so the fact that she'd even contemplated it gave me hope. When she told me she'd think about telling me next week, I told her that was fine. I could wait. Just because I'd spilled my guts, didn't mean that she was ready to spill hers.

CHAPTER TWENTY

Introspection

*"When the act of reflection takes place in the mind,
when we look at ourselves in the light of thought,
we discover that our life is embosomed in beauty."*

—*Ralph Waldo Emerson*

Micah and I went to Applebees for our third sister-date. It was pretty much a replay of our other times together, but it seemed a little less tense. We still talked mostly about me since she wasn't quite ready to open up. When I asked her how the last week of her junior year had been, she deflected and tossed the question to me, knowing that I was done with school for the summer as well. We talked about that for a little while, then she asked about my family.

"No," she said when I'd started telling her more stories about the Terrible Twosome, "your first family. Parents. Siblings. You know."

"Oh," I said, puzzled. "I'm surprised you're interested in them when you're just barely interested in me," I said with a smile.

She smiled back and said, "Well, maybe knowing about them will help me know a little more about you and you might get interesting." We'd fallen into this dynamic where we said things that sounded unkind but were not actually intended to be so. I think it kind of helped Micah with the ice breaking and, since I was no stranger to meanness, I was able to handle it, apparently to her satisfaction. She was most definitely loosening up. I was silently grateful that I didn't have a hangover.

Since I'd just thought about it the previous evening, I decided to tell her the story of my first binge.

"Oh my God!" she said after I'd finished the tale. "That must've been a helluva night. No wonder it had an affect on you!" Micah exclaimed, seeming not only interested now, but concerned. "What happened the next day?"

"I don't really remember," I admitted. "I think my dad left before my mother got home. Sally hung on to her as long as she could the next morning, but she finally walked her back. Thankfully, she'd loaned mom a light jacket and carried mom's robe over her arm. My mother would have been mortified to have been seen half dressed by the neighbors. As I watched them approach, I noticed that the pockets of her robe were bulging with the rollers she always slept in and that she'd tried to do something with her hair before heading out into the world. When dad got home that night, they both acted as if it had never happened. We, none of us, ever spoke of it again."

"Wow. How did you deal with that?"

"Repression," I chuckled. "It's a handy little device! And with food, binge eating, trying to stuff it all down, I guess. I remember that night every once in a while. I have a poem surface now and then, but not so much about the incident. More about the effects. One came up just last week when I was journaling."

"Let me hear it."

"No, it's dumb, and I am so not a poet."

"Would you let me get away with a cop out like that?"

"No. But anyway, I don't remember it."

"Bullshit. I know you have your journal with you. You told me in the car that Logan gave it to you, you love it, and it's helping you. I know you have it in that humungous bag. Don't lie to me. Read me the damn poem."

Logan had given me that journal, a beautiful book with an antique map of the world spanning both covers, as a gift the Sunday before the last week of school. She said it would help me navigate the crazy, and it did. I'd opened it for the first time that night and began writing, trying to work out why I had so much trouble abstaining from junk food and legal poison, and had recalled the episode with the gun. I'd written a few lines retelling it to myself on the page, then this poem materialized as if from nowhere. Logan told me that I should just go with whatever flowed, so I had, and I let the poem pour out of me unencumbered by analysis or revision.

"Okay," I acquiesced with a sigh. I knew I couldn't avoid this now and cursed my own big mouth for having brought it up in the car on the way to the restaurant. Micah had asked me why I had such a big purse and I told her it was because I had gotten into the habit of carrying that journal wherever I went, so I couldn't pretend I didn't have it. I dug through, pulled out the book, and opened it to a page marked with a long green ribbon. "Okay," I said again, "but no judgment. It's raw."

"Who the hell am I to judge it whether it's raw or burnt to a crisp? I don't care. I just want to hear it."

"Okay," I said, "It goes like this:

Chocolate and beer
That's what I fear
Cuz it's all I hear

Calling my name
I think I'm insane

I should meditate
But that can wait
Meditate
Hesitate
Wait
Fate
Too late
Self hate

And fear
Of chocolate and beer
Because it's all I hear

Because they own me

Appetite
Can't be right
Weight to height
Lost the fight
Far from light
Can't ignite
Can't fly right
Can't stay tight

Who am I?
Why can't I fly?

I want much more
I've been so sore
I've hit the floor
But I need to soar

I wonder why
I cannot fly

Out of control
I've lost my soul
What's my role?
This takes a toll
On a lonely soul

I'm in a trap
Stuck in a gap
When will I snap?

Will I learn to fly
Or will my soul die?

Of chocolate and beer
Or this constant fear?

She waited a second or two, then asked me to read it again. I did. She pondered for a moment or two again, then asked, "What are you going to title it?" I was beyond grateful to her. She didn't criticize what I knew was a juvenile attempt to sort out my insanity. She didn't give me false praise. She didn't try to psychoanalyze me. She just wanted information

"I was thinking about 'Insatiable.'"

"That works," she said after considering it for a moment. "And that poem can be the first in a trilogy. The second part can be about how you're working through it, like you are now, and the last can be about how you finally got your shit together."

"How old *are* you!?!?" I asked with a laugh. Who needed to pay a fortune for therapy when you had Micah around?

"I'm older than I'm supposed to be, that's for damn sure, and so are you."

"Hey!" I said jokingly. "What the hell does that mean?"

"It means that you've had more than your share of shit, just like me, and it ages us. I don't mean how we look. I mean how we had to grow up faster than we should have and that takes a toll, even if nobody can see it. I think we should make a pact to try to make each other younger. Whaddya think?"

"God knows I'd like to find my inner child and let her loose! I haven't seen her for years! That's a great idea, Micah. You ever write?"

"Nah, nothing but school stuff. Who has time?"

"That's what I said to Logan when she asked me. Then she gave me this journal so I'd have to take the time. It'd be rude if I didn't use the gift, right? Hey!," I thought out loud, "I'm going to buy one for you –– shut up, don't argue with me –– and we can share what we write. And we'll do it like you did just now. No judgment, either positive or negative, only questions. Waddya think?"

"Well, since you won't let me argue with you, what choice do I have?" I could tell by the look in her eyes that even if she didn't love the idea, she was intrigued by it.

Finally, we had something solid to connect us. Something that was creative and, quite possibly, therapeutic for both of us. I was an English teacher so I already knew the value of writing to learn, but it was

Logan, and later Micah, who showed me the value of writing to grow, to reflect, that kind of stuff… of writing to survive.

I found out that it was not only a great way to process information, but emotions as well. It helped me settle inner turbulence, sort things out, solve problems, and spark ideas. I wish I'd learned this earlier in my life. Maybe I wouldn't have binged or boozed so much. I wasn't an alcoholic like Dick. I'd go for long periods without imbibing at all, but I'd be lying to myself to say that I didn't self-medicate more than was good for me. I knew that even then.

I found myself really hoping that this could help Micah get through her shit better and sooner than I'd been able to get through mine. Then I had an epiphany: I *was* getting through mine! Maybe not all the way yet, but still… It may be taking me longer than I'd have liked and it may have been a harder road than I'd have wished to travel (and I wasn't technically done getting through mine yet by any stretch), but I was okay. I knew I was going to be okay, I couldn't remember the last time I had the thought that I was okay. I was starting to feel better.

"Come on," I said, standing up and grabbing my bag. "Let's go to Borders and buy yours now, and I'll get another one for me cuz I want to be ready when this one is full, and I think I'll buy another one as a thank-you gift for Logan." Micah lifted an eyebrow at my excitement over such a thing.

"I don't want you spendin' all that money," she resisted. She always had a problem with feeling like a freeloader, and I admired her for that. She had asked to contribute to the meals we'd had together, but I had flatly refused to allow it.

"Don't worry. I have a 30% off coupon in this humongous bag, and this is a gift. If you ever feel bad about me spending money in the future, you can pull my weeds or something if it makes you feel better."

"Fat chance!"

"Come on" I pleaded, "let's go!"

* * * * *

We spent over an hour browsing through the bookstore. Neither Dick nor Reagan would ever have condescended to spend time with me doing such a thing, I knew. Micah chose a small journal, five by seven, that had a colorful abstract impression of a pensive-looking woman whose face was partly covered when the magnetic flap (adorned with her flowing hair) was folded over to close and secure the book. It was rendered in gold and other rich jewel tone colors and a tiny blue tear perched on the woman's left cheek. The triangular point of the flap sort of pointed to the tear, so it was more prominent when the book was closed than it was when it was open. It was really unique and beautiful. I also insisted on buying her a pretty mechanical pencil with an amethyst where the eraser should be.

"What if I need to erase?" she asked.

"You don't erase in a journal. You write what's real and leave it there. No one will ever see it but you."

"Okay, but that'll be hard. Is that what you do?"

"Yeah. That's how Logan told me to do it, and sometimes it really *is* hard. I'm a perfectionist by nature and it was really difficult to train myself to just write. I'll admit that I have drawn a line or two through some stuff I really hated and I've scribbled out some stuff that I was embarrassed about, but I am beginning to understand that in order to work through stuff, I've got to own it. I can't be in denial about it or try to get rid of it or hide it."

"That makes sense, I guess."

When I wanted to get her a book mark for the journal as well, she drew the line. "Look," she said, "This one already has this cool ribbon thing attached that I can use to make the page. Quit spending money on me. In fact, I'm gonna pull those weeds for the pencil."

"You don't have to do that!" I said. "I was kidding about that."

"I know, but I want to contribute to this relationship, too, and since I don't really have any money and can't really invite you over for a meal or anything, then I can at least do that. And it can count for more than the pencil. It can count for the next bunch of lunches or whatever."

She planned on continuing with me! I was elated.

"Besides, I wanna meet this whack-ass family of yours," she said with a smile. As embarrassed as I was about my "whack-ass family," I suddenly realized that staying in denial about that and keeping Micah away from them would be a disservice to all of us. It would be like scribbling out something in my journal.

"Okay. What about next Saturday, instead of eating out? We can weed -- yes, I'm going to help you -- then you can have dinner with the whack-ass family, and I'll take you home after."

"Perfect. And don't worry about them," she read my mind. "I can take whatever they dish out."

"I know you can. And you have a friend there, no matter how rude they might be. Just remember that."

"No worries. Saturday it is."

As I drove home after dropping Micah back at her house, my mind was simmering. Having relived it while telling Micah the story of my first binge drove home to me both the futility of my food orgies and the very real danger of my undeniably excessive alcohol consumption. I realized that neither had ever really brought me any real relief at all. Neither had ever done anything other than make things worse all those years.

I thought about Logan, about all I had already learned from her in the short time we'd known each other, and about what a great role model she was for me. I realized that I wanted to be just like her, and I wanted Micah to feel about me the way I felt about Logan. I fell short of my goal to stop drinking and binging many, many times, but the goal was set on that drive home and finally achieving it has made all the difference in the world to my life.

CHAPTER TWENTY-ONE
Summer

"The earth laughs in flowers."
— *Ralph Waldo Emerson*

The weekend after that lovely last day of school went as weekends always do, except that I spent time with Logan tinkering in our yards, chatting with her, gliding in her glider. It was always the first week or two of week*days* that were weird in the summer. Weird, but wonderful. It was a mix of feeling lost and feeling free at the same time.

On Monday, after getting up way too early out of habit and making my morning coffee, I walked around aimlessly for a while, wondering what normal people did on weekdays. People who didn't work ten hours a day, six to seven days a week, people who normally had some leisure time after work and on weekends, who didn't hit the ground running at 5:00 a.m. and collapse in exhaustion between 8:00 and 9:00 like most teachers did during the school year, people who didn't spend their evenings grading papers and planning lessons to try to keep their heads above water. It took a while to decompress from all that and to get used to the different normal. It happened every year. As weird as it felt at first, I loved it, and once I got used to it, it always felt as if a ten-ton truck had been lifted from my shoulders.

I sat down at the kitchen table and started a list of the hundreds of things I never had time to attend to during the school year, like cleaning out closets and cupboards, scrubbing floors, stuff like that. I felt both overwhelmed and bored at the same time. It was like this every year. Uncharacteristically, I decided that the list could wait and I headed out to the backyard with my coffee but, instead of plunking down in the saddle swing, I decided to walk the perimeter of my yard instead. It was still pretty dark, but I could see well enough. There were tall, overgrown bushes along two of the three fence lines. The only one that looked the least bit cared for was the one on the side I shared with Logan, which was backed up by her box hedge, and that was because she trimmed it back as soon as she moved it and attended to it regularly to keep it looking pretty, like a lovely low green wall. When I got to that part of the yard, I looked over to her house, as I often did. She was either still sleeping or doing laundry in the basement because none of the lights on my side of her house were on.

As I surveyed her yard, it occurred to me that maybe I was more comfortable and serene at her place because of the beauty that surrounded me there. Since I really didn't have any weeds for Micah to pull on Saturday (my yard was an overgrown mess), maybe she could help me clear out a flowerbed along the back fence instead.

My mood darkened when I recalled the day that I'd cut down that burning bush that had blocked my front window, the day I was pretty sure my baby had died, but I put this thought in a pink balloon and released it into the clouds, as I had become accustomed to doing with negative thoughts. As the sun started to peek over the house behind mine, I could see more clearly that the clouds were white and fluffy, and that they were moving slowing across a lightening azure sky. They seemed to be intentionally moving out of the way of the sun so that she could shine on me, and I felt a warmth on my bare arms that invigorated me as much as seeing the sunshine did. I went in and grabbed my journal. I refused to dwell in darkness anymore. Screw the to-do list. I was going to plan my garden.

It's hard for people who are used to getting up at five every morning to sleep in much later than that, so I had left my bed way before the Terrible Twosome woke up. Dick would leave twenty minutes after he got out of bed and Reagan would probably sleep past noon. I loved the morning peace and quiet and I had grown to love writing in my journal, especially outside in the yard. That morning, though, it didn't last very long.

About a half hour into my garden fantasies, Dick got up. He meandered into the bathroom in his boxers and wife-beater tank to shit-shower-shave-and-shampoo. That's what he called his morning ablutions. Classy. While he was at it, I tried to keep the creative juices flowing, but I couldn't help being distracted by thoughts about how the hick who had just passed down the hall had transformed from the handsome man I'd met and married nineteen years before. I tried to puzzle out what had gone wrong, but I realized as I closed my journal and went to refill my coffee cup, that figuring that out would be a waste of time. What would it accomplish besides making me sad?

Dick finally left the bathroom and returned to our room to get dressed for work. I went into the bathroom soon after myself, but was stopped before I could turn the water on to wash my face. The sink was full of dark brown whiskers. The cap was off the toothpaste. The hand towel was on the floor. This didn't surprise me in the least. It was a daily occurrence and a situation that I'd compliantly cleaned up every day for years. What stopped me that day was the realization that I didn't *have* to do that…and I didn't have to listen to his snoring, or make excuses about why he wasn't with me whenever I went to gatherings of family or friends, either.

I made another decision right then and there, and didn't even stop to accomplish the tasks that I'd gone into the bathroom to do in the first place. I went down to the basement and brought up a laundry basket, which I filled with everything in that bathroom that belonged to me. I took it all down to the bathroom Dick had built in the basement years before. I think at that point he had wanted the basement to be his man-cave, but he found it was too close in proximity to the other people who lived in the house so he vacated that space in favor of the garage. So, I decided to take that bathroom as my own. My *own*. I wasn't going to clean up after him any more. I'd just shut the door on the bathroom upstairs the way I shut the door to Reagan's room and I'd just walk right by, so I wouldn't have to see it.

Having accomplished this spontaneous undertaking, I embarked on another, even more daring endeavor that had occurred to me and that I contemplated while finishing up that first task. The nursery was empty and would never enjoy the presence of another child, ever. I had claimed the bathroom, now I'd claim that room, too. I'd emptied the upstairs bathroom while Dick was dressing and he left (without saying goodbye, of course) while I was downstairs putting my new bathroom together. I decided I'd go shopping later and get some pretty towels and a throw rug so it would be an attractive room, in spite of being so small. I wouldn't have to step out of the tiny shower stall onto the cold tiles of the basement bathroom floor, either, if I put a pretty rug there.

So he was gone. I could do whatever I wanted and I had all day. Reagan would sleep until much later, so I had a good five or six hours all to myself.

I started to walk into the nursery, but was stopped at the door by the flood of sadness with which that room filled me. Well, I'd have to get over that. I boxed up all my poor baby's things, disassembled the crib, and took almost everything out of the room. I'd store all this for a garage sale later in the summer and I would make this space my own. My own space. I wanted to achieve the peace, serenity, and joy that invariably emanated from Logan. I knew now that it wouldn't drop out of the clouds into my lap, and that I'd have to make some real changes if I wanted to embark on that journey — and I did. I got more excited about the whole project as the morning raced by.

My first issue was getting a bed. There was a twin bed in the basement where Reagan slept on the rare occasions that my mother visited and occupied her room. That would do nicely. I'd have to dismantle it in order to get it up the stairs, but I'd managed to take the crib apart so I felt pretty sure I could do it. I spent the morning taking crib parts down and bringing bed parts up. I bet I burned a thousand calories!

I could use the dresser that was already in the room. It was as old as Reagan, but it was a nice woodgrain and didn't look the worse for wear. Maybe some new drawer handles... The closet was already empty, waiting to be house the clothes I would soon empty out of the closet in Dick's room. All I'd need would be a bedside table, a lamp, new curtains and bedding, and maybe a few pictures and a couple of plants to make it really nice! Way nicer than the room I had occupied until that morning, in which I was constantly picking up socks and underwear, putting shoes back in the closet, and generally feeling like I was living in a pig stye.

Around 1:30, Reagan finally made her appearance, just as I was making a list of the things I'd need while I was out shopping. The nursery door was closed so she was none the wiser. She didn't seem to notice anything amiss in the bathroom because when she came out and saw me sitting with my journal, the look on her face was contempt rather than surprise.

"I need to be at Lauren's in forty-five minutes," she announced.

"Better start walking then," I replied, not looking up from my list. She'd apparently become accustomed to not getting a rise out of me because she just turned her back on me and returned to her room. I spent the next ten or fifteen minutes finishing up my list and searching for coupons for Bed, Bath, & Beyond, then I walked into her room. I never had taken the door off as I'd threatened, but she knew now that I could — and possibly would — so she just looked up and didn't object to my not knocking.

"Turn that down," I commanded. When she lowered the volume on that God-awful music, I told her that I was going out and would be gone for a couple of hours.

"What about breakfast?" she whined.

"You mean lunch?" I corrected her. "It's almost two in the afternoon, Reagan. Make yourself a sandwich or have some cereal." She just looked away and shook her head in apparent disgust.

That trip to Bed, Bath & Beyond was the highlight of my year! I had decorated our house years ago to my own taste because Dick didn't give a shit about anything, but choosing things for my two new rooms seemed so much more *mine*, my own, somehow. I also hit the At Home Store and Target before the day was through and I was beyond thrilled.

The walls in the nursery were a pretty pale green, the color of newly sprouted leaves and, since I didn't want to deal with repainting the walls, I used that as a starting point. I got a really lovely white bedspread with pink rosebuds and tiny green leaves that closely matched the walls. I got a pretty silver curtain rod and a long white shear curtain panel to drape around it and down both sides of the window to the floor. It was so light and airy and it looked great against the bud-green walls and the blue sky visible through the window. It seemed as if nature had come indoors. It seemed almost as if the clouds themselves had come in through the window to rest on the rod. That window faced the backyard so when my garden was finished, I'd be able to enjoy it from inside as well as out.

I had picked up a small white bedside table and a 3-way lamp, so I could illuminate the room sufficiently for reading (I intended to do a lot more of that!) and writing in my journal, but I could also dim it for relaxing, meditating (even though I hadn't quite gotten the hang of that yet), doing yoga, and listening to music. Just thinking of all this brought me such joy. *"These* are the things that normal people do!" I thought. I was so looking forward to my new space, and I was also looking forward to my new life. I was beginning to feel like I could see it on the horizon.

I cleaned up the old bentwood rocker in which I'd nursed Reagan in a thousand times, tightened the screws, and brought it in from the living room. No one would ever even notice it was missing, I was certain sure. The room was small, but the mirrored closet doors made it appear larger than it was and they reflected the sunshine coming in from the window so the natural light was phenomenal. I was still able to fit in a small wooden bookcase without making the room look too overcrowded. It didn't quite match the wood of the dresser or the headboard, but I didn't care.

It took me all day to reassemble the bed and arrange the furniture, put the curtains up, arrange the bedclothes, move all my clothes into my new closet, and generally settle in. I brought a couple of pothos plants (the only kind I managed not to kill) in from the living room, putting one on the dresser and the other on the bookshelf. I filled my bookshelves only with novels and other fiction. None of my school stuff would live in here. This was not a work room. This was a play room, a writing room, a serenity room, a love room, a perfect room.

I worked well into the night to finish all this up. Of course, by then both Reagan and Dick had come home and wanted to know what the hell was going on. I couldn't help myself and said, "What do you mean, 'what's going on?'" Looking back, I feel kind of bad about being so mean to them, although most likely they didn't even notice it. They deserved it, for certain sure, but they didn't *understand* what was going on with me so it wasn't really fair. The problem was, I still didn't really understand it myself, so I couldn't really enlighten them. I was moving on. That was that.

They were also miffed that I didn't have dinner on the table. I'd made myself a turkey sandwich and told them to do the same or figure out something else.

When the day was done, I rocked in my bentwood and took it all in. All it needed still was a couple of throw pillows, a soft throw blanket to tuck around my lap on cool nights while I rocked and wrote, and some pictures for the walls, dresser, and nightstand. I slept like the dead that night in my new room and when I awoke in the morning, I didn't feel disoriented or out of place; I felt like I was home.

* * * * *

I went out again the next day to pick up the few things I still needed in order to finish creating my new abode and I officially moved into what I came to think of as Shangri-la. Dick never said a word about it. Not, "Are you okay, honey? Is anything wrong? Why did you move out of our bedroom?" Nothing. He didn't care. Oh, he did scream about the money I'd spent, but I just told him that he didn't make all the money and he didn't control the purse strings (even though he actually had for the last nineteen years). He eventually realized that he wasn't going to phase me so he dropped the argument because it wouldn't ignite. There wasn't a modicum of guilt in me and I was happier than I'd been in years.

Of course Reagan never said anything, I have no idea whether or not she understood the significance of this move. Years later she told me that she really hadn't, but that it was the beginning of her becoming aware that something wasn't right. At the time, though, just like her father, she never spoke about it. Just like after the almost-shooting of my mother, it was as if the event had never happened. It faded away like smoke from an extinguished fire and became hardly real at all.

* * * * *

I worked on this project all day Monday and Tuesday and, once I finished it so successfully, I turned my attention back to creating an outside space for myself as lovely as the one I'd made inside. I decided to discuss my garden plans with Logan. Her advice was to start small and build the gardens over the years. She was fortunate to have moved into a house with nice beds already dug and some perennials already nicely placed, but it would be back-breaking work to dig out all those scraggly shrubs and small trees that lined my yard. No baby to lose this time, though.

Logan offered to help me, so on Wednesday and Thursday we dug out all the brush and small plants along the fence on the side opposite Logan's house. The back fence line was more of a mess, so we left that for another time, and Logan's side had the hedges which, even though there was no color there (a situation that would eventually have to be remedied, we agreed) it looked fine at the moment.

We got the bed cleared and the dirt turned so that, when Micah came on Saturday, ostensibly to pull weeds, we'd have a much more creative and enjoyable chore: arranging and planting flowers. I was more excited than I'd been in ages.

* * * * *

On Thursday, Logan and I went to Farmer John's Greenhouse so she could help me choose what I wanted to plant. I had no idea then that you had to concern yourself with bloom time, sun requirements, plant height, soil condition, and all kinds of other things. I'd thought that I could just buy pretty flowers and plunk them in the ground. Live and learn!

When Dick came home that night and saw the pots and flats laid out on top of the newly cleared bed, he apparently realized that to harangue me about the additional expense would be a waste of time. "Good," I thought. I was in for another silent night and that suited me just fine.

* * * * *

On Friday morning, I went out to sit on the swing to anxiously anticipate the next day when Micah and Logan would be over to help me put the plants in. Then it occurred to me that, unless they also wanted to sit in a saddle swing when we took breaks, needed refreshment, or were finished, I'd need to get some furniture. I walked over to the hedge to look over the fence to consider Logan's yard. She had a glider, a dining-type glass-top table with matching chairs under the retractable awning that emerged from the back of her house, and a few Adirondack chairs around a fire pit, which we hadn't used yet, but which I was certain sure that we eventually would.

I knew I couldn't push my luck too much with Dick so I didn't go too overboard with spending on the furniture. I went to Big Lots and picked up a couple of brown rattan swivel chairs and a matching rocker with pretty red floral cushions, a couple of small side tables with glass tops, and a matching coffee table.

I didn't get an umbrella table or dining-type chairs because my intention was to have my yard area serve as more of a parlor than a "formal" dining area. As far was I was concerned, I only needed the three chairs: one for me, one for Logan, and one for Micah. I didn't see Reagan or Dick in my new space (which Logan later dubbed "The Oasis") at all. It wasn't until years later that Reagan told me how hurtful it had been for her that I had thought about seats only for Logan, Micah, and myself, but not for her. At the time, however, it didn't even occur to me.

After I'd unloaded the furniture from the rented truck I'd acquired to get it all home, Logan came over and gave a nod of approval. She helped me with the minimal assembly and said she had a couple of small red pots that I could have and we'd plant some pretty yellow flowers in them for the glass-top tables. They'd match the chair cushions perfectly, she said.

I decided then and there that, next summer, I'd have a patio poured or bricks laid so I had a floor more stable than the grass and that I'd get a retractable awning like Logan's, too.

By the time Friday night came, I was exhausted, but so happy, and I felt so at peace. I grabbed an iced tea and some grapes and went to rock in my new chair, leaving the saddle swing behind. As I rocked there envisioning my new yard, I decided that it was time: the swing set had to go.

CHAPTER TWENTY-TWO
Garden

"Build therefore your own world."
— *Ralph Waldon Emerson*

I had no idea what an eventful day that Saturday was going to turn out to be. Micah and I got back to my house around noon, and Logan came over as we were getting out of the car. The Terrible Twosome were nowhere to be seen, so the three of us went into the backyard to get started on what Micah surely must've thought would've been a horrible day laboring over weeds.

I introduced Micah to Logan and her response was similar to Bria's when she had been introduced to me, and again I was struck by the difference between the two most important teenagers in my life. It was really hard to not criticize myself for having been unable to raise Reagan to be as mature, polite, and respectful as Micah and Bria apparently were. They had become that way in spite of having a "bitch of a mother," as Micah referred to her. I must have already grown at least a bit at this point because I remember taking that thought (of me being a bad mother) and putting it into that pink balloon and letting it sail into the sky to catch up with the clouds. That day they were white and fluffy and they glided slowly across a deep blue sky. I prayed that the weather would be like this all summer!

My neighbors on the non-Logan side of my house had put up a six-foot wooden privacy fence several years before on their side of my ugly cyclone fence and, once we were finally able to remove the jungle that had sprouted up in front of it, I saw to my immense pleasure that was really in pretty decent shape. It would be a beautiful backdrop for the new plants, which would eventually grow up to cover most of the metal fence on my side and hide it from view. I couldn't believe that I had never really noticed it before, but had I never bothered to look. I guess I was just paying attention to different things back then, or not paying attention at all.

I was glad Logan was working with me and Micah in the yard, otherwise, in my neighborhood, Micah might appear to be hired help. My neighbors would look at her and make assumptions and prejudgments, I was certain sure of it.

Logan spaced and placed all the perennials along the fence first (hostas, coneflowers, black eyed Susans, day lilies that would grow tall and multiply). Once we confirmed that we liked the arrangement and got those in the ground, she arranged the annuals in front of and in between them. The three of us discussed the look of the bed and moved things around until we were in agreement about the aesthetic. It didn't take us very long with all three of us working. I'm so glad that Logan had extra gardening tools because it hadn't even occurred to me to get some. She said she'd take me to the nursery later in the week to get some plants for the front and she'd show me what I needed then so

I could get my own tools.

We finished planting, watered the new inhabitants of my yard, and took a break. I had some iced tea left and I brought out some hummus and pita bread that I'd cut up before I picked Micah up that morning. We hadn't done too much talking as we worked, other than to discuss our creation, so it was during this little break that Micah and Logan got to know each other a little better. It was mostly small talk, but it was pleasant.

We ended the day by putting yellow marigolds and tiny purple petunias into the red pots Logan had given me. They so brightened up my little Oasis and I could not have been happier. My world was taking shape, on my terms, and anyone who didn't like it could just go straight to hell. I needn't have worried. Neither Reagan nor Dick ever said a word about my beautiful backyard, except, of course, Dick's griping about what it cost, but I knew it was worth every single cent. I now had Shangri-la inside and my Oasis outside.

* * * * *

The planting had gone well, but the interaction with my family couldn't have gone worse. They embarrassed me thoroughly. As we were finishing up getting the annuals in the ground after our lovely break, Dick came out to see what we were doing and asked me, right in front of Micah, why I was doing some of the work and wasn't it her job to pay me back for all I did for her? Micah and I exchanged glances at this and she surprised me by ignoring his ignorance. She smiled and made a silly cross-eyed, tongue-out face behind his back as he turned to go back into the house. Too funny!

He wasn't phased at all by my ignoring him completely. I'd been so afraid Micah would be offended and angry. I followed her lead by lifting the spade I was using and giving it an air jab in his direction as he walked away. The two of us broke down into hysterical fits of laughter at this, as did Logan who had witnessed it all. I'm sure Dick thought we were nuts. "Way to lighten the mood, kiddo!" I thought. I knew for a fact that, were I in Micah's place, I wouldn't have dealt with that as well as she did.

Around four o'clock or so, Reagan came home from wherever she'd been. Instead of going in the front door after she was dropped off, she came around back to see us finishing up bagging all the empty plastic pots and flats. I asked her if she'd mind giving us a hand with this last little task since it was starting to get late and it was approaching dinnertime, but, not surprisingly, she refused.

"You're kidding right?" she snapped, hoisting her heavy purse higher up on her shoulder. "That's not my job, and it wouldn't have to be yours either if you had any sense." Again I was surprised by Micah's reaction. I'd expected the same kind of levity that Dick's insensitivity had caused, but I could tell that she was furious. I could see the muscles of her shoulders tighten through her T-shirt and the veins standing out on her neck, and she let out a barely audible sigh that sounded more like a growl. She held on to it though. If Reagan had had enough sense to see three feet beyond herself, she'd have seen the suppressed rage in Micah's eyes, but she just tossed her hair over her holier-than-thou shoulder and marched inside as if she couldn't condescend to waste any more of her precious time on the likes of us.

We finished cleaning up the debris, cleaned the tools, and put them back in Logan's tool caddy by a little after 5:00. I'd decided to order pizza (again) for dinner so I didn't need to worry about cooking. Gardening was hard work and cooking always stressed me out. I was already on pins and needles at the idea of Micah dining with the Terrible Twosome, so I'd decided to eliminate that one stressor and just order in. However, rather than go inside to do that and to make sure they were eating by 6:00 as usual, I suggested to Micah that, if she weren't too hungry yet, we could follow Logan (who'd left just moments before) back to her house, return her garden tools, and give her the journal we'd bought for her the week before.

"You haven't done that yet?" she asked. "What's takin' ya so long?"

"Well, when I knew you'd be here today, I thought we could give it to her together, from both of us. Lord knows you've earned more than the cost of that pencil and half of that journal today. Besides, she's kind of like a big sister to me, which I hope helps me be a better one for you, so we're kind of all connected. Don't you want to?"

"No. Sure. It's okay. What does she think about me?" I found it interesting that *this* girl was curious about someone else's opinion of her.

"Oh, she already loves you! I talk about you all the time!"

"What the hell?" she spat, suddenly angry. "You sharin' my private personal shit with a stranger?" She was clearly enraged and I rushed to set her right.

"Oh no! I don't tell her anything but how wonderful you are! Like how you put me at ease after you coaxed me into reading my poem.

Like how smart you are. Like how mature you are and how unfair life's been to you. Besides, you haven't told me much 'private personal shit' anyway, and she's not a stranger."

"She is to me."

"Well, let's go fix that. You guys got along really well all day, but I know the situation didn't allow for you to get to know each other much, which is why I made the suggestion. It's totally up to you, though." And that's when it all began, really.

CHAPTER TWENTY-THREE
Ideas

"It's not what you look at that matters, it's what you see."
—*Henry David Thoreau*

Micah acquiesced so we left my backyard, walked down along and then around the fence between my house and Logan's, then back around Logan's side to her back door wall. I knew that by this time she'd be in her kitchen getting ready for dinner. She'd declined to join us for pizza, suggesting (most likely rightfully so) that it would be too much for the Terrible Twosome to handle both her and Micah at the same time. I disagreed because I thought that maybe Logan's presence might stave off any more rude or racist comments from them, but I understood her point.

Unsurprisingly, Logan was delighted to see us. She always seemed delighted to see me (which was so refreshingly different from how I felt at home) and Micah having accompanied me was a welcome variation.

Logan told us to just drop the garden tools outside the sliding glass door as she slid it open for us. As usual, her house smelled wonderful, a combination of baked goods and scented candles.

She hadn't started preparing her own dinner yet so she brought out tea and freshly made muffins. Everything was always fresh and whole and natural with her. I had one, even though I knew it might make dinner happen a little later than the Terrible Twosome would prefer, but they were capable of taking care of themselves. Besides, I had to! The smell was too intoxicating to resist.

Logan was delighted beyond words with the journal and the story of how we had come to purchase it.

"I'm so glad you two are getting on so well," she said after we all settled down. Micah and I snuggled down into the two large, soft chairs that faced a matching couch, which was decorated with a few pretty accent pillows. Logan took the spot at one end of the couch after placing refreshments on the coffee table and reaching for her tea. "It makes me happy because I know how happy getting on with Alison makes me. Hey, what do you think about forming a little club of sorts? Not like a book club, but like a writing club?" I was intrigued, but Micah looked skeptical. "We all have journals now. We could share and discuss our thoughts and our writing…"

"I'm sorry, but I'm not much of a joiner, ma'am," Micah responded, "and I have a lot of responsibility already. I don't know that I could take on much more, even if I wanted to." I was glad that she was pulling out her more sophisticated persona for Logan and left what I had come to think of as her "street self" secluded for a moment. Then I chastised myself for that thought. She was who she was and I liked who she was so why was I judging her, wanting to change her? I refocused on the conversation.

"Oh, there's no pressure," Logan said. "Here's what I was thinking, then we can all take it or leave it or tweak it: What about if we meet like this, oh, I don't know, once a month or every other week and just share whatever we wanted to share from our journals, like you shared with Micah, Allison? It doesn't have to be deep, intense, personal stuff. I'm working on a novel right now and I would love some feedback on it as I work out the scenes in my journal. And I think the non-judgement rule is perfect — questions only. No feedback other than that, either positive or negative. We'd have tea and goodies. I'd love the company, and I think the fact that we're different sisters would give us a well rounded exchange of ideas."

"Different sisters?" Micah asked.

"Well," Logan explained, "I believe that all women are sisters, even if they're different and it's the differences that make life interesting. You're young and black, Allison is enjoying (well, sort of!) midlife and has a family, and I…" she hesitated for a moment. "Well, I won't say I'm old, but I've been around a while and I've seen and known a few things in my day, so I think I can lend some perspective to whatever we end up talking about."

"I love the idea, Logan!" I beamed. "I feel so much more at home with the two of you than I do in my own house," I admitted, surprised at how easily that had come up and out. "I think it'd do me a world of good. If nothing else, I'd get to spend some more time with my two favorite people." Micah tried to dilute her smile, but it was in her eyes anyway.

Micah was obviously pleased with the reference, but it was hard to gauge what she was thinking about all the rest. I think the idea intrigued her, but it was so out of her element, and she *did* have so much on her plate already, that she couldn't really come to terms with it.

"Well," Logan said, as if I hadn't already expressed excitement about it, "we don't have to decide now, certainly. Just give it some thought. But we *are* here right now so do you guys want to hear a couple pages of the latest scene I'm trying to come to terms with for my book?" She smiled pleasantly at us as she poured more tea from her beautiful blue porcelain teapot into our matching cups. I deferred to Micah, glancing over at her and giving her a look that said, "The ball's in your court."

"Sure," she said. Our appetites had been slaked by the warm muffins and tea. I decided to text Dick and tell him to just order for himself and Reagan, that Micah and I were eating at Logan's. That way, I wouldn't have to rush home and I wouldn't have to listen to him whine and argue later about dinner being late.

Logan leaned over the arm of the sofa and opened the drawer of the end table to retrieve her old journal and, unbelievably, it was the exact same one that Micah had chosen for herself! We both audibly gasped at the coincidence and so had to explain to Logan. She was thrilled. "Great minds think alike," she laughed. "We'll have to put our names on the inside front covers if we continue with this, just in case they get set down side by side. One reason I love this journal is because the tear is only on the left side of her face. You can see it when the flap is open, but it's even more obvious when the flap is closed because of the way the flap comes to a point that rests right next to the tear. Oddly, to me, that represents balance and reality. We can't deny the tears and look only on the right side/bright side. We have to feel everything or we appreciate nothing. To me, when the book is closed, the flap points to the tear as a reminder that we have to open the book and look at the other side, the hidden side, of the face as well to get the full picture. It doesn't cover the tear, because covering emotions never works. You have to feel and deal."

Micah seemed enthralled by her philosophy. I was hoping that Logan's comment about "great minds," the coincidence of their choice of journal, and Logan's easy, open manner (to say nothing of the great food!) would convince Micah to give Logan's idea a try. I could only see good things coming from this "club," if you could call it that, and Lord knows I wanted to continue my relationship with both of them. Maybe this would give us something to do besides just go to lunch every Saturday and take in the occasional movie when her boyfriend (about whom I was beginning to worry, just as her father did) didn't require her presence.

Logan read to us for about twenty minutes. Her novel, she said, was still very rough (she called it 40-grit sandpaper), and what she read to us was a very poetic description of the setting: a commune out west where several like-minded friends lived together. It made me think of Sally and Sam, and the cohort of cronies who had come and gone at their house so many years ago.

Micah didn't need to be reminded of the rules. She made no judgments, but asked Logan where she planned to take the draft next.

She also said that she'd be very interested in meeting the characters. I couldn't top that. I had nothing to say and so found myself glancing around the room, at the mantel, at the clock…

"Oh my God, it's 7:30!" I cried.

"So?" asked Micah. "It's still early. I told my dad what we were gonna do today so he said I don't have to be home until 11:00."

"I'm just worried about the Terrible Twosome."

"Why? They're grown people. They can order a pizza without us, can't they?" Micah pointed out. They could, but I knew they wouldn't and that they'd be sitting, waiting, starving, brewing to attack the minute I came in the door. Still, I had to take Micah home and that would take another hour almost for me to get there and back.

"I know it's ahead of your curfew, Micah, but we've had a long, labor-intensive day, and we really should have something more substantial than muffins for dinner before I take you home. We'll drive through McDonald's and eat in the car on the way, if that's okay. We'd better go. Logan, thank you *so* much for everything. It was a truly lovely evening and a phenomenal day!"

"Well, hopefully we'll have more of them, planned ones, when you won't have to rush off. Micah, thank you so much for the journal and for your input. It means a great deal to me."

"My pleasure. I really enjoyed the tea and muffins Ms…." She hesitated. She wanted to be respectful, but she'd never heard me call her new friend anything but Logan, and I realized at that moment that I didn't even know Logan's last name!.

"Call me Logan. That's my name. And we're all on equal footing here. Mutual respect. Nobody's doing anything, like adhering to formalities, to separate herself from her sisters!" She hugged Micah like she'd known her for years and Micah hugged her back in spite of herself. You couldn't help but love Logan. She was too open and accepting. Too sure of herself and of everything else. It was infectious, and I had to admit that I was jealous and wanted to be just like her.

CHAPTER TWENTY-FOUR
Embarrassment

"Go often to the house of thy friend, for weeds choke the unused path."
— *Ralph Waldo Emerson*

When we got back to my house to get my car keys, both Dick and Reagan were right where we'd left them, doing what we'd left them doing. I don't know how they knew when we came in the front door, but they materialized as soon as we set foot in the room. Dick was clearly buzzed and held on to the door frame to steady himself as he came in from the garage, and Reagan's scowl was louder than her music.

"Where the hell have you been?" Dick demanded as he followed Micah and I into the kitchen where we'd gone to get our jackets off the hooks by the back door. "We've been starving to death over here."

"Yeah Mom, what the hell?" Reagan added, with her hands on her hips.

"Watch your mouth, young lady," I commanded. If they hadn't been so disrespectful, I might have tolerated their abuse.I could feel Micah almost shaking with anger behind me. I could tell that she wasn't angry about anything having to do with her; she was angry about seeing me being treated like this, I knew.

"There are twenty fingers between you to push buttons on a phone and order in to feed yourselves. You don't need me to take care of you. If you're starving to death, it's your damn own fault, not mine. I texted you that we would be late and that we were eating at Logan's. It's not my problem if you don't check your damn phone."

"Well, excuse us for not wanting to eat before our *guest* returned." The way Reagan spat out the word — her smart mouth — it was about to throw me over the edge.

"The way you treated her," I snapped as I whirled around to face her, but then I hesitated, corrected myself, and used Micah's name rather than the pronoun, "treated Micah, this afternoon, how would you expect either of us to know that you thought of her as a guest? And the way you treated me… what makes you think I owe you anything? Why should I interrupt a perfectly lovely evening to take care you? Come on Micah, let's get out of here. This place is toxic."

Micah still, somehow, managed to keep her cool even though I could see that she was seething, even as Reagan yelled after us, "Oh great. Dump your own family for a…" and she stopped. She saw the look on my face as I whipped around to confront her and something in my expression — fury — stopped her mid-sentence. I walked up to her and slapped her across the face with all my might. Both she and Dick were so stunned by such an act from someone as passive as I usually was that it took a second for Reagan to scream, and I mean *scream,* "Oh my God! Daddy, are you going to let her get away with that?"

"Ali-Cat, Jesus Christ! What the hell…"

"Just shut up Dick, and don't call me that. I've had it with the both of you. Micah has treated me with more love and respect in two weeks than you two *ever* have. Take care of yourselves, cuz I'm outta here."

Micah still kept her cool and only added her two cents by smiling brightly at me and holding the door open for me as we marched out of the house. That small act meant more to me than I could have told her. It was silent respect that obliterated the blatant disrespect I'd had to endure in my own house.

When we got into the car, before I could back out, she stopped me. "Wait a second. I wanna tell you somethin' before we go. You don't have to take me out. I'm full from the muffins at Logans. Just drop me off and come back here… and give 'em hell all night! God, I wish I didn't have to go home! I'd love to be a fly on the wall in there right now!" She was beaming and more excited than I'd ever seen her. "You ROCKED! The looks on their faces…" She broke into hysterical laughter! "You SO rocked!"

I couldn't help but laugh as well, which was great because as I was walking to the car, I was having huge misgivings about what I'd said and done and major apprehensions about how I'd manage to live there anymore after that. Her laughter was contagious and we both broke down so much that tears flowed, sides cramped, and I was unable to drive for several minutes. I realized then how much I'd missed laughing and how often I'd enjoyed it since I'd met my new "sisters."

I wasn't surprised that no one came to out stop me or to see what was going on. It just reinforced my sense of isolation from my family, but even the sadness that I should have felt about that couldn't get into the car with us. We shut the door on that and welcomed mirth instead. I was starting to love this girl.

When we recovered ourselves, I told her, "No way are you going home. I need someone to celebrate with… and besides… I'm starving and there's no way I'm eating with those two." Saying that, a sentiment so true at that moment, I did feel a pang of guilt. They were my family, but… what was family anyway? Micah and Logan were more like family than they were. Before I had them in my life, I was miserable — I didn't even realize how miserable — and I had thought I was stuck there. No more.

"You can't always choose your family," Micah observed as we backed out of the driveway, "but you can choose what you'll put up with and what you won't from the family you're given. That's why when that woman came back that one time, I chose to deny her." This was a chapter in her life she hadn't spoken of before.

CHAPTER TWENTY-FIVE
Trainwreck

"A good indignation brings out all one's powers."
—*Ralph Waldo Emerson*

We decided to get Mexican food on the way back to Micah's that night and have a real meal rather than eating junk in the car. As we drove to the restaurant, she told me the story. Her mother had stopped by the previous Sunday to see Bria on her birthday. She was unannounced and just materialized on the front porch that afternoon. Their father hadn't been at home (he had been out on a handyman side job), so Micah felt like — was — the head of the house at the time.

Micah's mood got darker as she spoke. "When I answered the door and saw her standing there, I said, 'What the hell do you want?'" Micah told me that she wished she'd had the foresight to look out the window first. Had she known who it was, she wouldn't have answered the door.

"Hi Honey!" Her mother greeted her as if she would be a welcome guest. When I suggested that maybe her mother was having guilt and thought that the girls might have been missing her, she said, "One more piece of proof that the woman is an asshole." I knew by the tone of her voice, the look in her eyes, and the determined lift of her chin that she would never forgive this woman. Still, it hurt me to hear her — anyone — talk in such a hostile way about a parent. My mother and I had been close when I was Micah's age, but my relationship with Reagan was anything but... but I didn't interrupt her to mention that.

"What the hell do you want?" she had repeated when her mother ignored the question the first time and attempted to circumvent Micah and enter the house, but her way was blocked by her stubborn daughter.

"I come to see my baby Bria on her birthday," she chirped. Micah was about to turn her away when Bria came up behind her in the doorway and placed a warm hand on the small of Micah's back. Bria had a calming effect on her and she realized that she couldn't make the decision for her sister. Micah stepped aside, and Bria advanced to join her behind the screen door, still closed between them and their mother.

"Happy Birthday, Baby! I come to surprise you!" their mother effervesced when she saw Bria and tried once again to open the door to get to her daughters. Micah grasped the inside handle and pulled it tight, barring her entrance. Bria slid her small hand into her sister's unoccupied one and said, "It's okay Micah. I'll go out there for a little while." Bria knew that Micah wouldn't be able to tolerate admitting her mother into the house that she had so carelessly abandoned and that Micah had worked so hard to preserve and to make into a home for them all in her mother's absence. "I'll only be a little while."

"Oh come on you guys! Let me in! It's me!" their mother chortled.

"No," Bria said, respecting Micah's wishes. "I'll come out for a few minutes, but it will hurt Micah if you go in, and I won't have that." She spoke to her mother as if *she* were the adult. She turned to her sister and said, "Micah, it'll hurt mom if I don't go out, and I can't have that either." Micah was right. Bria was awfully intuitive and astonishingly mature for her mere twelve years. Micah had referred to her previously as "the balance" and now I could see why. I found myself wondering if it were nature or nurture (or lack thereof) that had taken these children and thrust them into premature maturity.

Bria and her mother spoke on the porch for about a half an hour, out of Micah's earshot. Just when Micah was ready to call her in because she was worried about her being out in the increasingly dark evening (to say nothing of her fear of their mother's influence), Bria came in and carefully closed the storm door behind her. When Micah asked what they'd talked about, Bria hesitated. "You can tell me. I just gotta know," Micah coaxed.

Bria told her that their mother was happy, living with some guy in Kalamazoo, and that she was a little miffed that her elder daughter didn't want to have anything to do with her and made her spend her short visit, which she had hoped would be much longer and more intimate, on the front porch out in the gathering night after she'd made the two hour drive to come see them.

Bria said that she had listened to their mother, but hadn't said much (no surprise there) until her mother insisted that they go shopping for her birthday. Bria refused. She was conflicted because she knew that whatever she did, she would hurt someone's feelings and it reveals a great deal that she opted to spare Micah rather than their mother. This placated Micah somewhat and earned Bria her forgiveness for having spoken to the woman at all. I never heard Micah call her "mother" or "mom." It was always "that woman," or something worse.

"Did you tell her to keep her slutty ass away from here in the future?" Micah asked, not wanting Bria to misunderstand her condoning what she did for liking it.

"Yeah, those were my exact words," Bria laughed. Micah knew she'd said nothing of the sort.

By this time we'd arrived at the restaurant, ordered, and started devouring our fajitas. In spite of the muffins, the events of the day had rendered us famished.

"I worry about her," Micah admitted, pausing her story as she reached for her iced tea. "I don't know how to be a mother." Micah worried that Bria was turning inward too much, but I pointed out that someone with her maturity, empathy, and obvious sense of humor would certainly be all right. Their mother's abandoning them was hard on her, especially at her age, but she'd come to terms with it, especially since she had such a wonderful, caring older sister. Micah looked doubtful.

"Nobody knows how to be a mother," I consoled her, "and even the good ones have to contend with forces beyond their control more often than not, I think. Besides, you're not her mother. You're her sister. Just be that."

"You're a good mother," Micah said, surprising me.

"How can you *say* that?" I asked, shocked. "You saw Reagan. I tried so hard to raise her right. Everything I did, every decision I made, I did with an eye toward how it would affect her, shape her. I envisioned raising a smart, confident, loving, strong young woman. Well, she's a smart *aleck*, that's for sure, and she's confident in her disrespect. She's not loving to anyone that I know of, except herself and maybe Dick when she wants something, and the only strength she has manifests itself in how she manipulates him and her fearlessness in insulting me. How is *that* a success?"

"Because, like you said, you have to contend with forces beyond your control. Like her dad (and I don't care that he was hot back in the day. What the hell did you ever see in that guy?) and like her friends," she continued. "You got no control there and there's nothin' you can do 'bout them cuz the minute you try to stop her from seeing 'em, she just gonna do it anyway and then there's a bigger split between you. You're screwed. You're a success because you tried so hard. You're a success because you love her even though she's a bitch to you. You're a success because you stood up for yourself in spite of your embarrassment and hurt and impending guilt. She'll learn from that, too. Sometimes it's not what you say but what you do, or don't do."

"Wow," I exhaled. "Bria isn't the only mature one in your family. You're so wise beyond your years Micah... and you had a helluva bad hand dealt to you."

"Well, my dad rocks, unlike Reagan's. Jeeze what an asshole!" That started us laughing again.

"I guess I understand him, a little, though. He works ten hour shifts a lot and his job is really stressful...

"Don't you *dare* defend him!" she barked. "There's nothing on the planet that can excuse the way that shit treats you. Period." I smiled at her determination to be on my side.

"Well, he *is* a hard worker and a good provider…" I began, but I didn't get into it because the waitress came by to see if we needed anything, which also prevented Micah from continuing her argument that I shouldn't defend him. Why was I doing that, anyway? Old habits die hard, I guess. We ordered refills (my wine, her tea) and when the waitress left, Micah gave me an interesting look.

"What is it?" I asked.

"I do wanna do the club," she said, changing the subject, "but can we not call it a club; that's so lame!"

"Okay," I answered, pondering for a moment. "Let's call it a Gathering. We'll just schedule and get together for a Gathering. How's that?"

"Perfect. I really like Logan. I like her whole "sisters" thing. I like that she doesn't just ignore differences, but embraces them. She sees the similarities instead and wants us to learn from each other. I like that she likes me and wants to know me."

"I know exactly what you mean. That's how I felt when I first met her. Like I was destined to meet her. Like she was destined to help me. She already has, so much. I don't know if I'd have had the balls to stand up to those two nimrods…"

"Seriously… 'nimrods?'" she laughed.

"Well, what would you call them?"

She considered for a moment. "Well, 'assholes' is too trite." I loved when she chose to sound as educated and well-spoken as she really was. I derided myself for the thought — let her be who she is at each moment, I reminded myself — and I waited. "I heard you refer to them before, one term for both, that was kinda spot-on. What was that?"

"The Terrible Twosome," I laughed.

"Well," she mused, "that *is* fitting. Let's stick with that."

"Okay," I agreed. "Anyway," I continued, "I don't know that I'd have had the balls to do what I did tonight if Logan hadn't taught me to meditate and start taking care of myself." I glanced down at my glass of wine and the two remaining tortillas on my plate that I knew would be consumed before we left, and realized that I still had a long way to go. "I know it's a long process, but she's the one who put me on the path, and I'm grateful to her, more than she'll ever know."

"And I'm grateful to you, too. I know I don't show it much, or say it out loud, but I am."

"Thanks Micah. That means so much to me, especially after tonight. How the hell am I going to survive in that house now?"

"You'll find a way, just like I did. Anyway, I wanted to ask you something."

"Shoot."

"I wrote a poem in my journal, and I want to know if you think it's okay to read at the first Gathering."

"I'd love to hear it — but remember, we can do anything we want at the Gathering and we don't *have to* do anything at all."

"Yeah, I know, but I don't want to embarrass myself the first time. Will you listen? Same rules though. No judgment." I realized then that she really did understand the point of the Gathering and intended to stick to the rules. She just wanted to share with me first. I was so touched. I nodded and she began slowly: "It's called: 'Not Now,'" she said and she opened her journal to the marked page and read:

Not now
I'm on the rage train now
An express
No stops

You just stand there
Silent and
Watch it go by
Observe

Do not put a penny on the track
Do not try to ride these rails
You won't find an open door
On any car
Nothing to hold on to
You'll be thrown
You'll get hurt

Better to catch up with me
On the return trip
When the steam's run out
And empty are the
Bare, black, cold coal bins
Of everything but dark dust
That will streak and stain
But cannot drive the train

It will slow, if not stop
But at least
The steam can't burn you when
The coal's used up

It's a full bin now, though
The whistle screams

Pulling out
Pulling past
No wave goodbye for you

I don' t know
I may be back
Just not now

I was so blown away that I almost broke the rules and told her I loved it. Then I remembered how her nonjudgmental reaction to my poem had helped me so much that I stopped myself in mid-compliment and switched gears. I could see in her eyes, though, that she appreciated the almost-uttered praise and the fact that I stopped myself before I'd actually given it.

"When did you write that?" I asked.

"I wrote the first half, just up to the part before 'better catch up with me on the return trip' just after you bought me the journal, and I finished it after that woman came to the house on Bria's birthday. I never thought I'd ever want her to catch up with me… you knew this was about her, right?"

"I thought so, but that was going to be my second question, just to make sure. Would you read it to me again? I don't know if you ever learned this, but the very bare minimum number of times you should read a poem is three. Poems are a lot like onions and each reading peels back another layer."

"Sure." She started, then stopped when the waitress came with our refills, then started over again.

When she finished, I had tears in my eyes. Especially knowing that it *was* about her and her mother, as I had suspected. Knowing that for sure lent me a whole new ear for the second reading. "What prompted you to write the second part, the part after 'the return trip'?"

"It's hope," she said. "I seriously doubt that I'll ever forgive that bitch, but I found myself hoping that you'd find a way to reach Reagan someday –– dump the nimrod, though, he's not salvageable –– and that even though it'd be damn near impossible, I like to think there's always hope. I think the end of the poem comes back and speaks to the unlikelihood of reconciliation, but at least there was a glimmer of hope in the middle."

She could see the water pooling at the corners of my eyes, getting ready to spill over. "Don't you dare break the rules!" she warned, pointing her finger at me.

"I won't," I said, grabbing napkin to stifle the flow of tears, "but I am allowed to thank you for sharing that. I love you for sharing that." It came out before I'd given it a second thought. I was afraid that I'd stepped over some line she'd still have drawn between us, but I was wrong.

"I love you for listening –– and for following the rules!" she added to keep the moment from being too mushy, and she laughed, holding up her glass in a toast. I clinked my glass against hers. We were there. We were sisters for real. It was the most enjoyable evening I'd had years, the only possible exceptions being the times I'd spent with Logan.

About half an hour after I'd dropped her off that evening and was heading home, my cell phone rang. To my surprise, it was Desi. I hoped I hadn't gotten Micah into trouble. We'd been close to her curfew, but we'd broken it nonetheless. We had been having such a great time that we both forgot to watch the clock and call him to let me know that we were okay and were just running late.

"Oh Desi, I'm so sorry that I got Micah home late. Please don't be angry with her! It was entirely my fault and I should've called. We were just having such a nice time…"

"No worries *at all*," he interrupted. "I'm just calling to thank you, so much, for everything you're doing with her. She's still spending time with Darry, but her focus is shifting. She showed me her journal (the book, not the contents) and told me about the Gathering. Looks like I've lucked into getting her a second big sister with this Logan. I just don't know how to repay you."

"Seriously Desi, don't even think about it. I'm getting more out of the relationship than she is, I'm certain sure of it." And I really was.

CHAPTER TWENTY-SIX
Meditation

"Feelings come and go like clouds in a windy sky."
—*Thich Nhat Hahn*

Logan and I had been walking every morning for twenty minutes or more, around the block at least. Sometimes we went a little farther in the neighborhood, or we went over to the trails at Hiram Sims or to Kensington, depending on the weather and how much time we had. Now that school was out and since Logan was retired, we were able to manage our time so that, most days, we spent close to an hour just walking and talking. We were growing closer and I was becoming more and more aware of how her presence in my life was helping me in a multitude of ways.

The Terrible Twosome were most definitely *not* changing as I was changing, as I was growing stronger. It seemed like they went especially out of their way to either piss me off or to not see me at all, but I was getting better at not letting that bother me. Sometimes, though, especially in the evenings, I was lonely, so I'd vent to Logan and she never failed to steady me.

I had been very moved by Micah's sharing of her story and I had a hard time getting it out of my mind, so I shared it with Logan on our walk the next day. It was Sunday, so Reagan would be sleeping late and Dick would be putzing in the garage, so we took a nice long walk while I divulged the tale. Logan and Micah had gotten along so well when we were planting and later that evening when we came up with the idea for the Gathering that I was certain Micah wouldn't mind me having Logan help me deal with my whirling thoughts about it all and give me suggestions about the best way to help Micah.

As we drew nearer to Louie the Lamppost on the last leg of our stroll, Logan suggested that I should meditate on my swirling thoughts, and said that it would help me ease them down to something more easily handled. When I admitted to her that I really hadn't had much luck with meditating so far, she invited me in, promising to help me get past whatever my limitations or reservations were. Of course, I agreed. What was the alternative? Go home? Nothing there for me except housework. I could work in the garden later when it warmed up a little, but at that moment, I was entirely free. The gardening would give me some peace and joy and keep me out of the house later, and so would spending some time with Logan learning to mediate now, so I readily agreed.

Logan had on another beautiful, colorful scarf draped casually around her neck that day, the fringed ends hanging freely over her shoulders on either side of the section that was wrapped around her neck. She wore her scarves even when we walked. No work-out wear for Logan. She draped her slim body in flowing skirts and tank tops or shorts and T-shirts, even when we were working up a bit of a sweat on a walk. It gave her such a spontaneous, Bohemian look, and I loved it. She had silver rings on almost all her fingers, too, whenever she wasn't working. When she was gardening in her overalls or doing yoga, even then she wore scarves, just shorter, less elaborate ones. Bandanas in the garden and shorter, loosely knotted, fabric without hanging ends in the yoga room.

That day, her long dark skirt was topped with a white tank and she wore several strands of beads to adorn it, which were framed on the top and both sides by the dark green fabric draped around her neck. To me, she looked absolutely wonderful.

Logan had suggested that I try meditation as a way to cope with my issues and to "channel some good energy." Apparently, she thought that would counteract the negative energy she had perceived in my house the day she met the Terrible Twosome. I'd given meditation a shot a couple of times, but I still couldn't get the hang of it or see the appeal. Still, I so respected Logan that I figured I'd give it another shot. After all, Logan seemed to make it work easily enough. She attributed her tranquility and sense of peace to it, and God knows I needed some of that, so I agreed to let her to guide me through a meditation so I could maybe figure out what I was doing wrong, remedy that, and learn to derive the very obvious benefits Logan got from the practice.

We sent into Logan's meditation room, which she called her studio. It was located in her house where Reagan's room was in mine. She had painted the walls a lovely, muted yellow, which Logan told me was the color of joy, happiness, and imagination. There was good natural light in there for when she wanted to do other things like write or do yoga, but she pulled down the pleated shade to soften the illumination for our meditation session. She lit several scented candles and pulled out her zafu and zabutan for me to sit on. She made me run home to put on more comfortable clothes so I swapped out my jeans and T-shirt for stretch pants and a tunic. When I returned, I sat down, crossed my legs, raised my arms in a wide circle, and drew in a deep breath at her suggestion. I had to admit that even after just a few of these, I felt better.

I began to feel frustration building again when I couldn't keep my mind clear. My thoughts raced around in my head like kittens chasing a laser dot and I couldn't settle them down no matter how or what I tried. Logan could tell that I was having trouble so she reminded me that this was normal and that it happened to all meditators, but I had a hard time believing that. I figured I must just suck at it.

Logan eventually told me to open my eyes and I looked at her with what I'm sure was an exasperated glare. She asked me what the trouble was and I told her. She took a sip of her tea and said, "That's monkey mind."

"Ha! I was thinking kittens or squirrels!" I laughed.

"It doesn't matter what you call it, but you have to believe me when I tell you that it's normal," she reiterated.

"I thought I was supposed to empty my mind of thoughts and sit in silence."

"Environmental silence, not mental silence. That's impossible to sustain, Allison. The human brain was created to *think*. There's no way to keep thoughts from entering your brain unless you're dead."

"Well, I'll admit that I have contemplated that in the past, but thankfully, and in a lot of ways thanks to you, I'm beyond that now."

"Good deal," she laughed. "Now, the point of meditation isn't to empty your mind; it's to observe it. Thoughts *will* come and, when they do, you just notice them, let them pass through, then send them on their merry little way (kind of like you do with the pink balloon), and return your attention to your breath or to a mantra. That's why they call it 'yoga practice.' You practice it. There's no perfection involved or any goal other than that. Maybe you should try a mantra if you're having trouble focusing on your breath."

"No, I'm good I think. Let's keep going and if I'm still struggling, we can try a mantra next time."

"Good deal," she said again. "Okay, keep your spine erect. Pretend there's a string connected to the top of your head that's pulling you up straight. Here, that zafu might be too tall for you. Try sitting on this pillow instead." I took the proffered cushion, which was quite a bit slimmer than the zafu on which I had been sitting, and placed it on the zabuton, the soft meditation mat that she'd lent me. I sat back down and it really was easier to imagine that string pulling me up, lengthening my spine. I was immediately more comfortable.

"Better?" she asked. When I answered in the affirmative she smiled. I loved that all the lines on her face went up. Her wrinkles were barely visible, but her minute smile lines, crow's feet, and brow lines all slanted upwards, even when she wasn't smiling. She must have spent a good deal of time in her life smiling for that to be the case, I thought.

I took a few more deep breaths and began again. I felt myself settling down to the rhythm of my breath. After a few minutes, a random idea surfaced my mind. I tried again to refocus on my breath. Nothing. I opened my eyes.

"Okay, let's try something else," Logan said, understanding immediately. "There are multiple ways to enter a meditative state — and you should really try a variety of them even when you are comfortable with one or two, just to see how they all work for you. Try this: picture yourself in a lovely, peaceful place, then just watch yourself meditating there as if you were an entity entirely separate from yourself, a separate person, a watcher. The image might give you something more substantive on which to concentrate than your breath. I know that can get boring if you're not used to it and that it can sometimes bring the monkeys (or kittens or squirrels!) back to the party."

I had created a mental "sacred place" once before when listening to a visualization CD that Logan had lent me after a particularly rough night with the Terrible Twosome, so I tried to go there in my mind. It had so relaxed me that first time that I'd fallen asleep and never even heard the end of the CD, but I had gotten as far as creating, imagining, my sacred place and I remembered it. I guess I could have just listened to the CD again instead of bothering Logan with all of this, but I'd already learned so much from her and she had given up her morning to help me, so I rededicated myself to the endeavor and began again.

I imagined my sacred place in as much detail as I could. I was walking though an old growth forest in early summer and everything was green and fresh. There was a slight warm breeze stirring the leaves and the small branches and they were making gentle music with their movement. The streams of sunlight coming through the crowded branches overhead looked like the gossamer threads of a web, but there was still enough light to make the forest far from gloomy. It almost glittered with the light's reflection in the dew drops that still clung to the foliage.

In my mind, I followed a well-worn path through the woods toward the sound of water, and came to the edge of the forest. It ended abruptly at a three foot embankment, like a tiny cliff. At the bottom was the beginning of a narrow, sandy beach leading to a vast ocean. Soft waves were breaking against the shore a short distance away and seagulls were circling, calling to each other, their white, graceful bodies dancing in the air above and beyond me, tying invisible air currents into lovely loose knots as they waltzed to the music of the waves.

I imagined myself dropping down from the top of the embankment and landing softly in the sand with a little poof. I was wearing loose, flowing, white cotton drawstring pants and a tunic, which was weird because I owned nothing remotely like that. My clothes billowed gently around me, kind of caressing me, as I moved slowly through the light ocean breeze toward the water.

I rolled up my pant legs, removed my sandals, and carried them with me as I walked to a point half way between the embankment and the shore. Here, I resumed my cross-legged meditation position and observed my surroundings. By this point, I'd totally forgotten that I was really sitting cross-legged in Logan's studio. I was so focused on watching myself meditate at the ocean in my mind.

On either side of me the land curved outward, away from me, in arcs that wanted to head off into the distance but thought better of it and circled back around toward each other instead, only to give up before they actually touched. It felt like the outcroppings were outstretched arms that cradled the water of the small bay between them.

Along those arms, the forest gave way to hundreds of beautiful wild flowers of varying heights and colors that were swaying rhythmically in the warm breeze. They carpeted the ground all the way to the water's edge along the ends of each of the arms. I was situated on a warm swatch of sand between them, looking out at the water ahead of me, which was framed by their dancing blooms.

I could see and hear small creatures playing in the flowers and in the forest behind and beside me and in the air above. I was surrounded by every kind of natural and beautiful miracle I could ever imagine. Life was pulsating all around me in my mind.

As Logan had suggested, I watched myself through all this and then I watched myself just sit there. I was lost in all of it. All my senses were engaged and I totally forgot where I really was.

Logan had originally suggested meditating outside (she said everything was better in nature and I was certainly coming to agree with her), but I had been too apprehensive about possibly embarrassing myself should I be seen by anyone, so I'd said I'd prefer the studio. Now, though, everything other than the beautiful place in my mind was outside of my awareness. I *was* outside, but on the inside, if that makes any sense. Even the cramp in my left leg and the ache at the base of my spine that had plagued me only moments before had vanished, and I swear I could actually feel the breeze in my hair and smell the freshness of the air.

I watched myself breathe. I watched myself smile. I watched myself relax even as I maintained the upright posture that had been so difficult for me to hold on to earlier. I watched as the tension in my shoulders released and my neck elongated. I felt peace and joy entering the space I had made in my body. Peace and joy looked like colors as they filled me up: yellow and blue, sunshine, water, and sky.

Then, inexplicably, my point of view began to move and change. The watcher I had become transformed into a ball of yellow-white light and began to slowly circle the me that was sitting on the beach in my visualization. I was now watching the watcher (now a light), circling me, watching me on the beach. Weird, right? But it was so cool! This was so much better than a wine buzz, and I would learn soon enough that the residual affects were way better, as well!

I was watching myself (the light) floating around my sitting self, viewing me from every angle, and I started to appreciate things about myself that I had never noticed before, or had forgotten. How straight my back was, how square my shoulders were, what a beautiful long, slender neck I had, how my hair moved across my forehead and across my back so delicately in the breeze, how lovely my eyes were even when they were closed, how exquisite I was in my serenity.

As I watched, the light that had been the original watcher continued to circle the sitting me as it ascended, moving higher and higher into the sky, until it reached what seemed like some sort of heaven and was looking down at me from there. The sitter was me. The light was me. The observer watching it all was me. I was seeing myself as a being of light in the heavens, looking down at my meditating self. It made me feel like part of me was divine. I knew all three of me — the sitter, the light, and the me watching all of this — were one being. I felt it just as surely as I felt the air moving in and out of my lungs, slow and cool coming in, warm and comforting going out.

I actually enjoyed the sight of myself in this peaceful place, in this peaceful state, and this totally amazed me. I usually only found fault with myself and criticized myself and felt badly about the way I looked. Not here, though. Not in this place, in this space.

After a while, the me that was the light began to descend, slowly, calmly, joyously, in a circular motion around the sitting me in the opposite direction to that in which it had risen. It finally came to rest within my seated form and its light filled me up. My perspective became that of my sitting self once again, and I became aware of the forest and the flowers and the ocean and the creatures as separate from myself once more. The feeling of unity that I had just experienced lingered and made me happy, happier than I'd felt in a very long time.

As I became re-centered in my sitting self on the beach, the studio began to creep back into my awareness. I could feel the cushion and zabuton beneath me, I could smell the lemon scent of Logan's candles, feel the warmth of my own skin, and the hear sound of my breath — it all became real once more. I opened my eyes and realized that I had just had an amazing meditation experience and I was overjoyed. As I took a deep cleansing breath, I marveled at the sense of peace and joy it left behind.

Logan said, "I'm willing to bet that was an enjoyable meditation. You're getting the idea, right?"

"Absolutely," I said, pushing myself up off the floor with the help of an adjacent armchair. I couldn't wait to share the experience I'd had with Logan. I was certain sure she was the only person in the world with whom I might be able to do so and who would understand and not think I was crazy. She was very interested to hear about my experience, but she cautioned me not to expect that every time I sat to down to meditate.

Of course, I didn't believe that any real part of me had left my body and gone to heaven or that I had really split into three separate entities. That would be ridiculous -- but I didn't care. If I could capture this feeling, this freedom and groundedness, even something remotely close to it, even once in a while, nothing else would ever matter. Logan told me that I could expect all sorts of experiences when I tapped into source energy like that. She told me that I was nurturing my spirit and that made me feel strong.

Did I become a master meditator after this experience? No, but I did learn that there are other ways besides whining, wine and Wonka bars to help me get centered and deal with the challenges of my life. It was incredibly liberating and I had one more for thing for which to thank (and love!) Logan.

We went out into her yard so we could have some ice water and crackers under her Maple tree and I could tell her about my experience. We sat in her glider and rocked back and forth together.

She listened attentively as I related my tale, then we sat there in silence, enjoying another glorious day.

I commented that I was afraid that it would be short-lived since it looked like rain clouds were heading our way.

"You've got to love the clouds, all of them, even the dark ones," Logan mused.

"Really? I'd rather have that glorious morning than the impending drizzle. I was hoping to work in the garden this afternoon."

"Here's the thing about clouds," she said, "besides being beautiful, they are constantly on the move. They never stay still. When they're there, you know that they'll eventually leave. When they're gone, you know they'll eventually be back, in one form or another. Like the rising of the sun, you can count on it."

"I don't know if that makes me feel better or worse," I laughed.

"Better, for sure. Think about it. The sun is always there, even if you can't see it. If you can remember that, you'll appreciate the clouds for what they are. They're just as important for life as the sun is. The sky is ever-changing and variety is good. The constant progression of clouds is not only necessary, but beautiful. I saw a red sky after a shower once that was absolutely breathtaking. That couldn't have happened if the clouds hadn't brought the rain or hadn't been there to help paint the sky. It's the same with rainbows. You just have to remember, know in your heart, that the sun will shine again. It's the natural way of things."

"Logan," I said, "sometimes I can't tell if you're talking about what we're talking about or if you're philosophizing again!"

"Both," she said. "Thinking about that always gives me hope, no matter how bad things get. It helps steady me when things go wrong and it makes me grateful when things are good."

We sat watching the dark clouds pick up speed as they crossed the sky until it started to rain, and I remembered to remember that the sun would shine again for certain sure.

CHAPTER TWENTY-SEVEN
Poem

"The finest poetry was first experience."
—*Ralph Waldo Emerson*

It was Wednesday and I'd been working on and enjoying my
meditation practice every morning before my walk with Logan ever
since she had helped me open that door. She was also teaching me
yoga. We'd had a couple of sessions in her studio and one in her
backyard. I was feeling stronger physically as well as emotionally,
thanks to her.

That morning, I left my bed just after the sun rose, did a twenty-
minute meditation, and decided to take a walk by myself, since Logan
had something going on that morning (I can't remember what) so was
unavailable. I was really craving some communion with nature, so I
laced up my Nikes and stepped out into the beauty of the day. I found
that I was appreciating things like that more and more.

As I walked, I realized that I was pondering positive things more
than negative ones, as I usually would have done. I'd had a call from
Eunice the day before and shared with her how well my Big Sister-
Littler Sister relationship with Micah was going. I told her about Logan

and our idea for the Gatherings and she not only approved, but was impressed. She said she'd be checking in with Desi as well to get his input, but I had no doubt that he'd have nothing but positive things to say.

When I tuned the corner and was walking with the morning light behind me, I saw my shadow move ahead of me on the sidewalk and I remembered how much I liked my neck and shoulders. No one had ever commented on them, so I don't know why I liked the way they looked, but there on the pavement, as my body blocked the sun, I just did. I think I liked them even more because I was the first to appreciate them, first in the meditation and then again on that walk. The odd thing was that whenever I looked in the mirror, I saw nothing to admire. I could only find fault with my short stature, baggy green eyes, overweight and under-toned body. It was only in my inner space and in shadow that I could compliment myself and feel physically attractive. Still, that was certainly better than before, when even the shadows seemed to be against me. I wondered if Desi ever noticed my neck and shoulders.

When I got home half an hour later, I hesitated for a moment after closing the storm door behind me to gaze out into the day once more. When I turned and faced the interior of my home, I instantly remembered all the things I needed to do: laundry, grocery shopping, meal planning...and the peace and joy I'd experienced during my meditation and on my walk began to evaporate before the onslaught of waiting tasks that permeated my brain like a mist moving in before a summer rain.

I was too intrigued by the conflict between my mirror and my shadow to care about any of that for long, though. I normally would have been stressed about not getting to it all right away, afraid that I wouldn't get everything done but, for some reason, that day, I didn't care. I just blew that mist away. Maybe people with pretty necks didn't care about stuff like that.

I went into my new bedroom, opened the drawer of my nightstand, and pulled out the new leather-bound journal that Logan had given me. I hadn't used it yet because I had only just filled the last page of my old one the night before. As I closed the drawer, I thought about what *should* be in the nightstand drawer of a woman with beautiful shoulders: condoms, lubricant, silk scarves… "Oh stop!" I thought, chuckling at myself for having the thought and pushing out the thought of Desi that immediately followed in its wake.

I popped into the office and grabbed the fountain pen I'd given Dick on his last birthday, the one he'd never even touched, then I went back into my room. *My* room. The thought of it as the nursery seemed to be fading and I was feeling more and more at home there. I sat down in the rocker, the one in which I'd rocked slowly back and forth while I nurtured or nursed Reagan so many years ago. Now it was time to nurture myself.

I opened the journal, which was stiff with newness, and smelled the pages. There is nothing like the smell of pages, blank with promise or filled with wisdom or reflection or imagination, either way. I took a deep breath and tried to open myself to the watcher again, the one I'd experienced when Logan taught me to meditate, to see what would happen. I breathed and thought about loving myself, not just the newly discovered neck and shoulders but my whole self, and about how good it felt to do that.

Logan had told me that when you learn to love yourself is when the world really and truly opens up to you, so I knew I had to try. I waited and waited, and nothing happened but, eventually, and *so* surprisingly, a poem took shape somewhere between my soul and my mind and worked its way down my arm, through my hand, and onto the page. I have no illusions about the quality of this rough, straight-from-the-muse poem, but I'd learned that judgment is the creativity killer, so I didn't dwell on that at all. I wrote:

I love my legs
They are heavy and pocked
I love them not because they're beautiful
But because they can and have carried me through life

I love my breasts
They are long and low
I love them not because they're beautiful
But because they can and have cradled the soft head of my child

I love my arms
They are short and white in summer
I love them not because they're beautiful
But because they can and have embraced so many and so much

I love my eyes
They are clear and bright
I love them not because they're beautiful
But because they can and have shed tears of joy

That was all that came out of me, but it was enough. I understood that

I could feel gratitude even for the parts of myself that I had heretofore disparaged. I had learned from my sisters, from both Micah and Logan, not to judge, so I didn't criticize my thinking, my feelings, or my writing. I just appreciated it for what it taught me, what it showed me, how it made me feel to have brought all that onto the page.

I closed the journal and my eyes. I held the book close to my heart and allowed myself several deep breaths. That, too, had been a meditative experience. Things were certainly turning around! When I got up to tackle my chores, it was with an entirely new attitude, a lighter heart, a more satisfied mind. I was doing these things for *me* now, and I was worth it. There was such satisfaction in knowing that, and there was also joy.

CHAPTER TWENTY-EIGHT
Gathering

"The best writing has no lace on its sleeves."
—*Walt Whitman*

For our first official Gathering, Logan made gorgeous blueberry scones and fresh lemonade, and she set up what was as close to a British tea party (without tea!) as I'd ever seen. Her table was beautiful! She had a blue and yellow floral tablecloth (appropriate for those refreshments, I thought), and daisies in a dark blue vase adorning the center of her dining room table. She used her good china for us, too. It was so classy: ivory with gold trim. The glasses also had that same gold trim, and the flatware had a subtle gold inlaid design on the handles. We really felt special. Neither Micah nor I had ever had anyone go to so much trouble (even though Logan insisted it wasn't any trouble at all) to make us feel so welcome, so special, and so happy.

After Logan filled our glasses and plates, we settled down in her living room in what eventually became our customary places, and complimented her on the refreshments and the attractive presentation. She told us that the china, glasses, and flatware came to her as wedding gifts. This was the first we'd heard about a husband and we pressed her to provide details. We could tell almost immediately that it wasn't something she was ready to talk in depth about. She only told us that her husband, a police officer like mine, had been killed in the line of duty many years before, after only ten years of marriage. We didn't press her for details because we could tell the time wasn't right.

"Let's begin the Gathering!" Logan announced, smiling in spite of what must have been a painful memory. She started us off by reading a character sketch of one of the inhabitants of that commune she'd described to us before and it had us rolling with laughter. If all her other characters were that colorful, her novel would be amazing! Micah read the poem about her relationship with her mother that she had shared with me, and it drew me near to tears once again. Logan loved it and was able to convey that by the questions she asked. We all stuck to the rules.

When it was my turn, I hesitated. Their stuff had been so good. Logan was a great writer and had such color in her prose. Micah was so passionate and articulate even with teenage angst. What did I have? I had chosen to read the second poem I'd written for the trilogy that Micah had suggested. It was really rough, but I got over my inhibitions in light of their obvious interest, so I read my as-yet untitled poem.

I will get there
But I must beware
And take great care
To avoid the snare
It's everywhere

But I will dare
The stress I'll bear

I'll pay the fare
And face the glare
Of my reflection's stare

I will get there
Life seems unfair
But I am aware
That a tortoise's care
Will take me there

With far more care
Than the racing hare
I will get there
Slowly… steadily…

"Let me guess," Micah joked. "You'll title it 'The Tortoise and the Hare'!" She was smiling and making fun of my apparent tendency to not title my work.

"Sounds a little trite and maybe plagiaristic — is that a word? — but what the hell?" I laughed.

We explained the trilogy idea to Logan and they insisted that I read the first part to her. She conveyed her approval by asking when I thought the third part might come to pass. I had no idea, and it was great that nobody seemed to want to pressure me. Still, they were obviously looking forward to it. It motivated me for certain sure. The problem was, I still didn't know how the story would end, so the third part would have to wait until I figured that out.

Logan asked if she could read something else. She left the room and came back with a different journal. It looked old and worn. She sat down, rearranged the scarf around her neck, and told us that this was one of her old journals from the late seventies.

"Wow, you've been writing that long?" I asked.

"Every day since… every day for a long time. I number and date every journal. The one you gave me will be number fifty-eight. They've saved my life, actually. The journaling and the yoga. But I want to read you a certain one…."

"You know what's in each journal?" Micah asked, astounded.

"Well, I remember roughly where I was in my life in most years so I can narrow it down. Then, I've made a rough table of contents in each one. When I start a new journal, I number the pages at the bottom right then, on the inside front cover (which sometimes carries over to the back cover as well), I write the page number and a brief description of what begins on that page. Most of them just say 'rambling,' but every now and then I write something that I suspect I might want to find later, and those notes give me kind of a map to it. You'll see why this one was important I think. It's called 'The Beast.'" I saw her glance at Micah, who gave her an approving nod at the title and lifted an eyebrow at me as if to say, "See? Was that so hard?" Logan read,

He is such an evil beast
Mistaken often, feared the least
Controllable it sometimes seems
But the evil in his eye just gleams

Bestowing pleasure in disguise
Unsuspecting victims so unwise
Influenced by society
Which foolishly rejects sobriety

The victim ultimately will be taken
Surely eventually will be shaken
By hints of the Beast's enormous power

And its intent to utterly devour

The victim tries then to break free
But sadly too soon comes to see
That the Beast has claws quite deeply in
And it thinks it knows that it will win

There's guilt, relapse, another pledge to quit
You're sure in your heart this time is it
Then something inside you just breaks loose
You take a drink, tightening the noose

Self loathing, denial, remorse, self-hate
You fear that already it's too late

But wait, there is yet a real true hope
There IS a way that you can cope
All of a sudden, you see quite clearly
That those you love so much, so dearly
Are worth any difficult sacrifice
So you no longer need think twice

Though he'll never quite completely vanish
The Beast, at last, you know you'll banish
To a cell down deep inside your soul
You now know that you have control

Although you know it'll be very hard
You know in your heart that love'll stand guard
And keep the Beast corralled in its cage
Where it still smolders in a seething rage

It'll try to break free every once in a while
But you can take heart, you can actually smile
You have the strength, you have what it takes
Because your love makes no mistakes

Focus on that as the days go by
And soon the Beast will become too shy
And will fade away into memory

He'll have no power; that's all he'll be

He'll be locked up tight, toss away the key
You can do this, I guarantee
And you will finally be set free
To live your life the way it should be

Joy you'll then see fill your world
And your beautiful future can be unfurled
And no matter what the future brings
No Beast puppeteer will pull your strings

You'll live life under your own power
Blossoming like the most beautiful flower
Wih petals unfolding to greet the sun
And you'll know in your heart that you've finally won

"You were an alcoholic?" I asked, amazed. That was *so* like the third poem of the trilogy that *I* wanted to write!

"Yes, and my son, too. That poem is a combination of some thoughts of mine and parts of his suicide note." We were stunned. Logan was always so joyful and peaceful, we'd just assumed that she'd had that kind of life. She lost her husband to street violence and her son had killed himself. I didn't think I'd ever be able to get over that at all, let alone shine with peace, love, stability, and creativity all the time like she did! I was speechless, but Micah knew exactly what to say.

"You've gotten strong as well as sober. Good for you!" Follow the rules.

"It must've been more painful than I can even imagine. I'm so sorry Logan."

"You're both right. It was unbelievably painful, not just his suicide, but what he'd done to his life, and it did make me strong. I had to either get strong or die."

An out-load laugh escaped me and they both looked at me incredulously. "I'm so sorry," I explained, rapidly recovering myself. "It's just that those are the *exact* same words that I said to myself right before I met you, Logan…right after I found out that my baby was dead."

"What baby?" they cried simultaneously.

I told them about my son and how losing him had indirectly led me to both Logan and Micah. Micah pointed out how the loss of her mother had indirectly led her to me. We talked about how loss can lead to good things in the end, and we all felt so much better about everything after that discussion.

It was an amazing afternoon and we decided to do it again the same time every week. It was just a given that we'd return to Logan's. It was the most serene place either Micah or I had ever been and there was certainly no way I would subject them to the negativity that papered the walls at my place. Even in my Oasis, there was an off chance that the Terrible Twosome would intrude. I offered to provide the refreshments, which caused me considerable, but well hidden, distress because of my inability to cook and my aversion to entertaining, but as with the tea to which I'd invited Logan before, I'd make it work for my sisters. That experience had taught me that making things simple worked just as well as perceiving them as complicated, so I put that stress in a pink balloon.

CHAPTER TWENTY-NINE
Bitch

"I have learned that to be with those I like is enough."
—Walt Whitman

The week went by well enough. Logan and I walked in the mornings and on Tuesday and Thursday we had yoga "classes," as well. Logan had assured me that meditation would be helpful in my quest to get strong, and I was having more success with that the more I practiced, which I tried to do every morning. She insisted, too, that I'd love yoga as another vehicle to personal growth and she was right. She taught me Hatha, Vinyasa, and Kundalini yoga and I enjoyed all three practices. It was a lot more strenuous than I'd thought it would be, but I felt somehow whole after doing it so I agreed to continue. I also found myself traipsing around the fence and through Logan's back door wall on several of those evenings to sip tea and just talk. It was so wonderful to be wanted and Logan ensured that I had no difficulty understanding that I truly was welcome. We talked a lot about Micah. I was really looking forward to seeing her again.

* * * * *

On the drive home after that first Gathering, Micah and I had decided to start meeting on Wednesday evenings as well as at the Gatherings so that we'd still have some regular sister-dates in addition to those focused on sharing our writing with Logan. We'd still have some time with just the two of us to go shopping or out to dinner or to the movies. School was out, so that was fine, and we were both on board with seeing each other twice a week.

When I picked Micah up that next Wednesday, Desi wasn't there, which I have to admit I was a little disappointed about. I got a shy smile and a small wave from Bria when she walked Micah to the door. I wondered if I should invite her to join us some time, but I thought better of it. This was Micah's time and as much as I could tell that I'd enjoy Bria's company, it wasn't time for that, at least not yet. I so looked forward to our sister-dates and I got the impression that Micah was starting to feel that way, too.

After we'd been seated and served, Micah took a long draw of her Diet Coke, broke off the end of a breadstick, and leaned back against the booth. We were at Library Pub that week, having appetizers and mozzarella bread. After a few moments, and with no segway, Micah began telling me about her mother's departure.

"Bria and me was squatin'…" she paused and began again. "Bria and I were kneeling upstairs, looking down between the slats in the railing that dad put up there to keep us from falling over," she continued. "There's just one big room up there that we have shared since we were born." It sounded a lot like the attic room I'd had at my parents' house. "We were just twelve and seven years old. I was the age Bria is now. It seems weird. I had turned twelve just the day before.

"Dad gave me my party. It was a lame 'dad party.' Men don't seem to know how to do it right, really, but there was cake and ice cream, and he found out most of my friends from Bria, and from the ones he found, he found a few others, you know. He did this for me, even though I know he didn't really care much for some of my friends, even back then. They were all fine, but entertaining a bunch of twelve-year-olds? Well, I'm sure he would rather have been doing just about anything else.

"We didn't do anything but have the cake and ice cream, but he did it all for me. No goody bags, no games. Obviously no clowns or blow-up houses," she laughed. "He did his best with no help from her. She wasn't even there. She was hardly ever around by that point. Oh, she showed up at the tail end though, totally shit-faced again, just in time to embarrass me in front of all my friends, fallin' down drunk — or stoned I later learned — slurrin' words, inappropriate ones, to a bunch of little girls."

I could see Micah tense up under the weight of the memory and I could tell we hadn't gotten even close to the meat of the story. I noticed again that she never used her mother's name or called her "mom" or "mother." She always referred to her as "that woman" or some other term that clearly demonstrated their estrangement and Micah's animosity toward her.

"Dad tried to hustle her into their bedroom, suggesting that she might want to change her clothes — which *were* a little on the slutty side for that occasion and time of day, I remember that — but really it was just to get her out of there," she continued. "When he suggested it, she mimicked his words and rolled her eyes (just like a child), and made exaggerated air quotes to indicate to everyone there that she knew it was a ruse and that she had no need to or intention of changing anything. She was trying to make him look like an idiot, but she only made herself look downright pathetic. She apparently assumed he wanted sex or something because she started berating him, telling him that he was a pervert who was just turned on by all the 'young tail' in the room.'" Micah rolled her eyes and used air quotes herself to indicate that her mother used that exact phrase. "She seemed to just boil up as she spoke and she shouted that she hated him and had just come from a real man anyway so why would she go with him… you get the idea.

"Oh, Micah," I sighed. "I'm so sorry."

"Oh, it gets worse. Turns out this kinda shit had been goin' on for a long time, but we just didn't know 'bout it. Dad had been telling us that she worked nights. Maybe he thought she did. Maybe she even did, but that wasn't all she'd been up to. He'd been laid off so he was always home for us after school, for dinner, books at bedtime, the usual mom stuff. She slept late on weekends which seemed normal to us since we thought she 'worked' nights and she was fine, it seemed, on weekend afternoons as long as we let her sleep in. We played cards, went to movies. We were a family two afternoons a week…six or eight hours a week. We were young and that tiny slice of normality fooled us into thinking everything was okay."

She paused and I could see that this memory and her reflection on it made her sad (in spite of her having told me that she was over it) and that there were cracks in that solid cement persona she wore like armor. She was tough on the outside, but she had a tender heart on the inside.

She looked up at me and must have read empathy in my expression because she put up her shield once more and continued."Bria deserved so much more, so much better. She's such a good kid. She was such a good little kid, even when she was that young. You think I'm smart? You should meet her, get to know her. Maybe you will some day."

"I really do hope I so," I said. An "in" I thought! I almost started to tell her about my brief meeting with Bria and how impressed I had been with her, but I overcame the urge and let her go on.

"Anyway, as me and my girls just stood there — frightened, fascinated, fixated on this fuckin' crazy woman — my poor father… He could see no way to stop her so he gave up on her and ushered my friends out the door, thanking them for coming and for being so kind to me…" she paused again at this point and didn't even try to cover up the hurt that the memory produced.

"Damn it," she spat suddenly. "I spent a hell of a lot of energy repressing this shit, and now you makin' me dig it all back up. Shit."

I didn't apologize. I hadn't asked her to tell me this story since I had suggested it at our first meeting. I just sat and waited as she recovered herself. I saw such strength in her.

She took another sip of her Diet Coke, then a deep breath, and went on. "So, anyway, Bria and I were watching them from upstairs the next day when they hashed this all out. It was Sunday and for some reason not yet known to us, that woman was up at 9:00 a.m., so we knew something big was happening.

"Even Bria, who was such a little kid at the time, with a short attention span and everything, knew to hush and not fidget, not give away that we were there, listening at the railing in the upstairs bedroom… and she told him she was done. She had thought she wanted that life… wife and mom, home and family… but now, not at all." Her frown deepened and her tone become bitter. "She wanted to party instead. She'd gotten a job at the bowling alley bar and had met some loser who apparently interested her more than we did, so she traded in her apron for a push-up bra and a mini-skirt. She traded in my dad… my wonderful, caring, sensitive dad," (here she sniffed as if trying to holding back tears and the bitterness intensified), "for a new high-roller primp or something, who the hell knows or cares? She left me and my sister like we were dolls she was tired of playing with, to be tossed under the bed and forgotten. She walked out the door. Never even said goodbye to us. Left it for the old man to explain."

I couldn't hold myself back any longer and I whispered again, "I am so sorry Micah." She gave me a slight nod, and looked away for a second. I swear, I could almost see her willing her tears to recede before they could fall, pulling herself together, so she could go on.

"He just stood there, like a morbid stone, looking after her, at the door she had closed behind her like it was any other day. Not gently like she was sneaking away, not slammed like she was pissed. Just closed, no big deal. Nothing important.

"That was when my twelve year old heart broke right in fucking

241

half. From my perch at the top of the stairs I saw a single tear roll down my father's face. It moved so slowly, it amazed me, like gravity didn't work on it or like time was standing still or something. It was really weird. It finally reached his chin, hung there for like a second, then dropped to the front of his shift, making a tiny dark spot… that's when time turned on again for me, but he still didn't move and neither did we."

I was so tempted to reach across the table and take her hand, try to comfort her, let her know that I really cared about her, but the time didn't feel right, so I waited. I didn't want to make it more difficult for her to stay strong.

"I don't know how long we all three hung there like in suspension," she went on. "Finally though, Bria got up really slowly and went down to him. She has a sixth sense for people's feelings that girl, and for timing. She even did at that age. She walked slowly and silently down the stairs, tiny hand gliding along the rail and, when she got to the bottom, she put her arms around his legs. She was so small. That's only how high she could reach. He dropped to his knees and hugged her close, then broke into convulsive sobs. The heart I was sure had already broken when that bitch walked out, broke again and again as I watched him fall apart.

"I ran down the stairs, knelt down behind him and hugged him from the back. I could barely get my arms around them both. He pulled me around so that he was embracing both of us, soaking us with his tears. I realized then that he really loved that birch for some crazy reason and that her leaving had torn a huge hole in his big-ass heart." I had a lump in my throat and thought my big-ass heart would break as well, or maybe explode — it was so full of compassion for her.

"Well, not me," she declared, her face hardening as she reached for her drink, probably so she wouldn't clench her fists. "I've hated that bitch from that moment on, and it only grew more intense as the years passed by and I grew to love my father even more because of who he is and what he's done and because he so deserves better than what life's given him. The only reason I don't wish that she never existed at all is because then Bria wouldn't be here and the world needs people like my sister."

"How did she handle your mom's leaving?" I ventured to ask, resisting the urge to remind her that the world needed people like her, too.

"Hard to say for sure. She never said a word about it. In fact, she hasn't said very much at all since then. She may be really quiet, but she can read people better than anyone I've ever heard of or read about or seen on television or anywhere, and she knows just what to do to put them as right as they can be. Like she knew when to go down to him, how long he needed to rock us in his arms, and when it was time for him to let loose. She was the one who finally broke up that little family hug. She let him cry and let me boil with hate for only a little while, then she pried herself loose and took him by the hand into the kitchen, sat him down at the table, and got him some cereal. She was only seven. Seven, for God's sake! I was the older sister, but I was paralyzed." I could see something akin to wonder on her face as she spoke about her little sister. "She poured some cereal for me too, then for herself. We were all silent the whole time. It was kind of eerie now that I think about it.

"Anyway, when we finished eating, dad had come back to himself a little bit and said, 'You heard.'" A rhetorical question. Hell, it wasn't even a question. It was a statement. Two words that encapsulated the gargantuan rift in our tiny world. I said, without a hint of the anger that was raging through me, 'I suppose I'm the mom now' and he hugged me and said, 'No, no. Don't you worry honey. I can be both mom and dad, too, you'll see.' Well, we'd already seen, hadn't we? He had really been both parents for a long time. That was the way it had been for a long, long time," she repeated, as though she was realizing it all over again.

She paused and sat in silence for a little while. I could hear the clinking of plates and the scraping of silverware, the animated chit-chat from nearby tables, but I don't think she was aware of anything but this memory. I was almost sorry that she had decided to share the story and dredge it and all its attendant emotions up at all, but I did think that knowing this might help me help her, so I continued to sit silently and wait for her to continue or to end the conversation, whichever she preferred.

She continued, "Things didn't get much better at all for a while. My rage simmered like a pot on the stove and my poor father wore his pain in his eyes. We were silent a bunch, especially Bria. The night after that bitch left, dad ordered pizza and said he wanted to sit at the table 'like a family.' He meant it to be comforting, I know, but all it did was tornado the rage inside me. We were not a real family. That bitch saw to that.

"As I sat there pretending to be part of a family, trying to keep it all bottled up for both their sakes, I remembered his valiant attempt at my birthday party and how many traditional components it lacked (games, goodie bags… twelve-year olds like that shit), and I knew we were in for a rough ride despite his best efforts. I silently promised him and myself that I'd do whatever it took to keep that family afloat and that Bria would never miss anything because of the disappearance of that whore." She took a deep breath.

"Dad always had made his best effort to make us all happy," she said, softening as she often did when talking about Desi. "I decided then and there that I might be too young to be the mom, but that I'd never do anything to make his job harder or to cause him any more pain. I had just witnessed him experience more than his share. My anger transformed into determination and I swore that nothing, nothing, would hurt either of them ever again if I could prevent it. It was so weird though. Right after I made this resolution in my head, Bria looked over at me and smiled. I knew I'd have to look out for her, too, but I had a feeling she'd be the easy one."

After another long pause, Micah raised her eyes to meet mine and said, "So maybe that's why I'm 'mature' and not spoiled. I had no chance to get spoiled and a life like mine grows you up quick. I've kept my word, too. I've managed to stay out of trouble and I work hard in school — which is where your 'intelligent, articulate and well-read' shit probably comes from. But all that just makes it harder for me to survive where I live, not easier.

"I'm so sorry, Micah."

"Don't be. I'd rather be strong than spoiled."

"Me too."

"So which are you, anyway? Strong or spoiled?"

"Neither. I don't know. I don't have any clue who or what I am."

CHAPTER THIRTY
Darry

"Nothing is to be so much feared as fear."
—Henry David Thoreau

The following Saturday, we were enjoying our second Gathering. We were all growing closer on these lovely afternoons. Logan shared the opening chapter of the novel she was working on. I shared another poem I'd written. I wasn't sure if this was really the third in my trilogy, but it was a start. Still having neglected a title, this is what I read:

For a timeless age, a slender string
Sliced through
my clenched, clamped fist
Burning
Friction from futile fighting
Slashing palm skin, painful

I was fearful of failure, but
I could no longer fight it,
So, just to spite it,

I surrendered

I let it go

My resistance soared silently into the sky
With an undulating weave-wave farewell
No more staccato strain to restrain, to resist
No longer tightly tethered to trouble
It was weightless now in a calm, cloudless sky
Where only moments before, in a tempest it had torn me

I watched it float, fly, minify…

Astonished
No stick snapped
No paper shredded
No knotted tail whipped wildly in the wind
It only waved smooth smiles back down to me
In the balmy breeze
As it drifted drowsily away

All that remained was
A dancing diamond, diminishing in the distance
Wordlessly writing peace across the sky
A vanishing friendly foe, a flyspeck only now

I surrendered
And fear and frustration just floated away
Now my fist is open

And my palm has healed

When I finished, Micah, unsurprisingly, asked me about the title. I shook my head and smiled, saying, "Well, since you're always giving me grief about it, I thought I'd throw it out there for you to bombard me with brilliant suggestions."

"Well," said Logan, "I'm up for that, but let's give you a little feedback first. Did you notice the metaphor, Micah?"

"Yeah, it's like you're comparing the third episode of your life to letting go of a kite." So Micah thought this might really *be* that third component of the trilogy. I must have done something right. "I liked the alliteration, too, cuz it makes it kind of like a song in some places. How about "Surrender" for a title? It shows that something really hard can be accomplished by something really easy, like by just letting go." I wondered if she was thinking about maybe letting go of the hatred she felt for her mother, but I doubted it.

"Yes," said Logan. "I like that. Oops! I didn't mean to judge."

"It's okay," Micah assured her. "You're only agreeing to a title, not judging the work." Logan smiled at her.

We talked about that poem for a while. Logan said she agreed about the alliteration and pointed out how some stand-alone stanzas provided emphasis, stuff like that. All very helpful. I actually toyed with the idea of someday putting together a collection of poetry. Me! Who'd never even considered writing poetry until it just bubbled out or escaped of its own accord. Still, I had several rough ones in my journal that I was beginning to think I could polish up someday.

After ten minutes or so, I could tell that Micah was ready to move on, so I asked what she had decided to share.

"Well, it's kind of a stream-of-consciousness thing from my journal. I know Allison shared the story of my mom's abandoning us with you Logan, which is fine, so I thought I'd round out my 'story' with some reflection on my friends so you can get to know me, maybe, a little better."

We said we thought that was a great idea, and Logan and I were secretly thrilled. We'd spoken about Micah's friends on more than one of our walks, and we were concerned that she never really mentioned any girlfriends and only briefly alluded to her boyfriend, Darrius. She called him Darry, and we were still worried about him.

"Sorry, but it's not creative at all. Just some venting, really. It didn't start out that way, though. It started as sort of bunch of character sketches, like the one Logan read us before, but it sort of morphed into a rant."

"That's totally okay," Logan reminded her. "Journaling needs to stay open and free and what comes up, comes up. I cannot tell you how many rants fill my journals, and I also can't tell you how many of them taught me something or inspired me somehow. Remember, too, that you're not allowed to judge yourself either!"

"Yeah, I know, but after listening to the stuff you guys read… Okay. Here goes." And then she began.

"I have/had three friends. Not good friends. Okay friends. Tanisha, Mel, and Sasha. We used to hang out, go to the mall, go to the park. Not so much anymore. They've drifted. More like deserted. Or maybe I drifted… When I

started hanging with Darry, I guess I spent less time with them or something and they got pissy. No great loss. I'm not one for gossip or nail-doing or slumber parties with a bunch of airheads anyway, which they really kinda are. They're either failing out of school or about to. No ambition. No dreams other than to meet a boy and fall in love. Bria told me that they're jealous of me, but I think they're just nimrods." She glanced my way and smiled.

"I know how annoying *they* can be," I smiled back, nodding for her to continue.

"I don't need them anyway," she went on. *"I have my dad and Bria, I have my new sisters, and I have myself. That's five to three so screw 'em. Then, there's Darry. Man, he's so hot. I've been feeling lately, though, that maybe that's not enough. Being with a hot guy didn't turn out too well for Allison."* She shot me an apologetic glance and I responded with a "what the hell" shrug.

"We met in eighth grade and stared going out, if you could call it that, during freshman year. Wow, that means I've wasted two years of my life." She paused to tell us that she'd never really thought about that until she wrote it and that it made her realize how quickly time flies by. *"Two years. The worst part, though, is that I'm just now starting to see that it* was *wasted. At first, being with him made me more popular, so who needs those bitches, right? I got to know a lot of people through him, but nobody I really liked or could relate to. Still, it was nice to belong to him. It was a security. And we did okay for probably the first year.*

"We were young so we never really went out like on real dates, but we had fun, and he was good to me. Last year, though, our junior year (maybe a little at the end of sophomore year too, though), he started changing, and not for the

251

better. I'm stressing about how the hell I'm going to get into and afford college, and he's just trying to get tougher, sell more drugs, move up the ranks in his gang. He got himself mixed up with the NWO." She glanced up to explain that it stood for New World Order, a pretty well-known Pontiac street gang.

"At first, he was just buying in bulk and selling weed to friends, but since he's gotten involved with that gang, he's getting worse, and he tells me less and less about what he does, which not only makes me worry, but makes it weird because we don't have that much to talk about any more. He's not interested in my studies or my family or my dreams. He doesn't want me to do anything but hang on his arm and sleep with him." She paused again to vehemently deny that she *had* slept with him. *"He's pressuring me now, more than ever before, though. For sex and to do drugs. Apparently I'm not cool anymore since I won't, but I can't because it would kill my old man if I did.*

I know most of my friends have done the deed and most of them smoke weed at least, but I can't take a chance of anything going wrong. I've got my dad and Bria to think about. Anyway, he gets high more often now and I think he's into harder stuff, too. He bullies little kids now, too, trying to act like a tough guy, and I guess he is one. Actually, he kinda scares me sometimes, and he's getting more and more possessive. He wants to see all my texts, know where I am all the time and who I'm with. I've started avoiding him cuz he kinda scares me sometimes." Her repetition of that caused Logan and I to exchange a concerned glance.

She continued in that vein for another five minutes or so and Logan and I locked eyes more than a few times as she did. We weren't allowed to judge and it didn't seem right to offer advice at this point, so we thanked her for sharing it and asked that she keep us up to date. I knew we'd converse later about the best way in to which stage a sort of intervention and help her disentangle herself from Darry because he really did sound like dangerous bad news, and I was pretty sure it was worse than her short journal rant made out. If he's stopped telling her things and started pressuring her for sex and to do drugs... not a good sign at all.

Ironically, we were about to find out just how bad the Darry situation really was.

* * * * *

Just as we were getting ready to end what had been a lovely afternoon, all hell broke loose. There was a deafening, violent, rapid pounding on Logan's front door and a man's voice yelling, "Micah, you get yo' ass out here!"

"Shit, it's Darry!" Micah whispered, stunned. "How the hell did he find me?"

Logan got up, putting up a hand to indicate that she wanted us to stay where we were. She moved at a leisurely pace to the door, but didn't open it. She spoke calmly and clearly through it. "Darry, Micah is here, but we aren't letting her out as long as you're here. You're acting irrationally and violently and we've called the police." She motioned to me and I came back to life, found my phone in my back pocket, silently dialed 911, and walked into the kitchen to make the call so they could hear me over the Darry's continuous yelling and pounding. Micah stayed where she was, unsure about what to do.

"Darry," continued Logan, still sounding serene in spite of his vicious hollering and attack on the door, "I'd advise you to leave now or you'll get into trouble that you don't need. When you straighten up and can behave like a gentleman, you can call Micah and the two of you can talk, but not now. There's nothing you can do here, so please leave. We're busy."

He ignored her and continued to yell obscenities and pound on the door and I was terrified that he'd break through before the police arrived, so I called Dick. I don't know what I expected from him. I was surprised that he even answered the phone considering it was my number that would have shown up on his screen. "Dick!" I said breathlessly, "Micah's boyfriend is stoned and outside trying to break the door down. Keep Reagan inside until the police arrive, please!"

"Is that what all that racket is?" he asked, obviously annoyed. "I'll be right there." He hung up before I could protest and before I knew it I heard his voice, thick with drink, shouting to Darry.

"Get outta here you fuckin' low-life nigger punk before I shoot off your sorry ass!" I could not believe what I was hearing! That he even cared enough to answer my phone call had shocked me enough. Now, here he was threatening a very large teenager, obviously hopped up on something -– not a smart move in my estimation – and with a gun! A gun! I could see it in his raised hand as I watched from behind Logan's shear curtain panels and saw him round the fence and stomp and stagger toward Logan's front door.

I had expressly forbidden him to have a gun in the house after Reagan was born and now I knew that he had one anyway and probably had all this time. It immediately occurred to me that I should not have been surprised by that. He told me that he kept his service revolver in his locker at work. I was so gullible. Why would I have believed him? He'd always told me what I wanted to hear just to shut me up, then he did whatever he damn well pleased anyway. Even though I was thoroughly frightened at this turn of events in what was obviously a dangerous situation, I was still enraged at the deception and at the fact that he'd put our daughter in danger.

I asked Micah in a whisper if Darry had a gun. She lifted her shoulders in a gesture indicating that she had no idea.

"You heard me asshole!" we heard Dick shout. "Beat it! Now!" Micah and Logan joined me at the window once the thunderous knocking and Darry's yelling stopped and he turned around to face Dick. We could see the muscles strain in this back as he strode down the walk toward my husband. "Where the hell is Reagan?" I thought in a panic.

"Oh my God," Micah breathed. "He's volatile when he's high, Allison. This is bad. This is really bad," and she was right. Darry was walking toward Dick as if the gun in Dick's hand were nothing but a twig he intended to snap in half. Surprisingly, Dick stood his ground and leveled the gun at Darry. Drink makes you brave, I guess, or stupid.

I had flashbacks of the gun incident with my parents and moved to head outside to defuse the situation on instinct. Both Micah and Logan put their hands on me to impede my advance. "Don't," Logan said. "Let it play out. This is too big for you, or me, or Micah."

Thankfully, before it accelerated to the point of injury (or worse!), the police arrived in two squad cars, sirens blaring, lights throwing red and blue dancers across nearby homes as they skidded to a stop between the two houses. Everyone in the neighborhood was alerted now, even those whose attention hadn't been drawn by Darry's loud shouting and pounding or Dick's slurred shouts. It was late Saturday afternoon and almost everyone in the neighborhood was home, out mowing or working in their gardens, walking dogs. At this commotion, everyone seemed to stop and move inside, doors either cracked open with curious eyes peaking out to watch the spectacle or quickly shut against the commotion. I have no doubt that seeing an enraged, strung out black man in that neighborhood stoked at least some white middle-class fears.

Two officers from the first car wrestled Darry to the ground and handcuffed him. A third officer emerged from the second car and took the gun away from Dick while his partner came to the door to check on us. It occurred to me that they were treating Darry way more roughly than they were treating Dick, even though Dick was the one brandishing a firearm. Damn him! Damn them! I certainly *did* want Darry taken care of, but Dick was guilty of at least as much…but Darry was a black kid and Dick was a white cop. It shouldn't have surprised me, and I could tell from the expressions on the faces of Micah and Logan that it had surprised neither of them in the least.

The rest of the afternoon was spent sorting through the mess. Darry was arrested for disturbing the peace, drunk and disorderly conduct, and probably a couple of other things. We never found out for sure.

Dick was given a warning about using his service revolver in a personal altercation when off-duty, blah, blah, blah…. Something like that. He's lucky they didn't lock him up for drunk and disorderly conduct, too. He knew the officers, so I guess it makes sense that they let him off with a warning, but I really didn't think it was fair… because it wasn't. So many assumptions made by so many people in this world.

About an hour and a half later, I was finally able to drive poor Micah home. She was visibly shaken, something very uncommon for that strong young woman. "You okay?" I asked.

"Yeah, just a little… I don't know. He's never done anything like that before. He's pissed because I cancelled our date tonight because I didn't want to have to rush back from the Gathering. But how the hell did he figure out where we were? Oh my God! Bria! Allison, please drive faster! I swear to God if he hurt her there's nothing that can save his sorry ass! Drive!"

I stepped on the gas and risked arrest with the speed and recklessness of my driving, but the same fear had taken hold of me and we were both consumed by a rising panic.

When we got to her house, Bria was sitting quietly in one of the chairs on the big covered front porch with her feet up on the other one, looking so like the day I first met her, doing her homework. "Are you okay?" Micah cried, as she took the front porch steps two at a time and hugged her startled sister.

"Sure, why wouldn't I be?" Bria asked. Micah related the events of the afternoon and Bria said, "Well, that explains it then." As usual,

Micah had to coax her to speak, but we eventually gathered that Bria had gone to the park to read earlier in the afternoon and when she'd come back, the front door was unlocked.

"Micah! You didn't give him a key, did you?" I asked, appalled, swinging around to face her. She just shot me a look that asked if I'd lost my mind, then she urged Bria to continue her story. Apparently, when Bria came in, the place was empty and nothing was out of place, so she just figured that she'd forgotten to lock the door. But when she went over to the desk to get a pencil to do a crossword puzzle, she noticed that the address book was open and a page had been ripped out — the page with my address and phone number. Good thing Desi resisted using technology or we may never have figured out how Darry got our address. Still, that didn't explain how he found us at Logan's. That mystery was solved soon enough.

I called home to tell the Terrible Twosome that I wasn't leaving Micah and Bria alone and would wait with them until their father got home. We had decided not to call him at work and worry him and, most likely, cause him leave work early and lose the hours and hence the pay. Reagan answered the phone and, in her usual catty voice, said, "Great. Once again we take second place. Too bad I told that jerk where you were. If I hadn't, maybe you'd be back by now and I'd have my laundry." What a bitch, I thought.

"You know I don't do your laundry anymore... and *you* told him where to find me? Why?"

"He wasn't looking for *you*. He was looking for *her*, and I was just as happy that one of her own was here to take her back where she belongs. When are you going to stop this crazy crap anyway and come back to do your job?" She sounded just like her father. I was so livid that I couldn't even speak. I hung up the phone. Both Micah and Logan could tell I was upset, but said nothing about it. I explained to them that it had been my own lovely daughter who had put us all in harm's way. Bria tried to make the excuse for her that she couldn't have known what Darry was like.

"You didn't hear her reason for sending him to us," I said, and I could tell that Bria, even as young as she was, understood.

"Darry's like an open book when he's high," Micah added. "He's a monster and, even as shallow as Reagan can be, that could not have been lost on her."

"I'm so sorry Micah…" I began.

"Don't you dare," she snapped at me. "Don't you dare apologize for that bitch. She and I will get into it one of these days, but you don't ever worry about me. I'm fine." I sincerely doubted that.

Just minutes after we decided to vacate the porch in favor of the living room where there were more comfortable chairs, Desi came in, obviously pleased to see me. He'd recognized my car outside and was probably happy that I'd stopped in instead of just dropping Micah off, as I usually did.

He could immediately tell that something was wrong and we told him about the day's events. I could see him visibly reign himself in instead of lashing out about Darry. I'm sure he wanted to kill the kid, but he knew that expressing that would be counterproductive and I admired his insight and restraint.

"I'm worried," I said. "He'll be in jail tonight probably, but what about when he gets out?"

"Oh, he's harmless when he's not high," said Micah.

"Micah!" In my astonishment that she'd make excuses for him after this, I had really raised my voice at her. I simmered down a bit and said, "I'm sorry for yelling, but *are you kidding me*? How often is he NOT high? What are the chances that he'll just let this slide?"

She sighed. "You're right. I don't know. I know he loves me, but he's just not himself when he's wasted. I don't know what to do."

"Well, I do," said Desi, finally snapping. "I'm getting a restraining order against that punk yesterday!" They argued about it for a short while, but Micah was too level headed not to see the danger she was in, so she finally capitulated, knowing that it wasn't really up to her anyway. I really think she was thinking more about Bria, Logan and me, but in any event, she finally agreed that it was the right thing to do and that she'd never see him again.

"Don't worry," Micah said to all of us. "I wouldn't date a *total* loser…" Her father and I exchanged glances and Bria got up and put her arm around her sister's waist.

"Okay, " Desi said, formulating a plan. "I'll change the locks tonight. I'll give you girls, and you, Allison, keys that you will guard with your lives." I thanked him, promised to keep my key safe, and said that I'd stop by the next day to check on the girls.

"We don't need to be checked on. Jeeze you guys. It's not that big a deal."

"Yes, it is," said Bria, surprising all of us by chiming in. "Alison doesn't have to come. It'll be light out until dad gets home. But it *is* a big deal Mic."

"Fine," Micah answered, with mild (or maybe feigned?) exasperation in her voice. "I'll keep you on speed dial, okay?" she asked, looking at me. I was touched that she understood my very real need to have some kind of role in protecting her, that I couldn't just walk away from all this.

"Good deal," I said gratefully, sounding like Logan.

When I got home, I was completely exhausted. The day had taken an emotional toll for certain sure. It was almost 9:00 o'clock and The Terrible Twosome were pissed at me, of course. One, because it was apparently *my* fault that Dick had been forced (he actually said "forced") to pull out the gun that he'd lied to me about all those years and that he was now in trouble at work because of it. He hadn't identified himself as an officer, he got involved in a domestic dispute to which he had not been dispatched while obviously intoxicated... blah, blah, blah... and two, because I had hung up on Reagan after her vicious, racist remark that I refused to tolerate.

Both laid into me the minute I walked through the door, but I just ignored them. I knew that if I didn't, I would explode. I walked silently past them, through their torrent of dark, hateful complaints, but I let those blow past me like a strong wind and went into my room and closed the door against the storm. My room. Nobody would bother me there and the spirit of my little boy might just pay a visit to console me. I did't really believe in such things, but it was a comforting thought. I had way too many things on my mind to entertain the selfishness of the Terrible Twosome just then. I grabbed my journal and started to write. No wine. No food. Just thoughts that needed to be sorted and settled.

CHAPTER THIRTY-ONE
Peril

"Times of heroism are generally times of terror…"
—*Ralph Waldo Emerson*

The next day, I couldn't concentrate on anything at all. I was *so* worried about Micah. I was tempted to text her, but I didn't want to be that overprotective adult or worry-wart friend who over-reacts. I knew I wasn't needed at Micah's house, but I wanted to be there.

In spite of myself, I finally broke down around noon and called her to tell her I was on my way with tacos and not to argue with me. She didn't, which worried me. When I got there, everything was fine. We all enjoyed our lunch and I stayed for a couple of hours playing monopoly with the girls. When Desi came home we watched an episode of "Friends" together before I headed home. We all needed a laugh to break the tension that was pulsating through the air, even though none of us mentioned it. We were kind of in denial, I think, but still, what could we do?

In spite of the frightening reason for my being there, the whole afternoon and evening made me feel like part of a family again. We were all so easy together. With the exception of the multiple times that our eyes met and locked, Desi and I were relaxed. At those times, however, the sexual tension was so great that I was certain sure the girls must feel it almost vibrating between us. I think Bria sort of did. Once, after dragging my eyes away from Desi's, they crossed her gaze. She gave me a sad smile and an almost imperceptible shake of her head (had I imagined that?), as if to say, "It would be nice, but bad idea." I knew this to be true, but I could not deny that I wanted this man. Not only was he physically attractive, but his intelligence and the way he so obviously loved and cared about his daughters so touched my heart. That evening just intensified the feelings I'd been noticing more and more in his presence (and even when I was alone) and I couldn't shake it off. When he shook my hand as I left, the heat was almost unbearable. I'm sure he felt it, too, because when he moved forward to hug me, he thought better of it and just sort of waved instead.

As I climbed into the drivers' seat, I was on fire. My heart was beating at twice the normal rate, and I felt a yearning that I didn't even recognize — it had been so long since I'd felt anything even remotely like it. "Stop it!" I said out loud to myself to break the spell. It worked, but only slightly. I had wonderful dreams about Desi for a lot of nights thereafter.

* * * * *

When I got home, the shit storm was already in progress. Apparently, while I was gone, the Terrible Twosome had turned on each other to lay blame for my absence and what they referred to as my "ridiculous behavior." Dick actually used that phrase. He still thought he was my lord and master, I guess, or my father maybe. He still hadn't figured out that I'd already grown so far past that. Reagan called me selfish and told me she hated me. She still hadn't figured out that I'd finally learned the value of taking care of myself and that I didn't care if she hated me. By this point, I really didn't. Of course, deep in my heart I fervently wished this weren't the case, but in all the parts of myself that needed to get strong, I did not care. She had hated me for so long already and that fact had upset me for so long, but I realized then that I was so over it.

I remembered the night I met Logan, when I'd taken Reagan's phone away. I remembered how powerful my calm had made me feel that day and I fell back on that strategy. I just listened as they ranted and waited for them to run out of steam and stop. I figured it had to happen eventually and I was right. It was hilarious watching their tantrums sputter and die in the face of no resistance!

When the tirade subsided, I looked from one to the other and said, "Maybe you should have been nice to me. Maybe you should have shown me the respect I deserve. Maybe you should have given one flying fuck about me, but you didn't. I did everything I could think of to be a good wife to you" and I looked pointedly at Dick, "and a good mother to you." I moved my steady gaze to meet Reagan's eyes next. "I'm sorry if you feel I've failed you, but I always did the best I could with what I had, and I always loved you both no matter how miserably you treated me. Now it's over. I just don't care anymore. I still love you because you're my husband" eyes to Dick "and you're my daughter" eyes to Reagan, "but I don't feel love from either of you so I'm done. Fend for yourselves. You've both hurt me too much and too often. I have found other people who love me for who I am. I won't be abused anymore, and I won't be lonely anymore, either. I'm done."

"What do you mean, you're done?" I *so* hated when Dick did that, but it made me laugh because it was so predictable. I'd actually said the same words in my head simultaneously with him because I knew it was coming! My reaction seemed to completely baffle them both. It was hilarious!

"Done," I repeated. "I'm living my life for me from now on. If ever you choose to be nice to me, you can be part of it. Until then, we're roommates and all chores will be divided evenly. We'll discuss it later. I know no one cares, but I've had a rough couple of days." I headed toward the bathroom (the upstairs one, the only one with a tub) to draw a bath to nurture the calm that I felt was starting to unravel just a little bit. I *did* love them, and calling an end to my family was no easy thing. I guess they don't call it "tough love" for nothing. Neither of them came after me. I knew they wouldn't. I wished I had a tub in my new bathroom downstairs so I'd be more removed from their negative energy, but hey, this was my house too and I'd use whichever rooms I chose to use.

As I sank deeper into the bubbles, I thought that beyond that closed (and locked) bathroom door, they would probably be trying to figure out how to have me committed and replaced with a more subservient doormat, which is what they'd become accustomed to. Sorry guys. Not me. No more.

As I started to unwind beneath the water, the scented bubbles and candlelight drowning the stress that had so recently started to boil to the surface, it occurred to me that all this was as much my fault as theirs. Okay, maybe not *as* much, but I could've done things differently, too. I could have refused to be used. I could've been more forceful, demanded that Dick get out of the damn station or the damn garage (or wherever the hell else he hid out to avoid me) and take me out, take me seriously. I could have demanded that Reagan treat me with respect. But then I realized that, even if I had seen the value in that, which I really didn't, it wasn't in my nature so how could I have done it? If Dick wanted to avoid me, what good would it do to force him to be with me? If Reagan hated me, what good would it do to make her pretend otherwise?

It is what it is, I realized. I didn't have to like it; I just had to accept it. I'd just have to learn to live with it, and I could do that now that I had Logan and Micah… and Desi. I thought to myself that I could even count Bria among my friends, although she was so young… and Desi was so dangerous due to my obvious feelings for him. I was still a married woman after all, technically, if not practically. I was still an honest person. Nothing could come of our attraction to each other. Nothing. I repeated this to myself over and over. Although I had to admit that I really, really wished it could happen. I worked hard to let it go, but as someone who wasn't used to wishes coming true, I never really expected anything to come of it anyway.

I soaked for about half an hour then emerged to pamper myself some more with a glass of wine and a pedicure. I knew I didn't have to worry about running into the Terrible Twosome because Dick would have retreated to the garage and I was pretty sure I heard the front door slam just after I stole away to the bath, a sure sign that Reagan was having a tantrum and had left the house. No sense hoping Dick was dealing with her. That's not how it worked. She'd come back when she was ready and, rather than disciplining her for leaving the house without permission, he'd believe whatever excuses she made and give in to whatever demands she might make. That was their dynamic.

I had just put the nail polish away and was lighting some incense in my room after changing into my softest pajamas around 11:30, when I heard a loud pounding on the front door. I immediately flashed back to Darry, so I quickly grabbed my robe, put it on, and headed down the hall to the front of the house. I was almost blinded by the red and blue flashing lights washing over my living room walls, so I hastened my barefooted pace, my heart in my throat.

When I opened the door, there stood the same two officers who had wrestled Darry to the ground the day before, but this time, they were flanking my evidently distraught daughter. They looked as if they were literally holding her up. Dick had come in from the garage at the commotion, beer in hand. He undoubtedly imagined one awful daughter-embarrassed-me scenario after another because he started yelling at her, demanding to know where she'd been, what she'd done, what trouble she had gotten herself into. Showing off for his buddies, pretending to be a real father, I thought, and very obviously buzzed.

Reagan was visibly trembling and I rushed forward and took her into my arms. I knew something must be terribly wrong when she not only permitted my embrace but returned it and began sobbing against my chest. I led her to the couch, sat down next to her with my arm around her shaking shoulders, and let her cry, telling her that I loved her and that when she was ready to talk, I'd listen. Dick looked completely thrown by the whole situation. He had finally quieted down and was speaking with the officers rather than raging at a daughter he apparently didn't even really see.

I rocked Reagan back and forth like I did when she was a little girl and it felt so beautiful that I almost wept myself. I found myself wishing that she were still small enough to sit on my lap in the bentwood rocker like she used to when she was a toddler and had a fever or had scraped her knee. This was way worse than that, of course, and I knew not to press her. I just let her know that I was there. After a while, she whispered to me that she wanted to go to bed and asked if I would I take her.

The officers and Dick quite forgotten, I held her firmly, lovingly by the shoulders as I walked beside her to help her down the hall. She didn't feel steady to me at all, which increased my worry. I waited just outside her door while she changed out of her clothes and into her pajamas. When she called, I went in and only then, looking at the pile of clothing she'd dropped on the floor, did I notice that her t-shirt was ripped almost in half. How I'd missed that at the front door, how her father had missed it and had commenced accusing *her* of something, I had no idea. I kept silent about it and waited for her to be ready to talk. It was probably the hardest thing I'd ever done.

I tucked her in and brushed a stray hair from her forehead, a tear from her eye. "You okay?" I asked.

She started to nod, then went the other way and shook her head, wrapping her arms around me again. "Want me to stay?" This time she did nod. I slipped off my robe, turned out the light and slid in beside her. She turned her body toward mine and wrapped her arms around me. Who'd have imagined that, after that scene earlier in the evening, we'd be holding on to each other as if for dear life.

"When you're ready to talk, I'm here," I said. She nodded and sniffled but remained quiet. It was in the middle of the night, after we'd both been asleep for a few hours, that she woke me. She asked if I'd get her a glass of water. When I got to the kitchen, Dick was sitting at the table, several empty beer bottles and a full ashtray in front of him. He never smoked in the house. That worried me, but he was not my priority just then. I didn't even wonder why he hadn't come to Reagan's room to check on her. I went to the cupboard to get a glass, then to the fridge, and had just stared pouring from the Britta pitcher when he spoke.

"It was that goddamn black hoodlum. He's the one who hurt her."

"What?" I said, turning to look at his bloodshot eyes.

"It's a damn good thing they took my gun or that nigger'd be history."

I'd had it with him. "Oh shut up Dick. Don't you even care about your daughter? All you can think of are racial slurs and violence? What the hell's wrong with you?"

"With ME?" he shouted, standing in a stumbling whirl to face me, holding on to the back of the chair to steady himself. "You're the asshole who brought that whole fucking world into our lives, putting us all in danger, and now look what happened."

"What did happen? -- wait, never mind. I don't want to hear it form you. I'll hear it from Reagan when she's ready to tell it. Now go to bed or you'll never get through the day tomorrow. You look like shit." In spite of what the excessive drinking had done to *him*, I decided to take a glass of wine back to Reagan's room.

When I got back, I saw that she was sitting up in bed and had turned on the bedside lamp. I handed her the water and set my wine glass down on the nightstand. I got back into the bed with her, under the covers, and I propped some pillows up behind my back and head so I could comfortably sit up. She drank a little, then handed me her glass to put on the bedside table and snuggled back down, putting her head on my stomach and wrapping her arms around my waist. She seemed so young and sweet and innocent just then. "What happened, honey? Can you tell me now?"

"You promise you won't get mad?"

"Absolutely. I'm just so relieved that you're all right. I just want to make sure you're really okay. You can tell me. I won't be mad, and maybe I can help."

"Well," she began, then she paused and was barely audible when she finally spoke again. "I was *so* pissed, so I got on your computer and found Micah's address." I'd put it in my contacts the day I first met with Desi.

"How did you know the password to get on my computer?" I asked.

She raised her head and gave me a look that said, "I told you so."

She had advised me to come up with a difficult password when I got my new Mac, but she must've known I'd ignore the advice.

"It wasn't hard, Mom. My birthday? Really?"

"Lesson learned. Go on."

"I wanted to go over there and let her have it, tell her to go back to her own family and leave mine alone. I don't know if you've noticed, but even dad's been acting weird since you've deserted us."

I ignored the dig and answered, "I don't notice much when your father's always in the garage or at work. Sorry."

"I know," she conceded, softening, even though there had been no malice in her comment. "Anyway, when I got there, she was sitting on the porch writing in some gold colored book. I walked up and started talking to her."

"Talking?"

"Well, sort of bitching, I guess. Saying what I came to say. She just sat there and let me go on until..." she paused.

"Until?"

"Well, until I started dissin' you. I told her you weren't much of a mother (sorry), but that you were the only one I had and she couldn't have you."

I swallowed, but kept silent. I didn't want to turn her off before I found out what happened, even if it did hurt like hell.

"That's when she came at me."

"Came at you?" I asked, shocked. "Did she hurt you?"

"No, no! I mean just started yelling back at me. She said something like, 'You spoiled brat. You have no idea how lucky you are to have someone who loves you so much. All you do is abuse her and hurt her. You don't deserve her. Not that I deserve her either, but you sure as hell don't." I didn't say a word as she listed off Micah's sentences one after another like she was reading from a grocery list. I couldn't see Reagan's eyes because her head was back on my stomach, facing away from me, and I was glad she couldn't see mine because tears were welling up in the corners. I stroked her hair and waited. It took her a couple of minutes before she could continue. I think she was waiting for me to say something, but I stayed silent and just waited.

"Then, just as I was about to scream something back at her, this car pulled up. I recognized it as the same car that crazy black kid drove over here yesterday. Mom, I'm sorry I told him where you were. I wasn't thinking, I guess, and I was pissed."

"Anger makes us do things we wouldn't ordinarily do," was all I said.

"Well, he came storming up the front porch steps like I wasn't even there and grabbed her arm. The book she'd been holding flew out of her hands and she tried to jerk away, but he wouldn't let go. She yelled, 'Jesus Darry! Lemme go godammit! You crazy?' and she managed to get her arm loose -- it looked like it really hurt —and she went after her book, but he followed her and grabbed her by the back of her shirt as she tried to bend down to get it. I was just standing there and it all only took a couple of seconds, but that's all it took for me to see that he was stoned and that he was gonna hurt her. I yelled, 'Hey! Leave her alone!' and he swung around to face me. I don' t think he knew I was even there until then, and I don't think he recognized or remembered me at all, that I was the one who had helped him out yesterday. He came at me so fast that I couldn't even move!" I kept silent, but I was consumed by abject terror for certain sure.

She took a huge breath and I realized that she was choking down a sob. When she spoke, her voice went up an octave and was shaking. I was absolutely beyond anxious to hear the rest, but I kept rubbing her back to help her (and maybe me) calm down.

"He grabbed the front of my shirt and just ripped it! Just ripped it!" she sobbed. "Just tore it right down the front, showing my…" Another sob shook her and she held me tighter. "I was *so* scared! I didn't even have time to think because the force of it… he's a big guy… the force of it… just… When he grabbed me, he pulled me toward him and I could see his crazy eyes! I was so *scared*…" Her body was shaking again, vibrating with her voice. "And when he ripped it away, it brought me to my knees. The porch was hard and I felt a pain shoot from my knees right up my legs at the same time that I felt the cold air on my chest." She was starting to hyperventilate. I gathered her up higher and held her tightly to my chest to try to get her to feel the deep, slow breaths I was deliberately drawing in and out, hoping that she would feel it and be able to breathe that way with me and that it might calm her down. She was convulsing at the memory.

"Shhh. Shhh, baby. It's okay now." I was flooded with the memory of her when she was three and had a nightmare, but this was so real. We both knew how real this was for us both. She calmed just a little, and continued.

"Then, all of a sudden, Micah was on him. I mean literally *on* him.

She had struggled up from the floor of the porch where he had shoved her when he turned to attack me. It all happened so *fast!*" The pace of her breathing picked up again and I rubbed her back and shoulders, very slowly, to try to pacify her a little. "Micah was literally riding his back, strangling him with her arms. She had her legs wrapped around his body and he was moving around in circles and trying to get his arms around her neck he but couldn't grab her. She was *screaming* for me to run. "He's crazy high girl! Get the hell outta here!" she yelled over and over, but I couldn't move. I just couldn't move!"

Reagan cried then for several minutes, remembering her terror and, in the interim, I was in agony wanting to find out if Micah was okay, but I didn't push her. Eventually her sobs and convulsions subsided somewhat and she went on. "She was on his back and they were turning in circles. He was trying to shake her off or grab her, but she held her arms across his throat and just took it as he hit her wherever he could reach and bumped her into the porch and tried to grab on with his flailing arms and pull her off. They were both yelling and swearing like you wouldn't believe. I finally got up and pulled the torn parts of my shirt together to try to cover myself. My knees weren't working very well, so I kind of stumbled and staggered away, toward my car.

"But then I stopped. I knew she was in trouble. *Real* trouble. She had come to *my* rescue. I was so confused. I didn't know what to do. I started crying, but I couldn't move again. No one was paying any attention to me. Micah and that guy were tearing each other up. One of them was bleeding, but I couldn't tell which. I came to myself a little bit and figured out what to do.

"What was that, baby?" I asked, giving her a little squeeze.

"I staggered the rest of the way to my car as fast as I could and tried to find my phone in my purse, but before I could even make the call I heard sirens in the distance. While I was doing this, I guess the guy had thrown Micah off him cuz she was on the ground again when I looked back at them. He was still grabbing at her and she was kicking at him with all her might, trying to keep him from being able to grab her as she scooted backwards across the grass to try to get away from him. He was so high that he couldn't get a good hold of her and she kept wriggling out of his way, backing up on the ground, but he didn't look like he was about to give up until he heard the sirens, too." Reagan paused to sit up and take another small drink of water, then she settled back up against me and I repositioned my arms around her. She began again after another couple of minutes.

"When he heard them, he stopped in mid-grab, snapped his head up, then tried to plant a mighty kick on Micah's side. He missed her, though, and stumbled, then he went lumbering away toward his car. He almost fell on this first step, but he steadied himself with his hand on the ground and sort of lunged forward, got some kind of a weird rhythm going with his legs. It didn't look like he was walking but sort of running and stumbling at the same time. He made it to his car and squealed his tires as he sped away down the street.

"When I was sure he was outta there, I got over to Micah as fast as I could (which wasn't very fast because I was literally holding myself together, my knees were killing me, I was crying like a crazy kid…).

She was doubled up on the ground and moaning. I didn't know what to do! I just knelt there by her, afraid to touch her, crying, thanking her for saving me, asking what I could do for her… then, out of nowhere, this little kid shows up and puts her hand on Micah's head. It had this like magic effect. Micah didn't straighten out (I don't think she could have) but her head sprang up and she screamed, 'Bria! Get back in the house and lock the doors! He could come back! He could come back with a piece! Get the hell back in the house!" I'd never heard such real panic in anyone's voice before. Not even when you'd yell when you saw me getting ready to run out into the street when I was little. I was more scared by that than by anything that had happened so far. She grabbed my arm and said, 'Reagan, get her outta here, *please!*' She was literally begging me and I thought it was the least I could do, so I was about to try to help the girl inside, but she put her hand on my shoulder. Her other one was still on Micah's head, stroking her hair. 'It's okay," she said, 'the police are on their way. I had them dialed up before he even got out of his car.' Thank God, I thought, and just at that moment the officers pulled up. They came to me first and I told them I was okay, that they should look after on Micah. They helped her sit up and asked where her dad was. Bria said he was at work but that she had called him just after she called the police and that he was on his way, that he'd be there any minute.

"While they were taking care of Micah, one of the cops took my statement and I told him pretty much what I just told you, only it took a lot longer because it was all fresh and I was way more upset."

"Jeez," I thought, "more upset that this?" She couldn't stop shaking, she could barely get her words out, and more than once I wondered how I could manage to get a paper bag for her to breathe into without having to leave her side. I couldn't imagine how scary all this must have been to someone like her, so young and so sheltered and spoiled, who had been so protected all her life and had never, ever before felt even a whisper of danger. "Oh Reagan, I'm so, so sorry that this happened to you."

"It's not your fault. It's mine."

"No. It's no one's fault. Tell me what happened next."

"Well, the little girl, Bria… she's a weird little kid. It's like she's forty or something. So calm. So knowing what to do. It was weird. Anyway, once the EMS guys got there and checked Micah out she came over to the squad car where I was sitting in the back, rubbing my knees as best I could while trying to hold my torn shirt together. She was holding on to her stomach (I guess he must've gotten a kick in after all when I wasn't looking) and I could already see bruises coming out on her face.

I was sitting sideways with the door open and my legs stretched out because my knees hurt too much to bend them. The EMS guys looked at them, though, and they're okay. Just sore and bruised and a little swollen. Don't worry.

"Anyway, when she got to me, she took off her thick black hoody and said, "Here Reagan. Put this on. You gotta be freezing." I don't know why she said that because it was kinda warm out, but I appreciated it. I was having trouble holding my shirt together because I was shaking so much. Maybe that's why she thought I might be cold."

No wonder I hadn't noticed her ripped shirt at first. She had covered it up with what must have been one of Desi's sweatshirts. The one I now noticed on the floor next to Reagan's discarded clothes was too big to belong to either Micah or Bria.

"It was so sweet of her to take care of me like that," Reagan reflected, "and I felt so terrible. If I hadn't shown up, Micah might have noticed that asshole earlier and could have gotten into the house before he got to her. I'm so sorry." She broke down into sobs again and I held her until she recovered herself a little.

"Honey, if she was writing in her journal, she wouldn't have noticed him. She would've been too into it," I said, trying to take the blame from her. I had tried to explain the Gatherings to Reagan a couple of times, in a hopeless attempt to persuade her to join us, but she had just given me dirty looks as if to say that she wouldn't condescend to spend time with the likes of us, let alone write something in order to do so.

She lifted her head from my chest and pushed herself half way up. "So what's the big deal with this stuff? What can a middle aged woman (sorry), a black chick, and old lady have to do with each other?"

"We're sisters," I said simply.

"I so don't get it. You're all so *different*."

"That's the beauty part. We share, tell stories, learn from each other, help each other. We all come from different places and are in different places in our lives, but we're just as much the same as we are different. We're all lonely. We all have pain. We all have joy. And we share all that with love…" I saw the skeptical look on her face. "Yes, love. There are lots of different kinds of love in the world Reagan. They are my sisters."

"But I'm your daughter."

"I know, and I know you love me because I'm your mother. But I don't feel that love. I haven't in a very long time. Not from your father, either. This house isn't only cold and lonely to me, Reagan. I get hurt here. A lot. And when I lost my baby, I thought I was going to die. I actually thought that dying might be the best thing that could happen to me, to all of us. And my job sucks. I was drowning and not only didn't anyone notice, but I seriously doubt that anyone would've thrown me a line even if they had, as long as the work was getting done around here. It felt more like I was being pushed under dark water. My sisters taught me to swim, and they love me for who and what I really am. They show me that they do every day. I was dying here. Now I'm alive, and it's because of them."

Her sobs had stopped, but the streams of tears that ran down her face had become rivers. She looked so mournful.

"I'm *so* sorry mom," she said, dropping her head. "I know I've been terrible to you and I don't know why I was. I'm so…"

"It's partly my fault," I interrupted her. "If I hadn't taken it, if I had demanded respect, from you and your father both, then…"

"It's nobody's fault," Reagan amended, echoing what I'd said earlier. "It just is. And I don't want it to be. For a minute there tonight, mom, I really, really thought I might get really hurt or might even die. The first thing I thought of right when that fear hit me was that I might never see you again, then the next thing was that the last time I saw you I was such a bitch to you, then the next thing was — it was all jumbled up and kind of at the same time — was that I knew you wouldn't care that I'd been a bitch. You'd still love me and you'd still die if I were dead. I saw myself having treated you like shit... sorry... then killing you with grief. It's like it was the first time in like ever that I wasn't thinking just about me.

"Then," she sniffled, "when things calmed down a little and I was in the back of the police car waiting for them to get done talking to Micah's dad... he's hot... and drive me home, I realized that you are never like that. It's never about you... at least not until lately. I had a lot of time to think there in the backseat of that car and on the way home. We have to pick my car up tomorrow morning, okay? I mean your car. I took it. Sorry. I know it's like the phone, and I...." she had let that all breeze out of her like the air out of a balloon and it left her limp and empty. She collapsed back against me and sobbed some more.

I was torn between wanting to comfort her and wanting to get up to call Desi to find out if Micah was okay. Still, Reagan was my daughter and Micah was my sister. The former was my priority. Besides, Micah was stronger than the two of us put together, and had Desi and Bria with her, so I felt I could wait as long as I had to in order to get Reagan feeling better and a little more stable.

As though she had read my thoughts, she said, "Mom, do you think Micah's alright? Can we call somebody and find out? I don't know what would have happened to me if she hadn't had the guts to attack that crazy guy. God, I hope she's okay. She was on her feet. I saw that from the back of the police car when she handed me the sweatshirt, but it looked like she was hurting. She was trying to refuse to get into the ambulance, but her dad and Bria weren't taking no for an answer. Can we call someone, please?"

I was so relieved to be able to do this without offending or neglecting Reagan. "Sure," I said. "I'll go get my cell so they'll recognize the number and maybe pick up, even though it's so late... or early. You wanna come with me or... why don't you stay snuggled up here and I'll get it and come right back in there with you."

"Okay, but hurry, okay?"

"You got it." I grabbed my empty glass and went to the kitchen to refill it and get my phone. Dick was gone. I don't know whether he went back to the garage or to bed. I really didn't give a solitary single shit one way or the other.

When I got back into bed with Reagan, I dialed Desi's number.

"Oh, thank God!" he cried. "I was just getting ready to call you. They're just getting Micah settled in. How is Reagan? Is she okay? Jesus Christ, what a night!"

"Yeah, she's quite shaken up, but she's settling down now, too. She just told me what happened. Please tell me Micah's okay."

"Yeah, they said he was so high that that kick he managed to land on her just sort of glanced off. No broken ribs. Kidneys seem okay. They're going to keep her overnight for observation anyway. I can't believe this! My poor little girl!"

"Your brave little girl, you mean. According to Reagan, she pretty much saved my baby's life tonight!"

"Can I talk to her," Reagan asked, wiping her nose on her sleeve. She seemed so young just then, such a little, helpless child.

"Desi, Reagan would like to talk to Micah if she's up to it."

"Maybe tomorrow. She's pretty out of it right now. I'll call you when I get her home, okay."

"Great. Maybe we could stop by?"

"We'll see how goes."

"Okayl," I said. "Talk to ya then."

I hung up and asked Regan, "You got the gist?"

"Yeah. Can I come with you when you go?"

"Sure."

"I wonder what made her do that."

"What?"

"Jump on him like that, risk getting hurt or even killed, just to save me, who'd been bitching her out just five seconds before."

"She doesn't think about herself. She never does. She has too many other things to deal with."

"Why would she go with a boy like that?"

"She's torn. Torn between two worlds. She started to understand that a little more today at the Gathering, I think, when we were talking about the journal entry she shared with us. I don't know if she really understands it yet. She still needs to process, I think, but she said that she'd write more about it and would read it next week."

"Do you think she'd read it to me?"

"Maybe when she knows you a little better. It's pretty personal.

Maybe when you have something to share with her," I suggested.

"I can't write poetry," she said.

"Everyone can write poetry. You just have to want to."

"I don't know what you mean," she said, and I didn't know quite how to explain it.

"I think it's something you have to experience. No one can make you see it with ordinary words. You'll have to come to a Gathering and see."

"Will they let me? I mean, I was *so* mean to Micah. And Logan must think I'm a total bitch. Even if you didn't tell her how it's been around here, she could've figured that out just from our short couple of meetings."

"Logan doesn't judge anyone or anything and neither does Micah. You'd be more than welcome, I can guarantee that."

"How do you not judge?"

"It's *really* hard at first, but it gets easier. I think I'm getting better at it."

"You are."

"How do you know?" I was truly surprised by her saying that.

"Your daughter was brought home late at night in a police car. Her father immediately started yelling at her, accusing her of all kinds of bad stuff. You just loved me. That's all you did. And while we were sitting here, and you were holding me…" she choked up a little again and said, rapidly and through sobs, "you didn't get pissed or defend yourself when I said mean things, you didn't try to tell me what I should or shouldn't have done. You didn't judge me. You let me be me and loved me anyway."

"You'll sooooo fit in at a Gathering!" I laughed as I hugged her a little more tightly. "And thank you so much for saying all that. I do love you so much, Reagan. And I've so missed being close to you."

"I don't know why I needed to be the way I've been."

"I don't either, and I don't care. I just want it to be over. I want you to be my daughter and my sister."

"Me, too," she said as she snuggled deeper into my embrace. We slept the rest of the night holding each other with a kind of love and peace that neither of us had experienced with the other in almost a decade.

CHAPTER THIRTY-TWO
Fate

"Fate is nothing but the deeds committed in a prior state of existence."
—*Ralph Waldo Emerson*

We woke up the next morning still glued together. It was so wonderful. I made Reagan some frozen waffles with strawberries and bacon — her favorite. We decided that it wouldn't do for her to sit around ruminating about or reliving the events of the night before, so we picked up her girlfriend, Amanda, and I dropped them off at the mall. I wondered if Reagan would share her ordeal with her friend, but I never found out one way or the other. The plan was that Amanda's mom would pick them up later and they'd hang out at her house for a while. Reagan, understandably, wasn't really in the mood to see her dad. His reaction the night before had really hurt and upset her and, even though I advised her to talk to him about it, she wasn't ready.

Of course, when I got back to the house, I immediately went over to Logan's to unload. She had been really worried, having seen the flashing reds and blues through her front window. She'd called and left a message right after the officers left, telling me to call her immediately if I needed anything at all and to come over as soon as I possibly could in the morning to fill her in. Her reaction was exactly what I expected from her: concern, love, and understanding — for me, for Reagan, and for Micah — and a repeated offer to do whatever she could to help any of us.

Desi finally called mid-morning while I was at Logan's and told me that Micah was home and doing fine, but that a visit that day probably wasn't a good idea. She was tired, still a little shaken, and needed the rest. I knew Reagan would be disappointed. She'd asked me to come get her if I was heading over there, no matter what time it was. I'd shoot her a text when I got off the phone to let her know that Micah was okay.

Desi said Micah might be able to give me a call later in the day. We decided to touch base about our usual Wednesday sister-date to make sure that she'd feel up to it and to reschedule it if she felt that would be better. Wednesday would only be three days after the attack, after all, so she might not be ready to go out and socialize. It had been rough on her emotionally as well as physically. Desi said she'd certainly be ready for our next Gathering on Saturday, though.

As it turned out, Desi called Tuesday to say that, even though Micah insisted that she was fine, he'd feel better if she took it easy for few more days, so we ended up skipping our sister date that Wednesday. I missed her, but we spoke on the phone a few times and I could hear her strength coming back to her so I knew Desi had been right.

* * * * *

When Saturday rolled around and I pulled into Micah's driveway, it was Bria who met me on the porch. "Your daughter was awesome that night," she told me. "I knew Micah would kill me if I came out of the house, and there was nothing I could have done to help that crazy situation anyway, so I watched through the front window and saw the whole thing. She was mean to Micah at first, but she tried her best to defend my sister. Please tell her that I love her for that. She was in real danger, Allison." I pulled Bria into a bear hug and told her that she'd done the right thing by staying in the house and I told her how wise and brave she'd been. I told her that she would be able to tell Reagan herself one day and that Reagan would be happy to hear it.

I was sad that Reagan had declined to join our Gathering that day. She was still a little shaken up and embarrassed that she'd been so vicious to Micah. That had been her word when she shared her reasons with me: "vicious." I tried to convince her to forgive herself and join us, but only for a moment. She needed to heal, too, so there was no point in pressuring her. She said she'd definitely join us at some point in the future, when she felt ready, and that made me very happy.

Once the Gathering was underway that afternoon (which meant we were eating some awesome apple tarts and drinking sweet tea), I related to both Micah and Logan the story of what happened after the police brought Reagan home. Even though Logan had heard the tale once already, she listened with rapt attention. They were both amazed that even Dick could be such a dick.

"How the hell did you end up with that asshat?" Micah asked.

"It's actually an interesting story," I told them and they insisted on hearing it, even though I hadn't written about it. Our Gathering rules were pretty lax. The no-judgement rule, however, was always in effect.

Once I began telling Micah and Logan about how I met Dick, I was compelled to tell the whole story for some reason, not just answer that first question. The weather was so beautiful that we decided to hold our Gathering outside. We were sitting on a soft blanket under the shade of Logan's gorgeous Maple tree.

Micah had asked me several times how I'd ended up with someone to whom I was so obviously ill-suited, but I'd put her off. I don't know why. Maybe because I felt that the biggest failure of my life was my marriage, even though both Logan and Micah argued with me on this point. Not that it was the *biggest* failure, but that the dissolution of my marriage was not *my* failure, but Dick's. I still wasn't wholly convinced of this, but I figured that for all their support, the least I could do was tell them the whole story. The sun was shining in a cloudless sky and a warm breeze was blowing the end of July into the backyard for us as I told the tale.

As always, my sisters gave me their full attention. "So," I told them, "my mother actually commanded me to go out that night. She literally said, 'Sunny, you *ARE* going out tonight!' They always called me that, Sunny, short for Allison. In my mind, though, each of my parents spelled it, meant it, differently. My father, I know, meant S-O-N-N-Y. Like sonny-boy. He had wanted a son and he never let me forget that I wasn't that. No matter how well I did at anything, it was never good enough. Not as good as it would have been if I'd had balls, anyway. My mom, though, meant S-U-N-N-Y because I was her sunshine, at least I was back then when she liked me. And Dick calls me Alley, like the place behind houses where people put their garbage, and sometimes 'alley-cat' when he's trying to be funny and, once in a while, when he really wants to get my goat, he calls me 'alley-fat' instead."

"What a dick," Micah said, then added, "Don't your mom like you no more?" She sounded surprised and concerned.

"Of course she does, Micah," said Logan. "Mothers always love their children!"

"True." I said. "They *love* their children. They don't always like them. My mom loved me *and* liked me back then, when I was in my late teens and early twenties, but I don't think she likes me much now. She's completely uninterested in me or my life, at any rate, especially now that she's making a new one for herself. I'm okay with that, though. I'm just glad she's finally happy. She calls once in a while, but I think that's more to talk with Reagan than with me.

"But anyway, she did actually *command* me to go out that night. It was so strange that the mother who nagged at me for two solid years to stay home, now wanted me out of the house. On this of all nights. I had listened to my mother whine and complain over and over and over that I was never home. I'd heard this almost daily for almost the whole time -- two years -- that I'd dated Marc, and now that the relationship had finally ended and all I wanted to do was go to bed and talk myself into or out of calling him, my mother was rummaging through my closet pulling out shirts she wanted me to try on.

"'Look Sunny,' she said with overt enthusiasm 'This one is nice and I haven't seen it on you in a while.' She held up a blouse to show me. I honestly don't think she realized that I hadn't worn it because I'd just lost twenty-five pounds and it no longer fit.

'Mom, what's wrong with you?' I asked, starting to get really annoyed. 'There are people dead across the street and you want me to go to a party? Are you sick?' I could not believe my mother's cavalier attitude, considering what had happened across the street earlier that evening."

"Wait, what?" Logan asked, astonished.

"You kidding? Seriously? Dead people?" asked Micah. "You maybe shoulda started with that!" She raised one eyebrow which produced a look of such skepticism that I almost chuckled.

It was true, though, and I backtracked to tell them that story, too. "We had come home two hours earlier from a trip to the mall — my mother's idea to keep me busy and to keep my mind off Marc – and as we rounded the corner onto our usually quiet suburban street, it looked like a war zone. We were greeted with swirling waves of red and blue flashing light and the neighbors were gathered in groups here and there, their heads together, conversing in low voices.

"We pulled into our driveway, which was about four houses down and across the street from the crowds and confusion, totally forgetting the ice cream we'd just picked up on the way home. We trotted over to join the neighbors gathered on our side of the street. As Neapolitan licked through the carton and the grocery bag onto the floor of the backseat of our car, the sad and gory tale of the Ramseys slobbered through the neighborhood. The old man –- an odd guy with a real drinking problem, among other things I imagine — had finally lost his mind, shot his wife, and then shot himself. They were both were dead, and the police were taking statements from all the neighbors who had been around when it happened."

"God, that's awful," sighed Micah.

"It really was. I remember some little kids kept sneaking up to the house under the yellow caution tape to get a peek in the window when they thought the adults were preoccupied, only to be chased away again and again. They certainly were persistent little buggers!"

"Gross!" spat Micah. "Who would want to see something like that?"

"You know how kids are," Logan answered, and it wasn't lost on any of us that this was meant not only to answer Micah's question but to subtly let Micah know that we considered *her* an adult.

I went on. "I had never experienced death before — not of anyone or anything (unless you counted Susie the hamster when I was eight, but that didn't throw me for too big a loop). I never really knew my grandparents, never had a dog die. I didn't really know what to do with myself after I went back home.

"I cleaned up as much of the ice cream as I could from the backseat of the car, and put most of what was left in a bowl for myself. I tossed the sticky paper towels and half-ripped carton into the kitchen trash can that was always too small to accommodate our wasteful family, even though there were only three of us. It was overflowing again. Why it never seemed to overflow when my parents were around was beyond me. I lifted the paper bag out of the plastic bin. It was soaked with melted ice cream and ready to rip. I barely made it to the aluminum can outside the back door before it gave birth to its load. By the time I got back inside, the contents of my bowl looked like soup, too, so I dumped it down the drain."

I paused to reach for some of the grapes that Logan had put in a pretty blue bowl on the blanket, then continued. "Somehow, it just didn't seem right that I should be struggling with trash and feeling sorry for myself because I couldn't have ice cream when two people had just been killed a few hundred yards from my house. As I rummaged through the cupboards to find something as bad for me as ice cream in which to drown my sorrows, an ambulance passed by with a dull churning engine sound. No sirens. No lights. All was quiet. The end. It seemed so final.

"I was reading in my room to take my mind off everything when, a half hour later, my mom returned from the gossip-fest from which I'd managed to escape earlier. She came in, apparently wanting to relive the whole morbid thing and tell me what the neighbors had said. I told her that I didn't want to talk about it.

It was so strange though. The minute she finally left, I *did* want to talk about it — but not with her because she really thought I was perfect and I couldn't handle that shit just then. I know it sounds like a mean thing to say and a silly thing to fault her for, but it did a number on me nonetheless. I knew she'd tell me that my feelings were normal, that I was normal, that everything was normal. Nothing could dull her little ray of sunshine where I was concerned. But it was all a lie and I knew it. None of this was normal. I couldn't stomach the idea of listening to her go on and on about it.

"My problem was that I really had no idea what normal actually was. I only knew that I was not it. My father could find nothing right with me and my mother could find no fault, at least not back then. I had a completely whacked out sense of self. If I were to move a mountain single handedly for my father, he would have criticized me for not moving it far enough, or fast enough, or because it was too far to the left or too far to the right or whatever. But my mom… if I had pulled the trigger myself and blew the Ramsey's brains clear to the moon for no reason at all except to see the sight, my mother would've applauded, told me I was wonderful, that my aim was admirable, that I must have had a good reason, and so therefore I had done the right thing and, in fact, I had done it flawlessly. I was a wishbone constantly pulled apart by these two maniacs and I had no idea who I was.

"I know *now* that they both loved me in their own weird ways, but man did they screw me up back then. Who the hell *was* I? What *was* the right thing? What *was* good enough? What *was* normal? I could never figure it out."

"Okay, we get it," Micah said, anxious to end my tangent and get to the answer for which she was waiting. "You were screwed up. Now get on with the story. How did you ever end up with that dick Dick?"

"I'm getting to it," I laughed with feigned exasperation, then I resumed the tale. "So no, I could not talk to my mother. I had cried and died just a little on my walk back to the house after hearing the neighbors talk the way they had about the poor Ramseys, discussing their personal lives, habits and problems, speculating, guessing, suggesting... No compassion, just curiosity and gossip. My mother would never understand how I felt even if she managed to really listen, which was highly doubtful. I remember wondering at that point where the Ramseys' kids were. They were in their late teens and early twenties. Saturday night. They were out for certain sure. How would they hear about it? Where would they live?

"Still waiting…" Micah moaned again, drumming her fingers on the side of her glass to indicate her impatience and I realized that remembering my concern for the Ramsey kids hadn't really been necessary and had stalled my story.

"Be patient," Logan interjected kindly, putting a hand on Micah's wrist. "Sometimes you need the backstory to really understand the tale." Micah settled down straight away and nodded for me to continue. I gave Logan the grateful smile that her intervention deserved. I know how hard it is to hold a teenager's attention.

"No, my mom would not get it," I repeated. "Neither would my friend Sara, but I called her anyway after I shooed my mom out. I called her from the phone that I'd persuaded my parents to let me have in my room so I could close the door and have some privacy. There were no cells phones back then. I suddenly felt the need to vent a little and let some of it out before I could ever hope to fall asleep. I needed a little distraction. That was all I really wanted to do. Go to sleep, and hopefully not dream. Just sleep and forget about dead people, lost boyfriends, lunatic parents, and just leave the crazy world behind for at least a little while.

"But… my mom overheard my conversation with Sara (she'd been listening at the door) and, when she gathered from my end of it that Sara was heading out to a party, she sprang back into my room and snatched the receiver right out of my hand. She slobbered all over Sara like they were the best of friends. Then she told Sara to come and pick me up! Sara hadn't even invited me! My mom just went on in such a matter-of-fact, lighthearted way that Sara really had no choice but to agree to come get me. From the way my mother carried on, I couldn't believe that she even remembered about the poor Ramseys at all. She just told Sara that she should definitely come by for me and that I'd be ready in fifteen minutes.

"I understood her motives though. I knew that my mother had been overjoyed when I broke up with Marc and just didn't want me moping around the house or getting back together with him out of boredom."

"Kinda like you and my dad'd be overjoyed if I broke up with Darry? Is that what you gettin' at?" Micah interrupted with a scowl. "Skip that shit and get on with the story," she demanded.

"Wait," interjected Logan, incredulously. "You haven't broken up with him? After what happened after the last Gathering, after last Sunday?"

"Well, not yet," she admitted. "I haven't actually spoken to him so there was no opportunity. He hasn't called and my dad certainly won't let me call him, and there's still that restraining order."

"Well," Logan pondered aloud. "That makes sense, but you'll need to make it official at some point. Let's talk about that later."

"Yes, definitely," I agreed. "But no, that's not it at all, Micah," I reassured her, "and I *am* getting on with the story. I'm talking about me a hundred years ago, not you. Drink your tea. I'm getting to it," I retorted with a smile.

"My mom knew how much I had loved Marc," I continued, "and I really had. But she also knew, I knew, everybody knew, I still know, that he was going nowhere in a hurry and that staying with him was a serious dead end for me... I'm not kidding either...he was the personification of 'nice guys finish last.' My mom knew, and I knew she knew, that if we stayed together, I would have spent the rest of my life supporting him, looking at his legs sticking out from under that damn Mustang he loved so much, and that I'd never get anywhere in life at all. And I intended to get somewhere... out of the awful little world into which I had been born and out of which I was laboriously trying to raise myself even then, without much success. My mom was miserable with my dad, with her life. She wanted so much more for me and I so did not want to end up like her."

The afternoon sun was getting lower in the West. Rows of small, high cumulous clouds were moving in, and the yard darkened just a bit when they traversed the face of the sun. The air was still pleasantly warm, though, and a gentle breeze caused the leaves to gently wave to us from their branches.

"Marc was a great guy," I went on, "but he could not hold down a job. He was always suffering from one ailment or another. We never went anywhere or did anything. We just sat around his house watching TV or drinking with his dad.

"My mom saw her chance: I could go to this party with Sara and I'd finally meet someone *worthy* of me." When I air-quoted that, Micah rolled her eyes, but she smiled at me all the same.

"I hate to admit it," I continued, "but I knew even then that she was right. That's why I let her drag me around with her for a week after the break-up, keeping me busy. This, though, shoving me out the door at 10:00 o'clock at night... shit! But... she was right.

"She had no idea why I had suddenly showed up at home before 9:00 the previous Saturday night when I'd been over at Marc's, as usual. She didn't ask. She didn't care. I had ended it with him and that's all she cared about. It was so funny. She always used to ask me why I didn't date rich guys, like they were a dime a dozen and all out looking around for me! I used to ask her to point out where they all were and give me the money I'd need to be able to afford to go there. The sarcasm was lost on her, I think, but I know it hurt her that she couldn't do more for me."

I could see that I might be losing Micah again, but for some reason, I felt like I had to tell the whole thing, all of it. "I had so immersed myself in that relationship -- if you could call it that — with Marc over the previous two years that I'd lost touch with all my girlfriends," I confessed.

I stopped my reminiscence at that point and looked pointedly at Micah. "I will tell you one thing: Never, *ever* let go of your girlfriends, no matter what! That is, once you find some who are worthy of you."

She gave me a little side-eye, and said, *"Worthy* of me? Yes, mom." She smiled at me as she air-quoted that, and I thought I detected a tiny nod. I knew she knew what my point was, though, and she was thinking about us, her sisters, and not the lost girlfriends she'd written about in her journal. It was probably good that she had let them go.

I shoved that thought to the back of my mind and continued. "The fact that Sara was even home at 10:00 on a Saturday night was a miracle in and of itself, and not one that my mom was going to let slip by without capitalizing on it, no matter how much it embarrassed me or how much I protested. She needed an ally to help 'save' me and she wasted no time pressing her advantage as the favorite of all the moms in our high school click. All my friends loved her, so Sara agreed."

"Why did they love her so much when she drove you so crazy?" Micah asked.

"She was great to them," I answered, "and I really did appreciate that. She was kind of like a teenager herself in a lot of ways. She was always so happy when my friends were around and she inserted herself into our conversations as she fed us whatever she had on hand. Usually a lot of junk because she couldn't cook any more than I can. I think she was lonely. She had no family and she couldn't stand my dad. She just wanted some friends herself so she latched on to us. I really didn't mind. It was kind of nice being the one with the cool mom.

"Anyway, 'She''ll be here in ten,' my mother bubbled at me as she hung up the phone. 'Put on something nice.'

"'I don't even know where we're going,' I protested, but my mother already had dozen different outfits spread out on the bed for me. She told me that Sara said they were going to a party in someone's backyard and she held up another shirt, the one I'd worn yesterday so I couldn't poo-poo it."

"Poo-poo it? Really?" Micah shook her head at me.

"Yes, poo-poo it," I said and smiled. "I told my mom that I didn't have anything nice anyway, which was true. My mother sighed. She knew it was true, but there was precious little she could do about it, then or ever. She didn't have anything decent either. Well, at least it would be kind of dark at an outdoor party at that time of night, I reasoned. It was easier to pull off discount clothing and cheap jewelry in that situation.

"'You're so gorgeous you'd knock 'em dead in a potato sack,' she chirped. I rolled my eyes at that worn out expression, which had never been true. I'd had to buy my own clothes since I was fourteen if I wanted anything even close to having any style or quality at all, and babysitting money didn't go very far for things like that, not back then. My father never gave my mom more than a few hundred dollars a week and that didn't really stretch very far, not even in the late '70s and early '80s, and not even with a frugal homemaker like my mom."

I realized that I had been going on longer than I had intended with this side-story, but it was so nice to have someone interested in me for a change. Logan was definitely interested. Even though Micah gave no hint of it, I asked, "Are you getting bored? Do you want to do something else? Should we read? I know this probably isn't how you wanted to spend your afternoon, listening to an old lady whine about her past. We can do something else if you want."

"No," Micah insisted. "I'm starting to understand some things about you, I think. I am tired of sitting here, though. Let's get in the car and talk while we drive, okay?"

"Where do you want to go?"

"I don't care. Surprise me."

"I don't care either," Logan agreed.

* * * * *

We still had several hours of daylight available to us so off we went. We took the grapes and Logan grabbed some crackers she had been meaning to set out. She folded up the blanket, and we walked over to my house to get my car. I had no idea where I could take them, but after I pulled out onto the road, the car sort of went into autopilot and before I had even consciously thought about it, we were pulling into the Proud Lake pine forest trail. We'd traveled mostly in silence just to give Micah a break, but the break helped me, too. I felt clearer and less worried about what they might think of me after they heard all this. Some nice jazz was playing on the radio and we all enjoyed the lull.

I parked the car and insisted that they all spray down with insect repellant. "I don't wanna go nowhere I'll get bit!" Micah protested.

"Don't worry. I keep this in the car so when I stop by here to walk and think, I'll be protected. It's still pretty early in the day for the bugs to be out, but better safe than sorry."

"You come here a lot?" Micah asked.

"Yeah… no… I come when my need a for nature-fix coincides with me having a spare half hour, so I don't come nearly as often as I'd like."

"I have't been in the woods in ages and I'm so glad this place is nearby!" Logan said gleefully, obviously relishing the thought of wandering through the forest. She turned to Micah and said, "We'll try to get Alison out here more often, won't we Micah?" Micah still looked skeptical.

Once we'd sprayed down and locked the car, we started to stroll down a wide, well-worn road lined on either side with towering pines. The beauty of it never ceased to amaze me. The sun steamed in streaks from the top-most branches to the forest floor. There were warm, light gusts of wind gently caressing us as we strolled and it all seemed so peaceful. I could see Micah settling in to the rhythm of our walking and of the gently moving branches, so I resumed my tale.

"So… my mom had been looking out clothes for me and finally got just the tiniest bit irritated by my constant rejection of her suggestions and said, 'Then put on anything. She'll be here any minute.'"

"'I don't want to go,' I insisted yet again, 'I'm tired.'"

"'No, you're not. You're just upset. Seeing old friends and making new ones will help you feel better and sleep better later. Trust me.' I hated when my mother said that. I'd trusted her all my life and so far she hadn't been right about anything, Everything had been wrong, had been a let-down. Looking at what I saw as scraps of clothing on my bed, knowing that my friends would be decked out to the nines, even for a yard party, I felt so defeated at that moment that I almost cried.

"So I lied and said, 'I feel fine, and I want to sleep now, not later,' but I walked to the closet and pulled out my favorite shirt, one that Sara had seen me in at least a thousand times. When I wore it over my only pair of decent jeans, it did make me look a shade slimmer. I didn't realize it at the time, but I hadn't really been fat in those days, especially after I'd just taken off that twenty-five pounds, which didn't stay off very long, by the way," I digressed. "I look back now at pictures from then and I was just fine. I'd just been told so many times by my dad that I was 'fourteen axe handles across the stern' that I believed I was."

"What does that even mean?" Micah asked.

"It's some nautical term meaning really wide, but I didn't even know that at first. I could just tell by his tone that it was bad, and when he held his hands apart about three feet as he said it, I got the gist. I knew that he thought — and so I thought -- that I was that wide. Needless to say, I was pretty self-conscious about how I looked even after having lost that weight. Nothing like being insulted by a parent in nautical terminology. Well, at least he was original."

"That ain't what dads is supposed to do!" Micah seemed genuinely hurt for me.

I continued. "I knew what my mother was worried about and what she was trying to do, and I knew that her heart was in the right place, so I finally capitulated, knowing full well that sleep would elude me for quite a while anyway and that some distraction might, indeed, be a good idea after all.

"My mother didn't know that she didn't need to worry because I had no intention of getting back together with Marc. I knew the time had come for me to jump ship and find another one on which to book passage. I just didn't know which one or where to just yet, and I certainly didn't know that it would come in to port in the next few hours."

"Hold on. Bad metaphor. So you jump ship. Why can't you swim on your own? Who says you need another guy?" Micah wondered.

"It was a different time, Micah. No," I corrected myself, "I can't really blame it all on that. True, there were very few women making it on their own, going into careers other than wife-secretary-nurse-teacher jobs, but there were some. It was starting… but I'd been raised to be a wife and mom. It's all I knew. I mean, I knew I wanted to be a teacher, but I knew my parents couldn't afford send me to college so I gave up on that dream."

"I thought you *were* a teacher," said Micah.

"Oh, I am. I just went to college a decade and a half after I graduated from high school. At the time of these events, though, I thought my only real option was to find a good guy, get married, have a family, and live happily ever after. The problem was, you can't do that by yourself, and it would have been out of the question for me to try to have a family on my own even if I'd had the wherewithal to do it. There were very few single moms back then and it would have been looked down upon. So, even if I'd had what it takes to pull that off, I'd probably have been too worried about what others thought of me."

"That's bullshit. Why you gotta care what other people think?" Micah protested.

This, however, turned the tables a little bit. I stopped walking and she halted as well. "Seriously, Micah?" I said. "Look at *you*. You're freakin' brilliant and you act like you're a thug half the time… Oh God, I'm *so* sorry! I didn't mean that like it sounded!" I said, abashed. I so didn't want to alienate this girl and I never intended to insult her, only make the point.

But I need not have worried. Micah only smiled and said, "Touche!"

"Anyway," I continued, "I'd been waiting almost a year for the right opportunity to break it off with Marc so there was no going back now. I somehow knew I could handle whatever heartache or loneliness or overbearing mother crap I had to deal with. And in spite of everything I just said, though, I also somehow knew at some level that I was in charge of my own destiny and I did not — so, so did *not* — want to end up like my poor miserable mother who apparently planned to live vicariously through a daughter who was sailing without a rudder.

"I'm sorry – I must sound like an idiot -- but there were so many contradictions in me then. Anyway, my poor mother. While I was getting dressed and thinking about all this, a wave of pity and love flowed through me and, in my rising compassion for her and all her misguided attempts to help me, I walked over to her and gave her a genuine hug. My mom's life was all but over then because she didn't have it in her to make a change. She would never leave my dad, no matter how miserable he made her."

"Why?" asked Micah. "Why couldn't she leave him?"

"She had no family to turn to and no real friends to give her advice, to help her. She was kind of a loner and turned all her focus and energy on me. I'm sorry my dad's dead, but it was the only thing that could have freed her. I'm so glad she's happy now.

"I somehow knew that I'd be different and not emulate my mother. I had absolutely no idea how I knew -- but I *knew* — that I was supposed to do something, something important, with my life. And I knew that I couldn't do it in that house, with that family. And I knew after a year with Marc that I couldn't do it with him, either. Leaving him had set me adrift, but my mom was my anchor. I could always find safe harbor with her, even if the skies were gray and storms were brewing. But a vessel kept too long at port eventually rots, and I knew that I needed to set sail, and soon, so I let her shove me out the door."

"No offense," interrupted Micah as we rounded a bend in the trail, "but are you ever going to a) quit with the nautical shit, and b) to get to how you met that asshole you're married to?" She didn't sound impatient. It was more as if she were afraid I had lost my way in the story.

"Yes. I'm almost there, but I have to tell you all this stuff so you might have half a chance of understanding how I ended up getting together and then staying with him."

"Good then, because you staying with him don't make no sense to me at all."

"Are you guys in a hurry to get home?" I asked.

"No," answered Micah as Logan shook her head with a smile, "I'm just not the outdoorsy type and I'm afraid we'll get stuck out here in the dark. That'd suck!" said Micah.

Logan had been silent all this time, walking a few paces behind us, listening. She calmed Micah by saying, "Allison has walked these woods a hundred times. We're fine. No worries."

"We're almost at the bridge," I said. "We'll sit there for a bit, then head back. We'll be back to the car well before dark."

"Splendid. Proceed," Micah said with a smile, extending her arm with a flourish to indicate that we should resume our walk. I loved when Micah got sophisticated or… I don't really know what to call it. It's like she could get younger or older at will. Oddly, the wise, grown-up persona wasn't out of character for her even though you might think it would be had you only ever met "Street Micah." That's how she referred to herself whenever she talked about the culture into which she had been trying so hard to fit. She didn't always sound like a teenager. Sometimes she sounded like a wise old woman. It was so obvious that she was head and shoulders above her peers... hell, above a lot of adults I knew.

I smiled at this and continued. "Marc was truly a kind, gentle guy who treated me as well as an unemployed hypochondriac possibly could, and I truly was in love with him, and he with me. He had loved me, axe handles and all, even before I lost the weight. Maybe that's why I fell for him.

"He thought we were happy. It had broken his heart when I walked out the week before, leaving without a word, and that I wouldn't take his calls made him sad, I know. I felt so guilty, but I also knew it really was over and talking to him would only make it worse for both of us.

"I hadn't known how to leave him and it wasn't in my nature to purposefully offend anyone, let alone start a conflict or crush a person, so I had bided my time. Then, seven nights before the Ramseys died, we were at a local bar with Marc's father and brothers, slamming beers as usual. I couldn't even remember what was said, but something signaled me that the time had come. I made a speedy, quiet exit and used that as the springboard to plunge into the breakup. I walked back from the bar in the dark, much to my mother's chagrin when she found out, and made it the five blocks back to Mark's house to pick up my car (he never picked me up at home – I always had to drive to him, which I did over my mother's vehement protests).

I drove home from there and almost gave my mother a heart attack with my unexpected appearance. I headed straight to my room, pleading a headache. I usually stayed at Marc's till one or two in the morning, even on the rare occasions when I didn't feel well, so it was weird for me to be home and I don't think she bought the headache story. It wasn't until the following evening after she got off work, when she found me at home again and not making my usual excuses about why I had to go to Marc's that she really caught on.

"She couldn't get me to relay the details (frankly because I couldn't remember them clearly myself), but she knew she had to find a way to keep me occupied and away from the temptation to fall back into my old two-year habit.

"I knew all this and loved her for it in spite of the fact that she drove me crazy and was then trying to kick me out of my own house against my will. I finally concluded that getting out of her hair for a few hours was the least I could do, so I gently shoved her out of the room so I could finish getting ready.

"'You're going then?' she asked in disbelief from the outside of my closed door. I think in spite of her persistent efforts she really hadn't expected to get her way; she rarely did.

"'As obvious as you're making it that you want to get rid of me? How can I stay?' I called back. I could just see her victory smile. I felt like a defeated martyr who knows there's nothing for it so making the best of it is all there is to do.

"A car horn sounded impatiently just as I tossed the hair brush back on my dresser."

We had reached the bridge by this time and we stopped at the rail to admire the water. The river was beautiful with the western sun floating across it like an artist's brush against canvas, creating a masterpiece, and the pause felt good. I hadn't realized how much this story would take out of me. Micah seemed to understand so didn't press the matter and let me rest and reflect whenever I needed to do so. She knew I was too far in now to not finish.

I took a deep breath and suggested that we sit on a nearby bench, and I continued the story.

"So I ran out to Sara's car, telling my mom in a sing-song call that I'd be home 'later.' It was already 10:30 and my mother would normally have had a hard time with me leaving so late, but that night she didn't care. I was out. That's what she cared about.

"So I went with Sara to the party. It turned out that it was her boyfriend's birthday and there were a ton of people there, most of whom I didn't know since they were mostly his friends. I was a little shy and hung on Sara's coattails for most of the night until, around midnight, Sara's boyfriend introduced me to Dick, Richard.

"He was handsome — you can probably still see some of that if you look past the beer belly, the red nose, and the bloodshot eyes — and that night, at least, he was charming. We got along well and I was enjoying our conversation, when Sara said that she was ready to leave. I wasn't. Dick asked if he could take me home later and, even though I knew my mother would have a full-out shit fit if she knew, I took a ride from someone I barely knew, I told Sara to go ahead and that I'd be fine.

"That son of a bitch didn't hurt you did he?" asked Micah, concerned.

"No, and it was one of the very few nights that he didn't. I mean, he never hit me or anything. It was just the meanness and the neglect that hurt me. It hurt in a different way, but it was painful nonetheless."

"'Sometimes,' Logan said softly, "psychological or emotional hurt is worse. It doesn't heal as easily or as fast, and no one can see the scars, so you feel alone." I was so glad that she, at least on some level, understood, and I wondered how she knew.

"We talked until around 2:00, then he drove me home and we sat in his car talking until about 3:30 in the morning," I continued.

"That was a real idiot move, you know that right?" said Micah. "He could've been a real asshole. He could have hurt you!"

"Well, he is a real asshole and he hurts me all the time, but that night, and right up until we got married, he really seemed great. Once we were married, though, it all changed. He started coming home later and later and when he *was* home he spent less and less time with me. He'd go out without me and would never go out *with* me when I asked him to. It was hard to deal with. I kept wondering what was wrong with me. I thought when I got pregnant with Reagan, he'd come around. I thought having a little girl would bring him back to me. It didn't. I thought, later, that maybe a son would do it, so I was so happy when I found out I was pregnant, even though there would've been such an age gap between the baby and Reagan, and I'm so old…"

"You are *not* old!" Logan admonished me.

"You now what I mean," I said. "That didn't work either, though.

We never found out for sure if he was a boy but, in hindsight, I don't think it would have mattered. With Reagan, Dick at least pretended to be interested in the pregnancy, in me, in her when she finally arrived, at least a little bit for a little while. This time, nothing changed, that is until he told me that if I got fat he'd stay away more than he already does. That crushed me. Then the miscarriage…" I stopped, realizing how much I had actually dealt with in the recent past. "I am so very, very thankful for the two of you," I said, getting up from the bench.

"So what's his deal, do you think?" Micah asked as she rose to join me and Logan followed suit.

"I don't know. I guess I just wasn't as good a wife and mother as I needed to be."

"Stop that right now," said Logan. "This is not on you. It's on him." She saw the doubt in my eyes and continued. "Did you do the very best you could do to be a good wife and mother?"

"I tried everything I could think of. I read books and magazines. I tried to notice what worked in the relationships of my friends and even people on TV, and I tried to copy that. I even tried talking to Dick about it point blank and asking him what the problems were and how I could fix them, but he always just said that everything was fine even though it very obviously was not. When Reagan was born, I found myself focusing on her and neglecting my marriage, but Dick didn't even seem to notice. He always got his way so what did he have to complain about, right? He insulted me a lot, but he never really complained. He never really did anything at all. I did everything. I even let him name Reagan."

"Is that a family name?" asked Logan.

"Nope," I told her. "If you can believe it, I let him name her after Ronald Reagan. Dick's a way right-wing conservative Republican and it made him happy, so…"

"What the hell about that made *you* happy?" Micah sounded angry as hell that someone would treat me so poorly, or maybe it was because I had been weak enough to let it happen.

"Didn't matter back then."

"Does it now?"

I had to think for a minute, but I realized the truth of it. "Yes, it very much does. He was talking about naming this baby George, after Bush. I don't now for sure, but I think I could have put a stop to that. Maybe not, though, if I hadn't met you guys. It does matter now. What I want does matter now."

"Good," said Logan putting her arm through mine as we walked. "No more self-deprecation. We'll steer you out of it if you fall back in, won't we Micah?"

"Abso-freakin'-lutely," she said, slipping her arm through mine on the other side. The three of us looked so ridiculous, arm-in-arm in the middle of the forest, that Logan started skipping and singing 'Lions, tigers, and bears! Oh my!,' dragging us along with her. We fell in step, joined in the song, and within moments were doubled over with laughter.

When we got back to the car, Logan looked at Micah and said, "Next week, we'll hear more about your situation with Darry's, right? We'll figure out a way for you to get away from him, officially, so he has no doubt about it."

"Okay," Micah acquiesced as she climbed into the backseat.

"Good," I thought. I was anxious to hear more about this, especially in light of recent events,

As we drove home, Micah asked a few pointed questions related to my tale. I didn't mind. I didn't think of it as prying. I knew she was just concerned.

"Why the hell did he marry you if he was going to treat you like shit?" she wondered.

"Well, I obviously don't know for sure, but I have a theory. Put simply, it was time. He'd finished the academy, got a good job, life was moving on. All his friends were getting married and I'm sure his parents were after him about grandchildren. He was just at that stage of life and I just happened to fill the bill. I wasn't bad looking since I'd slimmed down, I was kind of smart, and I was the biggest doormat on the planet. It probably didn't take him long to realize that I'd be easy to control. The perfect wife, right? Now, I really don't think that was how *he* saw it, though. He's really not a bad guy, you know."

"Yeah, right," said Micah.

"No, really. I just think he thought he wanted one life and then decided he'd rather have another. He's just naturally a loner and, when he does want company, he just has more fun with his buddies. I don't think he's the type of guy who wants to be married. He wants his freedom, but he didn't figure that out until later."

"Sounds a lot like that bitch of a mother of mine," observed Micah.

"How do you know he didn't see it that way?" asked Logan.

"Because I didn't see my real reason for marrying him until much later, so I have to give me the same leeway."

"You didn't love him? Why *did* you marry him then?" Micah seemed utterly confused by this.

"Oh, I loved him, at least for the first few years, until he sandpapered it away with his indifference and unkind words. It just couldn't last, even though I really don't think he meant to be malicious. It's just his nature, I guess. Anyway, after a few years, I realized that I had probably married him as a way to escape the craziness of my childhood home. Makes sense, right? I so wanted to get out of there and here was this guy who actually wanted me (I thought), was nice to me at first, made a decent living... then, a few years in, I had the horrible realization that had married my father!"

"I was just about to make that observation," said Logan as she and Micah cracked up at this.

"Yep. Same neglect. Same heartless words, especially about my appearance... Still, there are a lot of differences. Dick's a very high functioning alcoholic and he has a good job that he loves, maybe too much. He even loves it now that he's off the beat and sits behind a desk. I think his demotion might have been a contributing factor to his deterioration from potential-happily-ever-after to currently-clueless-and-cruel. I could be wrong, but this stuff occurs to me from time to time." We drove the rest of the way in silence.

"Well, that's it then," Micah announced as we pulled up in Logan's driveway to drop her off before heading back to Micah's. "Allison, it sure sounds like you've done all you can do and you need to start putting your time and attention on *you* and not on him. "

"Well, that's getting easier, I think. The Gatherings, you guys, really do help me, more than you know."

"Oh, I know," Micah agreed. "They help me, too,"

"Me three!" chimed Logan, and we ended up in a huddle hug when we got out of the car.

* * * * *

After I'd returned home from dropping Micah off that evening, I got an unexpected call from Desi. When I asked if everything was all right, he put my mind at rest right away. We were still on tender hooks after all that had happened with Darry. Apparently, he hadn't resurfaced in their lives, so that was good news.

"I'm just calling to tell you that I'd love to have you come and have dinner with us sometime," he said. "You've done so much for Micah, for me. I'd love you to meet Bria, have you get to know her a little better. Let me do this as a thank you. Please. Nothing fancy, just a nice family dinner."

"Did Micah put you up to this?" I blurted. "I told her that her company is all the repayment I need. There's really no need to put yourself out."

"No really. I *want* to do this. I want to know you better and I want Bria to know you, too. You're making such a positive difference for this family already, even in this short amount of time, that I want you to know us, too. To be honest, Micah kind of bridled at the idea and complained that she'd have to clean the house and cook," he chortled. "I made a bargain with her and said I'd cook if she'd clean, so it's all settled."

"I'll come under one condition," I said. "No one cleans and we order in, or I don't come.

"Okay," he lied. "Can we do on Wednesday, say around 6:00, instead of your regular sister date?"

"Absolutely," I said. "I'd love that. Remember, though, no fuss." It was a date.

CHAPTER THIRTY-THREE
Celebration

"Love and you shall be loved."
—*Ralph Waldo Emerson*

The following Wednesday was one of the most wonderful evenings of my life. I told Micah I'd be there a bit early to make sure they were sticking to their promise of ordering in and keeping it simple. When I pulled up, I was happy (maybe too happy!) to see Desi's car in the driveway. It was only 5:00 so he must have gotten off work early for the occasion. When he answered the door, the familiar rush of excitement started to expand within me, but I was able to hold it down and not make a fool of myself (I hope!).

The living room and dining room occupied one large space so I could immediately see what they were up to. There were streamers hanging from the light fixture above the dinning room table to the four corners of the room and the table was beautifully set. Before I could comment on what was happening, Micah, Bria, Logan, and Reagan emerged from the hallway and rushed to embrace me, all singing "Happy Birthday" to me with open arms.

I was so taken aback that I could barely wrap my head around what was happening! I had mentioned to Logan and Micah at our last Gathering that my birthday had been the previous Friday, unnoticed and unmarked by my family. I had really just mentioned it in passing and didn't really express any regret (and certainly no surprise) about it having been ignored by the Terrible Twosome. It was exactly what I'd expected because it was what always happened. It had been my fortieth, so it was supposed to have been kind of a big deal I guess, but not to me. My birthday had passed without fanfare, without comment, for the last fifteen years at least, so I was used to it.

When I disentangled myself from the hugs, I realized that these lovely sisters (and Desi, Bria, and even Reagan!) had conspired to plan this party in just three days. I don't know how they pulled it off. I was so touched that it seemed like forever before I could recover myself enough to thank them.

They led me to the table and sat me in the place of honor at its head. I was presented with a ridiculous pointed birthday hat and a pink feather boa (that must've come from Logan!). Everyone took their places and donned their own silly hats. After we were all properly seated and hatted, Desi and Bria went into the kitchen and, when they returned, they placed a beautiful spread on the table before us. There was spaghetti with meatballs, garlic bread that smelled just heavenly, and a lovely spinach salad.

I asked who'd prepared the meal and Desi answered, "All of us. We each had a job. I did the spaghetti, Bria did the garlic bread, Logan did the salad, and Micah did the cake."

"There's a cake!" I was as excited as a child. I hadn't had a birthday cake since I was little. Reagan looked a little ashamed that she hadn't been mentioned in the line-up of prep work so I got up, went to her and hugged her around her shoulders from behind. "Reagan! I am beyond thrilled to see *you*! How did you get here? I thought you were going to Jordan's after school."

"Well, that was kind of a lie. Logan brought me. She picked me up right after school, and I did the steamers."

"Oh, sorry Reagan!" said Desi, who had only just met her that day. He was kind to her even though he must have heard about her behavior toward Micah. "I didn't mean to neglect your efforts! I was answering the question only about the meal. My bad!"

Reagan, I could tell, was very happy to hear him say that and she smiled shyly at Desi. "The decorations are *perfect*!" I said. "It makes the whole affair so festive! Thank you, Reagan!" I gave Logan a grateful look. I knew she didn't really like to drive, so her having gone to the high school at the getting-out time to grab Reagan was a gift in and of itself.

We had a lovely time and talked about so many things over that delicious dinner. It was just like the happy family meals I always wanted to have, but never could. Everyone had worked so hard and no one would even allow me to help them clear the table or clean up.

Once that had been done, Logan insisted that Reagan should be the one to bring out the cake. When she put in on the table, I was surprised to feel a sob well up in my chest and escape unabated. They all waited for me to come back to myself with satisfied smiles on their faces. The cake wasn't store-bought but was a Betty Crocker box cake. Those little confection peel-off-the-paper letters spelled out "Happy Birthday Sister" in yellow, pink, blue, and white on top of thick chocolate frosting from a can. My absolute favorite.

"I know Reagan, Bria, and I don't count as 'sisters,'" said Desi, "but we're on that cake in spirit…and, besides, that's what Micah wanted it to say and since the cake was her thing, she got her way." I took a few deep breaths to center myself and stifle any other sob or whimper or whatever it was that wanted to break free, then tried to speak, but couldn't. I really couldn't. I was that overwhelmed.

"This is exactly…and I mean *exactly*…like the last cake I remember my mother baking for my birthday a hundred years ago," I finally managed to choke out. "If you tell me it's a yellow cake under that frosting, I won't believe it!"

"Believe it!" said Micah with a satisfied look on her face.

"How on earth did you know? How did you have any idea that this would make me so, so much happier than a store-bought cake."

Reagan looked abashed. I found out later that she had not only suggested but insisted on a store-bought cake but, since that wasn't her job (and she didn't have any money), she'd lost the argument.

"Well, I kind of know you, ya know," Micah offered. "I know you're a serious chocoholic but that too much doesn't sit well, hence the yellow cake for balance. I wasn't about to try doing letters with one of those squeezy things so the little candy letters were what you were going to get. I didn't know that that's what your mom did, but I'm glad you like it!" I could tell she really, really was.

They made me cut the cake and distribute the slices, and Desi set glasses of milk in front of us as I did so. That milk was more enjoyable to me than any glass of wine I'd ever had. I was really proud of Reagan when she got up to gather the empty (scraped clean!) plates and take them to the kitchen without being asked. When she returned, she brought with her a small box wrapped in silver and gold paper, tied with a cobalt blue ribbon.

Desi and Reagan took their seats and I discovered that they'd all prepared short birthday messages for me. They went around the table, relaying their sentiments like regular families do when expressing gratitude on Thanksgiving.

Desi's was all appreciation. "Allison, this little birthday gathering isn't even a drop in the ocean of gratitude I have for what you have done for this family," he said. "We are blessed to have you and you are never, never allowed out of our lives!" He lifted his half-empty milk glass in a toast that was replicated by all.

Bria went next. "I really hope you understand how much you mean to us all, Allison and, when Micah heads off to college" (here she looked at her sister as if daring her to dispute the fact that college was a foregone conclusion and that she *would* be going), "I hope you'll be my big-sister, too." Nothing could have made me happier, until Reagan spoke.

"I really thought I'd feel out of place here," she said softly. "I really thought Micah would never ever want to see me again. I was so wrong...and I'm so, so sorry to all of you!"

She almost broke down at this point but everyone at the table, everyone, in different but equally sincere words, told her there was nothing to be sorry for. "We all grow up at our own pace," said Logan. "You belong with us." I found myself taking deep breaths yet again to try to maintain control of my run-away emotions.

Reagan continued, smiling at Logan in a way that I thought I might even be able to describe as loving. Reagan...loving! This night was... there are no words to adequately describe it. Reagan continued, "I know I am...was...am... a spoiled little girl sometimes and, Micah, I am so, so sorry about how I treated you, and Mom..."

Micah interrupted, saying gently, "No more apologies. Everyone is accepted by everyone here and all is forgiven and forgotten. Reagan, why don't you save your birthday wish until last." I could tell that Reagan was relieved by this suggestion. This was really difficult for her, and I found myself becoming so filled with love that I thought my chest would burst.

"I'll go," said Logan. She lifted her glass and recited a short poem she'd written and memorized for the occasion.

"People come and people go
Some speed away and some go slow

However true this thought may be
It'll never happen with you and me

We're sisters now and sisters later
Our friendship grows but could not be greater

Here's to Allison, my dear friend
And to a love that will never end!"

I was touched to tears, of course. How could I not be? I said, "Sorry,

Logan, I know I'm breaking the rule about non-judgment, but that was the most beautiful, touching..." I couldn't finish the sentence.

"Wait until you hear Micah's!" chimed Bria as Logan came around the table to hug me. I got up and we folded into each other's arms.

When we finally broke apart, I commented, "I love the line 'Our friendship grows but could not be greater.' It speaks to the uniqueness and depth of what we have, like it really *couldn't* be greater, but yet somehow, it constantly is." I wanted her to know that I felt the same way, that I loved her so much. I wiped the corners of my eyes with my paper birthday napkin. "What we all have is just so, so… rare and special. Oh, that doesn't do it justice…"

"Yeah, right, but stop trying to figure it out now!" laughed Micah. "It's my turn." She pulled her journal out from under her chair where she'd apparently stashed it earlier. I hadn't noticed it because she was at the opposite end of the table from me, but when I saw it, I knew she'd written something for me as well.

"In your honor," she said, "this has no title!" Logan and I laughed, but the others didn't get the joke.

"Perfect!" I said. She read:

I really wanted this to be longer
I have lots to say to you
But Logan said a short one would be stronger
So that's what I agreed to do

I know at first I was a bitch
I know now that was wrong
I'm so glad that we've found our niche
And you'll be my sister my whole life long

* * *

You accepted me for just being me
And I've accepted you
That acceptance and more has made me see
That what we have is true

I know this sounds like a dumb love letter
But I don't know how else to say it
Since I met you my life is better
But it's still hard to display it

Six stanzas, I'm afraid, is all you get
I said I'd keep it short
I know we have much to do yet
And I'm glad you're my cohort

On this adventure as we grow…
(Sorry, I had more to say) — here she looked at Logan and playfully stuck out her tongue!
It important to me that you know
I'm grateful for you every day

So stanza seven…

"Okay," she laughed when she saw everyone settling in for more, "I'm kidding! I'm done, but I do have so much more to say to you Allison, and Logan, but for now I'll shut up and just say thanks and that I hope you have the best birthday every."

"That," I said, "it most certainly is!" and I raised my glass to toast them all. I couldn't have been more moved, at least that's what I thought until Regan said her message. I could tell that she was nervous and I was so glad when Logan suggested a bathroom break.

When everyone was up from the table and either using the restroom or speaking quietly to each other, I cornered Desi to especially thank him. "You must have lost hours at work to pull this off, Desi. Thank you for doing all this. Thank you so much."

"Well," he smiled, "don't thank me too much. It was Micah's idea. She enlisted me and the others, gave us our assignments, oversaw our progress… it was actually so very sweet. Not like the hard-ass girlfriend of that loser Darry, not even like the angry little girl I used to know. She was like an adult on a mission. I'm telling you, I've almost cried a few times since you dropped her off on Saturday, watching her charge forward with this like a bull in a china shop! Bria and I knew to just stay out of her way and do what we were told, but we were so happy to do it for you, Allison. This is the very least you deserve."

I couldn't help myself. I reached up and hugged him around the neck and he leaned down to hug me back. For a second, it was like we were wrapped in blue mist and the whole world fell away around us, but we were both still cognizant of where we were and who we were with, and of the necessity of keeping our feelings at bay, so we let go and backed away from each other, turning back to the others, who were taking their seats. All except Reagan. "Where's my beautiful daughter?" I asked.

Before anyone could answer, Reagan emerged from the hallway carrying a smaller version of the exact same journal that Micah and Logan had, the one with the woman with the tear on her face. "Logan gave this to me on Monday," she said by way of explanation as she stood behind her chair. "When I got home from school, she motioned to me that I should come over to her place rather than go inside, so I did." she explained. "She gave me this. Thanks again, Logan." We both looked at Logan, who smiled at us as she straightened her scarf. "She didn't pressure me at all, but pointed out the symbolism of this cover. It's so cool." She looked at Desi and Bria to explain. "When the book is closed, it's just a beautiful woman with a tear on her face, but when it's open you see that the other side doesn't have a tear. The one on the left can be a tear of sadness, of wonder, of joy… whatever, but there are two sides to the face, sometimes there's a tear and sometimes there's not." It wasn't the best explanation of the symbolism we'd discussed, but she seemed inspired by it just the same. "It's a book for emotions and for looking inside yourself just like you're looking inside the book to write on the pages. I've felt really bad about everything that's happened, and I'm…"

"Don't say it!" laughed Micah, holding up her hand, palm out, in the "stop" gesture.

"Okay. Anyway, I wrote in it that night and last night, too, and it's true. It really did help me figure some stuff out, Logan. Anyway, then today at lunch at school I wrote my birthday message for you, Mom. It's really terrible…

"No judgment," Micah, Logan, and I all said simultaneously, with a little more vehemence than we'd intended. The looks on the others' faces were hilarious.

"Sorry," Logan said. "That's one of our cardinal rules at the Gatherings and we have to stop each other from judging every now and then. Sometimes we can get a little intense, I guess! Just say that it's raw, Reagan. Everything in a journal is raw. No judgment."

"Okay, it's raw. I started to write a poem, but I just couldn't, so it's more like a letter, a note. Don't worry. Logan told me to keep it short."

She read:

Happy Birthday Mom,

I'm sorry about everything. I really mean it. I think I understand you now, better than before. I know we have work to do to fix our relationship — to get a relationship — but I want to do that work. I could tell after the cops brought me home last week that you love me so much (and both Logan and Micah told me that, too). I want us to be as close as you guys all are. I've learned a lot in the last week. I want to be your daughter and your sister. I want us to be friends — all of us — if you'll all have me after all the horrible things I've said and done.

"That's all I could do. Happy birthday, Mom." I could tell she was embarrassed and afraid in this new place with all these new people. She'd never met any of them before, not really. It was like she'd matured ten years in the past week. I knew even then that this wasn't a miracle that would make everything okay, but it was a start, and I was so happy and so very proud of her!

I got up and went around the table to give her a hug, while everyone else applauded. I whispered in her ear how proud I was and how much I loved her and how incredibly happy her message had made me. As I disentangled myself from her embrace, Logan said, "Of course we'll have you Reagan! We'd love to have you!"

"Yeah," added Micah, "we've all had our crap happen. We get it." I know this meant the most to Reagan since it had been Micah to whom she's been the worst, even worse than she'd been to me. I smiled at Micah and I know she understood the gratitude I was trying to send her way.

I thought that nothing could top that, but in order to keep the evening from turning into a "mushy love-fest" (that's what he called it!), Desi suggested that we get to the gift. I'd forgotten all about that. He picked up the small box that had been on the table the whole time but, before he handed to me, he explained, "Now, this doesn't come close to showing you how grateful we all are for you or how much we all love you, but we chipped in and thought you'd like this. We all threw in ideas and this is what we finally came to consensus on."

I pulled off the bow, ripped through the paper, and saw to my delight that it was a pedometer. That may not seem like a personal or sentimental gift, but it was perfect. They knew I was trying to get healthy and had been walking almost daily with Logan. This was them *knowing* me, supporting me, encouraging me. Dick would never have thought of anything like this even if he *were* inclined to give me anything at all. He'd have sent flowers or given me a gift card, like he did the first few years we were married. *This* gift was personal. This was for *me*. The me I was and the me I was becoming. It was both a pat on the back and a helping hand up at the same time. It was perfect.

I bubbled out my surprise, my pleasure, and my gratitude as Desi took it out of the box and handed it back to me. I clipped it on the band of my jeans and really just couldn't say anything else.

"You need another piece of cake!" smiled Bria! "I know we just gave you a fitness thing, but it's your birthday so there are no rules today."

I acquiesced and went for more plates. Everyone but Bria joined me in finishing off what was left of the best birthday cake on the best birthday I'd ever had.

* * * * *

After that amazing evening concluded, Reagan drove home with me. She was quiet so I didn't push her, but as we turned left at the T in the road where Louie stood guard, she said, "Is the next Gathering on Saturday?"

"Yep, at 2:00. We're doing it at our house, in the Oasis, this time, just to change things up. Don't worry, Logan's bringing the food, so it'll be good!" I joked.

"You're not that bad a cook, you know."

"Lair!" I said and we both laughed. As I pulled into the driveway and stopped the car, I took her hand before she could get out. "Reagan, I meant what I said and I know you meant what you said tonight, and it makes me happier than you can ever know. Do you want to come to the Gathering?"

"I'm not sure. I did feel like Micah has forgiven me…"

"Oh, she has. She understands more than you'd imagine for someone her age." I turned off the engine and we sat there, holding hands. I couldn't believe she wasn't pulling away or jumping out of the car to get away from me as she would have any other time. Maybe seeing that some people really did love me made her think that maybe she could, too.

"Why? Why is she so much older than me when she's only a year older than me?"

"Well, she's gone through a lot of shit, Reagan." I couldn't believe that I used that kind of language with her, but it just came out. "You've had it easy. No offense, but you've had it too easy thanks to your father. You haven't had to really learn anything about life, real life."

"Yeah, I guess. Well, I've sure learned a hell of a lot lately!" We laughed at that and I squeezed her hand rather than chastising her for her language. I could actually feel our relationship changing. "I'd like to come to the Gathering, but just to sit and listen, not actually be in it. Is that okay?"

"Absolutely. Hey, all that cake made me thirsty. Let's go in and get something to drink. Whaddya say?"

She nodded, released my hand, and got out of the car. That was the beginning. That was the start of me getting my daughter back. It took a while, but that was the jumping off point for certain sure. I will be grateful to my sisters and to Desi and Bria for every second of that evening and for every second afterward until the day I die because of this as much as because of the birthday messages, the lovely party, and the touching gift.

My only concern about the evening was that, at one point, Micah answered her phone, then left the room to take the call. I was sure it was Darry. Based on the look on her face when she returned, I knew I was right.

CHAPTER THIRTY-FOUR
History

"There is more in every person's soul than we think."
—*Ralph Waldo Emerson*

It was such a sunny, beautiful afternoon the following Saturday that it seemed as if the very Universe was blessing this Gathering. Micah was in a particularly good mood, having spent an enjoyable evening with her family the night before instead of seeing that loser Darry. I didn't think that Logan and I had been entirely successful in convincing her that being true to herself —even if she wasn't entirely sure yet who she was —was more important than trying to fit in with him or others in her peer group who were holding her back rather than helping her forward, especially since she was so far and away beyond them by any measurement you wanted to take. I was struggling with the same damn issues, though, and, frankly, not moving forward as fast as I'd have liked either, so why should she listen to me? There was something still holding me to Dick, to that life in which I was so insignificant. How could I even suggest to Micah that she should switch gears, give up what she was used to, abandon a long-held goal (that of fitting in) that she'd worked so hard to achieve, when I couldn't yet do it myself?

Micah finally admitted that afternoon that Darry *had* been in touch with her and had begged her forgiveness and promised to do right by her from then on. She'd had several phone conversations with him while he tried to renegotiate their relationship, but she hadn't seem him since that fateful night.

Reagan joined us for this Gathering. I spread a blanket on the ground in front of the lawn furniture in my Oasis and Logan set out crackers and hummus, some grapes, and some nuts in pretty pink bowls on all the tables. She brought a pitcher of lemonade and she poured us each a glass and handed us some small pink plates to load for ourselves — no paper stuff for Logan, not even outside. She said that one of her goals in life was to reduce her carbon footprint to the size of a pea, plus it made her feel special to use "real" things, so she had a few different sets of plates and bowls. She always said it was up to us to make ourselves feel special, be happy… that we shouldn't rely on anyone else to do that for us, so she did this for herself because it brought her joy.

Reagan was quiet for most of the afternoon, but I could see her taking everything in. I so hoped that she'd enjoy it and eventually really become one of us. I knew she really wanted to, so I felt good about it. Micah and Logan did everything they could to make her feel comfortable and part of everything, even though she kind of wasn't at that point yet. She was a fly on the wall who would eventually, hopefully, actually fly with us.

Logan wore a particularly colorful scarf that day. It had an autumn leaf pattern in rust and green, even though that season was still a couple of months away. Logan didn't care about things like conforming — she wore what she wanted to wear and she did what she wanted to do. I hoped that I could be like that someday. My perfectionism would have caused me to hesitate mixing seasons, but Logan's scarf was proof positive that some things I'd long held to be important didn't really matter at all.

That scarf was beautiful and sported all the colors of fallen leaves mixed with the occasional thread of summer green that ran through it here and there like the last vestiges of the waning season. There were also some gold threads running through the pattern that picked up the sun as it shone through the passing clouds and the tree branches, and they sparkled like sunlight on water.

I loved all the scarves that Logan wore, and it seemed like she had dozens and dozens, and that she planned her outfits around *them* rather than using them to accent her outfits, as most people did. I wondered if she'd like a new one for Christmas or for her birthday. At first, I couldn't decide if she'd be easy or hard to buy for, then I realized that it would be easy because Logan would love anything because she loved everything.

That day, her long gray hair was pulled back and swept up at the back of her head against the heat and you could easily see her whole beautiful face. I was again struck by how all the lines on that face swept upward. I decided that I'd try to smile more so that, hopefully, I'd age as well as she had. She always seemed like she was filled with light from within and bathed in light from without. It was such a pleasant and calming aura and it seemed to wrap around all of us.

I read a relatively lame poem about stress because I'd been thinking about what September would bring when I went back to school. I was always so overwhelmed by work during the school year and it caused a good deal of negative anticipation. I almost hadn't written the poem, but I knew Micah would've thought less of me if I came to the Gathering unprepared, so I forced myself to do it the night before, just before I went to sleep, because it was what was on my mind.

"Well, that has potential," Logan said, without a touch of sarcasm. "I'm not used to hearing low writing from you though — not a judgment, just an observation…" This had become a standard line at our gatherings. "Isn't it a little early to start worrying about school?"

I laughed. "Well, teachers look at summer this way: June is Friday, July is Saturday, and August is Sunday, and it's August now! 'Friday' we can just enjoy. 'Saturday' we realize that we're halfway through the summer 'weekend' and we redouble our efforts to get all our personal stuff done and have some fun before we no longer have a life, and we start worrying just a little about how we'll get everything done on 'Sunday' so we'll be ready for 'Monday' when school resumes. When 'Sunday' does come, summer is essentially over, and we start planning stuff, setting up our classrooms, having 'teacher dreams.' It's an occupational hazard. I know it sounds funny, but those few summer months are the only months during which we can decompress, unwind, and get anything significant done in our lives and homes. I start having teacher dreams in early August so get ready for more low writing!"

"We'll try to keep you positive! I would miss hearing your more introspective, uplifting work, but I'd love to hear this again if you choose to revise it." How tactful she was! She'd managed to tell me to pitch it without being judgmental. How the hell did she do that off the top of her head? I'd spend days planning what to say to Reagan or Dick if anything important needed to be discussed so that I wouldn't say the wrong thing or sound wrong, and I'd still somehow manage blow it and not adequately communicate what I'd intended before giving it up as lost after their negative reactions.

"I had no intention of doing anything with that rant other than get the feelings out," I noted.

"Well, that's what journals are for, right?" Micah reminded me.

Micah, like me, didn't have the knack that Logan had for giving real feedback without judgement, but I still think she was better at it than I was. She asked a couple of perfunctory questions about my poem out of politeness then turned to comment on Logan's scarf in an attempt to change the subject.

"Why you wear scarves all the time?" she asked. "I really like 'em and 'specally that one, but I was wonderin' 'bout it." Her speech was casual today for whatever reason and no one commented on it. Sometimes I think she liked to assume her other persona just to see if she could drag a judgment out of one of us. We never took the bait.

"I think they're pretty, too," Logan replied, toying with the fringe on one long end, without a trace of self-satisfaction or vanity. She hesitated for a moment, then slowly moved her hand up to the knot at her neck, as if she were trying to make a difficult decision. There wasn't exactly tension in the air, but a sense that time was standing still just a little bit, that something was about to happen. "And they save me, a little," she added.

We knew that if we just waited, she'd explain. Reagan leaned forward almost imperceptibly, expectantly. We didn't need to fill the air with questions and I think Regan sensed this. Logan brought her other hand up to her neck as well and with long, slender fingers began to slowly untie the knot. When the long tails of colorful fabric fell away from each other, she pulled one long end, hand over hand, until the short end caressed the back of her neck and fell off, revealing to us the longest, most hideous, protruding scar any of us had ever seen. It started under her left ear, went under her chin and then pointed down toward her collar bone on the right. I silenced a gasp and brought my hand to my own throat in horror. Reagan froze. Micah made not a sound, but slowly got up, went over to Logan, knelt down in front of her, and looked up directly into her eyes. She so reminded me of Bria then. Logan nodded slightly and Micah reached up and traced her finger, very slowly, across the scar from left to right, like she was reading it.

"What the hell happened, Logan?" she whispered. I think it was the first time she'd ever used Logan's name to her face. She'd always avoided calling her anything before, I think because she felt she needed to show her more respect than Logan expected, even though she had asked Micah several times to call her familiarly by her first name. Looking at them now, they seemed on equal footing, two friends divided by years, by race, and by culture, but sisters just the same.

Micah could see that Logan had battle scars too. It was obvious that whatever had caused that scar had been no accident.

"My son, Shane," she said very slowly and clearly, still locking eyes with Micah. "He tried to kill me one night, in a spaced-out rage." Micah got up from her kneeling position and put her hand on Logan's shoulder. I could see her give it just the slightest squeeze. Then she sat back down, not in the chair she'd just vacated, but on the blanket next to Logan. She was still looking at Logan, waiting for the rest. I just sat, immobile, watching them interact and listening, feeling not a part of it, really, at all.

"It happened almost twenty years ago, but it sometimes seems like just yesterday. He came home one night, late, as usual. I had decided to try something different and confront him then and there instead of waiting until morning or ignoring it as I had in the past. Mornings he was hung over, but at least he pretended to listen. I knew, though, that it was, indeed, pretense and that everything I said to him went in one ear and out the other. So, I decided I'd go on the offensive that time and draw him out. I had a tape recorder going so I could play it back for him in the morning so, hopefully, he'd hear himself, how slurred he was, how…and then he might admit that he had a problem and let me help him or might try to help himself." She took a sip of her lemonade as if to cool a rising heat.

"I loved him so much," she continued, "even when he was like that. Even then. I still do even now, even after everything. But he was killing himself. I had to help him, but he was nineteen and much bigger than I was. I couldn't *make* him do anything. I'd lost my husband ten years earlier and my parents had been dead for years… no siblings… so I had no help. Back then I was worried about what people would think of me so my friends and coworkers didn't know anything about it. I had no help, no support. No one to help me make him understand.

"I had to find a way to make *him* care enough to get help, or I couldn't help him. In hindsight, it was a stupid idea, but I can't blame myself. I was at the end. It was either try this last thing, or throw him out on the street, and I couldn't even fathom doing that."

It was not lost on me that she'd said "can't" blame herself instead of "don't." She was apparently still struggling with this particular demon.

"His friends were all into the same things he was, so it was all on me. I just kept thinking, 'Find a way to save him or you'll lose him.' So, when he came in the door that night, I started in on him. I tried to be positive and calm, but I know that's not how he perceived it. To him, it was an attack. I reminded him about all the things he'd done wrong, I pointed out the hundred ways in which he was ruining his life, I told him about all the people he'd disappointed, how hurt and frightened I was… All the while he ignored me as if I weren't even there. He walked past me, past my judgment, and went to the refrigerator and got a beer, as if I were invisible to him.

"I never kept alcohol in there. He'd stuck a few beers in the back behind the apples in the crisper drawer and, since I'm not partial to apples, I'd never noticed them. How I'd missed them I'll never know, but I found two more two weeks later in another bin after it was all over. But I'm not blaming myself. I did the best I could." That she had repeated a form of that notion reinforced to me that Logan's life hadn't been as perfect as we always assumed it had been. She had issues just like the rest of us and it was a constant struggle to deal with them. Some hurts just don't go away. Like my lost baby. Like Micah's lost mother. I wondered if Micah had picked up on that.

"Anyway," she continued, "just after he opened the beer and took a long pull, I started in again on how he'd hurt me, how much I loved him, how much I wanted for him… and eventually he just lost it, yelling, 'Hurt you! Hurt *you*? I'll hurt you!'" She paused at this point to make another sip of lemonade and took a deep breath. I could see her struggling with the memory. It played out on her face in spite of her effort to keep the narrative calm and neutral.

"He just lost it," she went on. "It all happened so fast that I remember it as though it all happened in slow-motion in a dense, swirling fog." She took another deep breath before she could go on. "As he moved the beer bottle away from his mouth after that last sip, he raised the hand that held it almost like a toast, but then he shot it backward behind him, then he swung it forward again, hard, and released the bottle. Even thrown underhanded, it became a violent projectile that flew through the air just past my head and smashed into a thousand beer soaked pieces against the glass of the picture window behind me. The window shattered too. It was a spider web, dripping with foamy brew. It's almost beautiful in my memory now. A work of art.

"But at the time, the noise of the shatter of the bottle and the shatter of the glass was like a high-pitched gong signaling the end to me. With the same swift movement that he used to throw his arm back to hurl the bottle, that same arm swung forward again and, somehow during that swing, his hand had retrieved a small knife that he apparently had in his back pocket. Thank the Universe that it was small! If he'd grabbed one of the knives out of the block on the kitchen counter, I'd most likely not be here now. Anyway, his arm flailed upward and then down again in front, slicing the air in my direction. It was terrifying. It all happened so fast then, but it lives in slow motion in my memory now," she said again. Our hearts were breaking for her.

"Of course, I jumped at the sound of the breaking glass and then jumped back from the arc of his knife-wielding arm. I was more afraid than I'd ever been in my life, than I've ever been since. This was my son, but this was *not* my son. He was possessed by some demon he couldn't control, and he came at me.

"He reached me in seconds and knocked me to the floor with a backhand swing of that same crazy arm. Thank God it wasn't with the blade. When I look back, I often find myself wondering what his left arm was doing all that time. Just watching its crazy brother? Supporting him as he leaned on the back of the chair to keep from falling over from the momentum of the powerful swinging arcs of its counterpart? I don't know. I can't remember. It was only that right arm, the hand with the knife, and his bloodshot, crazy eyes that were not the eyes of my son, that I saw. They were the eyes of a madman.

"Then he did it. As I was backing away from him, I stumbled and fell. While I was lying on the floor, trying to scramble backwards and up, onto the coach, so I could regain my footing and run, he slashed out at me and he cut me. Here." She covered the part of her neck that bore the scar with her whole hand, as if hiding it from view could obliterate it from memory, or as if caressing it would make it hurt a little less. But she knew better. She brought her hand back down into her lap. It looked as though she had no strength left to hold it up. We all just sat in silence.

"I don't now why he didn't entirely slit my throat," she continued after a few moments. "I know that was his intent, well, not *his* intent, but the intent of that drug-crazed maniac who'd taken over his body. I like to imagine that the real Shane was still in there somewhere and may have heard my screams and calls for him to stop, as apparently half the neighborhood had, and that's why he didn't proceed with his attack. I like to think that my son saved me, that he came to himself in the middle of all that and stayed the monster's hand that would have killed me. He saved me. He saved me," she repeated. She lowered her head and I saw a tear drop onto her folded hands.

My son had saved me, too. My eyes were brimming and I had a lump in my throat the size of a watermelon, but I knew not to say anything. So did Micah. Even Reagan still sat in respectful silence. It wasn't time for words, or even hugs. Not yet. We just waited, using the time to try to compose ourselves.

"The doctors said that it was a miracle. He somehow missed the jugular veins and the carotid artery by a fraction of a fraction. Thank God." I rarely heard her use the word "God." She usually referred to the "Universe" or "Source Energy" instead. This was more personal, I think.

"One or two of the neighbors knew that we'd been having problems just through general observation, (although they could never have imagined *this*), so they called the police when they heard Shane's shouting and my screaming. When they heard the shattering glass and my impassioned pleas for him to stop (I never even thought of calling for help), two of my neighbors sent their husbands rushing over and they found me, bleeding profusely and incoherent, on the floor in front of the couch, and they found him, kneeling in my blood, just looking at me as if he'd just entered the room and was trying to figure out what had happened. They held him for the police and tried to stop my bleeding with kitchen towels until the ambulance got there. At least that's what I was later told." She picked up a couple of grapes, not putting them in her mouth but just holding them in her open palm, and breathed deeply for a minute or two. On impulse, I got up, moved to the blanket on the other side of her, and took her other hand.

When she resumed her story, she lifted her head and looked at each of us in turn as she struggled to get bay on track. "Of course I refused to press charges and he was released into my custody. When I got out of the hospital a few days later, I was still pretty weak, and he actually stayed clean and took care of me for a while. I think he was so horrified by what he'd done that he stayed clean while I was in the hospital and for short while after. At least he appeared to be himself when he visited every day. He was crushed, and nothing I said could abate his guilt or ease his conscience. If only I'd been able to make him see that I knew it wasn't really him…

"On the fourth day after I got home, he insisted on going out to get us some pizza, even though I'd suggested delivery. We were celebrating his twentieth birthday so he got his way. He came home three hours later, not entirely as high as I had seen him had been before, but obviously having done a little celebrating on his own. I didn't say a word — look what had happened the last time I'd spoken up — but I couldn't enjoy myself and it showed in spite of my best efforts. Even though I told him that I loved him, that I forgave him, and that I was just tired, he knew I was disappointed. He knew he'd screwed up again.

"He helped me, unsteadily, to my room and I tried to sleep. I kept seeing his demon striking out at me. I kept seeing his almost-week of sobriety going up in smoke.

"Apparently, after he'd put me to bed, he found the hand-held tape recorder I'd had used to record my unsuccessful and fateful intervention that night. It had fallen out of my pocket during the scuffle and somehow got kicked under the sofa where I'd found it the day before when I bent down to pick up a magazine I'd dropped. I'd put the recorder back on the desk in my office and didn't think another thing about it.

I have no idea why he would have gone into my office after I'd gone to bed, but he did, and he must have noticed it on the desk. He hadn't seen it the night I confronted him, I don't think. Apparently, and for reasons I cannot fathom, he replayed the recording of that whole night, the whole scene from the time he came in the door (I'd hit record when I saw his car almost crash into the garage) until the front door closed after the ambulance had taken me and the police had taken him. After that, it was just silence on the tape because the house was empty. It always seemed empty after that. I often wonder what he was thinking when he finished listening and landed in that silence.

"I found him hanging from the ceiling fan in his room the next morning. The tape recorder was on his bed, which he had pushed out of the way so he could... it was wrapped in a sheet of paper with a rubber band around it. The first line read, "I love you and I'm so sorry."

"I never heard the tape. He had erased it. He said in his suicide note that he didn't want me to relive it as he had. He said he was sorry again and again. He said that he loved me and that he wasn't strong enough to recover, so he might as well end it, that he was afraid he might do something like that again. He asked me to be happy. Not to grieve. Not to feel responsible...and I fell apart.

"He wanted to hear your voice," Micah offered softly. "That's why he listened to it. He loved you and he wanted to hear your voice is all. He wasn't spyin' on ya or tryin' to get anything on ya. He loved ya. He was messed up is all. It ain't your fault, Logan."

"Oh, I know. I've always known that. I never really had guilt about that or, at least, when I did, I managed to push it out of the way and let the love come back in." She began rearranging the scarf around her neck.

"I always did the best I could with what I had," she said. "His dad's death was really hard on him, on both of us, but there was nothing I could have done to stop that." Logan looked directly at me then. "He did what he thought he had to do to cope. It's just the hand that the

Universe dealt us, and we just had to play it out as best we could."

Logan took a deep breath and finished retying the scarf around her neck. "So," she continued, taking a deep breath that signaled that we were coming to the end of the tale, "I wear the scarves not so much to hide the scar, which is, to me, a reminder of how my son saved me, but because they're beautiful and I want to wrap that memory in beauty, like a gift with a bow. I see the scar every night and every morning and I remind myself to appreciate all the time I had with Shane before I lost him... before he was lost to me," she corrected herself. I could see that she was going to, rightfully, refuse to put blame on herself, even accidentally, even though it was a constant struggle to push it away when it crept back into her heart.

"I have to remember that this whole episode may have robbed me of my son, but it put me on the path to a more meaningful, more beautiful, more fulfilled life. Sometimes you have to lose in order to gain." She was looking at me with a knowing smile. She was offering me the theme of her life to make of it what I would. I loved her then, as ever before and as ever after, like an angle sent from Heaven to cradle me and love me and encourage me, but to also let me be me, the me that was emerging from the wreckage of my life as I had known it up until this past summer.

I wondered why Logan had no photographs of her son anywhere in her house. I asked her once, long after this, and she told me that she did have some, but that she kept them all in her bedroom (which I'd never had any reason to see before that point) because she felt closer to him there. I understood that. It was like how I felt closer to my son in his nursery, in my room. She said she wanted to keep reminders of that pain in one space so that it would be up to *her* when the memories would be resurrected, when she would mourn and when she would celebrate his life on her terms, rather than having those feelings intrude on their own, when she wasn't ready. She said that she told him good morning and good night every day, and that sometimes she just sat with his pictures in her room and let her emotions roll through like rain clouds until they passed.

"Wow, Logan," I finally said after a long silence. "I am *so* sorry you had to suffer all that. I can't even imagine it. I know how destroyed I was when I lost my son, my baby, and I hadn't even known him four months, hadn't even held him or pressed his little face to mine. You had yours for twenty years. How much more devastating that must have been."

"That's one of the things I'm most grateful for," she said after she popped one of the grapes into her mouth. "The Universe gave me twenty years with my Shane. I'm so sorry that you didn't get that, Allison."

"Wow," said Micah. "That's kinda the theme of my poem this week, too."

"Way to segue, girlfriend!" I thought. Micah never ceased to amaze me. I found myself wishing I could have met her mother. What an amazing combination of genes, life experiences, and parenting (or lack thereof) must have gone into making Bria and Micah both so extraordinary.

"It's about Darry and my former friends."

"We'd love to hear it," Logan smiled.

"Me, too." These were the first words Reagan had uttered. We all turned our full attention to Micah.

"Well, I had dinner and a game night with Bria and my dad last night," she said by way of introduction. "We had some Taco Bell and played Jenga and Scrabble and, when I finally went to bed around 10:00, I realized that I felt happy, really happy, and that I hadn't really experienced that in a long time, except here with my sisters." I could hear her moving back into more formal speech, the poet's. "I realized that I hadn't had to second guess myself," she continued, "or worry about fitting in, or saying something 'wrong,' or any of that. I had been myself all night with my family and had really enjoyed it. And they enjoyed it, enjoyed me, just for who I was. It was kind of peaceful. Do you know what I mean? Do you know how that feels?"

Since it was a direct question, I felt that responding wouldn't really be interrupting. "I only feel it here, with you guys," I said. I glanced at Reagan and couldn't read her expression. Was she realizing that she wasn't the only one who wanted to find her way? There was still a real frigidness in her interactions with Dick after the way he'd acted the night the police brought her home. She wasn't over it. He had really hurt her, but he seemed oblivious to that fact.

"I feel it all the time, everywhere, but I had to lose what was most precious to me to set me on the road to figuring out how," Logan mused. I squeezed her hand.

"Well, I sat in bed, trying to figure out what to write for this Gathering, and," Micah continued, smiling at me, "you can't say a damn thing about waiting till the last minute, not this week! You did it, too!" We all laughed and then let her go on. "I couldn't write, so I just sat there and thought. I thought about it all, thought about it all night. Then, at 4:13 this morning, my hand started moving across the page, and this came out. It's called "Introspectacular.'" She looked at me again and telepathically sent me the message that I really needed to start titling my poems. She read,

"I am me, whole and alone
But together,
with and without
without and within
I am filled with, surrounded by
What?
I am never empty if I look
Everyone and no one matters
Just my Self
My beautiful who-the-hell-am-I Self

My love is for
Everyone, and no one, and me
I breathe with my sisters
I sit alone or with them
And I see
Who loves me
And, more importantly
Those I love, even me

It's the love that matters
Not who or what or when or how or why
Just the love
And the who-the-hell-am-I Self
May never be clear
But will always be here
And will be fine
Forever true

To my Self

She stopped, closed and lowered her journal (which was getting full — she'd written the last few lines on the back of the back cover) into her lap and smiled up at us. I had the overwhelming urge to applaud but sat on my hands instead. I know she knew why. And I know she knew why I had tears in my eyes. I waited for her to challenge me with, "No judgment!" but she beamed at me instead. It may not have been the greatest of poetry, it was raw like almost everything we shared, but it revealed such personal growth and it signaled to us that she had finally moved past her long-held belief that she had to be someone she wasn't in order to fit in where she didn't really want to be. It also sounded the death knell of her relationship with Darry, which caused both Logan and I to breathe a sign of real relief. However, there was still the problem of how to actually go about getting him out of her life for good.

Logan gathered Micah into a big hug. Micah surprised me by settling into the embrace, then raising an arm for me to join them. The three of us hugged and I broke into uncontrollable sobs, as did the other two. Sobs which almost instantaneously turned into hysterical laughter and we fell apart and rolled backward on the blanket, clutching our bellies and wiping our eyes. It was one of the most painful, emotional, glorious, wonderful, healing days I'd ever experienced.

Reagan just looked at us like we were insane. I can't image what she was thinking, but she later told me that she'd never felt so many different emotions at one time in her life as she had that afternoon. She told me that, even though so many of them were negative emotions, feeling them had made her feel alive and a little cleansed somehow.

As we struggled to sit back up and try to control our laughter and recover ourselves, Micah raised her arm to Reagan and invited her into another "family" hug. That little invitation was what made Regan a sister, too, I think. She has referred to it often over the years as a legitimate turning point in her life.

Once we regained our composure, Logan poured out more lemonade for all of us and we spent the rest of the afternoon hours discussing the experience. How I felt my son had saved me, too. How Logan managed to overcome her guilt and how, even she, still felt like the "who-the-hell-am-I-girl" sometimes. Micah offered that maybe that's what keeps her young, her openness to the "whatever," as she called it.

Reagan participated more openly once the reading was over and the afternoon progressed so pleasantly. At one point she turned to me and said, "Mom, I never thought about what losing the baby did to you. It never occurred to me that you were in so much pain. I'm sorry I didn't know." She was developing awareness and empathy, I thought, and I was thrilled.

Toward the end of the afternoon, Logan asked the question I lacked the courage to broach. "So," she said to Micah, "what are you planning to do about Darry?"

"He's gotta go. I know it," she said with a hint of sadness. I knew how she felt. It's so hard when you really want something but know in your heart that it has to go. "I really do still love him and I don't want to hurt him, but I see now that I can't really be myself if I'm with him. He can't let me. It's not his fault. I don't think I can make him understand, and I'm a little scared about how he'll take it, so I decided I'd write it all out to make sure it sounds right and so that he can't interrupt me and start arguing. Then I'll make sure he's straight when I sit him down and make him read it, or maybe I'll read it to him. I think I'll make the rule that he can't talk to me until it's finished, no matter who reads it, then he can ask me or say anything he wants." I highly doubted that Darry would respect any rules.

I was reminded by this that she was, in fact, still a kid and that, while this sounded like a good plan, she didn't realize the very high probability that it wouldn't pan out as she hoped and intended. I didn't know whether or not to caution her. Logan jumped ahead and beyond that to practical matters. "You have to make sure you're in a public place, Micah. Somewhere you can get instant help if he gets crazy. You can't take a chance of him hurting you. We could be there for you, just sitting nearby where he can't see us."

"Oh, for sure. I'll keep you posted. I'll text you guys when and where so you don't worry. You can be in the vicinity if it makes you feel better." It did. Logan and I exchanged a glance of hopeful apprehension and our Gathering came to a close at dusk. Things were certainly about to change for Micah.

CHAPTER THIRTY-FIVE
Plans

"The task ahead of us is never as great as the power behind us."
—Ralph Waldo Emerson

I got Micah's call in the middle of a lovely afternoon that I was spending with Reagan. I was beyond thrilled that I could even describe it as such. It had been so, so long since Reagan and I had connected in any meaningful or positive way.

We were sitting out back in the Oasis the Tuesday after learning about Logan's son. My yard was really becoming beautiful after all the work we'd done and the result was a really peaceful, calming environment, colored by flowers and shaded by trees. The lilacs bushes and the roses that Logan had given me were flourishing along the back fence and I could hear the singing of the colored glass wind chimes I'd put up on a pole near Logan's fence so we could both enjoy their quiet, calming music.

Reagan had grabbed a Diet Coke from the fridge (I really need to quit buying that stuff, I thought) and I had a tall glass of water with lemon and mint that I grew myself in a corner herb garden we'd put in as an afterthought. I didn't need the herbs for cooking, God knows, but

I loved their amazing aroma and my sisters teased me because I frequently put bunches of them in vases of water as if they were bouquets. Well, they kind of were and my sisters stuck their noses in them to inhale their heavenly scent as often as I did.

Reagan and I sat next to each other in the wicker chairs, sinking into the cushions, with our feet up on the coffee table. We had some apple slices, Ritz crackers, and peanut butter on a plate to share. The day was warm, but not too hot or too humid, and the sun was shining, its rays sliding down and touching the lawn and flowers like magic wands that seemed to brighten their already beautiful colors. The occasional tall, billowy cloud crossed the sky, floating above us and moving to the East as the warm breeze hurried it along.

"So," I asked Reagan, "we haven't really had a chance to talk and I really wanted to hear your thoughts about the Gathering. It was pretty intense for your first one, I so hope you'll come again. It's not always that way. It's usually a lot more… a lot less… I don't know… emotional."

"I figured. Who could take that kind of emotional drain on a regular basis?" she joked. "I did enjoy it, though, and I learned a ton, about a ton things, but really I learned a lot about you, and that was nice. It helped me understand some things, about myself, too."

"Good. That's the whole point. Well, no, it's not. The Gatherings are also about love and support and sharing, and introspection, and self-expression…

"Oh, I get that. I still don't know if I'm up to sharing yet but, if I can, I'd like to sit in again until I am. Is that okay?"

"That's absolutely perfect," I replied, reaching over and giving her hand a squeeze. "There's a lot I need to learn about you, too."

She hesitated a moment, then said, "I just feel so overwhelmed. It's like I'm for sure not who I was, but I don't know who I am now, and I have absolutely no idea who I want to be," she lamented. She was just getting to that stage in life when she needed to start thinking about her future, I thought, and it seemed as if that fact has just occurred to her of late.

"Ah, you're the who-the-hell-am-I girl, too," I mused to myself.

"What?"

"It's something that Micah wrote in the poem she shared, remember?"

"I do, now that you mention it. I really can't believe that *Micah* doesn't know who she is. She seems to really have her shit together, at least way more than me," Reagan said. I let the language slide.

"Well, she thought she did, but then she learned some things and grew up a little more and, like you, she's at an in-between place. Like me, just after I lost the baby and like Logan after she lost her son. There's nothing wrong with you sweetheart. You're just in one of those transition periods that life throws our way every now and then. They happen to everyone and we all have to reinvent ourselves from time to time. I've learned that it's better to do that consciously, though, rather than to just let the winds blow you any-which-way."

"That reminds me of what my teacher said when we studied 'A Road Not Taken,' you know, the Robert Frost poem? We were talking about choices and how not making one is really making one and she said it's better to have both oars in the water than to let the stream dictate where you end up. It's kind of like that, isn't it?"

"It's exactly like that."

"But I feel so lost, like I've dropped my oars into the water and they either sank or have floated so far away, and I'm going in circles and bouncing off banks and I don't know what to do."

I asked her to look up at the clouds and I pointed out how none of them stay in the same place. They always pass by, I told her, whether because of the wind or the rotation the earth. "Your confusion and overwhelm will pass by too. The progression of clouds is constant, and so it the progression of the phases of our lives. They come and they go, too. Keep the faith, Reagan. You'll be just fine. Do some reading, some observing. Learn everything you can. Stay open to everything. Make some decisions, learn from your mistakes. You'll find your oars again. You'll find your way. That's what I did when my clouds were black and threatening to lightening-strike me to death after I lost my baby, and it's working out beautifully now. The sun is shining for me again, especially now that it looks like I'll have my daughter back!" I squeezed her hand again and she smiled at me. "And I know that I'll have dark days again, but knowing that the sun *will* shine eventually will help me get through the dark times until it does."

"Look, here comes Logan," I pointed out when I saw her emerge from her back door. She leaned slightly over her hedge and asked, "You guys going to be out for while? Feel like company?"

"Of course!" we said.

Logan walked toward the front of our houses, rounded the fence that separated our yards, came around back, brushing her hand gently across at the wind chimes as she passed them, and took a seat with us.

"Can I get you something to drink," asked Reagan. I beamed at her! She was really becoming a different young lady already, slowly growing out of that spoiled child she had been and thinking about others for a change. I knew we still had a long way to go and I reminded myself not to get too far ahead of things, but still, it felt wonderful.

Just after Regan returned with an iced tea for Logan, my cell phone rang. It was Micah.

"Hi! We were just thinking about you!" I said when I answered the phone. "We're out in the Oasis and we're missing you. What's up?"

"Well," she said, "I made the date with Darry. To break up with him. Officially. I wrote out everything I want to say, but I'd like to run it by you guys before I read it to him."

"Sure. I'll put you on speaker. Go ahead."

"*Darry,*" she read, "*thanks for meeting me. I need to tell you that, even though I still like you and hope we can stay friends, I feel like I need to take a break from this relationship. It's not you. I just need to spend more time with my dad and my sister. They're both struggling right now and they need me.*" She hesitated, then said, "That's kind of a lie, but he'll understand that better than the truth — that I just like them better than him!" She continued reading her letter. "*I don't want it to seem like I'm ignoring you or make you think that you did anything wrong and that's why I asked you to meet me… so I could tell you this, explain things to you. It's not you, really. It's just that I need to take a break. I hope you understand.*" She paused for our reaction.

Logan and I looked at each other. Reagan said nothing. In keeping with our Gathering rules, I wanted my response to be nonjudgemental but, in this instance, Micah was really asking for some judgment. I kept it positive, though. "Well, I like that it's short and sweet. I wouldn't feel bad about the lie, either. In fact, it's not even really a lie. They *are* both struggling — worrying about you — so it's kind of true. This move will make them really happy and end their worrying. That's a good thing."

"And," Logan added, "I like that you put it on *you* (even though it's really not) rather than on him. You used a lot of "I" statements, which is less confrontational."

"Thanks," Micah said. "I really *do* want to avoid confrontation. I doubt that he'll be high that early in the evening, but you never know. Can you guys come and be there, hidden in the back, just in case? I scheduled it for tomorrow because I want to get it over with so I don't keep stressing about it. I know it's our sister date night, but this shouldn't take long and we can go out to eat afterward. We're meeting at 4:00 for coffee at the Panera at Fourteen Mile and Haggerty. He wanted to do Starbuck's, but I don't think it's big enough for you guys to be there and stay out of sight. At Panera, if you have on maybe hats and sunglasses and sit around the corner, I think we'd be safe."

I could tell that she had really tried to think this through. She didn't seem too nervous, but I certainly would have been were I in her situation, knowing what we knew about Darry, and especially that he apparently thought they were getting back together rather than breaking up. Micah hadn't talked about him much, but from what I'd heard from Desi and from what we experienced of Darry so far, we certainly had enough information to justify apprehension.

"Sure," I said, "we can be there, right Logan? Reagan, I think you should sit this one out." She nodded in agreement. I wasn't really sure how much she actually understood about what was going on, so I decided I'd fill her in after Logan left. She should know.

"Absolutely," said Logan. "We'll get there at 3:30 to make sure we have a good spot — somewhere out of sight but from which we can still observe you guys. My question is: how do you see this playing out after you read it to him?" That's what was concerning me as well. "Also," Logan continued, "it's short enough that you might want to consider memorizing it and saying it rather than reading it (you can have it in your hands to fall back on if you need to). I think he might be more receptive to it that way."

"That's a good point," said Micah. "I can do that and I think you're right. As to how this will go after that, who the hell knows? Somehow I don't see him saying, 'Oh, I totally understand and let's be friends forever.' He's not the type. Actually, I *am* a little worried about how he'll react so I'm glad I'll be in a public place (good idea, Logan!) and that you guys will be there to have my back."

"I'd advise getting out of there as soon as you can," offered Reagan, surprisingly. "Based on what we saw of him the last time, even if he's not high, it could be dangerous. He probably won't make a scene in the restaurant with so many people around, but who's to say he won't follow you out and… sorry, just a thought."

"And it's a good one," Logan said, smiling at Reagan. "Here's an idea: When we see you get up, we will, too, and we'll head out the side door at the back, then come around and meet you in the front. We can pretend it's a chance meeting so Darry won't suspect anything. We could put you in our car and drive away. Who's dropping you off? Do you need a ride there?"

"My friend, Turron. I've known him since we were little. He knows Darry and understands the situation. He also pointed out that Darry will be violating the restraining order if he shows up so if he gets belligerent, we can call the cops and that'd be that. I'd be partially at fault for arranging the meeting but, hey, I'm a kid, right? Great idea, though, helping me get outta there!

"Actually," she went on, "at first, I was going to ask my dad if I could use his car. I could drive him to work and take it for the day (we've done that before sometimes in the summer when I'm off school and he's always pretty cool about it), but I didn't want to take the chance that Darry might follow me out and hurt the car. I'd never forgive myself." So, she had given at least some thought to possible outcomes of this meeting.

I took another sip of my water and was, once again, impressed by this girl.

"I was going to have Turron either wait outside in his car or come get me when it's over, but I think this idea is way better, safer. It'll keep Turron out of it. I was worried that Darry might see him or recognize his car and I don't want him in harm's way either. Darry can be the jealous type, plus then I won't inconvenience Turron any more than I already am. We've have been friends since first grade and he's been after me about dumping Darry, too, so he's happy to help me. So I'll have him drop me off at 3:45 (so I can pick the table, hopefully, rather than Darry), then he can go and I'll drive home with you guys. Okay?"

"Good deal," agreed Logan. We had a plan.

CHAPTER THIRTY-SIX
Done

"Letting go gives us freedom, and freedom is the only condition for
happiness."
—*Thich Nhat Hanh*

During our morning walk, Logan and I ran through possible scenarios that might develop that afternoon at Panera. Very few were good. What *were* the chances that Darry would just say, "Okay, nice knowin' ya" and be done with it? Maybe? Unlikely. And what could we do if he lost it? We were both pretty nervous about it, but agreed that whatever happened, the bottom line was that Micah got him out of her life, and this seemed as safe a way as any.

We decided to spend the whole day together to get ready, whatever that meant. Reagan had borrowed my car to go to the zoo with a couple of friends and, by this point, I neither knew nor cared what Dick was up to. It would be the same ol', same ol' for sure: work, then home to the garage to drink alone. I was so over it.

Logan and I went to the mall for a while once we'd cleaned up after our walk, which was a little more strenuous than usual that day, probably because we subconsciously wanted to walk off our apprehension. We didn't buy anything, but window shopped for an hour or so.

We went to Kensington Metro Park after that and had a late picnic lunch that Logan had packed the night before. Peanut butter and jelly sandwiches, chips, pineapple slices, bottled water. It was wonderful because the day was…well I think glorious might be the best word to describe it. It occurred to me as we set out our picnic blanket that this entire summer had been especially beautiful. That afternoon, the sun sparkled on the surface of the lake, and a gentle breeze sent ripples chasing each other across the water and occasionally brushed wisps of our hair across warm skin. We sat on top of a small rise under a sprawling tree, an Oak, I think. We watched as children laughed and played happily down at the beach below and to the right of us. It was hard to imagine that anything could go wrong on a day like this.

After lunch, we headed back in Logan's VW convertible. She normally didn't like to drive, but thought that maybe Darry might have seen my car the day he crashed our Gathering and she didn't want to take a chance that he'd recognize it in the lot. We agreed that he probably wasn't that observant, but it was better to be safe than sorry. Plus, it was a perfect day to ride with the top down. Logan was a good driver, but her dislike of the chore (as she thought of it) made her overly cautious. Better that than the opposite, I thought.

Logan had arranged her scarf so that it covered her head to hold her hair in place as well as embrace her slender neck. It reminded me of the film *Thelma and Louise,* and I fervently hoped that our day wouldn't end in disaster as theirs had at the end. I shook it off and reminded myself to say positive.

We headed over to Panera and found a table near the window at the side of the restaurant. That section was partially blocked by a wall that separated that part of the dining area from the coffee counter on the other side. Fortunately, we were able to get the table closest to the front where Micah and Darry would be and we could turn our chairs so the backs were against the window and we were both facing the front dining area rather than each other. This way, we could both observe without sitting on the same side of the table, which might have looked suspicious. Were we paranoid? Who knows?

We each grabbed a hazelnut coffee and we split a bagel while we waited. We were in a good position to see them, especially if Micah got the table near where the bagels were, but we knew we wouldn't be able to hear the conversation or see Micah's face because, if all went as planned, she'd have her back to us so we could watch him. Logan had her phone out and 911 pulled up, ready to hit "send" the moment we got worried.

When Micah came in, she winked at us, but did not come over to us. Wise move, I thought. Darry could have planted another gang member like Micah had planted us. Yes, definitely paranoid.

Micah took a seat at the exact table we'd hoped she'd get at the side of the front section of the restaurant closest to where we were. She sat with her back to us, just as she said she would. We already knew what Micah was going to say, so it was better for us to be able to see the front of Darry and the back of her, rather than the other way around, even if it made me nervous. We had no way of knowing whether she'd be able to stick to her script if Darry started getting out of hand. There were so many unknowns in this endeavor.

The minutes dragged by while we waited for Darry to arrive. He was half an hour late and my nerves were starting to fray. I thought that might actually be good, though, because it meant there was no way he could have seen Turron drop Micah off, and it afforded her a little more time to rehearse her message and feel stronger and more confident. I hoped that's what she was doing there, alone, waiting, and that she wasn't stressing too much.

Finally, he came in, saw her, and took the seat opposite her. He seemed steady enough. He'd leaned down to kiss her before he took his seat and Micah turned her head just slightly to ward it off, but it was enough to alert him that what she wanted to talk to him about probably wasn't good. We could see his body change into a more defensive position. He leaned back in his chair, straightened his legs and stretched them out under the table, and folded his arms across his chest. "Here we go," I thought.

It only took Micah a couple of minutes to tell him what she'd planned to tell him. He didn't say a word while she spoke and was silent for what seemed to us like forever afterward. Micah was sitting up straight with her head held high. She wasn't afraid, but I was.

After however long it really was, we could see that he was saying something to her, but we couldn't hear him or read his lips or see her reaction, other than observing that her spine stiffened slightly and she squared her shoulders just a touch. His response only lasted a minute, then he stood up, put his closed fists down on the table, balancing himself on his knuckles, and leaned menacingly toward her. He said something else that we couldn't discern, then he turned and stormed out. Whew.

Logan and I went out the side door as planned and re-entered through the front door since Micah hadn't yet come by the time we got there. She was still sitting at the table, and it was difficult to tell how she was.

"Come on, girl," said Logan. "Let's get the hell out of here."

Micah followed us out to Logan's car and we put the top up so we could talk more intimately and not have to struggle to hear each other over the wind and passing traffic. By this time, it was a little after five. We decided to drive to Hirim Sims park and walk since none of us was hungry yet. Logan and I had split that bagel and Micah said she was too "fucked up" to eat at the moment. Profanity didn't phase any of us anymore.

Once we were settled in the car and the top was secured, Logan said, "Okay. Short version before we drive, then as we drive and walk at the park, we'll dissect the situation and decide what to do next."

Micah told us that, as least as far as she could tell, Darry had been clean and sober, but she noted that she could've been wrong about that because she had been before. He'd listened carefully, as we'd observed, then seemed to pause take it all in. Finally, he said, "Fine, bitch. If that's what you want. Who needs *you*? You're no fun anymore anyway and I can do way better than you. You won't even put out, you selfish bitch. Hell, I've done better than you already, even while we've been together. I only stayed with you cuz I felt sorry for yo ass, but no more.

Good luck with everything, and by that I mean your luck has just run out." Micah noted that he often said things like that, things that he thought were clever but to any clever person sounded idiotic. Good, I thought. She realizes that *she's* a clever person. She told us that, after he'd stood up and he'd leaned over toward her, he whispered, "You'll be sorry." This worried me, but hopefully it was just macho bravado and, anyway, the restraining order was still in effect.

It obviously worried Logan, too, because she said, "I don't like the sound of that. Is there anything you can think of that he can do to hurt you, other than actually, physically hurt you?" I hadn't thought of that. He could conceivably hurt her, somehow, from a distance.

"I don't know," Micah replied, thoughtfully. "I'll make sure I'm never alone, but I guess he could try to alienate my friends, our friends, from me. I don't care about that, though, cuz that's been over for a while anyway. I told you I realized that group of friends is *not* where I belong. Besides, I have you guys." We all smiled at that.

Then Micah's face darkened and she said, "You don't think he'd try to do anything to Bria or my dad, do you?"

"God, I hope not!" I said, starting to feel distressed again. Would he? How big a deal was this?

"I doubt it," Logan reassured us both. "He admitted to cheating on you in order to hurt you so how in love can he be? You just hurt his pride and hopefully he'll get over that by hooking up with another girl and getting high. Still, it's a legitimate concern and we should tell your dad about all this right away. We should be able to get that restraining order extended if we need to since the police had to be called on him twice already." Micah must have been more concerned than she was letting on because she agreed to that right away.

By this time we had pulled out of the lot and were heading toward the park, but then we thought better of it, changed course, and headed toward Micah's house. Desi would be home from work around 6:00 and we figured it would be best to fill him in right away and get his input about where to go from here.

Unfortunately, Desi had no more ideas than we did, but he agreed about the restraining order and said he'd get on that first thing in the morning. He was obviously overjoyed that Micah had ended that relationship. We decided to keep in constant touch with each other to monitor the situation, at least until we were sure that Darry had moved on.

Logan and I offered to pick Micah up and keep her with us during the daytime, but she worried so much about leaving Bria so we abandoned that idea. We had suggested bringing Bria with us, but Micah didn't think her little sister would handle that too well and Bria agreed. She was so shy and introverted. She preferred to read and draw by herself to being with others most of the time. We decided that Micah'd be okay and that she would call one of us immediately if she saw anything that concerned her.

We made sure that she had both Logan and me on her speed dial. Bria and Micah both promised to call if anything seemed even slightly amiss, so we got up and hugged them both, telling them (and ourselves) that everything would be okay and that we were so proud of them for being so brave and of Micah for taking charge of her life.

Then Bria retired to her room and left the rest of us to say our good-byes.

Desi expressed to me again how grateful he was and he hugged Logan and told her the same. He apologized for getting us into "this mess." We reassured him that we loved Micah and would never let anything happen to her, that he had nothing to worry about. Damn.

CHAPTER THIRTY-SEVEN

Endings

*"For each storm cloud — a rainbow... For each shadow — the sun...
For each parting — sweet memories when sorrow is done."*

—*Ralph Waldo Emerson*

I was so happy to learn that Micah had reached out to her friend, Turron. Turron had always liked her, and she felt that he could be a strong ally. She had, for the most part, ignored him since she'd been with Darry, but he held no grudges. He was tall and muscular, but gentle as a lamb, she'd told us. We're all pretty sure that he'd have liked to date Micah himself, and he'd have been way better for her, but Micah was just focused on the matter at hand and was just trying to move on after the break-up. She'd planned to spend Friday with Turron, then we had the Gathering on Saturday, so that would keep her distracted and safe for the next few days at least.

She'd arranged to have coffee with Turron on Friday around 4:00, then they were going to a movie, then maybe a late dinner. Turron knew the whole sordid tale, but wasn't afraid of Darry and would have done anything to protect and spend time with Micah. If Darry showed up somewhere, somehow, Turron could most likely diffuse the situation one way or another. Darry was too macho to let anyone think that a mere girl could hurt him, so with Turron there, Micah could hopefully stay out of harm's way if a dangerous turn of events should occur. We hoped.

She was alone when Turron got to her house to pick her up. Desi was at work and was planning to hit a side job on his way home so he'd be late. Bria was at another friend's birthday party one block over, which she'd let them talk her into attending. Logan and I knew about the plans with Turron, and it put us somewhat at ease.

We found out later from Bria what happened.

Just as Turron was holding his car door open for Micah, Darry came screeching around the corner and jammed his car to an abrupt halt at an angle in the street blocking any chance of Turron moving his car backward out of Micah's driveway. "What the hell is this?" he hollered, slamming his car door behind him and rounding his vehicle in two bounding steps. "Whachu doin' Turron?" He was nose to nose with Turron, grabbing him by the front of his shirt, by the time these few words were spoken and Micah saw instantly that he was stoned, and stoned hard.

"Nothin' man! I..." Turron sputtered, also alarmed by Darry's condition and obvious intent on violence.

"Darry!" Micah spat the word out before Turron could finish, loudly and sharply enough to direct Darry's attention from Turron to her. She'd seen him in this same condition before and knew that a firm hand had a better chance of diffusing him than groveling would. "Let go a him!" Darry was twisting the front of Turron's T-shirt into a tighter and tighter knot around his fist. "He was just gonna give me a lift to the library, dude! It's too fucking far and hot out for me to walk."

Darry abruptly thrust Turron, who'd been scrambling to keep his toes on the ground, upward and backward so that Turron ended up splayed out on his back on the grass, then Darry turned his full force to Micah. "Yeah Bitch? That so? You lie! I know that guy has the hots for you and you know it, too!"

"That's bullshit, Darry! He's my friend, just like he's yours." He wasn't really, but it was worth a shot.

"*That's* bullshit, Bitch!" he yelled. By now he had her arm in a vice grip and she winced, baking down, as he wrenched her closer to him. "…and you know it's bullshit!" He whispered that last in her ear, which seemed to have scared Micah more than his shouting had.

"Really, honey," she panted, trying to keep the panic out of her voice, and her arm in its socket, "I don't know no such thing. You my man. I know what I said yesterday, and I meant it, but it's only temporary, till I get my shit together, that's all. I know you don't want your woman walking the streets alone, and the library's far, you know." She knew that he had no idea where the library was. She was hoping that he didn't think to ask why she hadn't called *him* for a ride.

"Bullshit! Library, hell. I know you two always had the hots fo' each other." There was no way this could be true because Micah rarely hung around with anyone other than Darry when they'd been a couple, at least before the sister dates and the Gatherings. If he should be angry at anyone, I thought, it should be Logan and me.

Turron had recovered his breath by this time and was struggling back to his feet. He was fearfully angry about the situation. He started to advance menacingly toward Darry, yelling, "Hey man, this ain't your biznez! And take your hands offa her, dude! She ain't done nothin!'" Apparently, to Darry, this sounded like an admission that he, Turron, *had* done something and so he dropped Micah's arm with whipping force and turned on Turron once more.

"Then what you doin' with my girl?" he yelled, apparently having already forgotten the explanation he'd just been given for that. "Why didn't neither of you think to fuckin' call *me*?"

Darry had worked himself up into a fever and now had his hands on both of them. There was a moment's hesitation when neither Turron nor Micah could come up with a sufficient answer to this since they knew he never left his phone out of arm's reach and that if he'd seen either of their numbers, he'd have picked up.

That short silence was the catalyst to the explosion. Simultaneously he grabbed Micah's upper arm again as she tried to disentangle Turron and he threw Turron back to the ground once more, hard. He savagely kicked Turron once, then twice, then a third time for good measure, even while Micah was struggling violently to free herself and yelling for him to stop. All he did in response was to move his grip from her upper arm to her wrist, where he could do more damage if he chose to tighten his grip or snap a bone.

When Turron had stopped moving, Darry turned his attention to her. "I know whose fault this is! It's that bitch 'sister' you've been spending so much time with. Bad enough that you don't see me no more so you can see *her*, now she's got you not seeing me to just sit at home or go hanging out with that loser," he hollered as he cocked his head in Turron's direction. "Whadya think I had to do last night after you dissed me? Just think about missing you? Hell no. I scored and went with my boys and got some nice sassy tail, but tonight I'm havin' *you*, Bitch, and there's nothin' you can do about it. But first I'm gonna take care o' some biznez. I'm gonna solve me a problem. Get in!" he shouted as he wrenched her arm behind her back and forced her into the passenger seat of his Malibu. He banged her head on the door jamb and almost shut her legs in the car door, but she managed to recover her senses and pull them in just in time before he slammed the door shut. She tried to open it and get out as he ran to the driver's side, but she was disoriented and fumbled with the handle and he was too fast. He had her by the hair and smacked her face with the back of his hand in an instant. She slumped against the seat, whimpering and holding her injured head and swelling jaw, surely realizing for the first time just how much trouble she was in.

He squealed his tires as he pulled out . He gave her one final shove back into her seat as she jolted forward after he slammed on the breaks to miss a squirrel who had come scampering across the street.

Of course, I knew none of this until later. All I knew was that my cell phone rang while I was loading the dishwasher after another unappreciated meal. Dick still complained and hid out in the garage, but Reagan *was* coming around. She gave me a small hug as she left the room and said, "Thanks for dinner, Mom. It was great." That meant more to me than she'll ever know because it was a sign, another small sign, that our relationship might be salvaged to some degree at least.

I finished stacking the last two glasses, closed the dishwasher, and picked up the phone on the third ring. I was surprised to see Bria's number. What was even odder was that when I answered, it was a panicked man's voice I heard.

"Get outta the house!" he screamed. "Get outta the house, now! I already called the cops, but he's coming…" I didn't recognize the voice but by the obvious panic in it I knew instantly who he was talking about and I knew I'd better be scared. I dropped the phone and ran into Reagan's room, hit the power button on her stereo, but before she could even get her earbuds out and protest, she knew from the very look of me that something was very amiss.

"If you love me," I pleaded, "if you care about me at all, even a little, for me, yourself, or your dad, do NOT leave this room!" I yelled. "Lock the door…" damn, I'd removed her lock! "…push the dresser in front of the door and stay down!" I turned to leave, but then thought better of it and ran back to her. I hugged her close and placed a passionate kiss on the top of her head. "Please, please Reagan. Don't let this be the time you don't trust me!" I ran out then, slamming the door behind me.

I ran into the front room, but didn't know what to do. I circled around and ran back to the kitchen, but there was nothing I could do there either. I picked up the phone to call Logan, but thought better of it because I didn't want to endanger her. I was just about to call 911 when I heard the car roaring down the street even as I raced back down the hall to warn Reagan one more time.

Why had it taken so long for whoever that was to call me? How did

Darry get there so fast? My mind and my body were both whirling around in a directionless panic. I stopped before I got back to Reagan's room and, for a moment, thought about racing out to the garage to warn Dick, to tell him to hide himself, or to burst through the front door onto the lawn to confront Darry myself. I was in an indescribable panic, but by that time I was also in a rage at the idea that he'd put me and my family in danger, and what about Micah? I was simultaneously furious and petrified.

I instantly dismissed any thought of warning Dick. He never listened to me. Why would he start now? Why waste my time? He had probably snuck his gun back in and that could make everything much worse. I couldn't hide. I was done hiding. I didn't care if he killed me, but there's no way I'd stand idly by while he threatened my family. This was *my* family, such as it was, and I would protect it, and Micah, too, somehow.

I raced for the front door and, just as I threw it open, I head the sound. I'll never forget that sound as long as I live. It reminded me of Logan's description of her son's bottle shattering the window, but this sound was infused with thunder, roaring, loud and deep, yet it occurred in a fraction of an instant. By the time I'd reached the first porch step, I saw it. Darry's car. I recognized it because I'd seen him arrive at and leave Panera in it just two days before. Now, it was wrapped around Louie The Lamppost, exploding into flame.

In the harsh light I could clearly see two heads in the front seat silhouetted against the flames, struggling with seatbelts, but I knew. I knew.

I broke into a high pitched scream that never seemed to end and ran toward the blazing vehicle. I could feel the heat of it on my face before I even got to the sidewalk. I felt like a train engine, whistle blowing, turbines turning as my legs started to run toward the wreck, but I was stopped. Stopped! I struggled, panic-stricken, against the hands that held me back and tried violently to wrench myself free, but Logan held me hard. At her age, I had no idea how she'd gotten out of her house and over to me in time to keep me from lunging into the fire to save Micah, which I totally intended to do, or how she managed to hold on to me as I struggled violently against her grip.

"Micah! Micah!" I screamed and cried as soon as I could form words as I continued to try to fight my way free, my breath coming in huge gulps and making my voice shrill as a shrew. "Let me go! Let me go!" I demanded, and I threw one shoulder forward then the other in an attempt to unscrew myself from the coil that held me, but Logan's strong yoga-arms had me pinned tight and the motion only served to wind me down into a lump of sobbing flesh on my knees on the sidewalk in the driveway between our houses. Logan followed me down to the pavement and her strangle-hold morphed into firm hug as she wrapped her arms around me and held me tightly. I was sobbing on her chest, sobbing that evolved into screaming then devolved back into sobbing, and Logan was sobbing into my hair herself as she held me. We were a tangled wet mess of heaving, bawling disbelief and anguish. We both knew that no one was walking away from that wreck.

We found out later that Darry had a two-liter pop bottle filled with pseudoephedrine pills and some other household chemicals in his glovebox, which apparently could produce enough methamphetamine to provide a high. When Darry hit Louie at such a high speed as he tried to take that corner on two wheels, the bottle exploded on impact, and the car was instantly engulfed in flame.

The car burned until the fire truck arrived a hundred years later. The sun hadn't fully set yet, but the world seemed to be in shadow. The only things that were visible to me were the flailing yellow arms of flame around and above the car that looked like they were trying to capture the roiling clouds of black smoke that were rising from the wreckage to darken the world, and the skeleton of the Malibu that could be seen against the light of the fire that was consuming everything. Consuming Micah.

Once they'd extinguished the flames, neither of the two heads in the front seat were discernible any longer. I was hollow. Completely hollow... empty. There was nary a tear nor a breath left in me. I truly think the only way I stayed alive to rhythmically draw air into my body and to permit the expulsion of breath was Logan, still holding me, even though, by this time, we'd managed to haul ourselves up from the pavement and stood, watching, in horror. I would have died right there had it not been for her, that's for certain sure.

We hadn't spoken. I couldn't have spoken if my very life depended on it. Neighbors had emerged from their homes, from their usually quiet lives, to gather, watch, discuss, speculate... It reminded me of the night the Ramseys died. I could understand curiosity, watching, but I was enraged later when I found out from some neighbors about some of gossip they heard from certain of the other neighbors who were saying ridiculous, racist, hurtful things about a girl they didn't even know. My girl. Logan's girl, and Reagan's, her dad's, Bria's... They knew nothing.

After countless ages, Logan somehow sensed that it was time to let me loose a little bit. A light blanket materialized from somewhere and she placed it gently around my shoulders and held it there, but more gently than she had before. She didn't need to hold me back anymore. There was nowhere to run, nothing anyone could do.

"She never had a chance," I whispered to no one in particular. "I wanted so much to help her. I wanted so much to love her. I did so love her." I didn't even bother to try to wipe away the tears that were waterfalling down my face, working with the cool evening breeze to redden and chap my cheeks. "I so wanted to help her," I whispered again.

"You did," said a small voice beside me. As I heard it, I felt a tiny hand slip into mine. It had been hanging at the end of a lifeless arm, which was now resurrected by the warmth and the sound. That warmth traveled up my arm, across my shoulder, and somehow enabled me to turn my head away from the smoldering steel-covered pole to see Bria standing next to me.

"You did help her," she repeated. "She heard every word you ever said, and she repeated them all to me. I heard you, too. You helped me, too. And she loved you, too."

I collapsed back down onto my knees once more and took Bria into my arms. She had either cried herself out long before or was just that strong to hold off for me, but in any event, she wrapped her arms around my neck and stroked my hair, saying, "There, there. The Universe gives us the cards, and we have to play the hand, don't we?" I wasn't sure if that was Bria or Logan. It seemed that the words were Logan's but the voice was Bria's. "You made her strong, stronger, in a different way," Bria told me. "You made her happy. I mean you helped her find her happiness, and even if she doesn't get to have a future, you helped her find herself, her very own real self, and I can guarantee you that she lived and died a better person because of you. Thank you Allison,." I was simultaneously comforted and destroyed.

Still, I was more comforted by that little girl than by Dick's awkward, canned words later on. He didn't understand. Reagan honored me by having stayed in her room until Dick went to get her after he heard the sirens and stumbled out of the garage into the light of the fire. I thanked her from the bottom of my heart for having trusted me and for not putting herself in danger. I thought she'd give me hell for so falling apart for Micah, but oddly enough she seemed to understand. She was some comfort, too.

Logan and Bria, though, were the ones who pulled me to my feet once again, both literally and figuratively. The three of us stood, watching, for what seemed like years but was only hours, until everything was cleared away, statements were taken, and neighbors returned to their homes, to their own little lives, comprehending nothing.

Bria, it seems, had only gone to that birthday party to appease her father and had headed back as soon as she could extricate herself without offending anyone. She saw and heard the whole confrontation between Darry, Turron, and Micah from behind a bush at the side of their neighbor's house where she'd hidden as soon as she saw Darry's car racing around the corner, fearing to come out and distract Micah, whom she'd hoped could get away. When Darry peeled out, she ran over to Turron and, after what seemed like forever, managed to revive him. He ran to his car and jumped in, only to find Bria already in the passenger seat. He knew how volatile Darry was so, even though he would have preferred to make Bria remain at the house, he dared not take the time to argue about it… and he could see from the determined look on her face that he'd have lost that fight anyway.

Turron threw the car in reverse just as Bria was volunteering that she knew where they were headed. At Turron's command she handed over her phone so he could call the police. Bria had already called them, but they needed to know that their destination had changed. Then Bria told him to hit my number on speed dial and warn me. It had been his voice that sounded the alarm and, most likely, saved us all.

Unbeknownst to me, Bria and Turron had pulled up to my house only minutes after the explosion. Bria never even had the chance to say goodbye. Neither had I, nor Logan. Bria had stood and stared, transfixed like the rest of us, for a long little while before coming over to find me, standing like a statue, folded into Logan.

There were so many breaking hearts surrounding that firestorm. I had never met Turron, and I never saw him again after that night. He had come up behind us after Bria took my hand, and he stayed back, out of our way, until he knew she was safe with Desi. I asked Bria to convey to him my immense gratitude for having taken care of her and for warning me, but I never found out whether or not she did.

Darry had taken Micah from me, from Bria, from Logan... and from Desi. As soon as Turron had called to warn me, Bria had grabbed her phone from him and called Desi. It could have taken him ten minutes or ten hours to get there. I couldn't tell. Time had stopped moving for me, but he *was* there. I could tell he wanted to take me in his arms to comfort me, to let me comfort him, but thought better of it, seeing Dick leaning against his car at the top of our driveway. Apparently, he'd cracked another beer and was watching from there. Like it was a show, like it was a movie, and not real lives being lost, real hearts shattering to pieces.

* * * * *

I don't know if Desi ever really got over it, but we three looked after him, Logan, Bria and me. The next few days after the crash are still a blur, but I remember clearly that Desi, like Bria, expressed gratitude for my help with Micah, in spite of how it all ended. Gratitude for *my* help. How ironic! Micah had saved *me*. It wasn't the other way around.

After the funeral, Reagan sat with me in the Oasis for a while and surprised me by saying that she thought Micah had sort of saved her, too. At my quizzical look, she explained that seeing Micah's strength and her relationship with me sort of held up a mirror for her, and she hadn't really liked what she saw — a spoiled daddy's girl was not who she wanted to be. She told me then that she intended to turn her life around because she wanted to be more like us, the different sisters, and she asked if she could come to the next Gathering, if there'd still be one without Micah. At the time, I thought she was only trying to comfort me and tell me what she thought I'd like to hear, just like her father always did, but time bore out her commitment to "growing the hell up" as she put it.

I have no guilt about Micah's death, Logan saw to that, but I'll never stop trying to convince them all that I got more out of the relationship than Micah did. She was, is, and will always be my savior, my soul sister, my friend, and I will never, ever forget her.

Her tombstone reads:

Here Lies Micah,
Beloved Daughter and Different Sister

August 16, 1989 - August 11, 2006

"To be yourself in world that is constantly trying to make you different
is the greatest accomplishment."
—Ralph Waldo Emerson

CHAPTER THIRTY-EIGHT
Love

"Smile, breathe, go slowly."
—*Thich Nhat Hanh*

I kicked Dick to the curb twelve months after the crash. It was an inevitable and uneventful breakup. I'd followed through with my decision (at Logan's suggestion) to give it a year and try, every three months or so, to sit him down, talk honestly with him, try to make him understand, and to see if he would or could care at all about me. He never did. Six months in, I knew it was hopeless. One person does not a relationship make. So, he knew it was coming.

He moved out and, even though it was weird at first, it brought me a real measure of peace. I wasn't afraid of being alone any more, and I could more easily turn my attention to my own personal growth and to living my life in joy and peace, at least when life's occasional dark clouds blew past and permitted that. I had learned to wait them out.

When I confided to Reagan that I had decided to leave her father, I was astonished to find that she not only understood it, but had actually expected it and was pleased by it. I'd never heard of a child actually wanting her parents to divorce, especially when it was the parent she liked the least who'd initiated it. Although that was beginning to change. She never really forgave her father for the tirade he unleashed on her the night Darry attacked her.

Reagan and I started family counseling and we, eventually, did come to understand and love each other. It was weird though. We love each other now more like sisters than like mother and daughter. Maybe the possibility of a traditional mother/daughter relationship died with my marriage, or maybe it was the night of her attack, or the night we lost Micah. Who knows? And who cares? I think I actually prefer it this way, especially now that she's older.

But what helped more than family counseling, I think, was that Reagan started coming to the Gatherings regularly after Micah's death, which Logan and I decided should continue even though Micah was gone because she wasn't really gone. She lived on in us and that's for certain sure. "It's like how George and Candy should've still gotten their little place and lived off the 'fatta the lan' even after Lennie dies, right?" Reagan commented once during a discussion we had about whether or not it was right to continue the Gatherings. "I think they could've made it if they'd tried. I think you should keep the Gatherings. They help you. They helped Micah. They even help Logan."

"How do you know that?" I asked, surprised.

"Well, remember the day Logan showed us her scar? That couldn't have been easy. Did it ever occur to you that she was strangling in those scarves, keeping all that to herself?" Wow! Such insight from my girl! She really was growing up.

"You might be right," I replied.

She then surprised me by saying, "You told me once that you wished I were your daughter *and* your sister. When will I be old enough for that?"

"Yesterday!" I cried and I folded her in my arms. I had so wanted, had dreamed and prayed *so* many times, that she'd come back to me, but I had never entertained even the remote possibility that she'd want a relationship like that with me as well. Reagan was insightful enough to realize all this through the trauma of Micah's death and her parents' divorce and the peace and tranquility of our Gatherings.

She's been with us ever since. I remember her first poem. She didn't read until her fourth Gathering, which we'd agreed was okay so that she could ease in and not feel any pressure. She certainly seemed to have picked up on the energy of the Gatherings, though, because from her sixteen year old heart, she read:

I need to be brave
Or myself I'll enslave
I'll come out of my cave
That so feels like a grave

I'm really no knave
I'll return what you gave
My inhibitions I'll shave
My problems to stave

Let me ride on this wave
About which you all rave
And therefore me save
And help make me brave

* * *

"Oh my God!" Logan had exclaimed, "She writes like you!" Reagan beamed at me. I'd abandoned that style some time before and Reagan hadn't yet heard any of my earlier poems so it was really just a coincidence. "It must be genetic! What's it called?" she asked, turning to Reagan.

"It doesn't have a title," she responded. We burst out laughing so merrily at this that Reagan had no choice but to laugh with us, even before we explained the cause of our hilarity. When we had controlled ourselves enough to explain about my early avoidance of titles, Reagan laughed again, and she seemed genuinely pleased. I couldn't have been given a greater sense of bonding with my daughter than I had that day.

CHAPTER THIRTY-NINE
Epilogue

"The mighty oak was once a little nut that held its ground."
— Anonymous

We still hold a Gathering every Saturday, even if it's just Logan and me. We follow the same rules and derive the same joy from them as we did that long-ago summer when it began. It's been thirteen years since we lost Micah and, even though we all still miss her terribly, every single day, we've learned to celebrate rather than to mourn because we know that's what Micah would have wanted. Our Gatherings are still non-judgmental events, so when one of us tears up at a memory or momentarily feels the loss rather than gratitude for having had her in our lives, we say nothing and just hug it out. It works for us.

Yesterday was our August Gathering. We always have a special August Gathering on the Saturday after the anniversary of Micah's death, and we always make it a celebration of her life. Depending on the weather (it's Michigan so you never know, even in August!), we either have hot chocolate and molasses cookies or lemonade and blueberry muffins, Micah's favorites. We read the poems from her journal, which Desi gave to me as a treasured keepsake.

My relationship with Reagan has blossomed over the years and she has truly become my sister-daughter. She's is a child psychologist now, working primarily with young people, helping them have better lives. She and Kyle have been married for about five years and at yesterday's Gathering, she announced that she's going to have a baby in February. I'm going to have a grandchild! I couldn't be more thrilled! Reagan is happy with her life and that makes me unbelievably joyful.

When things finally settled down after Micah's death, I became Bria's Big Sister and have enjoyed every minute with that amazing girl, who has turned into an even more amazing young woman. She's starting law school at the University of Michigan in a couple of weeks, and she wants to focus her efforts on social justice. She's been coming to the Gatherings since she was thirteen and she has been as lovely an addition as Reagan has been.

Both girls —I mean women — are happy and successful and living relatively nearby (Regan in Farmington Hills and Bria in Ann Arbor) and we see each other often, not just for Gatherings, but for holidays, occasional game nights and dinners… we are really and truly a family, all of us. We have all learned that it's not biology that makes a family, it's love.

I retired three years ago, a little early and for a smaller pension, but I couldn't take the insanity which had been mounting rather than abating at school. I finally got my Master's degree once Dick wasn't around to prevent me from doing so. It was a lot of work, but it allowed me to earn more money to save for Reagan's college and to save for retirement. I studied Creative Writing at University of

Michigan and now that I have more time in my life, I'm expanding my horizons and entertaining Logan with more interesting and creative poems and stories these days. My journal is still my lifeline and I write every single day.

Logan still lives next door and we are still soul-sisters. She's in her mid-70s now and still looks beautiful with her up-lines and her scarved hippie style. She insists on hosting the August Gathering every year. Louie the Lamppost is on her property, she says, so that gives her jurisdiction. Louie, of course, burned to the ground that horrible night, but he was replaced before winter's early darkness would have caused us to miss him too much. It doesn't really make sense that Louie makes Logan the perpetual hostess of our annual tribute to Micah, but we decided that it's as good a reason as any. I know how much Logan, too, loved Micah. We planted a beautiful flower bed (roses, surrounded by annual... we change it up every summer) around Louie and he also sports a seasonal wreath that faces our houses rather than the street so we can see it from our front windows. It reminds us of Micah and how beautiful and colorful she was.

Logan and I still walk every morning, and we meditate and do yoga together. All that has caused me to drop my extra weight and now I'm as fit and svelte as Logan, and the excesses in which I wallowed before that fateful summer have evaporated. I'm healthier and happier than I've ever been.

Logan and I supplement our retirement income by hiring ourselves out as amateur gardeners here and there in the summer. I do some tutoring. Sometimes Logan leads "Yoga In The Park" classes in the warmer months and I join her there. We save all the extra money we make and take trips to see as much of the world as we can. We try to do one big vacation in the fall and one or two weekend get-aways at other times during the year. We walk the pine forest. We visit the girls. When we're driven inside by inclement weather, we read and write together. Life is good.

This August Gathering was especially joyful because both Reagan and Bria were able to rearrange their busy lives to be there with us. Reagan was nostalgic and read a poem she'd written about Bria and how they'd become as close as sisters. Bria's poem was about Desi, whose passing two years earlier was still a rubbed raw sore for all of us. He had succumbed to prostate cancer, leaving us inconsolable, just as Micah's death had. Some clouds take a long time to pass by.

Logan's poem this year had been about possibility, like hers almost always were. And mine? Mine was as yet untitled. I wanted to pick the brains of my sisters on this one. And mine wasn't a poem. It was this, this story. And all of us —Logan, me, Reagan, and Bria — (and I think Micah, Desi, and my son and Logan's son, too, in spirit), decided on the title because it is the notion of the constant progression of clouds that has helped hold us together all these years (with each other and within ourselves), in spite of everything, and has ultimately saved us all.

Acknowledgements

There truly are so many people without whom I could never have even begun (let alone completed!) this novel. My family has been my anchor. My wonderful sons have been a rich source of support and inspiration for me, as has my daughter-in-law, Lyndsay, who was also a fabulous sounding board and idea rocket. My beautiful granddaughters, Scarlett and Lucia, keep me loving and laughing all the time, and I find this to be the best state in which to write (or do anything else, really!), so thank you my beautiful girls!

My dear, dear friends, the English Bitches (Ann Watson, Joyce Spletzer, and Kristie Hannan Syron), and my unofficial tech crew and talk-me-off-the-ledge pals Kim Paullin and Laura Palowski have my gratitude for more reasons than I can count, but especially for being the driving force behind my own personal growth and transformation and for still brightening my life in a thousand ways just by being in it.

I am also grateful for the great creative work of Books Covered, Ltd for designing my cover and for Christina Trader at Fina Foto for the headshots and for being so patient with me. Finally, I want to thank Mark Dawson and everyone at SPF. What I learned from them has been invaluable in making this project and my first book, *Creative Writing...In A Nutshell*, actually come to fruition.

Thank you all from the bottom of my heart!

About the Author

Sandra Hodde holds an Associate Degree in Liberal Arts from Oakland Community College, a Bachelor Degree in Education from The University of Michigan, a Master Degree in Teaching from Marygrove College, and a Master of Arts Degree in English from Oakland University.

She taught English and Creative Writing at Walled Lake Western High school for over twenty years. She has video courses in both Creative Writing and College Writing published with Lernsys.com.

Sandra is the sole proprietor of Your Coach for College, LLC, through which she provides tutoring and coaching services and offers a variety of support for high school and college students (yourcoachforcollege.com).

She lives in Walled Lake, Michigan with her ridiculously lovable cats Livia and Elliot, and enjoys visits from her sons, James and Michael; her daughter-in-law, Lyndsay; her beautiful granddaughters, Scarlett and Lucia.

Sandra can be reached at her author website (sphodde.com), her business website (yourcoachforcollege.com), and on Facebook (click here).

Also by S.P. Hodde

Creative Writing...In A Nutshell

Get the full book description and look at a preview by clicking

https://amzn.to/3vtLS8H

Praise for *Creative Writing...In A Nutshell* from Amazon reviews (verified purchasers). Click the link above to see these complete reviews and more.

- I've read nearly 50 books on writing this year and for some reason this little hole-in-the-wall KU Unlimited trounces them all.
- Ms. Hodde's style is so warm and encouraging, that I found myself wanting to try something new.
- SP Hodde's ebook on creative writing is helping me in ways I never would have come up with on my own. It's hard for me to stay focused on instructional materials, so I appreciate the concise and enthusiastic manner in which the author conveys her extensive knowledge. Recommend to anyone, on any level, to those thinking of writing a book.
- As a former English teacher who was really more of a writing teacher (according to my students), I would have LOVED to use this book in my classroom. As a freelance writer how, I consider this book the best writing course EVER! The links and resource lists alone make it a winner. If you are into writing in any way, shape or form, you will enjoy this book.

Free Short Story

Building relationships with readers is one of the very best things about writing. I would love to be able to let you know about upcoming book launches, promotions, and giveaways, so I invite you to join my author mailing list. Of course, you can unsubscribe at any time.

As a thank-you for joining my mailing list, I would love to send you my short story, "Pretzel Crumbs & Wet Sand." Get this short story for free by signing up to my author mailing list using the link below:

https://storyoriginapp.com/directdownloads/7e8ab58f-e86b-4444-b584-0f2593114aab

If you're reading the print version, you can get your free short story by visiting my author website (**sphodde.com**) and clicking the link there. Thank you so much!

Synopsis:

When a typical holiday weekend turns into a nightmare, Dana and her friend Kate experience terror they could never have imagined. As Dana tries to hustle the children to safety ahead of a monster storm, they are carried away on the wings of the wind and she has the fight of her life to save them. Can they all survive it? Will it tear the family apart or bring them together?

Made in United States
Orlando, FL
23 March 2022

16060415R00236